"There is something else you must do." Tigerstar swung his broad head around to face the warrior.

Hawkfrost narrowed his eyes to icy slits. "What?"

"There's another apprentice," Tigerstar told him. "She has great power. She must join us to make the battle even. Walk in her dreams. Teach her that our battle is her destiny." He flicked the tip of his long, dark tail. "Go."

As the broad-shouldered warrior turned away and padded into the mist, Tigerstar growled after him, "You should have no trouble. She is ready."

WARRIORS

THE PROPHECIES BEGIN

Book One: Into the Wild

Book Two: Fire and Ice

Book Three: Forest of Secrets

Book Four: Rising Storm

Book Five: A Dangerous Path

Book Six: The Darkest Hour

THE NEW PROPHECY

Book One: Midnight

Book Two: Moonrise

Book Three: Dawn

Book Four: Starlight

Book Five: Twilight

Book Six: Sunset

POWER OF THREE

Book One: The Sight

Book Two: Dark River

Book Three: Outcast

Book Four: Eclipse

Book Five: Long Shadows

Book Six: Sunrise

OMEN OF THE STARS

Book One: The Fourth Apprentice

Book Two: Fading Echoes

Book Three: Night Whispers

Book Four: Sign of the Moon

Book Five: The Forgotten Warrior

Book Six: The Last Hope

DAWN OF THE CLANS

Book One: The Sun Trail

Book Two: Thunder Rising

Book Three: The First Battle

Book Four: The Blazing Star

Book Five: A Forest Divided

Book Six: Path of Stars

Warriors Super Edition: Firestar's Quest

Warriors Super Edition: Bluestar's Prophecy

Warriors Super Edition: SkyClan's Destiny

Warriors Super Edition: Crookedstar's Promise

Warriors Super Edition: Yellowfang's Secret

Warriors Super Edition: Tallstar's Revenge

Warriors Super Edition: Bramblestar's Storm

Warriors Super Edition: Moth Flight's Vision

Warriors Field Guide: Secrets of the Clans

Warriors: Cats of the Clans

Warriors: Code of the Clans

Warriors: Battles of the Clans

Warriors: Enter the Clans

Warriors: The Ultimate Guide

Warriors: The Untold Stories

Warriors: Tales from the Clans

MANGA

The Lost Warrior

Warrior's Refuge

Warrior's Return

The Rise of Scourge

Tigerstar and Sasha #1: Into the Woods

Tigerstar and Sasha #2: Escape from the Forest

Tigerstar and Sasha #3: Return to the Clans

Ravenpaw's Path #1: Shattered Peace

Ravenpaw's Path #2: A Clan in Need

Ravenpaw's Path #3: The Heart of a Warrior

SkyClan and the Stranger #1: The Rescue

SkyClan and the Stranger #2: Beyond the Code

SkyClan and the Stranger #3: After the Flood

NOVELLAS

Hollyleaf's Story

Mistystar's Omen

Cloudstar's Journey

Tigerclaw's Fury

Leafpool's Wish

Dovewing's Silence

Mapleshade's Vengeance

Goosefeather's Curse

Also by Erin Hunter

SEEKERS

Book One: The Quest Begins

Book Two: Great Bear Lake

Book Three: Smoke Mountain

Book Four: The Last Wilderness

Book Five: Fire in the Sky

Book Six: Spirits in the Stars

RETURN TO THE WILD

Book One: Island of Shadows

Book Two: The Melting Sea

Book Three: River of Lost Bears

Book Four: Forest of Wolves

Book Five: The Burning Horizon

Book Six: The Longest Day

MANGA

Toklo's Story

Kallik's Adventure

SURVIVORS

Book One: The Empty City

Book Two: A Hidden Enemy

Book Three: Darkness Falls

Book Four: The Broken Path

Book Five: The Endless Lake

Book Six: Storm of Dogs

THE GATHERING DARKNESS

Book One: A Pack Divided

Survivors: Tales from the Packs

NOVELLAS

Alpha's Tale

Sweet's Journey

Moon's Choice

OMEN OF THE STARS

WARRIORS

FADING ECHOES

ERIN HUNTER

HARPER
An Imprint of HarperCollins*Publishers*

Special thanks to Kate Cary

 For information address HarperCollins Children's Books, a division of HarperCollins Publishers, 195 Broadway, New York, NY 10007.
www.harpercollinschildrens.com

Library of Congress Cataloging-in-Publication Data
Hunter, Erin.
Fading echoes / Erin Hunter. — 1st ed.
p. cm. — (Warriors: omen of the stars)
Summary: As Dovepaw, Jayfeather, and Lionblaze strive to understand and fulfill the prophecy that promises them great power, the cats of the Dark Forest begin to teach battle skills and techniques to different Clan cats through dreams.
ISBN 978-0-06-238259-7 (pbk.)
[1. Cats—Fiction. 2. Prophecies—Fiction. 3. Dreams—Fiction. 4. Adventure and adventurers—Fiction. 5. Fantasy.] I. Title.
PZ7.H916625Fad 2010 2009026328
[Fic]—dc22 CIP
AC

Typography by Ellice M. Lee
16 17 18 19 CG/OPM 10 9 8 7 6 5 4
❖
Revised paperback edition, 2015

For the real Ivypaw, and all of FarDriving Clan

ALLEGIANCES

THUNDERCLAN

LEADER **FIRESTAR**—ginger tom with a flame-colored pelt

DEPUTY **BRAMBLECLAW**—dark brown tabby tom with amber eyes

MEDICINE CAT **JAYFEATHER**—gray tabby tom with blind blue eyes

WARRIORS (toms and she-cats without kits)

GRAYSTRIPE—long-haired gray tom

MILLIE—striped gray tabby she-cat

DUSTPELT—dark brown tabby tom

SANDSTORM—pale ginger she-cat with green eyes

BRACKENFUR—golden brown tabby tom

SORRELTAIL—tortoiseshell-and-white she-cat with amber eyes

CLOUDTAIL—long-haired white tom with blue eyes

BRIGHTHEART—white she-cat with ginger patches

THORNCLAW—golden brown tabby tom
APPRENTICE, BRIARPAW

SQUIRRELFLIGHT—dark ginger she-cat with green eyes

LEAFPOOL—light brown tabby she-cat with amber eyes

SPIDERLEG—long-limbed black tom with brown underbelly and amber eyes

BIRCHFALL—light brown tabby tom

WHITEWING—white she-cat with green eyes

BERRYNOSE—cream-colored tom

HAZELTAIL—small gray-and-white she-cat
APPRENTICE, BLOSSOMPAW

MOUSEWHISKER—gray-and-white tom
APPRENTICE, BUMBLEPAW

CINDERHEART—gray tabby she-cat
APPRENTICE, IVYPAW

LIONBLAZE—golden tabby tom with amber eyes
APPRENTICE, DOVEPAW

FOXLEAP—reddish tabby tom

ICECLOUD—white she-cat

TOADSTEP—black-and-white tom

ROSEPETAL—dark cream she-cat

APPRENTICES

(more than six moons old, in training to become warriors)

BRIARPAW—dark brown she-cat

BLOSSOMPAW—tortoiseshell-and-white she-cat

BUMBLEPAW—very pale gray tom with black stripes

DOVEPAW—pale gray she-cat with green eyes

IVYPAW—silver-and-white tabby she-cat with dark blue eyes

QUEENS

(she-cats expecting or nursing kits)

FERNCLOUD—pale gray (with darker flecks) she-cat with green eyes

DAISY—cream long-furred cat from the horseplace

POPPYFROST—tortoiseshell she-cat (mother to Cherrykit, a ginger she-cat, and Molekit, a brown-and-cream tom)

ELDERS (former warriors and queens, now retired)

MOUSEFUR—small dusky brown she-cat

PURDY—plump tabby former loner with a gray muzzle

LONGTAIL—pale tabby tom with black stripes, retired early due to failing sight

SHADOWCLAN

LEADER **BLACKSTAR**—large white tom with huge jet-black paws

DEPUTY **RUSSETFUR**—dark ginger she-cat

MEDICINE CAT **LITTLECLOUD**—very small tabby tom
APPRENTICE, FLAMETAIL (ginger tom)

WARRIORS **OAKFUR**—small brown tom
APPRENTICE, FERRETPAW (cream-and-gray tom)

ROWANCLAW—ginger tom

SMOKEFOOT—black tom

TOADFOOT—dark brown tom

APPLEFUR—mottled brown she-cat

CROWFROST—black-and-white tom

RATSCAR—brown tom with long scar across his back
APPRENTICE, PINEPAW (black she-cat)

SNOWBIRD—pure-white she-cat

TAWNYPELT—tortoiseshell she-cat with green eyes
APPRENTICE, STARLINGPAW (ginger tom)

OLIVENOSE—tortoiseshell she-cat

OWLCLAW—light brown tabby tom

SHREWFOOT—gray she-cat with black feet

SCORCHFUR—dark gray tom

REDWILLOW—mottled brown-and-ginger tom

TIGERHEART—dark brown tabby tom

DAWNPELT—cream-furred she-cat

QUEENS

KINKFUR—tabby she-cat, with long fur that sticks out at all angles

IVYTAIL—black, white, and tortoiseshell she-cat

ELDERS

CEDARHEART—dark gray tom

TALLPOPPY—long-legged light brown tabby she-cat

SNAKETAIL—dark brown tom with tabby-striped tail

WHITEWATER—white she-cat with long fur, blind in one eye

WINDCLAN

LEADER

ONESTAR—brown tabby tom

DEPUTY

ASHFOOT—gray she-cat

MEDICINE CAT

KESTRELFLIGHT—mottled gray tom

WARRIORS

CROWFEATHER—dark gray tom

OWLWHISKER—light brown tabby tom
APPRENTICE, WHISKERPAW (light brown tom)

WHITETAIL—small white she-cat

NIGHTCLOUD—black she-cat

GORSETAIL—very pale gray-and-white she-cat with blue eyes

WEASELFUR—ginger tom with white paws

HARESPRING—brown-and-white tom

LEAFTAIL—dark tabby tom with amber eyes

ANTPELT—brown tom with one black ear

EMBERFOOT—gray tom with two dark paws

HEATHERTAIL—light brown tabby she-cat with blue eyes
APPRENTICE, FURZEPAW (gray-and-white she-cat)

BREEZEPELT—black tom with amber eyes
APPRENTICE, BOULDERPAW (large pale gray tom)

SEDGEWHISKER—light brown tabby she-cat

SWALLOWTAIL—dark gray she-cat

SUNSTRIKE—tortoiseshell she-cat with large white mark on her forehead

ELDERS

WEBFOOT—dark gray tabby tom

TORNEAR—tabby tom

RIVERCLAN

LEADER

LEOPARDSTAR—unusually spotted golden tabby she-cat

DEPUTY

MISTYFOOT—gray she-cat with blue eyes

MEDICINE CAT

MOTHWING—dappled golden she-cat
APPRENTICE, WILLOWSHINE (gray tabby she-cat)

WARRIORS

REEDWHISKER—black tom
APPRENTICE, HOLLOWPAW (dark brown tabby tom)

GRAYMIST—pale gray tabby she-cat

APPRENTICE, TROUTPAW (pale gray tabby she-cat)

MINTFUR—light gray tabby tom

ICEWING—white she-cat with blue eyes

MINNOWTAIL—dark gray she-cat
APPRENTICE, MOSSYPAW (brown-and-white she-cat)

PEBBLEFOOT—mottled gray tom
APPRENTICE, RUSHPAW (light brown tabby tom)

MALLOWNOSE—light brown tabby tom

ROBINWING—tortoiseshell-and-white tom

BEETLEWHISKER—brown-and-white tabby tom

PETALFUR—gray-and-white she-cat

GRASSPELT—light brown tom

QUEENS

DUSKFUR—brown tabby she-cat

MOSSPELT—tortoiseshell she-cat with blue eyes

ELDERS

DAPPLENOSE—mottled gray she-cat

POUNCETAIL—ginger-and-white tom

CATS OUTSIDE CLANS

SMOKY—muscular gray-and-white tom who lives in a barn at the horseplace

FLOSS—small gray-and-white she-cat who lives at the horseplace

OTHER ANIMALS

MIDNIGHT—a star-gazing badger who lives by the sea

CAT VIEW

TWOLEG NEST
GREENLEAF
TWOLEGPLACE
TWOLEG PATH
TWOLEG PATH
CLEARING
SHADOWCLAN
CAMP
SMALL
THUNDERPATH
HALFBRIDGE
GREENLEAF
TWOLEGPLACE
HALFBRIDGE
ISLAND
STREAM
RIVERCLAN
CAMP
HORSEPLACE

MOONPOOL

ABANDONED
TWOLEG NEST

OLD THUNDERPATH

THUNDERCLAN
CAMP

ANCIENT OAK

LAKE

WINDCLAN
CAMP

BROKEN
HALFBRIDGE

TWOLEGPLACE

THUNDERPATH

KEY
To The
CLANS

THUNDERCLAN

RIVERCLAN

SHADOWCLAN

WINDCLAN

STARCLAN

NORTH

HAREVIEW
CAMPSITE

SANCTUARY
COTTAGE

SADLER WOODS

LITTLEPINE
SAILING
CENTER

LITTLEPINE ROAD

TWOLEG VIEW

LITTLEPINE
ISLAND

RIVER ALBA

WHITECHURCH ROAD

KNIGHT'S
COPSE

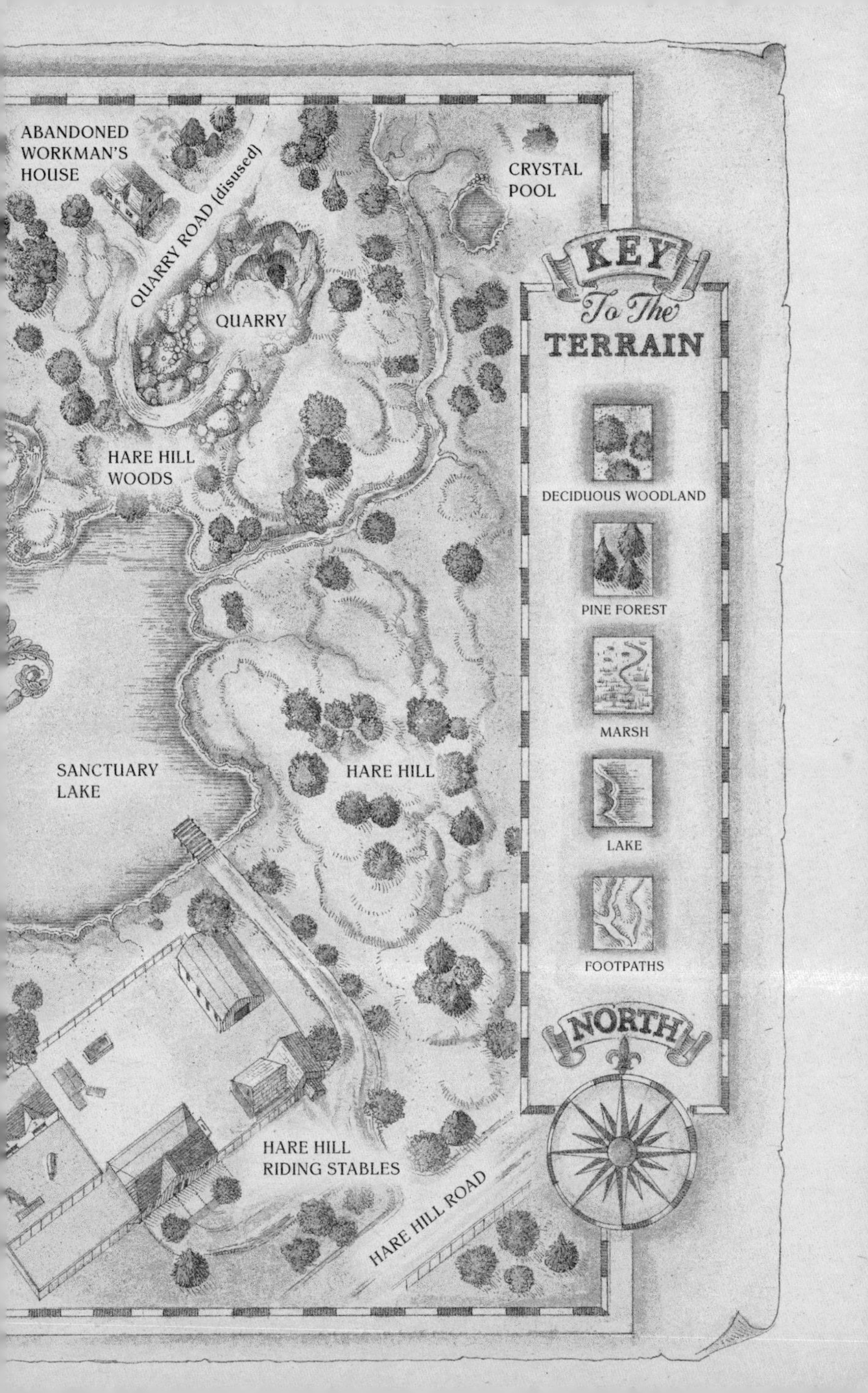
ABANDONED WORKMAN'S HOUSE
QUARRY ROAD (disused)
CRYSTAL POOL
QUARRY
HARE HILL WOODS
SANCTUARY LAKE
HARE HILL
HARE HILL RIDING STABLES
HARE HILL ROAD
KEY To The TERRAIN
DECIDUOUS WOODLAND
PINE FOREST
MARSH
LAKE
FOOTPATHS
NORTH

Prologue

Trees whispered, branch to branch, above the lifeless forest floor. Mist wreathed their smooth trunks, pale as bone, and swirled through the night-dark forest. Above their branches, the sky yawned, starless and cold. There was no moon to cast shadows, but an eerie light glowed through the trees.

Paws thudded on the dead earth. Two warriors reared on their hind legs and launched themselves at each other, their bodies heaving and twisting like ghosts in the gloom. One brown. One black. Wind rattled the trees as the brown tom, his broad shoulders heaving, aimed a vicious swipe at his lean opponent. The black tom dodged, not taking his gaze from his rival's paws for a moment, his eyes narrowed in concentration.

The brown warrior's strike missed and he landed heavily, too slow in turning to avoid a sharp nip from the black tom. Hissing, he reared again, twisted on one hind paw, and lunged, his forepaws falling like rocks on the black tom's shoulders.

The tom collapsed under the weight of the blow. Breath huffed from his mouth as his chest slammed against the ground. The brown warrior raked thorn-sharp claws along his opponent's pelt, and his nose twitched as blood welled in the wound, scarlet and salty.

Quick as a snake, the black tom slithered out from his rival's grip and began to swipe rhythmically with his forepaws, swaying one way then the other until the brown warrior flinched back. In that flinch—a single moment of distraction—the black tom sprang forward and sank his teeth deep into the warrior's foreleg.

The warrior yowled and shook the tom off, his eyes flaming with rage. A heartbeat passed as the cats stared at each other, both gazes glittering with calculation. Then the black tom ducked and twisted, raking his way under the brown warrior's snow white belly. But the warrior pounced on him before he could scramble clear, hooking his pelt with long, curved claws and pinning him to the ground.

"Too slow," the brown warrior growled.

The black tom struggled, panic flashing in his eyes as his rival's jaws began to close around his throat.

"Enough." A dark tabby stepped from the shadows, his massive paws stirring the mist.

The cats froze, then untangled themselves. The brown warrior sat back on his haunches, one foreleg raised as though it hurt. The black tom scrambled to his paws, spraying droplets of blood across the forest floor as he shook out his fur.

"Some good moves, Hawkfrost." The dark tabby nodded to the broad-shouldered warrior; then his gaze flicked to the black tom. "You're getting better, Breezepelt, but you'll need to be even quicker if you're going to outfight stronger warriors. If you can't match an opponent in weight, look to speed instead and use his weight against him."

Breezepelt dipped his head. "I'll work on it, Tigerstar."

A fourth tom slid from the shadows. His silver stripes gleamed in the half-light as he wound around Tigerstar. "Hawkfrost can match any warrior," he purred, smooth as honey. "There aren't many cats with such skill and strength."

Tigerstar curled his lip. "Quiet, Darkstripe!" he hissed. "Hawkfrost knows his own strengths."

Darkstripe blinked. "I wasn't—"

Tigerstar cut him off. "And there's always room for improvement."

A fifth cat slid from behind a tree, his dark brown pelt ragged against the smooth gray bark. "Hawkfrost depends too much on his strength," he muttered. "Breezepelt too much on his speed. Together they would make a great warrior. Separately they are vulnerable."

"Brokenstar." Hawkfrost greeted the matted tabby with bared teeth. "Are we supposed to take advice from the warrior who failed to silence Jayfeather?"

Brokenstar twitched the tip of his tail. "I did not expect StarClan to fight so hard to save him."

"Never underestimate your enemy." Hawkfrost stretched his forepaw, wincing.

Breezepelt licked the deep scratches along his flank, his tongue reddening with his own blood.

"We must be ready," Tigerstar growled. "It's not enough to be able to beat one enemy at a time. We must train until we can take on a whole patrol single-pawed."

Breezepelt looked up from his wound, his eyes flashing. "I can already beat Harespring and Leaftail in training."

Tigerstar's eyes darkened. "Training is one thing. Warriors fight harder when they're defending their lives."

Breezepelt clawed the ground. "I can fight harder."

Tigerstar nodded. "You have more reason than most."

A growl rose in Breezepelt's throat.

"You have been wronged," Tigerstar meowed softly.

Breezepelt's young face looked kitlike in the gloom. "You're the only ones who seem to realize that."

"I have told you that you must seek vengeance," Tigerstar reminded him. "With our help, you can take revenge on every cat who has betrayed you."

Breezepelt's gaze grew hungry as the dark warrior went on.

"And on every cat who stood by and did nothing while others claimed what was yours as their own."

"Starting with Crowfeather." Breezepelt snarled his father's name.

Brokenstar swished his crooked tail through the air. "What did your father do to defend you?" His words were laced with bitterness, as though soured by his own memories.

Darkstripe slunk forward. "He never valued you."

Tigerstar shooed the striped warrior back with a flick of his tail. "He tried to crush you, make you weak."

"He didn't succeed," Breezepelt spat.

"But he tried. Perhaps he valued his ThunderClan kits more. Those three kits should never have been born." Tigerstar padded toward the young warrior, his eyes gleaming, holding

Breezepelt's gaze like a snake mesmerizing its prey. "You have been suckled on lies and the weakness of others. You have suffered while others have thrived. But you are strong. You will put things right. Your father betrayed his Clan and betrayed you. Leafpool betrayed StarClan by taking a mate."

Breezepelt's tail was lashing. "I will make them all pay for what they have done." No heat fired his gaze, only cold hatred. "I will have vengeance on each and every one of them."

Brokenstar pushed forward. "You are a noble warrior, Breezepelt. You cannot live a life spawned on lies. Loyalty to the warrior code runs too strong in your blood."

"Not like those weaklings," Breezepelt agreed.

Hawkfrost was on his paws. "More practice?" he suggested.

Tigerstar shook his head. "There is something else you must do." He swung his broad head around to face the warrior.

Hawkfrost narrowed his eyes to icy slits. "What?"

"There's another apprentice," Tigerstar told him. "She has great power. She must join us to make the battle even."

"You want me to visit her?" Menace edged Hawkfrost's mew.

Tigerstar nodded. "Walk in her dreams. Teach her that our battle is her destiny." He flicked the tip of his long, dark tail. "Go."

As the broad-shouldered warrior turned away and padded into the mist, Tigerstar growled after him, "You should have no trouble. She is ready."

CHAPTER 1

Dovepaw trembled in her sleep.

"Dovepaw! Dovepaw!" Voices wailed around her as she struggled in the current, dragging at her fur, swirling her through darkness. "Dovepaw!" The cries were jagged with fear. Trees and branches tumbled past her, sweeping away downstream. Darkness yawned below, stretching so far beneath her that horror caught in her throat.

"Dovepaw!" Rippletail's desperate, lonely whimper rang in her ears.

With a start, she blinked open her eyes.

Her sister, Ivypaw, stirred beside her. "Were you dreaming?" The silver-and-white tabby raised her head and gazed anxiously at Dovepaw. "You were twitching like a mouse."

"Bad dream." Dovepaw fought to keep her mew steady. Her heart was pounding and Rippletail's cry echoed in her mind. She stretched forward and licked Ivypaw's head. "It's gone now," she lied.

As Ivypaw's sleepy eyes began to close, Dovepaw breathed in the soft scent of her sister. *I'm home,* she reminded herself. *Everything's okay.* Yet her heart still pounded. She stretched in her nest, a shiver running to the tip of her tail, and clambered to her paws. Padding carefully between the nests, she headed out of the den.

Moonlight bathed the deserted clearing, and above the rock walls that encircled the camp, the horizon was milky with dawn light. The mewls of Poppyfrost's newborn kits drifted from the nursery, and snores rumbled from the dens. The air felt strange, cool and wet on her muzzle. For many moons, Dovepaw had known nothing but the parched wind of drought, dry on her tongue. But now she could taste the green freshness of the forest, heady and mouthwatering.

Thin clouds drifted across the star-speckled sky, draping Silverpelt like cobwebs. She wondered if Rippletail was watching from among her starry ancestors.

I'm sorry. The words echoed in her mind like the lonely call of an owl.

Even though the long journey upstream was a quarter moon ago, the memory still ached in her muscles. Dovepaw had traveled with Lionblaze and two cats from each of the other Clans to track down the beavers that had blocked the stream and starved the lake of water. Together they had destroyed the dam and unleashed the torrent that had filled the lake once more. And now life was returning to the territories. She felt it in the rustling of the forest, heard it in the stirrings of prey beyond the edges of the camp.

Pride coursed through her. She had been the one to sense the beavers as they worked to block the stream. She had helped break their dam to pieces and now all the Clans would survive. But the memory was bittersweet, like yarrow on her tongue. The RiverClan warrior Rippletail had died fighting the large brown creatures, their heavy bodies stronger than foxes, their snapping yellow teeth deadlier than claws.

Memories of the journey had thronged in Dovepaw's mind since she'd returned, and Rippletail's death haunted her dreams. Did Lionblaze feel the same? She didn't dare ask. Nor could she confide in Jayfeather about how much the journey still clung to her thoughts. They might think she was weak. She had a great destiny ahead of her.

How could she ever live up to the prophecy that had been given to Firestar many moons ago? *There will be three, kin of your kin, who hold the power of the stars in their paws.*

Dovepaw was one of the Three, along with Lionblaze and Jayfeather. The realization still shocked her. She'd been an apprentice less than a moon and now she carried more responsibility than a senior warrior on her shoulders. What could she do but hone the power she'd been given, the power that made her one of the Three? She practiced each day, reaching out with her senses as deep into the forest as she could, listening, tasting, feeling for sounds and movements even Jayfeather could not detect.

Dovepaw crouched outside the den, her pelt ruffling in the damp air, and closed her eyes. She let the sensation of earth beneath her paws slide away, reached beyond the sound of Poppyfrost's kits fidgeting in the nursery, and let her senses roam. The forest trembled with life, filling her senses with smells and sounds: birds shaking out their feathers before they began their morning song, an early ShadowClan patrol padding sleepily out of camp, their paws clumsy on the slippery, needle-strewn ground. The sharp scent of catmint growing beside the abandoned Twoleg nest bathed her tongue. The sound of water chattering over the rock-cluttered stream on the WindClan border stirred her ear fur.

Wait!

Why were two cats slinking beside the lake at this time of day?

Anxiety pricked at Dovepaw's pelt. She blinked open her eyes. She should tell someone. But how could she explain without giving away her secret power? *Lionblaze?* No. She couldn't go to her mentor. He'd be asleep in the warriors' den and it would be impossible to wake him without disturbing his denmates.

Jayfeather? Of course! He slept alone in the medicine den since Leafpool had joined the warriors. Dovepaw hurried across the clearing and pushed through the lichen that draped the entrance to the shadowy cave.

"Jayfeather!" She opened her eyes wide, trying to adjust to the gloom. Hurrying to his nest, she nudged him with her nose.

His gray tabby pelt was ruffled by sleep, his nose tucked tightly under his paw. "Go away," he grumbled.

"It's important," Dovepaw hissed.

The medicine cat lifted his chin and blinked open his sightless blue eyes. "I was dreaming!" he snapped.

Dovepaw tensed. Had she disturbed a message from StarClan?

"I was about to catch a mouse." Jayfeather held his paws a whisker apart. "It was *this* far away."

Dovepaw stifled a purr. It was comforting to know that Jayfeather had regular mouse-chasing dreams like any other cat. "Sorry."

"It's not funny!" Jayfeather stood and shook out his fur.

Dovepaw ducked out of the way as he sprang from his nest and landed lightly beside her.

"What's the matter?" Jayfeather licked a paw and drew it along his whiskers.

"Two cats are walking around the lake."

Jayfeather let his paw drop and met her gaze. Dovepaw blinked. She still wasn't used to the way Jayfeather acted like he could see even though he was blind.

"Are they heading for ThunderClan territory?"

Dovepaw nodded. She was relieved that he hadn't asked her if she was sure. He just believed her. He trusted her completely. He had faith in her power. She really was one of the Three.

Jayfeather let out a long, thoughtful breath. "Do you know which Clan they're from?"

Why hadn't she checked that already? Dovepaw cast her senses out again, let them stretch back to the lakeshore and wreathe around the two cats still padding steadily onward. "RiverClan," she breathed, tasting their fishy scent. She could make out the shade of their pelts: one dappled gold, one gray.

The dappled cat was smaller, a she-cat. "Mothwing." The scent of herbs on the medicine cat's pelt was strong.

The gray was a she-cat too, but larger, with the muscled shoulders of a seasoned warrior. "And Mistyfoot." The River-Clan deputy.

Jayfeather nodded, his eyes clouding.

"What?" Dovepaw leaned closer.

"They're grieving," he murmured.

She recognized sadness in the slow, dragging steps of the RiverClan cats. But the sorrow sharpening Jayfeather's mew told her that he could actually feel their grief as though it were his own. "What are they grieving for?"

"Leopardstar must be dead." He sighed.

"Dead?" Dovepaw stiffened. "She's lost all her lives?"

"She'd reached her ninth. It was just a matter of time." Jay-feather got slowly to his paws and headed for the crack in the rock at the back of the medicine den. "Mistyfoot and Moth-wing must be heading for the Moonpool," he called over his shoulder. "So Mistyfoot can receive her nine lives."

He disappeared into the cleft, his voice echoing from the shadows. "Now that we're awake so early . . ."—reproach edged his mew—"we might as well make ourselves useful."

Dovepaw hardly heard. *Leopardstar, dead?* She cast her senses far across the lake, reaching for the RiverClan camp. Images of the stricken Clan filled her mind. Cats circled restlessly around a body laid in the clearing, while others smoothed rosemary and watermint onto its spotted pelt in an attempt to hide the odor of death. A queen shooed her kits in a flurry of paws back toward the nursery.

Jayfeather emerged from the cleft carrying a bundle of

herbs. "Mistyfoot will make a good leader," he mewed, dropping the herbs and heading back to his store. "She's fair and wise, and the other Clans respect her." He returned with another large bundle of herbs and dropped it beside the first.

"Will Leopardstar hunt with StarClan now?"

"They will welcome such a noble warrior." Jayfeather began to separate the leaves into smaller piles. The tang of them made Dovepaw's nose wrinkle.

She dragged her attention back to the medicine den. "What are you doing?"

"We need to spread these herbs out to dry them."

"But what should we do about Leopardstar?"

"Nothing." Jayfeather pushed a clump of herbs toward her. "Rain got into the store and I don't want them to rot," he explained.

"Shouldn't we tell Firestar?"

"Do you want to wake him?"

Dovepaw stared at her pile of leaves. She supposed it wouldn't really make any difference if she waited till he was awake and out of his den.

Jayfeather was already expertly separating the leaves in his pile, laying them one by one out on the dry ground. Dovepaw began carefully peeling a wide, floppy leaf away from the clump. "Is it always the deputy who becomes leader?"

"So long as no other warrior believes they can lead the Clan better."

Dovepaw stared at him in surprise, a leaf dangling from her paw. "Has that ever happened?"

Jayfeather nodded. "In WindClan, Onestar had to fight for his leadership."

"Fight?" Dovepaw laid the leaf beside the others, trying to keep her paw steady. Could Clanmates really turn on one another like that?

"Mudclaw thought he'd make a better leader," Jayfeather answered matter-of-factly. His line of drying leaves was already a tail-length long. Dovepaw tried to work faster.

"Careful!" Jayfeather warned. "If you rip them, they lose some of their healing juices."

Dovepaw hesitated before she drew another leaf from the soggy pile. "Does it happen often?" Her belly churned. "I mean, Clanmates fighting to be leader."

Jayfeather shook his head. "It's rare. And if Mistyfoot is already on her way to the Moonpool, clearly no one's challenged her." He began to straighten the leaves Dovepaw had laid out. "Though there might have been a time when she would have been challenged."

"When?" Dovepaw cast her senses back to the RiverClan camp, searching anxiously for any flicking tail or unsheathed claws that might suggest discontent. She found nothing, only the slow steps and drooping tails of a Clan in mourning.

"Hawkfrost." Jayfeather half spat the name. "Mothwing's brother."

"Hawkfrost?" Dovepaw had heard the name in the stories that elders told about the days when the Clans first made their homes around the lake.

"He's dead, thank StarClan." Jayfeather didn't look up

from his work, though his paws slowed down as if memories distracted him.

"Have you seen him in StarClan?" Dovepaw asked.

"Hurry up." Jayfeather ignored her question. "I want all these leaves laid out by the time the sun's up, to give them enough time to dry."

Has he seen Ripple tail? she wondered, laying out a new leaf. The memory of the dead RiverClan warrior stabbed her heart.

Jayfeather padded away to the cleft and fetched a new bundle of damp leaves. "Was it Mistyfoot and Mothwing who woke you so early?"

Dovepaw looked up, blinking.

"Did they disturb your dreams?" he pressed.

Dovepaw shook her head. She didn't want to share the dream that had broken her sleep.

"Were you dreaming of Rippletail?"

Dovepaw looked up sharply, as surprised by the gentleness in Jayfeather's mew as she was by the question. Had he been there in her dream?

The medicine cat shook his head. "I didn't walk in your dreams."

Is he reading my thoughts right now? Dovepaw flinched away, but Jayfeather went on.

"I can tell that you're troubled and I can feel your grief. It's like a nettle in your heart, stinging any paw that tries to pluck it out."

Dovepaw began peeling and laying out leaves as though it

were the most important duty she'd ever had. She'd tried so hard to hide her feelings. What would he think of her now that he knew how soft she was? Would he be disappointed that she was one of the Three?

But Jayfeather carried on calmly separating the herbs. "You might feel as if you are responsible for his death, but you're not," he told her. "You have a destiny, but so does every other cat. Rippletail was always going to be part of the quest to unblock the stream. He was born with courage, and you couldn't have succeeded without him. His death steered your path, helped you find another way to defeat the beavers. He died saving the lives of his Clanmates. StarClan led him to the battle that killed him, not you."

Dovepaw stared deep into the medicine cat's blue gaze. "Is that true?"

"It's true." He rolled a torn leaf into a tight knot and wrapped it in another. His mew grew brisk once more. "The fresh leaf's juices will leach out and make the damaged leaf stronger," he explained.

Dovepaw nodded without really hearing. Jayfeather had managed to touch the nettle in her heart and release its sting. For the first time since Rippletail's death, she felt peace. Was it that simple? Should she just follow her own destiny and leave the rest to StarClan?

But one day she'd be *stronger* than StarClan. Lionblaze had promised her that. What then?

She sat back on her haunches. Sunshine was beginning to ripple through the trailing brambles at the cave entrance.

Long lines of leaves lay drying in front of her. "Firestar will be awake by now. Should we tell him about Leopardstar?"

Jayfeather's eyes flashed. "And how would you explain what you know?"

Dovepaw frowned. "Shouldn't Firestar know about my power?" Firestar had assumed that she had learned about the beavers in a dream sent by StarClan, and Dovepaw had said nothing to change his mind. But how likely was it that she would dream about the death of another Clan's leader?

"No." Jayfeather plucked up a leaf, dark with the beginnings of rot, and flung it to the edge of the den. "Things are complicated enough."

"Doesn't he know about your powers?"

Jayfeather began to sweep dust away from the leaves with his tail. "He doesn't even know we're the Three."

Worry dropped like a cold stone in Dovepaw's belly. "Doesn't know?" *Why not?* Why should they hide their powers if they were going to protect the future of the Clans? And the prophecy had come to Firestar first of all. "Surely StarClan wouldn't have shared the prophecy with him if they hadn't wanted him to know—"

Jayfeather cut her off. "You should join a patrol," he mewed. "I'll finish up here."

She opened her mouth to argue but Jayfeather went on. "I can hear Brambleclaw coming out of his den. He won't want to be kept waiting."

Reluctantly, Dovepaw turned away. Jayfeather wasn't going to give any more answers. As she nosed her way out of the medicine den, she saw Brambleclaw sitting beside the tumbled rocks leading to Highledge. Cinderheart was pacing in front of him while the other warriors emerged from their dens to hear their duties for the day. She saw the flash of surprise in the deputy's eyes as she padded out of Jayfeather's den.

"Are you okay?" Brambleclaw called.

Dovepaw forced her ears to stop twitching. "Just a bit of a bellyache," she lied. "It's better now."

Brambleclaw nodded. "In that case you can join the patrol with me and Lionblaze."

"Did someone say my name?" Lionblaze was emerging from the warriors' den, yawning.

"You're joining the dawn patrol," Brambleclaw told him.

The golden warrior's eyes brightened. Then he spotted Dovepaw and frowned, his gaze questioning. He could clearly sense that something was up. She gave a quick shake of her head.

The nursery rustled and Poppyfrost's kits tumbled out with their mother padding behind them. The tortoiseshell queen was wearily shaking her head. "Why do kits have to wake up so early?" She steered Cherrykit and Molekit with her tail as they began to skip toward the warriors gathered by the rocks. "Stay out of the way," she warned.

"But I want to hear Brambleclaw," Cherrykit complained.

"We won't disturb them," Molekit promised.

Dovepaw stared blankly at the kits. The knowledge of Leopardstar's death churned inside her while her Clanmates surrounded her, aware of nothing but the hunting patrols that lay ahead. She suddenly felt as though she were trapped behind a waterfall, separated from her Clanmates by the glistening torrent, her voice drowned by its thundering.

Ivypaw bounced up to her. "It's so early!" she complained. But her eyes were sparkling with excitement. "Doesn't the forest smell great?" She took a deep breath and licked her lips. "The air tastes of prey."

Brambleclaw nodded toward the silver-and-white apprentice. "Perhaps you and Cinderheart should join our border patrol."

"Yes, please!" Ivypaw looked at her sister. "I bet I catch the first prey today," she teased.

Cinderheart padded past them, flicking her tail. "We won't be hunting until we're sure the borders are safe," she reminded her apprentice.

"Yes, but after that." Ivypaw bounded after the gray tabby she-cat.

Dovepaw followed, catching up to Lionblaze at the thorn tunnel. Brambleclaw, Cinderheart, and Ivypaw were already filing out of the camp.

Should I tell Lionblaze about Leopardstar?

"Come on, Dovepaw!" Ivypaw was calling her.

No. I'll tell him later.

She slid past her mentor and plunged after her sister into the still-dripping undergrowth. The rainstorms had left the forest soft and yielding, the earth springy underpaw and fragrant. The sun was beginning to warm the forest so that steam drifted up through the branches.

Newly fallen leaves littered the ground, some still green,

shriveled by the recent drought and battered early from their branches by the torrential rain. Dovepaw kicked her way through them as she reached Ivypaw. Purring loudly, she flung a pawful over her sister's back.

"Hey!" Ivypaw shook the leaves from her pelt and sent another bundle showering over Dovepaw. Then she turned tail and ran.

Dovepaw pelted after her sister as Ivypaw bounded onto a fallen tree, her claws scattering bark shreds that caught in Dovepaw's whiskers. Leaping up beside Ivypaw, Dovepaw nudged her sister off balance and yowled with amusement as she watched Ivypaw wobble, then dive dramatically down the other side.

Ivypaw squeaked, staggering into a thick clump of ferns and disappearing behind the fronds.

"Ivypaw?" Dovepaw sniffed at the ferns, her tail stiffening as she detected no movement. "Are you okay?"

The ferns shivered and exploded as Ivypaw hurtled out and rolled Dovepaw onto her back. Triumphant, Ivypaw pinned her littermate to the ground. "Even Cherrykit wouldn't fall for the play-dead trick!" she purred.

Dovepaw pushed with her hind paws, knocking Ivypaw away easily, aware of how strong she'd grown from the long journey to find the beavers. Ivypaw scrambled to her paws, scooting out of the way as Dovepaw leaped at her.

"Ha! Missed!" Ivypaw crowed before scrambling down the slope that led lakeward.

Dovepaw raced after her, bounding down to where the trees began to thin. She nearly bundled straight into Ivypaw, who had skidded to a halt.

"Wow!" The silver-and-white apprentice was staring open-mouthed at the lake.

The vast, dried-out lakebed, which had been dotted with shallow muddy pools where fish had huddled while the Clans paced jealously, had vanished.

Shining silver water rippled in its place, gleaming in the dawn sunshine. The lake was brimful, shivering beneath overhanging trees and bushes, lapping lazily at the shores. It heaved and swirled, and the taste of it bathed Dovepaw's tongue, as fresh and rich with the promise of life as the damp forest.

"Come on!" Ivypaw was already dashing out from the trees.

Dovepaw gave chase, her paws slipping on the damp grass so that she nearly toppled over the short sandy bank at the top of the shore. Pebbles clacked as she landed at the water's edge and sprinted after Ivypaw.

"I've never seen so much water!" Waves were lapping at Ivypaw's claws.

Dovepaw hung back, remembering the torrent released from the beavers' dam that had toppled trees, uprooted bushes, swirled like a storm around her as it carried her back to the forest. Then the water had been terrifying, a foaming beast roaring with fury at being pent up behind the dam for so long. Now the lake lay peacefully, like a plump silver tabby, curled beneath the blue sky.

"Where did all the water come from?" Ivypaw pressed. "The sky? The stream?"

Dovepaw cocked her head, listening. She could hear streams splashing and tumbling all around the lake, refreshed by the recent rains. "The streams are back," she told Ivypaw. "Not just ours, but all of them, thanks to the rainstorms."

"Good." Ivypaw nodded. "I hope the lake never goes away again." She bent her head to lap from the sparkling water, then leaped away as a tiny wave splashed her muzzle.

An angry yowl sounded from behind them. Dovepaw spun around and saw Brambleclaw bounding toward them, with Cinderheart and Lionblaze on his tail.

"This is a patrol, not an outing for kits!" he scolded. "The noise you've been making will have disturbed every piece of prey in the area. I don't envy the hunting patrol!"

Dovepaw hung her head and followed Ivypaw as she slunk back up the bank and halted in front of Brambleclaw. "Sorry." Her ears burned with shame.

"I know it's exciting to have the lake back," Lionblaze meowed with a hint of sympathy in his voice. "But you can play later."

Brambleclaw's gaze remained stern. "Have you re-marked the boundary here?" He swished his tail, indicating the scent line running three tail-lengths from the water's edge. "Now that the lake's full again, we need to reestablish old markers."

"I'll start now!" Ivypaw began to dart away. "Ow!" She skidded to a halt and lifted her paw, ears flat, eyes round with pain.

"What is it?" Cinderheart hurried to her apprentice and examined her paw.

Ivypaw winced and tried to snatch it away.

"Hold still," Cinderheart ordered. Grasping the apprentice's paw more tightly, she sniffed at the pad and began to pluck at the splinter with her teeth.

"Ow-ww!" Ivypaw yowled, still trying to wriggle away.

"Wait!" Cinderheart commanded through clenched teeth. "I've nearly got it." Keeping a firm grip on Ivypaw's paw, she gave one last tug and plucked out a ragged, bloody splinter.

"StarClan's kits, that hurt!" Ivypaw hopped in a circle, cursing, then sucked at her pad.

Dovepaw wove around her. "Are you all right?"

Ivypaw's pelt gradually smoothed. She shook her paw, then inspected the small cut in the pad, oozing a tiny drop of blood. "That feels better." She sighed.

Brambleclaw sniffed the splinter that Cinderheart had spat onto the ground, then glanced around the smooth grass at the top of the bank. His eyes darkened when he spotted the two halves of a broken stick buried in the long grass. "It must have come from that."

Dovepaw recognized them at once. "I trod on that last time we were here." She dragged one half out and laid it at Brambleclaw's paws before dislodging the other half.

Lionblaze stared at the broken pieces with wide, startled eyes. He opened his mouth as if he were about to say something, but Brambleclaw spoke first.

"Throw them in the lake," the ThunderClan deputy ordered. "I don't want any more cats injured."

Dovepaw picked up one half and dragged it to a high part of

the bank where the water lapped the sandy cliff. She tossed it as far as she could, enjoying the splash when it hit the surface, and returned for the second piece. But Ivypaw was already heaving it over the edge, flinging it into the deep water.

As the last part of the stick struck the waves, Dovepaw heard the agonized yowl of a cat in pain echoing through the trees. She froze, listening. Had another cat trodden on a splinter? She glanced back at her Clanmates, but they were calmly watching the two pieces of stick bob away from the bank. None of them had made a sound.

Dovepaw frowned. She cast her senses farther, ears pricked, listening, trying to tell which cat had howled in agony. A scent drifted to her on the damp breeze, tinged with the echo of pain.

Jayfeather!

She could hear his rough tongue scraping the fur on his flank. His movements were urgent, as though he was trying to find the source of the injury.

Fear brushed Dovepaw's pelt. When Jayfeather let out that terrible wail, it had sounded as if someone had sunk a claw into his heart. Now Lionblaze was standing beside her, his body tense as he stared at the pieces of stick floating out toward the middle of the lake. Worry clouded his gaze and, for a reason she couldn't explain, Dovepaw shivered.

CHAPTER 2

"Ouch!" Jayfeather staggered sideways as a pain, sharp as a hawk's talon, stabbed his side. He licked at it furiously, anticipating the tang of blood. But his pelt was unharmed.

Puzzled, he sniffed the air, tasting the herbs laid out before him on the floor of the medicine cave. Reaching tentatively forward, he felt the space around him for any brambles.

Nothing.

Then what had stabbed him?

He must have imagined it. Maybe the death of Leopardstar had pierced the air as StarClan mourned. Maybe Mistyfoot's naming ceremony had somehow touched him—the shock of new lives carried from her mind to his. He frowned. A change in a Clan's leadership *was* an important event; perhaps it was inevitable that it would affect him somehow.

He padded along the row of herbs once more, the pain in his side easing to a dull ache. The leaves were drying nicely in the breeze that filtered through the brambles trailing at the den entrance, and there was enough sunshine striking into the hollow to warm the air. There was nothing left to do but wait. Enough time to check on Poppyfrost and her kits.

Springing over the leaves, Jayfeather pushed his way through the entrance, the brambles stroking satisfyingly over his spine as he headed out of the den.

Firestar was dozing on Highledge, his breath clouding in the cool morning air as he rested his chin over the edge of the jagged rock. Sandstorm lay beside him. Jayfeather could hear their fur brushing as their flanks gently rose and fell. They must have been night hunting again. Jayfeather knew that the ThunderClan leader and his mate sometimes liked to slip out of camp while their Clanmates slept and run through the woods. Images of their hunt filled Firestar's dreams now, and Jayfeather sensed joy as the ThunderClan leader relished the freedom of the forest, his mate at his side, the worries of the Clan left behind at the barrier of thorns.

Jayfeather pulled his mind away, always uncomfortable at intruding on the thoughts of his Clanmates, though the temptation was never far away.

"Come on, Blossompaw!" Graystripe called to the apprentice. "You're supposed to be helping, not playing."

Blossompaw froze, her tail sweeping to a halt, leaves drifting from the stale-smelling bundle that she clutched between her paws.

"Ha!" Briarpaw's pads brushed the earth as she skipped out of the way, and Jayfeather pictured the scene: Blossompaw had been about to send a shower of leaves over her littermate and had been caught in the act by Graystripe.

"Sorry." Blossompaw swept her leaves toward Graystripe with her tail, and the gray warrior focused on his task once more; Jayfeather could hear his fur snagging against the prickles. "There are more holes in here than in a rabbit warren," he fretted. "I want them stuffed with leaves before the wind turns cold."

Berrynose was picking through the brambles on the other side of the nursery. "It's just as bad over here," he reported. The cream-colored tom began crunching pawfuls of leaves in between the branches. It was his kits, after all, who were in the nursery along with his mate, Poppyfrost.

Jayfeather was concentrating so hard on the two warriors working on the nursery walls that the flailing, fluffy bundle rolling into his paws made him jump.

"Sorry, Jayfeather!" Cherrykit scrambled back toward her mother, who was basking on the sandy earth outside the nursery.

"Watch where you're going," Poppyfrost chided.

"Jayfeather!" Molekit mewled. The tiny kit pattered toward him. "Watch what I can do!"

Jayfeather felt Poppyfrost tense at her kit's tactless words; he flicked his tail to let her know he wasn't offended. He liked the way kits didn't trip over themselves trying not to say the wrong thing to him. "Show me," he prompted Molekit.

A scuffle of paws and a sudden "Oof!" were followed by purrs of amusement from Cherrykit.

"That was the worst pounce I've ever seen," Cherrykit squeaked.

"You do better, then!" Molekit challenged.

Jayfeather heard her short, stumpy tail brush the ground

as she crouched and prepared for her jump. As she leaped forward, a falling leaf brushed her pelt. Her paws skidded clumsily as surprise flashed through her.

Molekit yowled with amusement. "Nice landing!"

"Shut up!" Cherrykit huffed.

"You're scared of a leaf!"

"Am not!"

"Are so!"

"Molekit!" Poppyfrost's mew was stern. "Cherrykit's your sister. You must encourage her, not tease! True warriors help their Clanmates."

Molekit scuffed his paws on the ground. "Okay," he muttered.

The nursery entrance trembled as Ferncloud slid out. Though she had no kits of her own, she preferred to stay in the nursery, along with Daisy, helping the queens as they came and went with the seasons. The two she-cats had helped raise so many kits that, these days, cats were as likely to see young apprentices visit the nursery for advice as the elders' den. Especially now that Purdy had moved into the honeysuckle bush. Once the old loner started one of his stories, it could be sunset before a young cat got a word in edgewise.

"How are you feeling?" Jayfeather asked Poppyfrost. He sensed the queen's weariness and felt a pang of sympathy. "The kits are doing well." He could hear Molekit scampering after Cherrykit.

"Look out!" Graystripe warned, staggering on his hind paws as the kits raced past him.

Poppyfrost purred. Jayfeather stifled an urge to ask exactly what it was about squirming, querulous, hungry kits that made queens so forgiving of the exhaustion, the endless demands, and the squabbles that flared up with every second heartbeat.

"Are you eating and drinking plenty?" he checked.

"I'm fine," Poppyfrost assured him.

He could smell moss soaked in water lying beside Poppyfrost. It carried Berrynose's scent. Her mate was obviously making sure she had everything she needed. And judging from the contented aura swirling around the tortoiseshell queen, all the fears she'd had that Berrynose still pined for her sister, Honeyfern, had disappeared.

The memory of Honeyfern, killed by an adder, was still strong in the Clan. Jayfeather sensed it like a lingering scent. But life moved on and Berrynose seemed happy with his new mate. Indeed, the whole Clan seemed content, the camp buzzing with soft mews. It was almost as though the drought had never happened.

Leafpool and Squirrelflight padded through the camp entrance, the fragrant scent of prey clouding around them. Jayfeather snorted, fury rushing anew through his paws. Some things could never be forgotten. Or forgiven. The lies and betrayals that his mother and her littermate had woven around his and Lionblaze's birth left a taste foul as crow-food in his mouth. If they hadn't hidden the truth, conspiring like vixens, his sister, Hollyleaf, might never have disappeared behind the mudslide that blocked the tunnels.

Bitterness rose in Jayfeather's throat. Despite what he and

his littermates had been raised to believe, Crowfeather was their father, not Brambleclaw. And it was Leafpool who had kitted them. Squirrelflight had never been their mother.

Mother! As far as Jayfeather was concerned, he had no mother now.

The second hunting patrol returned just before sunhigh. Sorreltail, dozing below Highledge, scrambled to her paws as Cloudtail, Brightheart, and Whitewing dropped their catches on the fresh-kill pile. Thornclaw stretched beside her, purring hungrily at the scent of fresh prey.

But it was a different scent that brought Jayfeather from his den. He'd been half expecting it all morning, ever since Dovepaw had woken him with the news about Mistyfoot.

"RiverClan!" Ferncloud's alarm set the whole camp stirring, and Firestar bounded down from Highledge as Mistyfoot padded through the thorn tunnel with Mothwing at her heels.

Jayfeather heard Ferncloud's tail swish the earth as she shooed Molekit and Cherrykit back toward their mother. Hostility prickled from Thornclaw and Dustpelt. Graystripe stopped work on the nursery wall and dropped onto four paws, curiosity pulsing from his pelt.

Firestar crossed the clearing to greet the RiverClan cats. "Is everything all right?"

Mistyfoot halted. "Leopardstar's dead."

Jayfeather found himself caught in a flood of memories swirling through Firestar's mind: a forest fire; a kit rescued from a river; mountains, snowcapped and scented with danger; courage and stubbornness flashing in Leopardstar's amber gaze. Jayfeather caught his breath as the ThunderClan leader's grief pierced his own heart.

Mothwing sighed. "We've just come from the Moonpool," she murmured. "Mistystar has received her nine lives."

Firestar's whiskers brushed the ground as he dipped his head low. "Mistystar," he greeted the new RiverClan leader.

"Mistystar," Graystripe echoed the name respectfully.

"Mistystar, Mistystar." The RiverClan leader's new name rippled through the watching Clan. Hostility faded like the morning dew.

Firestar touched noses with the gray she-cat. "How's RiverClan?" he asked.

"Greenleaf was harsh," Mistystar admitted. "We rely too much on the lake to survive without it."

Longtail padded stiffly from the elders' den, his whiskers twitching with curiosity. Mousefur's tail rested on his shoulder, guiding him forward as Mistystar went on.

"We lost three elders from thirst and hunger."

Mousefur tensed. "Who?"

"Blackclaw, Voletooth, and Dawnflower."

Jayfeather heard Mousefur's pelt brush Longtail's as the old she-cat pressed closer to her denmate.

Firestar sat beside Mistystar. "Take some strengthening herbs with you," he offered.

"Thank you, we will, if you can spare them."

Jayfeather wondered if Leopardstar would have accepted help so easily.

"Mothwing." Firestar addressed the RiverClan medicine cat. "Go with Jayfeather. He'll give you the herbs."

Jayfeather beckoned Mothwing with his tail. He relished the chance to be alone with her, intrigued about how she had managed Mistystar's naming ceremony when she didn't believe in StarClan. He held aside the brambles at the entrance to the den, unable to resist probing Mothwing's thoughts as she passed. But her mind was empty of everything except the ache in her paws.

"Rest there." Jayfeather slipped into the medicine store and bundled together some of the newly dried leaves. Carrying the wad in his jaws, he placed it gently at her paws. "I can give you some ointment to soothe your pads," he offered.

"No, thank you." Mothwing shifted her weight. "It's not much farther."

"But the shore is stony."

"I'll treat my paws when I get home," Mothwing insisted. "I'm already depriving you of enough supplies."

"We can spare them." *But only just.* The parched forest had yielded few herbs over greenleaf, and leaf-bare waited like a fox in the shadows.

"Longtail seems to be stiffer than ever," Mothwing observed. "Have you tried crushing poppy seed and combining it with marigold and comfrey in a poultice?"

Jayfeather looked at her in surprise. Why had he never thought of that? The poppy seed would reduce the pain at once while the comfrey and marigold worked on the inflammation. "That's a great idea!"

"It used to work on Voletooth's shoulder."

"Thanks." He spread the herbs in front of her. "There's tansy, watermint, and feverfew here." His mind was fizzing with curiosity. How had she felt overseeing Mistystar's receiving her nine lives? Did she finally believe in StarClan now that she'd seen it for herself?

As Mothwing bundled the herbs back into a wad she could carry in her jaws, Jayfeather gave his tail a casual flick. "How was Mistystar's ceremony?"

"Fine," Mothwing mewed levelly. "She's going to be a great leader. Have you got a blade of grass I can tie this bundle with?"

The RiverClan medicine cat wasn't giving anything away.

Jayfeather padded to the side of the cave and plucked a long stalk of grass poking from the base of the rock wall. As he carried it back to Mothwing, he took a deep breath and probed her recent memories.

Pale sunlight washed the Moonpool, reflecting the clear dawn sky. Jayfeather flinched at the bright images shimmering in Mothwing's mind. He was used to the night shadows of the Moonpool. Mistystar must have been in a hurry to receive her nine lives.

Mothwing was watching Mistystar. Jayfeather could sense the grief and disquiet of the Clan they'd left behind as the RiverClan deputy crouched at the pool, her paws tucked beneath her, nose tip dabbing the water.

Jayfeather cocked his head. Mothwing's sense of separation from her Clanmate felt strange. Her bond to her Clanmate was as strong as those Jayfeather felt for his own, and yet she was observing the ceremony like an outsider.

Mistystar suddenly flinched in her sleep with a cry of pain. Mothwing jumped, anxiety jabbing her. *Does it hurt?* The shocked thought echoed in her mind.

As Mistystar fell still once more, Mothwing fought the urge to creep forward and check that the RiverClan deputy was all right.

Was something *real* happening to her Clanmate?

No. Mothwing pushed away the thought.

Yes! Jayfeather willed her to accept it. How could she not believe? She was so stubborn. And yet Jayfeather was impressed by her determination.

They have not visited me; how can they be real? The thought burned like lightning in her mind.

Mistystar was stirring and Mothwing approached. "Are you all right?"

"You weren't there!"

Mothwing stiffened; then calmness flooded her. The discovery of her secret seemed to bring her relief. "No." She shook her head, meeting her leader's gaze without guilt or worry. "You will always visit StarClan alone. They don't exist for me in the way that they do for you."

"You . . . you don't believe in StarClan?" Mistystar's pelt rippled with shock. "But you've been our medicine cat for so long! Have you never walked with StarClan in your dreams?"

Mothwing felt the stone, cool beneath her pads, weathered by countless moons. "You have your beliefs; I have mine. The cats you see in your dreams guide you and protect you in ways that I have lived without so far. I am a good medicine cat and that has been enough to serve my Clan."

Mistystar gazed at her medicine cat a moment longer, then dipped her head.

Jayfeather blinked, darkness engulfing him once more as he slid out of Mothwing's thoughts.

He could feel her gaze like a breeze stirring his pelt. She was watching him curiously; she had known all along that he was inside her memories, reliving the scene at the Moonpool. "You know I have no connection with them," she reminded him. Her tail brushed the earth. "It doesn't make me any less of a medicine cat." She tied the grass around the bundle. "You need to understand that." She picked up the herbs, her jaws releasing their fragrance as they closed softly around the leaves. Then she turned and padded from the den.

Jayfeather listened to the bramble swish behind her, his paws tingling. Even without StarClan to guide and strengthen her, Mothwing was formidable. Instinctively he dipped his head to her, just as Mistystar had done. StarClan had made a wise choice after all.

CHAPTER 3

Jayfeather looked up as the brambles at the entrance to his den swished.

Lionblaze poked his head through. "Mistystar and Mothwing have gone."

Jayfeather could feel urgency rippling beneath the golden warrior's pelt. "What's wrong?"

Lionblaze hesitated.

"Let's go into the forest," Jayfeather suggested.

In answer, Lionblaze turned and headed for the camp entrance. Jayfeather let the thoughts and feelings of his Clanmates flood his mind for a moment, searching for any signs of need. All was well. Satisfied, he followed his brother out of the camp.

Lionblaze was already pounding through the trees toward the lake. As Jayfeather caught up to him, the scent of the water bathed his tongue.

"I can see RiverClan fishing," Lionblaze told him.

A cool, damp breeze rushed through the trees, sending leaves showering onto their pelts. The lake rippled and splashed below.

"So, what's up?" Jayfeather broached the question.

Before Lionblaze could answer, bushes farther along the shore crackled, and Briarpaw and Bumblepaw came crashing out of the undergrowth, dragging a fat rabbit between them.

They halted and Jayfeather could feel the happiness pulsing from their pelts. Graystripe and Millie's kits were growing fast. They'd be warriors come leaf-bare.

"Impressive catch," Lionblaze praised. "Where'd you find it?"

"It was grazing by the stream." Bumblepaw was out of breath.

"It was me who caught it," Briarpaw boasted.

"Only because I blocked its escape." Bumblepaw's purr rumbled deep in his throat.

"You just happened to be in the right place at the right time," Briarpaw retorted.

The leaves rustled on the forest floor as the littermates fell into a mock fight, tumbling between the slender trees. Jayfeather could sense the strength beneath their pelts. Their minds were filled with green flashes from running through the woods, a mixture of prey-scent and falling leaves and their own fearless pride. A sudden, fierce gladness caught him. ThunderClan was lucky to have cats like these.

"They'll make great warriors," Lionblaze whispered, echoing Jayfeather's thoughts.

"Yes," Jayfeather agreed, remembering the long, anxious days he'd nursed Briarpaw and Millie through a severe bout of greencough.

"You shouldn't leave prey unattended!" Lionblaze called to the two young cats. "Some warrior might claim it for his own."

The apprentices scrambled back to them, panting.

"Paws off!" Bumblepaw warned good-naturedly.

"Hey!" Blossompaw's petulant mew sounded through the trees and the tortoiseshell-and-white she-cat bounded out from the undergrowth. "I thought you were going to wait for me! Now everyone will think you caught the rabbit without me."

"We waited for ages," Bumblepaw objected. "We thought you'd gone back to camp without us."

Blossompaw sat down. "Why would I do that?"

"So you can moon over Toadstep some more?" Briarpaw teased.

"I do *not* moon over Toadstep!" Blossompaw snapped. "Why are you being mean?"

"Why are you being grumpy?" Bumblepaw didn't wait for an answer. "Let's take this rabbit to the camp. Mousewhisker is expecting me back for training." He began dragging the rabbit through the trees. Briarpaw hurried after him, her paws skidding on the leaves as she caught hold of the fresh-kill.

Blossompaw stomped after them, complaining, "You're leaving me behind again!"

Lionblaze stirred the leaves with one paw. "Did we fight that much?"

Jayfeather felt a prick of grief, remembering the games they'd played with Hollyleaf as kits and then as 'paws. "I guess." The breeze tugged his fur.

He could sense words on the tip of Lionblaze's tongue, hesitancy on his breath. At last the golden warrior spoke. "Ivypaw stepped on a broken stick earlier."

Jayfeather nodded. "I put ointment on her wound." He suddenly knew what was coming next. Ivypaw hadn't told him that her injury had come from a stick; he might have guessed Lionblaze's news earlier if she had.

"It was *your* stick, wasn't it?"

Jayfeather could feel Lionblaze's gaze prick his pelt, sharp with worry.

"Did you break it?" Lionblaze asked softly.

"Yes." Guilt surged in Jayfeather's belly. He'd had so many questions about the prophecy—he still did—but Rock would not answer him. And when the ancient cat had ignored his pleas, frustration had driven Jayfeather to fury and he'd broken the stick. With a shiver, he remembered the crack of the wood when it splintered. The scratches were destroyed forever, all connection with the cats from the past gone. The memory nearly choked him.

"Why?" Lionblaze sounded confused.

Jayfeather's pelt seemed to crawl with invisible lice. He had destroyed something sacred, something he didn't fully understand. *Why?* He wished with all his heart he hadn't broken the stick. "I—I . . ." How could he explain?

"I never understood why the stick was so important to you." Lionblaze's voice was distant; he was staring out over the lake once more. "But I know you used to go to it when you were worried or troubled." His fur brushed Jayfeather's as he leaned closer. "Was it a sign from StarClan?"

If only it were that simple. "There was a time before StarClan," Jayfeather ventured.

Lionblaze's fur sparked with surprise. *"Before?"*

"The stick came from then." Would Lionblaze understand? "The cats who lived here used to become sharpclaws by finding their way through the tunnels. . . ."

Lionblaze halted him midflow. "Sharpclaws?"

"Like warriors."

"Were they a Clan?"

Jayfeather frowned. "Not a *Clan.* Not then."

"But they had warriors?" He paced around Jayfeather.

"Sharpclaws," Jayfeather corrected.

"What did the stick have to do with them?"

"There were marks on the stick. The marks were a record of the cats who made it out of the tunnels alive and those who didn't." Lionblaze had to understand that. They had all been in the tunnels as apprentices—Jayfeather, Lionblaze, and Hollyleaf—when floods had swept underground. They all would have drowned if Fallen Leaves, one of the ancient cats, hadn't shown Jayfeather the way out.

Lionblaze stopped pacing and shuddered. "Cats *died* trying to become warriors?"

Jayfeather nodded.

"And these cats were here before us?"

"Yes."

"Do they still live here?"

"No." *Though I've met them.* But Jayfeather wasn't about to try to explain how he'd lived with those ancient cats, shared their food and their words, traveled back through time to learn their story, to help them leave in search of a new home. "I think some of them went to live in the mountains."

"Like the Tribe of Rushing Water?"

"I think they became the Tribe of Rushing Water."

Lionblaze's mind was whirling so fast Jayfeather had to block out the thoughts tumbling from his brother.

"How did you know what the stick meant?" Lionblaze asked finally.

"I felt it at first, and then I met Rock." He hurried on before Lionblaze could interrupt. "Rock lived in the tunnels a long time ago. His spirit lives there still, right beneath our territory."

Lionblaze halted, his paws and his mind suddenly still. What was he thinking? *Does he believe me?*

Tentatively, Jayfeather probed his brother's thoughts. He didn't like to pry in the minds of cats close to him. It felt unfair. And there were some things he didn't want to know. But right now, Jayfeather needed to know what Lionblaze was thinking. After all, his brother had his own associations with the tunnels underground. How did he feel, knowing that the caves were not as empty as they appeared?

Lionblaze was remembering Heathertail. He was standing in a cavern split by an underground stream and lit by a trickle of gray moonlight. Watching through his brother's eyes, Jayfeather glanced up at the ledge where he'd first seen Rock.

Rock wasn't there. But Heathertail was, watching Lionblaze with blue eyes filled with affection. "I am leader of DarkClan!" she announced.

Jayfeather felt a stab of grief pass through Lionblaze, then sensed Lionblaze shove it angrily away.

Lionblaze's memories held no image of Rock, yet Jayfeather could sense the ancient cat's presence in the cavern. Furless, ugly, and blind, he kept very still as the young cats played: not judging, hardly interested, just waiting, as though the outcome were inevitable.

"Stop that!" Lionblaze hissed. He must have guessed Jayfeather was walking through his memories.

Jayfeather snapped back to the present. "Sorry."

"Heathertail and I never saw any other cats down there," Lionblaze told him. "It was just us."

"They left long ago."

"Then why keep the scratched branch?" Lionblaze leaned closer. "Why *break* it?"

Jayfeather turned away, unable to describe the rage that had made him smash the stick. The prophecy had churned in his mind for so long; he *had* to know what it meant. What were their powers *for*? Why had the Three been chosen? What was their destiny? Rock knew the answers. Jayfeather sensed it in the very core of his heart. Yet Rock had chosen to stay silent.

Jayfeather swallowed back the frustration that had driven him to smash the stick. Anger hadn't worked then; it wouldn't work now.

"Why did you break it?" Lionblaze asked again.

Jayfeather stood up and shook out his fur. "We need to worry about what's happening now, not what happened in the past. If we're more powerful than the stars, then no cat can help us. We have to figure it out for ourselves."

"We haven't had much luck so far." Lionblaze padded forward to the very edge of the crest. Jayfeather followed him, the wind from the lake whisking through his ear fur so roughly that he could hardly hear Lionblaze's next words.

"Shouldn't we do something?"

"Like what?" Jayfeather raised his voice.

"Go and look for something. Try to find out what we're supposed to do." Lionblaze's mew grew louder as he turned to face him. "Instead of just waiting for things to happen."

Jayfeather shrugged. He didn't know the answer. He'd shared tongues with StarClan and with ancient cats and still he was no closer to understanding anything.

Lionblaze snorted and turned away. "I'm going back to camp."

Jayfeather stayed where he was, breathing the scent of the lake. An image of the stick swirled through his thoughts, its two shattered pieces drifting farther apart on the restless surface of the lake and then disappearing beneath the waves, sinking deeper and deeper, vanishing into the blackness.

Chapter 4

"No, no!" Lionblaze called to his apprentice. "If you climb up this side of the trunk I'll see you and know you're up there!"

Dovepaw slithered down the bark. The oak tree was shiny with rain. Drizzle had been soaking the forest all morning, the rainclouds so low that they seemed to drag over the tree-tops.

"Are you sure this is the right weather for a tree-fighting session?" Cinderheart queried. She was sitting beside her apprentice, Ivypaw. Both cats looked small, their fur plastered to their pelts.

"It's the best weather," Lionblaze insisted. "If they can cling to the branches when they're slippery, they'll find it mouse-easy when it's dry."

ThunderClan cats were the best climbers among the Clans because they hunted their prey among densely growing, thick-leaved trees; Firestar had recently decided that it was foolish not to take advantage of that skill in battle. From now on, all battle training would include tree-climbing practice, as well as techniques for attacking from among branches.

"Now climb up again," he instructed Dovepaw. "Imagine

I'm a ShadowClan patrol."

Ivypaw's whiskers twitched. "A whole one?"

"Concentrate!" Lionblaze was in no mood for silliness. He was hungry and wet and frustrated. What did training apprentices have to do with fulfilling the prophecy? *Wait,* Jayfeather had said. But Lionblaze was tired of waiting.

Cinderheart flashed Lionblaze a puzzled look. "I'll guide them up the tree and tell them what to do," she offered.

Lionblaze hesitated. He didn't like the thought of Cinderheart climbing trees after the accident that had nearly crippled her as an apprentice.

She rolled her eyes. "We'll be *careful*!" She nosed Ivypaw toward the trunk of the oak and watched her scoot up to the lowest branch. Then she nodded to Dovepaw. "You next."

Dovepaw darted behind the trunk. She reappeared a few moments later on a branch above his head. "Didn't see me that time!" she called.

He looked up, surprised by her speed. "Very good."

Cinderheart was scrambling after them. "This is an excellent branch for dropping from." She peered down at Lionblaze. "If you land squarely on his shoulders, he'll break your fall, and the surprise will give you long enough to get in a few good moves before he realizes what's happened."

"Can I try it?" Ivypaw mewed eagerly.

"I doubt if he'd be very surprised," Dovepaw pointed out. "He's staring straight at us."

"Let's try climbing onto the next branch," Cinderheart suggested.

"I'll wander around," Lionblaze offered.

"Concentrate on where your paws go," Cinderheart warned the apprentices. Leaves rustled over Lionblaze's head. "The bark's slippery. Use your claws to grip. Watch out!"

Too late. Ivypaw slipped from the branch with a yowl of surprise and plunged down straight onto Lionblaze.

He staggered, hoping his broad shoulders had broken her fall. "Are you okay?"

She scrambled off him and jumped to her paws. "Sorry!"

The shock on her face brought a purr to his throat, banishing his frustration. "I'm the one who's supposed to be surprised, not you!" he teased.

Pelt ruffling with embarrassment, Ivypaw scrabbled back up the tree.

"Careful, Dovepaw!" Cinderheart warned. "That branch is too narrow. It won't hold your weight!"

Wood cracked high overhead.

Heart lurching, Lionblaze looked up. "Dovepaw!"

The gray apprentice was gripping a thin, broken branch halfway up the tree. "I can't hang on!" she wailed. Her paws were sliding down the narrow strip of wood.

"Try to land on the branch below!" Cinderheart called up to her as Dovepaw reached the tip of the branch and tumbled down onto the next. She scrabbled for a grip, yelping as she fell again.

"Keep your claws out!" Lionblaze yowled.

"I am!" Dovepaw cried as she slid from branch to branch like a pebble bouncing down a slope. "I can't get a grip."

Lionblaze relaxed. The branches slowed Dovepaw's fall until she plopped out of the tree like a pigeon landing clumsily. She stood up and fluffed out her fur.

Lionblaze shook his head. "When Jayfeather told me it was going to rain today, he didn't warn me it was going to rain cats!"

Dovepaw brightened as she saw the glimmer of amusement in his eye. "I'll do better this time," she promised, dashing back to climb the tree once more.

Lionblaze padded away through the trees. He could hear the leaves rustling overhead as Cinderheart guided them from one branch to another.

While he was waiting for their "surprise" attack, he decided to hunt. With leaf-fall setting in, any extra prey would be welcomed in camp. He sniffed among the rain-soaked roots of the oak. Fresh squirrel dung made him wrinkle his nose. He climbed silently around the wide trunk, moving snakelike over the roots twining from the ground. The scent dipped between them and ran a few tail-lengths along a dried streambed fracturing the forest floor.

Lionblaze froze.

Rooting beneath the oak's dripping branches was a fat gray squirrel. Its back was toward him and it was so intent on nibbling a nut that it didn't even pause to sniff the air as Lionblaze dropped into a hunting crouch.

Whiskers stiff, tail just skimming the leafy ground, Lionblaze crept closer. A tail-length away he paused, waggled his hindquarters, and pounced. The squirrel struggled in his paws for a moment until he snapped its spine with a fast, clean bite. Pleased, he sat up with the fresh-kill hanging from his jaws.

A swish sounded above him. He looked up, his mouth full of squirrel fur. Two shapes dropped, landing one after another on his shoulders. He spat out the squirrel as his legs collapsed beneath him.

"We did it!" Dovepaw's triumphant mew sounded close to his ear.

Lionblaze shook her off, letting Ivypaw slither from his back. "Deafening the enemy," he meowed, his ears ringing. "Great strategy!"

Cinderheart scrambled down the trunk, looking pleased. "You didn't have a clue we were up there, did you?" She glanced at the squirrel lying at his paws. "Nice catch, by the way."

"Can we try it again?" Ivypaw begged.

"Why not?" Cinderheart flicked her tail back toward the trunk. "Up you go."

Ivypaw leaped for the tree, but Dovepaw had stiffened and was staring, ears pricked, into the trees.

She's heard something! Lionblaze could see anxiety darkening his apprentice's eyes.

"You climb with Ivypaw," he told Cinderheart quickly. "There's a hunting technique I've been meaning to show Dovepaw."

"Can I learn it too?" Ivypaw called.

"One at a time is easier," Lionblaze lied. "I'll show you another time."

Ivypaw shrugged. "Okay." She leaped up the trunk and disappeared into the branches with Cinderheart.

Beckoning with his tail, Lionblaze guided Dovepaw away from the oak. "What did you hear?" he demanded once he was sure they were out of earshot.

"Dogs!"

The fur rose along Lionblaze's spine. "In the forest?"

Dovepaw shook her head. "In WindClan territory."

"That's okay. Twolegs use dogs to chase sheep up there," Lionblaze explained.

But Dovepaw's eyes were still round. "They're not chasing sheep; they're chasing cats." She stared in alarm at Lionblaze. "We have to help them."

"No." Lionblaze was firm. "WindClan cats are used to it. Don't forget they can outrun rabbits if they want. They'll be fine."

"But *Sedgewhisker* is one of the cats being chased!" She froze, her eyes suddenly wild. "One of the dogs has caught up to her! It's biting her!"

Lionblaze stiffened. "Where are her Clanmates?"

Dovepaw frowned. "They're with her. . . ." She spoke slowly, describing the scene as it happened. "They're attacking the dog."

Lionblaze let out a sigh of relief. "Then Sedgewhisker will be safe."

"How do you know that?" Dovepaw hissed.

Lionblaze's heart sank. He'd been waiting for something like this to happen. Dovepaw was clinging to the friendships they'd made on the long journey; Sedgewhisker had traveled with them to destroy the beavers' dam. Dovepaw had to understand that they were back in their own territories now. "We're home," he told her. "Your loyalty lies with your own Clan. You can't be as close to Sedgewhisker or the others as you were before."

Dovepaw stared at him. "Why not?"

"Because the warrior code tells us we shouldn't make friends outside our Clan."

Her blue eyes flashed. "How can you be so cold?"

"I'm not being cold!" Lionblaze insisted. "Things have changed."

"*I* haven't changed," Dovepaw snapped. "I'm the same cat I was on the journey upstream." She kneaded the ground with her front paws. "What's the use of knowing what's happening far away if I can't do something about it?"

"Maybe you should figure out how to limit your senses to ThunderClan territory," he suggested.

Dovepaw looked at him as though he'd grown another head. "The prophecy is bigger than the warrior code, right?"

Lionblaze nodded, wary of where she was heading.

"So my powers aren't just for ThunderClan's benefit, are they?"

"We're *ThunderClan* cats," he reminded her. "That's where our loyalties should lie."

Dovepaw glared at him. "So am I loyal to the prophecy, or the warrior code?" The fur fluffed around her ears. "You and Jayfeather had better make your minds up before I decide myself."

Without waiting for an answer, she pelted back to the oak and disappeared up the trunk after Cinderheart and Ivypaw.

Lionblaze watched her go, his heart sinking. He was only just beginning to understand Jayfeather's abilities; now he was faced with another cat whose powers were beyond anything he could imagine. Stretching his ears, he strained to listen as hard as he could, but all he could hear was rain pattering on the dying leaves.

Ivypaw's mew sounded from high in the oak. "This branch keeps bobbing in the wind."

"Just hang on tight," Cinderheart advised.

"It's making me feel sick!"

Lionblaze's own power was far simpler. He could fight in battles, unscathed, fearless and stronger than any opponent. Did *that* seem strange and frightening to his Clanmates? He knew Hollyleaf had always felt uncomfortable about his readiness to fight, as though she didn't quite believe he wouldn't get hurt.

But then, she had no power of her own. She was never one of the Three.

And he *had* been hurt once. Tigerstar had drawn blood in their last dream encounter. Lionblaze glanced behind him, the fur lifting on his shoulders. Was the dark warrior watching him now? Ferns swished beside him and he swung around, uncurling his claws.

"Sorreltail!" He couldn't hide the relief in his voice. "Are you looking for Cinderheart?"

Sorreltail shook her head. "I'm joining Graystripe's hunting patrol. Jayfeather just told me that my shoulder's healed." The tortoiseshell warrior had wrenched it a few days earlier when her paw had caught in a rabbit hole. "Is Cinderheart with you?" She followed Lionblaze's gaze up to watch her daughter beckoning Ivypaw farther out along a branch. Cinderheart was balancing skillfully as the branch swayed beneath her paws.

Pride glowed in Sorreltail's eyes. "I never thought I'd see the day when she'd be strong enough to climb trees like a squirrel." She sighed gently and watched a moment longer before pulling her gaze away. "Leafpool healed her so well. She was a wonderful medicine cat."

There was an edge to her mew. Did she blame Lionblaze for Leafpool's decision to leave the medicine den and become a warrior? His pelt itched. It wasn't his fault Leafpool had thrown everything away by breaking the warrior code! She was the one who'd had kits with a cat from another Clan and then lied about them!

He held his tongue as Sorreltail headed away; then, remembering Sedgewhisker, he called hopefully, "Where are you hunting?"

"By the WindClan border."

Good. If the WindClan cats were really in trouble, the hunting patrol would notice; Graystripe could decide whether to help them or not.

As Sorreltail disappeared through a dripping wall of fern, Lionblaze scraped dirt over his catch and padded to the bottom of the oak. "How are you doing?" he called to his Clanmates.

"They're doing very well." Cinderheart landed lightly

beside him, Ivypaw and Dovepaw dropping down after her. "I think we can try something harder."

Ivypaw pricked her ears.

"Let's teach them to cross from one tree to another," Cinderheart suggested.

"Like squirrels!" Ivypaw squeaked.

"Yes, like squirrels."

Lionblaze's tail drooped. He wasn't a natural climber. "We could teach them battle moves instead," he suggested hopefully. "There are plenty they don't know yet."

"Firestar wants us to practice tree hopping," Cinderheart reminded him.

We're cats, not birds! Lionblaze always felt big and clumsy in trees. He'd rather be on the ground, fighting. Why sit up in the branches like a bunch of owls, watching the enemy, rather than tackling them head-on like warriors?

"Come on. Let's start in this maple." Cinderheart flashed him a determined glance. She knew he didn't like tree climbing. "In the old territory, Longtail swears he once crossed from the Great Sycamore to camp without touching the forest floor."

"How far was that?" Dovepaw sounded impressed.

"About the same as from here to the hollow," Cinderheart meowed.

Lionblaze snorted. *How do you know?* Cinderheart had been born by the lake, like him. She had never seen the old territory!

"I bet I could do that," Ivypaw boasted. She swarmed

up the trunk of the maple, eyes half closed against the rain dripping down through the branches. Cinderheart followed, Dovepaw on her tail.

Lionblaze stared up, wishing that the rain would stop. It was going to be hard enough without slippery bark. Sighing, he heaved himself up the trunk, digging his claws deep into the bark to stop himself from sliding down.

Cinderheart was waiting on the lowest branch, while Ivypaw and Dovepaw were already halfway to the end.

"We won't even have to jump this one," Dovepaw reported over her shoulder. The branch wove into the lowest branches of a neighboring willow.

"Perhaps we should take a different route," Lionblaze called to her. The willow had slender branches. "That might not take our weight."

"*Your* weight, you mean!" There was a sharpness in Dovepaw's reply. She was still angry with him for not helping Sedgewhisker. Lionblaze let it pass, though irritation pricked his pads.

Cinderheart nodded toward the willow. "It's an old tree." Dovepaw and Ivypaw had already crossed into its branches. "It'll be strong enough."

She was right. Lionblaze padded through its boughs easily, relieved to find them wide and sturdy. "Slow down!" he called. Dovepaw and Ivypaw were rushing on ahead, as though each wanted to be first to make it back to camp without touching the forest floor.

Dovepaw was balancing at the tip of the willow's longest

branch. An ancient oak sprouted beyond it, gnarled and twisted with age. "I'm going to try this one," she mewed over her shoulder.

"The bark's very rough," Lionblaze warned. "It looks old. There may be cracks in the branches you can't see." He quickened his pace, leaping past Cinderheart. "Wait until I've checked it!"

Too late!

Dovepaw was already leaping onto a branch of the oak. It cracked as she landed, snapping like a dry twig, and, with a yelp, she plummeted downward.

It was only three tail-lengths to the soft forest floor and she landed on her paws. But Lionblaze knew what was coming next.

"Look out!" He leaped from the willow, skidding across the forest floor and grabbing Dovepaw by the scruff.

"What?" she squawked as he dragged her backward. A moment later the ancient oak branch came crashing down.

Lionblaze screwed up his eyes, shielding Dovepaw with his body. When the branch had stopped rocking he turned on her angrily.

"However much you think you know, sometimes I'm right, okay?" he growled.

Dovepaw lifted her nose and sniffed. Then she turned and stalked away.

Chapter 5

Dovepaw stretched her aching legs. Her nest rustled as she fidgeted. Her denmates were fast asleep. They'd dozed off by the time the moon had risen above the hollow, tired after their training.

But Dovepaw felt wide-awake. She'd *seen* Sedgewhisker limping back to camp, supported by her Clanmates. She could smell the blood crusting over Sedgewhisker's wound, feel the heat pulsing from her swollen leg. She needed to know how badly injured her WindClan friend was!

"Are you okay?" Ivypaw peered over the rim of her nest. Her eyes were round with worry. "Did the fall hurt you?"

"No," Dovepaw answered honestly. Only her pride had been hurt. Lionblaze was so bossy! And now he was trying to tell her how to use her power. He should respect her, like Jayfeather did, not treat her like some dumb apprentice.

Ivypaw sat up. "You're not tired at all?"

Dovepaw flicked her tail. "No."

"Come on." Ivypaw stepped from her nest. Blossompaw was snoring again. "Let's go into the forest."

Dovepaw's heart gave a jolt as hope flashed through it. She

sat up. What was Ivypaw planning?

Briarpaw rolled onto her back, her paws folded in the air like a rabbit's.

"We haven't been out at night since you went to find the beavers." Ivypaw tiptoed to the entrance and slid out. The low branches of the yew den slicked Dovepaw's fur as she followed eagerly. The starlit clearing glowed like a pool in the center of the shadowy hollow. Dovepaw could smell the forest above, musty with the scent of leaf-fall, damp with night dew.

She cast her senses out past the thorn barrier and scented Rosepetal guarding the camp entrance, her paws shifting on the ground, her breath coming in billows.

"I know a secret way out," she told Ivypaw.

"Through the dirtplace tunnel?" Ivypaw guessed.

"Better than that." Dovepaw crept around the edge of the clearing, past the entrance to the medicine den. She squeezed through the tangle of brambles beside it until she reached the rock wall beyond. Stretching up through the twisted stems, she reached for a low ledge and hauled herself up.

"Are you coming?" she hissed down to Ivypaw.

Her sister's silver-and-white pelt was flashing beneath the bramble. "Coming," Ivypaw breathed.

Dovepaw jumped up to the next ledge, then the next, until the dens of the camp looked like small clumps of scrub below her. Fizzing with excitement, she scrambled over the lip of the cliff and onto soft grass.

Ivypaw bounded up after her. "How did you find out about that?"

"Lionblaze." He'd told her in case she ever needed to escape camp without being seen. *I bet he didn't expect me to use it so soon,* she thought with a glimmer of satisfaction. *I make my own decisions.*

A half-moon lit the treetops, filtering through the bare branches and striping the forest floor silver. Breathing the musty scents of the night-damp forest, Dovepaw scampered into the trees.

Ivypaw ran beside her. "I wonder if anyone else is out?"

Dovepaw cast her senses through the trees, feeling for signs of movement. The waves on the lakeshore murmured softly, like the lapping of her mother's tongue against her fur. Beyond the border, a ShadowClan kit wailed, waking from a bad dream, and across the lake, on the far side of RiverClan territory, Twolegs yowled in their nest.

"Where should we go?" Ivypaw's question jerked her back. "What about the old Twoleg nest? It's really spooky. I bet you're not brave enough!"

No. Dovepaw knew exactly where she wanted to go. She could sense Sedgewhisker stirring in her nest, her eyes flickering as though the pain in her leg wouldn't let her rest. "Let's go to the moorland."

Ivypaw skidded to a halt. "*WindClan* territory?"

"Right to their camp." Dovepaw paused beside her. She needed to make a challenge that Ivypaw couldn't resist.

Her sister stared at her, whiskers quivering as though she'd scented prey. "To their *camp*?" she echoed breathlessly.

"I haven't seen Whitetail or Sedgewhisker since I got back from upstream."

Ivypaw's tail drooped. "What do you want to see *them* for?" She sounded puzzled and hurt. "You don't need friends in WindClan. You've got friends here." She flicked her tail toward the hollow.

"But don't you want to see if we can make it?" Dovepaw coaxed. She couldn't explain Sedgewhisker's injury without giving away her secret. "We can always say we were lost if we get caught. We're only apprentices. No cat is going to think we're trying to invade." She had to see if Sedgewhisker was safe. *Just because Lionblaze couldn't care less doesn't mean I have to.* "Oh, come on," she pleaded with Ivypaw.

Ivypaw narrowed her eyes, then nodded. "Okay." She trotted away through the trees, heading toward the WindClan border. "If any WindClan cat catches us"—she ducked under a spreading yew bush—"we can say we were chasing a squirrel and hadn't realized we'd crossed the border."

Dovepaw's belly brushed the ground as she scrabbled under the low branches. "They'd think we're pretty stupid not to notice we'd run onto moorland," she pointed out.

"Okay." Ivypaw skidded down a bank. "We'll say we were sleepwalking."

"What, both of us?" Dovepaw wondered if her sister was taking this seriously enough.

"We can't just tell them we've come to visit Whitetail and Sedgewhisker," Ivypaw mewed.

Why not? They *had* been on the quest together. "We'll just have to make sure we don't get caught," Dovepaw decided.

They were nearly out of the trees and Dovepaw could smell

the moorland. She let her senses reach far out over the peat and heather, relieved that she could detect nothing but the soft breathing of cats tucked up in their nests in the Wind-Clan camp. "I wonder what the camp looks like?" she mewed.

Ivypaw padded from the trees and halted at the top of a steep bank. The wind tugged her whiskers and she shivered. "I'm glad I'm not WindClan." The border stream gurgled below them. "It must be weird to sleep out in the open."

"They must have dens."

"But no trees," Ivypaw mewed. "Just the open sky." She slid down the bank, pushing off with her hind legs as she reached the bottom and clearing the narrow waterway in one bound. She looked back at Dovepaw, who had paused on the bank. "Imagine what it must be like when it's stormy." She shuddered.

Dovepaw was staring across the moorland rising ahead of them like a giant sleeping cat beneath the pale night sky.

"Hurry up," Ivypaw urged. "It's spooky over here."

Dovepaw bounded down the bank and over the stream. Wind rushed over the grass and heather, buffeting her like a flock of starlings. She shivered, remembering the journey upstream and the exposed territories they'd had to cross to find the beavers. "It was like this when we—" She stopped herself.

"What?"

Dovepaw shook her head. "Nothing." Ivypaw was still upset that she hadn't been allowed to go on the quest. No wonder she wasn't interested in visiting Whitetail and Sedgewhisker.

Ivypaw scanned the moorland, her eyes wide and anxious. The tang of the WindClan scent markers tainted the air. "Do you suppose they have night patrols?"

Dovepaw pricked her ears, searching for WindClan patrols. A monster growled far in the distance and sheep mewled on the hillside, their greasy, pungent smell familiar from the quest, when she'd had to hide between their stinky, mud-encrusted legs.

She shook away the memory. There was still no sign of cats roaming the moor. "Nothing," she reassured Ivypaw. Worried that Ivypaw might wonder how she was so certain, she added, "With the wind blowing toward us, it'll be easy to scent any patrols."

Ivypaw's mouth was already open, tasting the breeze. "Come on." Her silver-and-white pelt glowed in the moonlight as she began to head up the slope, eyes half closed against the wind.

Dovepaw followed her across the scent line, anxiety yawning in her belly, not daring to speak now that they were on WindClan territory. They wove up the slope, the wind whipping more fiercely at their fur. A sheep bellowed close by and they both jumped, scooting through a clump of gorse and ducking lower as they pressed on between the heather bushes.

Ivypaw slowed. "Are you sure you want to go right to their camp?" There was a quaver in her mew.

Dovepaw could scent the camp just over a rise in the ground ahead. She could hear the gentle breathing of cats in dens. An image of the camp took shape in her mind: stiff bushes sheltering hollows scooped in the sandy soil; a paw-scuffed clearing; a gorse-shadowed dip, rich with the tang of medicine herbs. "Just a little farther," she pleaded. She could sense Sedgewhisker clearly. The pale tabby she-cat was lying in a den beside Whitetail. Their denmates surrounded them, a jumble of pelts, warm and sheltered from the wind. Only Sedgewhisker stirred. She kept sniffing gingerly at her wound. *It can't be too bad if she's not in the medicine den,* Dovepaw reasoned. Still, worry pricked at her pelt. She *had* to be sure!

But how in the name of StarClan was she going to get Sedgewhisker's attention without waking the rest of the den?

I'll worry about that when we get there.

They crested the rise. The earth dipped in front of them, a wide hollow denting the moorland. It was ringed by a grassy slope, edged at the foot by a wall of scrubby bushes. A sandy clearing glowed at the center, just as Dovepaw had imagined.

"That's it!" Dovepaw could hardly keep her excited mew to a whisper. "The camp!"

Ivypaw flicked her tail across her sister's mouth. "I bet Bumblepaw or Briarpaw'd never do anything like this!" she breathed. "You're not really going to look for Sedgewhisker and Whitetail, are you?"

"Of course!" Dovepaw began to slink down the slope.

"You can't!" Ivypaw protested. "It's too dangerous."

Dovepaw glanced over her shoulder. "You can stay at the top if you want!" she hissed.

Ivypaw darted after her. "No way! If you're going, then so am I! We're in this together, right?"

Dovepaw knew exactly where the warriors' den was and crept toward it, the moorland grass slippery beneath her pads.

Ivypaw pressed behind her, hardly breathing. "Is everyone asleep?"

Dovepaw's tail twitched. "Nearly everyone."

Ivypaw hesitated. "What do you mean?"

"It's okay," Dovepaw urged. "It's just a guard. He won't see us." She could see the silhouette of a single warrior in the clearing, his shoulders bunched with tiredness, his back toward them as he scanned the opposite horizon.

Ivypaw stiffened when she saw him and ducked lower as they slithered into the shadows around the scrubby camp wall. They slid through a gap between the stems and tiptoed toward a wide tangle of shrubs. *The warriors' den.*

Slipping into the darkness beneath the branches, Dovepaw felt a glimmer of relief.

Ivypaw was trembling beside her. "What do we do now?"

"Sedgewhisker is asleep just beyond the wall." Dovepaw touched her tail against the spiny branches, sensing her friend only a tail-length away. "Sedgewhisker!" she hissed.

"What are you doing?" Ivypaw gasped.

Dovepaw ignored her sister's protest. "Sedgewhisker!" she hissed louder.

Leaves rustled beyond the wall. Sedgewhisker had sat up.

"She's coming!" Dovepaw whispered to Ivypaw. She could hear Sedgewhisker picking her way between the nests on three legs, her injured leg tucked protectively under her.

The pale tabby appeared beside them like a moonbeam in

the darkness. "Great StarClan, Dovepaw! What are you doing here?"

Dovepaw tipped her head to one side. The WindClan warrior sounded cross, not overjoyed to see her old friend from the quest.

"Follow me!" Sedgewhisker hissed, and limped through the camp wall and up the grassy slope. She scrabbled over the top and crouched beyond the rise, wincing with pain.

Dovepaw and Ivypaw scooted after her.

"Are you okay?" Dovepaw looked anxiously at Sedgewhisker's hind leg, which was swathed in cobweb and reeking of herbs.

Sedgewhisker was scowling. "Why did you come here?"

Dovepaw felt her ears flatten. Wasn't she pleased they had come? "I—I was worried," she stammered. "I heard a dog chasing you." She didn't dare say more in case she gave away her secret, but it seemed she had said too much already. A growl rumbled in Sedgewhisker's throat.

"Have you been spying on us?" the WindClan warrior snapped.

Ivypaw swung her head to stare at Dovepaw, her eyes flashing with alarm and confusion. "You didn't mention a dog!"

Sedgewhisker leaned closer. "How did you know about it?"

Dovepaw flinched away. "I—I heard it while I was training."

Ivypaw blinked. "When? You didn't say!"

Sedgewhisker was watching them through slitted eyes.

Dovepaw felt a stab of disappointment. "I was worried you were hurt, that's all," she muttered.

Sedgewhisker bristled. "We can take care of ourselves, you know. We don't need a ThunderClan apprentice to watch out for us!"

A voice grumbled from the shadows outside the bush wall. "What's going on? Who are you talking to, Sedgewhisker?"

Dovepaw and Ivypaw froze. There was nowhere to hide! Paw steps padded up the slope toward them. Ivypaw unsheathed her claws while Dovepaw struggled to slow her breathing. This wasn't how it was supposed to be.

A lithe ginger shape appeared above the edge of the hollow.

Weaselfur.

His gaze flicked over the two ThunderClan apprentices, and then Sedgewhisker. "What are you up to now?" he mewed wearily. "Haven't you caused us enough trouble today, getting your patrol tangled up with that dog?"

Sedgewhisker bristled. "I was the only one hurt!"

Weaselfur looked back at the camp. "Invaders!" he called. There was no urgency in his yowl. "Why didn't you alert the Clan?" he asked Sedgewhisker, hardly paying any attention to Dovepaw and Ivypaw.

"I was handling it," Sedgewhisker growled.

Ivypaw straightened up, whiskers quivering. "We don't need handling," she mewed crossly.

"Hush!" Weaselfur turned on her, his hackles rising.

WindClan cats began streaming through the gaps in the scrub wall and swarmed up the bank.

A blue-eyed tabby she-cat circled them, tasting the air. "ThunderClan!"

"Is it an invasion?" A brown-and-white tom curled his lip.

A tabby tom lashed his tail. "I can't *smell* any others."

"They may have disguised their scent," snarled a black she-cat.

"Do you really think they're that clever, Nightcloud?" sneered the tabby.

Breezepelt slunk over the rise, his pelt bristling. "What are you doing here?" His eyes flashed with menace.

Dovepaw blinked hopefully as Onestar appeared and stepped in front of the young warrior. "Harespring!" The WindClan leader nodded to the brown-and-white tom. "Take Leaftail and Owlwhisker and search the area."

The three warriors raced away, tails down, hackles up.

The blue-eyed tabby watched them leave, her claws kneading the grass. "Can I go too?"

"Calm down, Heathertail," Onestar ordered. "They'll call if they need backup."

Dovepaw's heart was racing. "We came alone." She wrapped her tail around Ivypaw and tried to keep her chin high.

Onestar's gaze was stern. "Why did you come?" he demanded. "Did Firestar send you?"

Dovepaw shook her head.

Sedgewhisker looked at her Clanmates. "She knew about the dog. She knew it chased us." She flashed a look at Dovepaw. "Though it was nothing we couldn't handle."

Onestar widened his eyes. "How did you know?"

Dovepaw was ready for the question. "I heard it from the

forest, while I was training."

Heathertail growled. "How could you tell it was chasing our warriors?"

Dovepaw struggled for words. "I just . . . er . . . guessed," she mewed at last.

"You *guessed*?" The WindClan leader sounded unconvinced. His Clanmates exchanged doubtful glances.

Breezepelt slid around his leader and glared at the two ThunderClan apprentices. "What else have you *guessed* about us?"

A small white she-cat appeared over the rise. *Whitetail!* She bristled when she spotted Dovepaw.

Dovepaw stared at the ground. She didn't want Whitetail's disapproval as well as Sedgewhisker's. What had happened to the friendships they'd made?

Whitetail approached the two ThunderClan apprentices. "The quest is over," she told Dovepaw. "You must respect boundaries. Your loyalty should be with your own Clan." There was gentleness in her mew, as if she, at least, understood Dovepaw's disappointment.

"Don't they teach ThunderClan 'paws about scent markers?" A young WindClan apprentice was pacing angrily behind Whitetail, his lip curled.

"Of course they do," Ivypaw replied hotly.

Onestar swept his tail over the heather. "Go back to your dens," he ordered his Clanmates. "Heathertail and Breezepelt will take these foolish apprentices back where they belong."

Dovepaw's pelt flashed with heat. "We're not foolish!"

Onestar gazed at her. "Then why are you here instead of tucked up in your nest?"

Dovepaw couldn't meet his gaze. *I thought my friends were in trouble!* Anger and sadness squirmed in her belly. It was her stupid power's fault that she'd heard the dog attack Sedgewhisker! She was only trying to be a good warrior. *And* a good friend. But it seemed friendship counted for nothing. She hung her head as Heathertail nudged her down the flank of the hill.

"Let's get you home," the blue-eyed warrior mewed.

Dovepaw shrugged her away and stomped through the heather. Ivypaw padded beside her. "At least they didn't shred us," she whispered.

Remorse stripped Dovepaw's anger away. "I'm sorry I made you come."

"You didn't make me do anything!" Ivypaw answered indignantly.

The two WindClan warriors flanked them as they crossed the moor. No one spoke, but a low growl rumbled occasionally in Breezepelt's throat.

Heathertail swung her head and glared at her Clanmate. "Will you stop making that noise!" she growled.

"Do you want to make them feel *welcome?*" Breezepelt snapped back.

"I think they got the message from Onestar," Heathertail pointed out. "They don't need you snarling at them all the way to the hollow. They're just apprentices."

"It'll teach them not to do it again."

"Just shut up!" Heathertail snorted. "No one died and made you leader."

Breezepelt let out a hiss, then was quiet.

The four cats swished through the heather to the ThunderClan scent line, where the stream chattered through the gully dividing the two territories.

"We know the way from here," Dovepaw told the WindClan warriors.

Heathertail gazed steadily at her. "We're taking you back to your camp."

"You can't do that!" Ivypaw objected.

What would Firestar say if they brought WindClan cats to the heart of their territory? Dovepaw's fur ruffled along her spine. But the WindClan cats looked determined. She and Ivypaw couldn't fight them, and she wasn't going to make this situation more humiliating by begging them not to come.

Breezepelt had already leaped the stream. Reluctantly, Dovepaw led her sister down the bank and jumped the gully. Heathertail bounded after them. With heavy paws, Dovepaw headed toward camp.

"Firestar's going to kill us," Ivypaw whispered in her ear.

Dovepaw didn't want to think about it. She couldn't explain why she had taken Ivypaw to the WindClan camp without revealing her power. The whole Clan was going to think they were mouse-brained and reckless.

The WindClan cats padded ahead of them, weaving along

tracks and through bushes as though they knew the forest well. Heathertail veered along a fox track that led them around a wide swath of brambles.

Ivypaw flicked her tail. "How do you know where you're going?"

Without glancing over her shoulder, Heathertail replied, "We've been here before."

"But—" Ivypaw began to protest.

"She said, we've been here before," Breezepelt growled in a voice that put an abrupt end to the conversation.

As they neared the thorn barrier, Dovepaw scented Rosepetal bounding toward them. "What are you doing here?" she challenged the WindClan warriors, hackles raised.

Breezepelt halted. "This isn't an attack."

Heathertail stepped aside. "We're just returning a couple of strays."

Rosepetal stared at Ivypaw and Dovepaw in disbelief. "What are you doing out of the hollow? And with *them*?" She flicked her tail to the WindClan cats.

A cloud crossed the moon. Dovepaw was relieved by the sudden shadow. She stared at her paws, not knowing how to explain.

"We found them outside our camp," Heathertail told the startled ThunderClan warrior.

Shifting her paws, Rosepetal stared levelly back at Heathertail. "Thank you for bringing them home," she meowed. "I'll take them back to their den."

Breezepelt stepped forward. "We're coming with them," he

told her. "I want to speak with Firestar."

Rosepetal bristled. "He's asleep."

"So was WindClan before this pair woke us!" Heathertail growled.

Dovepaw felt herself shrivel inside her pelt.

Ivypaw's tail drooped. "I didn't think it could get worse."

Breezepelt glared at her. "I don't want any accusations that we took ThunderClan apprentices prisoner."

Ivypaw bristled. "We wouldn't lie!"

Rosepetal sighed and dipped her head. "Very well." She turned and led the WindClan cats through the thorns.

Dovepaw trailed after, her heart quickening as she heard Rosepetal's paws on the rock pile. *She's gone to wake Firestar.*

Cats were stirring in their nests, den walls trembling as they got to their paws and slid out to see what was happening. The nursery shivered and tiny paw steps pattered across the clearing. "What's going on?" squeaked Cherrykit.

Poppyfrost's nest rustled and the queen's fur scraped the brambles as she followed her kit out of the nursery.

Dovepaw tried not to hear what any of the cats were saying. Her Clanmates were gathering to witness her humiliation. How could she explain? With a rush of frustration that tightened her throat, she wished fiercely that there were no such thing as the prophecy, and that she didn't have any powers at all.

Why can't I just be an ordinary cat?

CHAPTER 6

Jayfeather jerked awake. The air was still damp with night, yet voices were whispering in the clearing. Stones shifted as paws descended the rockfall.

Firestar's awake.

Jayfeather sat up.

He tasted the air.

WindClan.

Jayfeather leaped from his nest and nosed his way through the brambles as Lionblaze and Cinderheart slid from the warriors' den.

"What's going on?" Lionblaze circled his apprentice.

Dovepaw didn't answer, but fidgeted beside her sister as they stood as uncomfortable as owlets caught in daylight.

Briarpaw pushed her way out of the apprentices' den, whiskers twitching with curiosity. "Come and see this," she hissed over her shoulder to her denmates as Brambleclaw joined Firestar in the clearing. Nests rustled behind him, while Whitewing and Birchfall watched from their den, their tails gently stirring the branches.

Dustpelt pushed past them. "What are they doing here?"

The dark tabby tom's mew rang around the rock walls of the camp, anger aimed like a thorn at the WindClan warriors.

Breezepelt and Heathertail didn't flinch.

"Keep your voice down, Dustpelt," Firestar ordered. "We don't want to wake every cat."

"Why not?" Daisy marched out of the nursery, her fur bristling. "There are WindClan cats in the camp!"

"It's not an attack," Whitewing reassured the anxious queen.

"Are you sure?" Dustpelt circled the edge of the clearing, distrust crackling with every paw step.

Heathertail's tail brushed the ground. "You seem to have lost two apprentices," she meowed. "We're returning them."

Jayfeather felt guilt pulse like a flame from Dovepaw and Ivypaw.

"*I'll* handle this." Firestar's gaze flashed around his Clanmates. "Any cat not directly involved can go back to their nest."

Dustpelt halted. The yew bush swished as the other apprentices scooted inside. Whitewing and Birchfall backed into their den.

"Lionblaze and Cinderheart, I want you to stay," Firestar went on. "You too, Jayfeather."

"What about me?" Brambleclaw meowed.

"Make sure everyone is settled and reassure the queens." Firestar padded toward the thorn barrier. "Follow me," he called over his shoulder. "I don't want any more disturbances in camp."

Jayfeather tagged along behind Dovepaw, Ivypaw, Lionblaze, Cinderheart, and the WindClan warriors as they followed the ThunderClan leader through the thorn tunnel. The night air felt heavy on his pelt, and his mind was ablaze with the tensions flashing among the cats.

Outside the camp, Firestar sat down. Lionblaze's paws scuffed the fallen leaves. An owl hooted overhead, then flapped away through the trees. Breezepelt and Heathertail stood stiffly beside each other, while Dovepaw and Ivypaw shifted on their paws. Cinderheart was tense and unhappy; Jayfeather could sense the knot in her belly. He shivered in the cold breeze.

Firestar cleared his throat. "Now, what's going on?"

Breezepelt answered. "We found these two outside our camp."

Dovepaw and Ivypaw shuffled closer together.

"Ivypaw?" Firestar's attention focused on the apprentice. "Is that what happened?"

"We . . ." Ivypaw hesitated. "We were just exploring."

"In the middle of WindClan territory?" Firestar's mew was ominously soft.

"It was my fault!" Dovepaw broke in. "I . . . I heard a dog on the moor while we were tree training and I was worried. . . ."

Jayfeather curled his claws. *Oh no! Dovepaw! You mouse-brain!* He felt Lionblaze stiffen.

A growl rumbled in Breezepelt's throat. "You were worried?" His tail swished the leaves. "About *WindClan*? Firestar, don't you teach your apprentices the warrior code?"

Firestar paused, then addressed the WindClan warriors calmly. "Thank you for bringing them back. I am sorry they disturbed you and your Clanmates. Nothing like this will *ever* happen again."

Jayfeather sensed irritation itching beneath Dovepaw's pelt, but she had the good sense to hold her tongue.

"We *do* live by the warrior code," Firestar assured Breezepelt, his mew tight. "And we will make sure these young cats understand how important that is." The ThunderClan leader was seething, embarrassed by his apprentices, but Jayfeather could also sense questions fizzing in his mind. What had these apprentices really been doing in WindClan territory?

Heathertail breathed out slowly. "Make sure you do." As she turned and began to head away from the ThunderClan camp, Jayfeather felt tension crackle like lightning between her and Lionblaze, and she aimed her final barb at the golden warrior. "You should keep a closer eye on your apprentice from now on."

Breezepelt swished after her through the undergrowth. "WindClan can take care of itself without your help!" he called before the ferns swallowed him.

Firestar waited until their paw steps had faded. "What in the name of StarClan did you think you were doing?" he demanded, turning on Dovepaw and Ivypaw.

"It was my idea!" Dovepaw insisted.

"Ivypaw isn't stuck to you like a piece of cobweb!" Firestar pointed out. "She could have changed her mind at any time."

"I wasn't going to let Dovepaw go alone!" Ivypaw objected.

"That doesn't explain what you were doing in WindClan territory!" Firestar snorted. "What's this nonsense about hearing a dog?"

When neither apprentice answered, he sighed. "Very well. Whatever the reason, it was a dumb thing to do!"

Was he really going to leave it at that? Jayfeather tipped his head to one side as Firestar went on.

"I'll leave your punishment up to your mentors, but I hope they will make sure you improve your understanding of the warrior code. Your training so far seems to have left little impression." Leaves rustled beneath his paws. "If you're going to behave like kits, then you should be treated like kits. Now go!"

Dovepaw and Ivypaw began to pad away.

"Dovepaw," Firestar called. "I want an extra word with you."

Ivypaw halted, puzzled. "Why not me?"

"Never you mind." Cinderheart nudged her forward. "Just do as you're told!"

Ivypaw's feet scuffed the ground as she was marched away by her mentor.

Jayfeather made to leave too, but Firestar called him back. "I want you and Lionblaze to stay."

He was circling Dovepaw, his mind sharp as a thorn. "How did you know about this dog?" he quizzed the apprentice.

"W-what do you mean?" Dovepaw stammered.

Firestar's attention flashed toward Jayfeather, crackling with suspicion. "What about you? Did StarClan send you a sign or a dream about the dog?"

Jayfeather shook his head. He wished he could lie to hide Dovepaw's stupid mistake, but Firestar wouldn't fall for it. "I've dreamed about dogs on the moors before," he mumbled. "But not recently."

Firestar's attention shot back to Dovepaw.

"So, how *did* you know about it? Did you dream it?"

"I told you," Dovepaw answered. "I *heard* it!"

A frustrated growl rumbled in Firestar's throat. "What about you, Lionblaze? You were tree training with her. Did *you* hear this dog?"

Lionblaze shifted his paws. "I was on the ground," he mumbled. "There was a breeze. It was impossible to tell."

Firestar cut him off. "Then it was just Dovepaw."

Jayfeather shifted his paws, his belly tightening. What was the ThunderClan leader getting at?

"Have you heard anything else other cats don't hear?" Firestar's question came out of the blue. "Like beavers blocking a stream, for example? That wasn't a dream, was it?"

Jayfeather froze. The shock from Lionblaze's pelt swept over him like an icy wind.

The Clan leader sighed. "Dovepaw, I've worked out that you know things other cats don't, and I don't think you're having dreams about them. So how *do* you know?" His tail-tip was tapping the ground. "I need to know. It's important. It helped save the lake, but it also just got you into serious trouble. Even worse, it could have caused a battle with WindClan, and that makes it my responsibility."

Confusion was flooding from Dovepaw, her mind whirling

as she searched for something to say.

Firestar snorted and flicked his attention back to Jayfeather and Lionblaze. "It looks like I'm going to have to be the one who says it, doesn't it?"

Lionblaze was holding his breath as Firestar went on.

"I think the three of you have something in common. Something we maybe should have discussed before."

The fur on Jayfeather's spine lifted.

"Haven't you wondered why you can slip so easily into other cats' dreams, Jayfeather? That's not something every medicine cat can do. And Lionblaze, do you think I haven't noticed the way you fight? You're not just brave; you're completely without fear. You must *know* that you're safe. That no mortal cat can hurt you. And then we have Dovepaw, who knows what's going on farther away than any of us can hear or see." Firestar paused to take a breath.

He knows! Jayfeather's heart beat faster. *He knows we're the Three!*

Chapter 7

"Long ago, I was told of a prophecy—" the ThunderClan leader began.

"We know!" Jayfeather interrupted. He had walked through this memory in one of Firestar's dreams. "We're the Three. Kin of your kin, with the power of the stars in our paws."

Shock flashed from Firestar's pelt, then ebbed into weary acceptance. "So you know already." He sighed. "I've been waiting for you a long time, since before Leafpool and Squirrelflight were born."

Jayfeather wasn't interested in Firestar's memories. "But what does the prophecy *mean*?"

"Mean?" Firestar sounded surprised.

Doesn't he know?

Before Jayfeather could speak, Dovepaw found her voice. "Did you think it would be Leafpool and Squirrelflight?"

"For a while," Firestar answered slowly. "I thought it might be them and Cloudtail. But nothing happened. Then Jaykit, Lionkit, and Hollykit were born." He stopped, and when he spoke again his tone was curious. "How long have you known about the prophecy?"

Jayfeather shrugged. "Since we were apprentices."

"Did StarClan tell you?"

"Not exactly." Jayfeather wanted to delve into Firestar's mind, find out everything the ThunderClan leader knew about the prophecy. But he was only one of the Three. Lionblaze and Dovepaw needed to know too. The whole thing would have to be teased out in words. "But it didn't need to come from StarClan, did it? This is not *their* prophecy."

"No." Firestar sounded perplexed. His paws shifted on the night-damp earth. "Do you know what your destiny is?"

"Don't *you*?" Dovepaw gasped. "I mean, if you know about the prophecy, how come you don't know what it means?"

"Didn't the old cat tell you?" Lionblaze meowed.

There was a moment of silence as Firestar digested the fact that the three cats knew who had given the prophecy to him. "I don't think even *he* understood what it meant," Firestar admitted. "He was just passing on a message."

Ice-cold fear spread along Jayfeather's spine. *No cat knows!* They were floundering in shadow, heading for what?

He felt Firestar's muzzle touch his head. "Skywatcher promised that you would come, and you have. We must have faith. There's nothing we can do but wait," the ThunderClan leader murmured.

Rage clawed Jayfeather's belly. Didn't he care what dangers could be lying in wait for his Clan?

"Tell me." Firestar turned his attention back to Dovepaw. "What exactly is your power?"

Jayfeather sensed her stiffen, like a hunted mouse. They'd

always told her to keep her power secret.

"It's okay," Lionblaze mewed. "You can tell him."

"Okay." Dovepaw hesitated for a moment. "I can sense things," she began tentatively. "Faraway things."

"How do you sense them?" Firestar urged.

"I—I hear them, and smell them, and sort of get glimpses."

"Do you hear everything all the time?"

"It's all kind of there—around me, in the background." Dovepaw fidgeted. "I'm used to it. Like . . ." Another pause, then, "Like *you* don't see every tree around you all the time but you know they are there; you know what they look like; you can remember which is which. You can focus on one tree or, if something's out of place or unusual, it'll catch your eye—it'll make you look harder."

"I see." There was warmth in Firestar's mew. "Now I know why you're so good at hunting." The ThunderClan leader's tail swished. "The Three have come at last." He sounded satisfied. "I will sleep a little easier from now on. Just be careful—your powers set you apart from other cats, but you are still members of this Clan. You are still bound by the warrior code, for as long as that stands."

Jayfeather leaned forward, heart pounding. "But we don't know what we're here for!"

"And there's nothing we can do until we find out." Firestar began to pad toward the hollow. "ThunderClan is lucky that you have come. Let's not ask for the stars as well. Tell me if anything changes," he meowed over his shoulder. "You will have my full support."

The thorns rustled as the ThunderClan leader disappeared into camp.

Lionblaze breathed out slowly. "How come he never said anything before?"

Jayfeather sat down. "I guess he was just waiting until he was sure."

"I gave us away." Dovepaw's mew was contrite. "I shouldn't have gone to WindClan."

"It might be for the best," Jayfeather reassured her.

"Yes," Lionblaze agreed. "And now it'll be easier to ask for more training time away from the other apprentices."

"But we still don't know what we're training for," Dovepaw pointed out. A yawn overtook her. Jayfeather was suddenly aware of the tiredness dragging at the young cat's paws.

He blinked at Lionblaze, but the golden warrior was already padding over to his apprentice. "Come on," he meowed, his fur brushing hers. "Let's get you back to your den. You'll need some rest before tomorrow's training." Lionblaze paused. "Are you staying here, Jayfeather?"

"I need to think."

Lionblaze yawned. "Can't you think in your nest?"

"I won't stay out long," Jayfeather promised.

"Okay." Lionblaze sounded too tired to argue. He followed Dovepaw through the thorn barrier, leaving Jayfeather alone under the trees.

Firestar doesn't know any more than we do. Jayfeather sighed. He walked down to the lake, following the scent of water and wind. As he emerged from the trees, the breeze whipped his whiskers back against his cheeks.

Jayfeather pictured the lake, wide, black, and silent, hiding the stick in its depths. *Why did I destroy it?*

He felt pebbles beneath his paws as he neared the water's edge. A yowl rose from his belly. "I'm sorry! Rock! I didn't mean it!" He drew the dank night air over his tongue, trying to catch some hint of the ancient cat's scent, but tasted nothing but dying leaves and water. Fear yawned like a dark pit in his belly. Rock knew about the prophecy long before StarClan crowded Silverpelt, and Jayfeather had broken the only link he'd had with the blind old cat.

"Oh, Rock! Please! I need to know!"

The wind blew Jayfeather's pleas back into his face. But he knew Rock heard him, could reply if he wanted.

Angrily, Jayfeather headed along the shore to where the stream tumbled out of the forest. He padded up the bank, picking his way carefully over the tangle of roots, heading upstream into the trees. When the stream narrowed, he leaped over it, careful not to let his tail fall into the cold, chattering water.

The damp earth felt good underpaw and he broke into a trot. He focused his senses harder so that he could run among the trees, sharply aware of the space around him, his whiskers and nose mapping his course, his ear fur pricked for the muting of sound that signaled the thickening of the undergrowth ahead.

Suddenly a leaf crackled. A bitter tang spiked his nostrils. *ShadowClan!*

Was he that close to the border already? He slowed and

padded forward cautiously, sniffing. Border markers dotted the trees ahead. They were fresh. Had ShadowClan started night patrols? He sniffed again. The scent belonged to a single tom. Why would one cat be out scent marking by himself?

A yowl ripped the air. Unsheathed claws slammed into Jayfeather's shoulders, thrusting him into the leafy soil. He spluttered and shoved himself upward, rage firing his muscles. He flung off his attacker, recognizing the scent.

"Tigerheart!"

It was Tawnypelt's son.

The young ShadowClan tom scrabbled to his paws. "S-sorry!"

Jayfeather sensed shame flooding Tigerheart's pelt as the young tom realized he'd attacked a medicine cat.

"I didn't realize it was you." The earth whispered as Tigerheart sheathed his claws. "I thought you were trespassing."

"Medicine cats can go where they need to," Jayfeather reminded him.

"I—I know," Tigerheart stammered. "What are you doing here? At night, I mean. Do you need something from ShadowClan? I can take you to Blackstar. Were you on your way somewhere?"

While Tigerheart gabbled, Jayfeather smoothed his ruffled fur and tasted the air, listening for waves on the shore and the tone of the wind in the trees, trying to figure out exactly where he was. Far from the shore, close to the ShadowClan border, close enough to be knocked onto the wrong side by a clumsy attack from a young warrior. Realizing the markers were behind him, Jayfeather carefully edged backward until he was sure his paws were back in his own territory. A medicine cat could roam where he pleased, but not without good reason.

"What are *you* doing here at this time of night?" Jayfeather hid his own discomfort by questioning Tigerheart. "Are you on patrol?"

"S-sort of." Tigerheart shifted his paws. "Anyway, it's none of your business." His mew hardened.

He's being very defensive. Jayfeather leaned closer. "Shadow-Clan doesn't usually send out lone patrols in the middle of the night."

"ThunderClan doesn't send out lone medicine cats," Tiger-heart countered.

Cheeky cub! "You should go back to your den," Jayfeather snapped. "You must have training tomorrow."

To his surprise, Tigerheart backed off. "Okay." Turning, the young tom scampered away into the trees.

As Jayfeather sniffed his fading scent, another touched his nose. It seemed oddly familiar as it wreathed around him but he couldn't place it.

The fur on his shoulders prickled. Stiffening, Jayfeather felt himself being watched. He spun around, tasting the air, ears pricked, frustrated by his blindness. Was a cat observing him from the shadows? No sound. No scent, other than those Tigerheart had left.

Jayfeather shook out his fur. *Don't be mouse-brained!* Tasting dawn, he ducked through a hazel bush and headed home.

Who'd be watching me at this time of night?

Chapter 8

Cold raindrops showered from the roof as Ivypaw pushed her way through the entrance and flung herself into her nest, making the whole den shudder.

"Hey!" Blossompaw sat up, shaking out her pelt.

Dovepaw blinked open her eyes. Was it dawn already? She felt heavy with sleep after yesterday's long training session with Lionblaze. He'd made her test her senses to their limit, insisting she keep her awareness spread to the very edges of their territory while she hunted for the Clan.

"Have a nice sleep?" Ivypaw asked crossly.

Gray light was seeping through the yew branches. Far above the hollow, the forest roared in the wind. Ivypaw's pelt clung, sodden and dripping, to her small frame.

Another stormy day.

Dovepaw stretched and yawned. "Have you been out already?"

"Dawn patrol," Ivypaw huffed. "I don't see why Brambleclaw made me go while he let you sleep in."

Dovepaw pricked her ears. Did Firestar tell his deputy about her powers so that *he* would make allowances too? Why couldn't they treat her like an ordinary apprentice? She stiffened as Ivypaw went on.

"What's so special about you?" Ivypaw muttered. "I've seen Firestar watching you when he thinks no one's looking. Now Brambleclaw's started treating you like you've just come down from Silverpelt."

"I guess they're just making sure we're following the rules," Dovepaw soothed, hoping Ivypaw would believe her.

"And the rule is that you get to lie in a warm den while I'm out trudging through the rain?" Ivypaw snapped.

Blossompaw was washing the drips from her pelt. "We all have to do dawn patrols sometimes," she pointed out.

"Some of us more often than others," Ivypaw growled.

"Perhaps Brambleclaw's got something planned for me," Dovepaw mewed.

"What? Like an extra rabbit for breakfast?" Ivypaw curled down into her nest with her back toward Dovepaw.

"I'm sorry you had to go out without me." Dovepaw began lapping at the raindrops caught in Ivypaw's pelt. *I wish they'd send me on the same patrols as Ivypaw, just to make it fair.* "At least we're allowed out of camp now," she mewed between licks.

"Huh!" Ivypaw grumped, but Dovepaw could feel her relaxing.

"They can't punish you forever," Blossompaw mewed.

The two apprentices had been confined to camp for a quarter moon as part of their punishment for crossing the border into WindClan territory. Dovepaw couldn't help thinking the elders' den and nursery had never been so clean. They had spent every day dragging bracken in and out of the dens until Ivypaw was convinced they'd made every cat in the Clan a new nest.

"Dovepaw!" Lionblaze's call sounded through the yew branches.

Ivypaw snorted. "Great timing," she complained. "You were just getting to my itchy spot."

"Sorry," Dovepaw apologized. "Got to go." She leaped from her nest and pushed her way out of the den into a haze of rain. "What is it?"

Lionblaze was sitting, whiskers dripping, in the rain-soaked clearing. "Hear anything?"

Dovepaw sighed. This had become his usual greeting. Did he think she was nothing more than a pair of gigantic walking ears?

"No," she hissed, her irritation deepening as she noticed Firestar emerge from his den, his gaze flicking straight toward her.

A ripple of dark fur caught her eye. Briarpaw was scampering toward her, brown pelt plastered with rain. Thornclaw, her mentor, padded slowly after her.

"We're going on border patrol!" Briarpaw skidded to a halt, slewing muddy water against Dovepaw's pelt. The wind, circling down into the hollow, tugged at her whiskers.

Dovepaw purred, cheered by her denmate's enthusiasm. It was as if the young cat hadn't even noticed it was raining.

Thornclaw clearly had. He shook his whiskers crossly, sending droplets spraying. "Are you ready?" he asked Lionblaze, casting a brief glance at Dovepaw. "Brambleclaw wants us to check ShadowClan's markers."

Dovepaw felt a surge of excitement. A run through the forest would warm her up. "Come on!" She raced for the thorn barrier, beckoning to Briarpaw with her tail, and slipped through, happy to be out of sight of Firestar's watchful gaze.

Thornclaw caught up to them outside.

"Which way should we go?" Dovepaw panted.

Thornclaw was staring along the gully. "We'll go by the ancient oak," he decided. He headed through the trees, his paws slapping over the wet leaves.

As they headed into the dripping forest, Dovepaw screwed up her face. Mud was clogging her claws and oozing up through her toes. Each time they pushed through a thicket a fresh shower of water seeped through her pelt.

Suddenly paw steps slithered behind them. "Wait for me." Graystripe was hurrying after them. "Firestar asked me to join you." The gray warrior was puffing. His leaf-bare pelt, normally so thick, was rain-slicked against his body and he looked unusually lean.

Thornclaw flicked his tail. "Has ShadowClan been crossing the border again?"

"No prey has been stolen." Lionblaze narrowed his eyes. "Just a few stray scent trails on our side of the border."

Graystripe shook the rain from his fur till it stood in spikes. "Firestar wants us to keep an eye on the situation."

Briarpaw's eyes were round. "Do you think Firestar will mention it at the Gathering tomorrow?"

"I don't see why not," Graystripe meowed.

Thornclaw peered up through the trees. "If there *is* a Gathering." Dark clouds swarmed the sky, heavy with more rain.

"There's a good breeze," Graystripe observed. "I think it'll have blown away the clouds by morning." A hefty gust buffeted its way through the canopy and whisked the undergrowth. Graystripe dug in his claws as the breeze streamed through his whiskers. "If it hasn't blown us away too."

The stream was in full flood and it took Thornclaw a while to find the narrowest place to cross. He leaped first over the gushing brown water and turned to watch Briarpaw safely over. Dovepaw jumped next, her heart lurching as her paws skidded on the muddy bank. Thornclaw grabbed her scruff while she found her feet. Graystripe and Lionblaze made the crossing in easy bounds.

"It's hard to believe the lake was ever empty," Graystripe commented, watching the water swirl away downstream.

Lionblaze was already pushing on, leaping onto a fallen tree. The bark was green and shiny with wet moss, and as he landed his paws skidded, sending him hurtling over the other side. "Oof!"

Dovepaw heard him grunt as he crashed down through the dripping foliage. The smell of wild garlic tainted the air. She stretched her front paws up the log, peering over the top. "Are you okay?"

Lionblaze was thrashing around in a patch of dark green leaves, turning the air sour with their scent as he crushed them beneath him.

Dovepaw swallowed back a purr of amusement as Lionblaze finally scrambled to his paws, his fur ruffled. "I'm fine," he snapped.

"Should we all disguise our scent?" Dovepaw asked as innocently as she could.

"That wasn't my intention and you know it!" Lionblaze flicked his tail and headed on through the forest while Thornclaw and Graystripe bounded over the fallen tree after him.

"Be careful," Briarpaw warned with a sparkle in her eyes as Dovepaw mounted the log. "It's a bit slippery."

Dovepaw snorted.

Briarpaw was purring loudly as they caught up with their mentors, but she hushed when Thornclaw flashed her a stern look. Instead, she wrinkled her nose at Dovepaw. "At least we won't lose him," she whispered, glancing at Lionblaze.

The golden tom stank of garlic, but was striding ahead as though he hadn't even noticed.

Dovepaw began to scent ShadowClan markers, so strong that even the smell of Lionblaze couldn't hide them. They mingled with the ThunderClan markers, which matched ShadowClan's scent for scent. She wondered whether to cast her senses farther, to try to detect ShadowClan movement beyond, but yesterday's practice had left her mind weary.

Light splashed in among the trees as they approached the edge of the forest. Dovepaw recognized the grassy space beyond, where she had charged unwittingly into a Twoleg pelt-den on the journey upriver. Fortunately the field was deserted now. Not even a Twoleg would be dumb enough to sit around in this miserable weather.

Lionblaze halted at the tree line, which was dotted with ShadowClan scent. Thornclaw and Graystripe began weaving among the undergrowth within the borderline, sniffing each bush and clump of ferns.

"Any sign?" Lionblaze called.

Graystripe shook his head, but Thornclaw had halted at a low hazel bush a few tail-lengths inside the border.

Briarpaw hurried to join him. "ShadowClan?" She sniffed the bush, the fur rippling along her spine. "They've been here!" she mewed in alarm.

Lionblaze and Graystripe crowded around her. Dovepaw hung back, the scent as clear in her nostrils as if she were standing beside it.

Tigerheart!

The scent pricked her memory. The young ShadowClan warrior had journeyed upstream to find the beavers with her. She knew his smell as well as any of her denmates'.

"Get back, Lionblaze," Thornclaw ordered. "That garlic stink is tainting everything."

That's why he doesn't recognize it! Dovepaw watched as Thornclaw sniffed again and found herself hoping that the warrior wouldn't identify the scent.

Graystripe padded to the border and started pacing, lashing his tail. "Patrol!" he warned.

Four ShadowClan cats were approaching across the grass, their pelts rippling. Thornclaw and Lionblaze squared up beside Graystripe to face them, keeping their paws on their own side of the border, but baring their teeth.

While Briarpaw hurried to join her Clanmates, Dovepaw padded to the hazel bush and sniffed. It was definitely Tigerheart. What in the name of StarClan had he been thinking, crossing the border? Was it an accident? Perhaps he'd been chasing prey and hadn't noticed until it was too late.

"What are you doing on our border?" A black-and-white ShadowClan tom stared challengingly at the ThunderClan patrol.

Dovepaw recognized Crowfrost from the Gatherings. He had halted a few paw steps from the ThunderClan cats. Beside him stood Ratscar, Pinepaw, and Tigerheart.

Graystripe curled his lip. "We're checking out the ShadowClan scents *inside* our border."

Crowfrost's hackles lifted. "What?"

"There's a hazel bush drenched in ShadowClan scent over here," Lionblaze snarled.

Tigerheart growled, "What would we want with a load of sodden old trees?"

Graystripe dug his claws into the muddy ground. "Then why did you cross our border?"

"No ShadowClan cat has crossed your border," Ratscar hissed.

Dovepaw was watching Tigerheart. His amber eyes gave nothing away.

Thornclaw stood aside. "Come and smell it for yourself!" he challenged.

"Don't tell us what to do!" Pinepaw was ripping at the

muddy ground, grass clumping between his claws. "Just because it was ThunderClan's idea to go upstream to find the river doesn't mean you're in charge of every cat."

"Just smell it!" Thornclaw growled.

"Don't be ridiculous!" Crowfrost spluttered. "If we cross your border then there will definitely be ShadowClan scent on your territory."

Ratscar curled his lip. "Are you trying to trick us into a fight?"

"Why would we do that?" Lionblaze stared levelly at the ShadowClan warrior.

Tigerheart stepped forward. "Okay," he meowed. "*I'll* check it. But remember that *you* invited me over the border!" He trotted over the scent line, his tail straight up in the air. "Where's this bush?"

Dovepaw narrowed her eyes. If Tigerheart checked the scent, he'd disguise his old scent with new. The evidence would be hidden. *Smart!* She felt a flash of admiration for his cunning. But still, he was up to something. What could it be? She stood her ground beside the hazel bush as he approached.

"Over here?" he called, shoving his nose into the brown leaves. "There's a faint scent here, but it's too old to tell if it's ShadowClan or ThunderClan." He turned, brushing his pelt against the bush, leaving strands of fur clinging to the spiky branches. "You must have bees in your brain, as usual." Nose high, he turned back toward his Clanmates. The two patrols were still facing each other, as if they were daring their rivals to make the first move.

Dovepaw hissed as he passed her. "It was *you*, wasn't it?"

Tigerheart swung his head to stare at her, his eyes startled.

"Don't deny it!" Dovepaw whispered, one eye on her Clanmates. They were busy outglaring ShadowClan. "I recognized your scent *before* you crossed the border."

"Don't tell, please!" Tigerheart's tail drooped. "I'll explain everything at the Gathering tomorrow."

He shifted his paws, glancing anxiously toward his Clanmates.

A wave of sympathy washed over Dovepaw. She didn't want to get him in trouble. He'd helped her defeat the beavers. She at least had to give him a chance to explain. "Okay," she agreed.

"Thank you." Smoothing his fur, Tigerheart recrossed the border and joined his Clanmates. "They're imagining it," he reported to Crowfrost.

"See?" Ratscar sniffed. "It was probably just scent drifting over the border."

Graystripe took a step forward. "There was definitely scent on that bush!"

Crowfrost leaned closer till their whiskers almost touched. Only the invisible border separated them. "Why are you so scared of a bit of ShadowClan scent?"

Briarpaw puffed out her chest. "We're not scared!"

No cat moved.

"Are you leaving?" Thornclaw growled at last.

"Why should we?" Ratscar flashed back at him. "We're on our own territory."

Graystripe snorted. "Come on," he ordered his Clanmates. "If they want to rot their paws by standing in the mud, let them." He turned, letting his tail flick over the border so that it brushed Crowfrost's nose.

Crowfrost growled, his fur spiking, but he didn't move as the ThunderClan patrol followed Graystripe into the trees.

Dovepaw glanced over her shoulder. Ratscar and Crowfrost were talking softly, their heads bent together. Pinepaw was pacing the border, hackles still raised, but Tigerheart stood calmly gazing after her.

Dovepaw caught his eye and looked away, suddenly feeling self-conscious.

What's wrong with him? He had been so open and straightforward on the journey upstream. She'd never thought of him as sneaky. At least he'd promised to explain at the Gathering.

As they approached the hollow, Dovepaw, out of habit, let her senses search for Ivypaw. Her sister was not in camp. She listened until she recognized Ivypaw's mew.

"Told you so!" Ivypaw was in the training hollow with Blossompaw. "You didn't get me that time."

Comforted, knowing her sister was safe and well, Dovepaw followed the patrol through the thorns. Firestar was pacing the clearing, his pelt dripping from the rain. He turned as soon as the patrol entered camp.

"Well?" he demanded, padding straight to Graystripe.

Graystripe shook the water from his whiskers. "More scents inside the border," he reported.

Firestar frowned. Dustpelt, who had been sheltering under ferns at the edge of the clearing, emerged into the drizzle. "Is ShadowClan still trespassing?"

Cloudtail, his white pelt gray with rain, sat huddled in

the clearing, ears pricked and eyes round. Sandstorm peered out from Firestar's den, her green gaze glinting from the gloom, and stared with narrowed eyes at the knot of warriors. Millie padded out from her den, touching Graystripe's shoulder with her nose before nuzzling Briarpaw, their kit. The brambles at the entrance to the medicine den trembled and Jayfeather padded out and sat down, his unseeing stare fixed on the returning patrol.

"I think it's just one warrior who's crossing the border," Graystripe reassured his Clanmates.

Sandstorm ran down the tumble of rocks. "Do you know which one?"

Dovepaw glanced at her paws. While angry murmurs rippled through her Clan as they speculated, she let her senses stretch back toward ShadowClan territory. Tigerheart was following his patrol into their camp. While Ratscar reported to Blackstar, he lifted a rat from the fresh-kill pile and carried it to the edge of the clearing, then lay down and began to eat, with one anxious eye on his leader.

"So what are we going to do about it?" Dustpelt's challenge brought Dovepaw's senses back to the ThunderClan clearing.

Firestar lifted his chin. "Since we don't know yet which cat is crossing the border, there's nothing we can do."

Thornclaw growled, low and hard.

"But," Firestar went on, "we will strengthen patrols on the ShadowClan border and hopefully catch this warrior and find out what he's up to."

"I'd like to be the one who catches him," Lionblaze hissed.

"Or *her*," Millie countered.

"Whoever it is," Firestar went on, "we can't be sure whether they are acting on behalf of ShadowClan or alone, and until we are, we must not overreact."

"You'll mention it at the Gathering, though?" Sandstorm prompted.

"If necessary," Firestar meowed.

"If *necessary*?" Dustpelt spluttered.

Graystripe wove between the brown tabby tom and his leader. "Why stir up ill feeling if none exists?"

Lionblaze lashed his tail. "Because ShadowClan will think we're weak!"

Firestar sat down and hooked his tail over his forepaws. "Strength doesn't have to be proved." He gazed intently at the golden warrior. "Remember, it may just be a single Shadow-Clan warrior, not the whole Clan."

"Then we should tell them!" Thornclaw snapped. "If they can't control their own warriors, every Clan should know it."

"I know, Thornclaw." Firestar dipped his head to the tabby warrior. "But sometimes it's better to wait and see before sharing our problems. I don't want the Clans thinking we can't protect our borders."

Thornclaw shook some of the moisture from his fur. "I suppose," he muttered.

Firestar and Sandstorm bounded up the rocks, back to the shelter of the leader's cave. Dustpelt followed Thornclaw to the shelter of Highledge, while Graystripe, Millie, and Briarpaw went to sniff the bedraggled prey on the fresh-kill pile.

"Are you hungry?" Lionblaze asked Dovepaw.

Before she could answer Jayfeather called across the clearing, "So?" The gray medicine cat hurried toward them. "Do you know who it is?" His gaze flicked anxiously to Lionblaze as he went on. "I caught Tigerheart sniffing around our border a few nights ago."

"Really?" Dovepaw couldn't hide her surprise. Then the ShadowClan warrior *was* up to something. Still, she held her tongue. She'd made a promise to let him explain first, and she wasn't going to break it. After all, the Gathering was tomorrow. She wouldn't have to keep her secret long.

"Tigerheart?" Lionblaze sounded equally surprised. "Why would he be up to anything on our borders? He was an ally half a moon ago! He helped us bring the river back."

But Jayfeather was frowning. "That was half a moon ago," he pointed out. "Not all cats think that one adventure makes everyone friends forever."

Dovepaw bristled. Was he criticizing her for going to check on Sedgewhisker? Guilt stabbed her. And now she had agreed to keep Tigerheart's secret. Perhaps Jayfeather was right to remind her of her loyalties.

A raindrop dripped from her ear tip and tickled the soft fur inside. She shook her head sharply. She would keep quiet until she heard what the ShadowClan warrior had to say at the Gathering.

CHAPTER 9

Dovepaw padded restlessly beside the barrier of thorns, anxious to be off.

Ivypaw sat watching her, her tail twitching irritably. "You'll tell me everything?" she asked again.

"Of course," Dovepaw promised. "As soon as I get back." Ivypaw seemed to have gotten over her suspicion about why Dovepaw was being treated differently by the senior warriors, until Brambleclaw decided that only Dovepaw would go to the Gathering tonight.

Ivypaw glared at the ThunderClan deputy as he padded past.

He paused. "Don't sulk," he meowed. "You're not a kit. You don't need your littermate by your side every moment of the day."

Whitewing sat up from where she'd been dozing after her evening meal. "As I recall, Brambleclaw," she teased, "you were never pleased to miss a Gathering." She glanced affectionately at her daughters.

Brambleclaw gave the white she-cat a stern glance, which lasted only a moment before melting into amusement. "Well, at least I had the decency to sulk in the privacy of my den."

Ivypaw scowled down at her paws, tail flicking.

"Don't worry." Dovepaw wove around her as Brambleclaw padded away to sit beside Graystripe. "When we're warriors we'll go to every Gathering together."

Squirrelflight slid out of the warriors' den and padded across the clearing. Her gaze darted toward Brambleclaw for a moment before she joined Leafpool beside the fresh-kill pile.

"Do you think Brambleclaw will ever forgive them?" Dovepaw whispered, staring at the two sisters. How could Brambleclaw be so cold toward his former mate? With a shiver, she wondered how two cats who'd been so close could suddenly start acting like they belonged to different Clans. That would never happen to her and Ivypaw.

At least Squirrelflight and Leafpool are still as close. Dovepaw watched the sisters as they leaned together, pelts pressing like littermates straight out of the nursery.

She nudged Ivypaw with her nose. "I'll make sure I get some juicy gossip from Petalfur," she mewed. She hoped that the shy RiverClan she-cat wouldn't act like they'd never shared an adventure.

Firestar bounded down from Highledge. As the stones clacked beneath his paws, the rest of the patrol hurried toward the thorn entrance. Sandstorm, Thornclaw, and Brackenfur wove restlessly beside the entrance as Foxleap, Rosepetal, and Brightheart emerged from the warriors' den. Lionblaze was still licking his lips after a hasty meal as he waited for Jay-feather to pad from the medicine den. Together they joined their Clanmates while Millie slid from the dirtplace tunnel and hurried to stand beside Graystripe. Birchfall slid in next to Whitewing while Blossompaw and Briarpaw came dashing from the apprentices' den, eyes bright with excitement.

Bumblepaw called after them, "I want to know everything that happens!" He'd be staying behind with Ivypaw.

As Squirrelflight left Leafpool's side and tagged on to the patrol, Firestar signaled with his tail before ducking out of the camp. His Clanmates streamed out after him. Dovepaw sensed restlessness in the patrol as they headed for the lake in silence. Graystripe had been right: The wind had blown the sky clear and Silverpelt glittered around a full, bright moon. But the forest still dripped from the heavy rains, and Dovepaw's fur was soon soaked as she followed her Clanmates through the wet undergrowth.

The chilly dampness seemed to have set everyone's fur pricking with irritation.

"We'd better not find any ShadowClan stench on our land!" Foxleap growled.

"Don't be ridiculous," Brambleclaw snapped. "We're heading around WindClan's side of the lake. Even ShadowClan wouldn't be dumb enough to stray that far!"

Thornclaw paused and tasted the air. "I wouldn't put anything past ShadowClan," he muttered.

Foxleap lashed his tail. "We should cross into ShadowClan territory and leave *our* scent. See how they like it!"

"Yeah!" Rosepetal agreed. "I bet they wouldn't be too pleased." These days the dark cream she-cat seemed to agree with every word her denmate uttered.

Mouse-brain. Dovepaw instantly felt guilty. Rosepetal was a good warrior. Still, Dovepaw hoped that she would never be too moony about a tomcat to stop thinking for herself.

"We should do it," Lionblaze growled. "Just to show them. Though their noses are probably too filled with pine scent to notice."

Squirrelflight bounded up the slope past the golden warrior. "Stop stirring up trouble," she warned.

Brambleclaw reached the top of the slope and stared down at Squirrelflight. "Sometimes aggression is necessary. StarClan gave us claws for a reason."

The orange she-cat's eyes flashed with shock, as though his words had raked her muzzle. Lionblaze winced visibly. The patrol regrouped at the shoreline and followed the lake's edge, keeping three tail-lengths from the water.

Dovepaw scanned the hillsides. No sign of the other Clans, and no fresh scent tainted the fallen tree spanning the watery gap between the shore and the island. As Dovepaw crossed, her claws unsheathed to grip the slippery bark, she listened past the water rippling below the trunk, beyond the wind stirring the island trees.

The clearing was empty. She hopped down from the tree-bridge. The shingle crunched beneath her paws and water soaked up through her paw fur.

"Come on," she whispered to Blossompaw. "Let's explore."

"But—"

She left Blossompaw trailing as she raced through the

trees. "It's okay," she called over her shoulder. "We're the first here."

Blossompaw burst from the ferns a moment after Dovepaw had skidded into the clearing at the center of the island. The air was foul with the stench of weeds rotting on the waterlogged shoreline. Dovepaw wrinkled her nose. How did RiverClan bear it?

"Wait for me!" Briarpaw hurtled from the undergrowth after them. She halted and stared around the deserted clearing. Their Clanmates were still traipsing through the bushes, tree-lengths behind them.

"Let's climb the big tree!" Blossompaw was already racing toward the Great Oak that loomed at the head of the clearing. In a blink Blossompaw had shot up the trunk and was sitting on the lowest branch, laying her tail regally over her front paws and puffing out her chest as though she were about to address the Clans.

"I, Blossomstar, welcome you—"

"Get down!" At Squirrelflight's stinging yowl, Blossompaw slid off the branch and tumbled to the ground.

Dovepaw spun around, startled. The orange she-cat's eyes blazed as Blossompaw found her paws and padded, shamefaced, back across the clearing.

"How dare you?" Squirrelflight scolded. "What must StarClan think?"

"Oops," Briarpaw whispered, pressing close to Dovepaw.

Millie jumped out of the ferns, her eyes darting from Squirrelflight to Blossompaw.

Blossompaw was limping slightly. The gray warrior darted to her daughter's side. "Are you okay?" She sniffed at Blossompaw's leg.

"It's fine," Blossompaw assured her. "I just landed awkwardly."

"What were you doing?"

Blossompaw hung her head. "I wanted to know what it was like to sit in the Great Oak. Squirrelflight made me jump by shouting at me and I fell out."

Millie shot an angry glance at Squirrelflight. "There was no need to frighten her! She could have hurt herself badly."

"She shouldn't have been sitting in the tree in the first place," Squirrelflight pointed out.

"She's just a 'paw," Millie reminded Squirrelflight.

"She's old enough to know better!" Squirrelflight turned as Jayfeather emerged from the ferns. "Will you check Blossompaw?" she asked. "She's had a fall."

Firestar slid from the bushes. "Who's had a fall?"

"It was nothing," Blossompaw mewed, as Jayfeather checked her leg. "I'm fine."

Firestar's gaze swept from Squirrelflight to Millie, their pelts ruffled.

Graystripe padded ahead of him, tasting the air. "Yuck!" He wrinkled his nose. "I don't know if this place smells worse when it's empty or when the other Clans are stinking up the air."

Dovepaw was grateful for the gray warrior's humor after all the bickering. Squirrelflight and Millie had retired to different parts of the clearing. Brambleclaw took himself off to sit underneath a beech tree far from both she-cats. Whitewing padded into the clearing and glanced from Squirrelflight to Millie, uncertainty clouding her gaze, then chose a shadowy spot beside a clump of ferns, midway between them. Jayfeather took his place among the roots of the Great Oak, where the other medicine cats would gather once they arrived. Birchfall paced the edge, sniffing warily, while the rest of the patrol sat to one side, their tails flicking in silence.

The air smelled of rain despite the clear sky. Dovepaw shivered as a breeze sent a flurry of leaves drifting down into the clearing. She was almost relieved when she heard undergrowth rustling on the far side of the island and smelled the fishy tang of RiverClan. They were leaving their camp and heading for the clearing.

She noticed Firestar following her gaze to the reed beds beyond the trees and watching the sleek forms of the RiverClan cats emerge. He lifted his tail in greeting as Mistystar led her Clan into the clearing. Petalfur broke ranks immediately and raced over the leaf-strewn clearing, skidding to a halt beside Dovepaw while her Clanmates wove among the ThunderClan cats and began sharing tongues.

"Hi!" The gray-and-white RiverClan she-cat puffed out her chest and lifted her chin. She seemed to have grown at least a mouse-span after her experiences on the journey upstream. "How's training?"

"Great!" Dovepaw was pleased to see her, and even more pleased to be greeted like a friend by at least one of the patrol who had helped find the river. And yet Jayfeather's words rankled in her mind. *Not all cats think that one adventure makes everyone friends forever.* She pushed the thought away. She could be friendly without being disloyal to her Clan!

"Aren't you finding everything is boring after our adventure?" Petalfur's eyes sparkled.

If only! Lionblaze was pushing her so hard to hone her powers that she hardly had time to find anything dull. "I have a really good mentor," she mewed, conscious of Lionblaze's gaze flicking over her. Was he scared she was going to give something away?

Her discomfort sharpened as she scented WindClan crossing the fallen tree and heading for the clearing.

"Are you okay?" Petalfur's eyes were round.

"What?" Dovepaw had been peering anxiously over her shoulder, wary of seeing the WindClan warriors who had watched her being unceremoniously marched home from the WindClan camp. She stiffened as Petalfur's gaze strayed past her.

"It's only WindClan!" The RiverClan cat hailed a familiar face. "Hi, Sedgewhisker!"

But the WindClan warrior turned pointedly away. "What's gotten up her nose?" Hurt glinted in Petalfur's amber eyes.

Dovepaw wanted to explain that Sedgewhisker's coldness was directed at her, not at Petalfur. But she couldn't bring herself to confess her ill-planned expedition into WindClan territory. And now Brambleclaw was staring at her, his eyes narrowed. *I bet he's wondering what Onestar will say about my crossing the WindClan border.* She wished Ivypaw were with her.

"Cheer up." Petalfur's mew startled her. "WindClan has always been prickly. If they don't want to speak to us, there's not a lot we can do about it."

Dovepaw flicked her tail. Petalfur was right. If her Clanmates wanted to snipe at one another and WindClan wanted to sulk, so what? She couldn't forget her most important mission tonight. Tigerheart had promised to tell her what he'd been doing in ThunderClan territory. She searched for his scent, surprised to find it close and fresh on the cool night breeze. ShadowClan had reached the island.

As they padded into the clearing, Blackstar at their head, Firestar glanced up at the moon. Clouds were crowding the horizon. The ThunderClan leader bounded up the Great Oak, settling on the low branch Blossompaw had fallen from. Onestar and Blackstar scrambled up after him. Mistystar glanced up the thick trunk, as though looking for clawholds, then hauled herself up and settled beside the other leaders.

Dovepaw watched the cats gathering at the foot of the tree, looking for Tigerheart's dark tabby fur. She caught a tiny glimpse of him, his pelt merging with his Clanmates', until a knot of RiverClan cats shouldered between them, blocking her view.

"Tigerheart!" she hissed. But he didn't turn around. Instead, sharp claws tweaked her tail.

"Ow!" Dovepaw looked over her shoulder.

Sandstorm was looking at her sternly. "It's time to sit down. The leaders are about to speak."

Frustrated, Dovepaw peered through the jumble of pelts and ears to where Tigerheart sat. Snowbird's white fur glowed beside his slick, dark pelt. She tried to catch his eye, but Redwillow slid in beside them and Tigerheart disappeared behind his Clanmate's wide, tawny head. Reluctantly Dovepaw turned to watch the leaders.

Onestar padded to the center of the branch. Dovepaw anxiously held her breath. *Please don't mention me!* "The return of the lake has been a blessing from StarClan," he began.

"I suppose the cats who went and found it had nothing to do with it," Blossompaw muttered under her breath.

"Our brave warriors who unblocked the river have returned safely and are happy to be with their Clan once more." The WindClan leader's gaze swept over the ThunderClan cats, and Dovepaw found herself hunching into her shoulders as he went on.

"WindClan will be forever grateful for the courage and strength of its brave warriors."

Briarpaw pressed against her. "He's acting like WindClan did it alone," she whispered. "What about you and Lionblaze and Tigerheart and—"

"Hush." Squirrelflight glared at them before turning back to the Great Oak as Onestar continued.

"As leaf-bare approaches, it's important we secure our borders. Rabbits are running well, but if leaf-bare is harsh, we must protect what is ours." He stared down at ThunderClan. "Any trespassers will be dealt with severely."

Dovepaw curled her claws, waiting for him to mention her

by name. Relief swept through her as the WindClan leader simply nodded and withdrew along the branch, making way for Mistystar. Silence gripped the Clans as the new RiverClan leader spoke for the first time.

"You all know by now that I am RiverClan's new leader."

Cheers erupted. "Mistystar! Mistystar!"

Firestar stood and dipped his head low to the gray she-cat, his eyes glowing with pride. Dovepaw pricked her ears. The ThunderClan leader seemed to have genuine warmth for the new RiverClan leader. *I suppose he's known her for a long time.* Besides, judging from the calls that came equally from every Clan, she was popular with all the cats, just as Jayfeather had predicted.

Mistystar nodded, her blue eyes round and unblinking, her gaze sweeping the Clans until they fell silent. "Leopardstar was a noble leader," she began. Murmurs of agreement rippled through the cats as Mistystar pressed on. "She was brave and loyal and would have done anything to protect her Clanmates."

"Or *Tigerstar*," a sour mew whispered behind Dovepaw.

She jerked around, puzzled. One of the WindClan warriors was whispering into her Clanmate's ear. Dovepaw frowned. Like every kit, she'd heard nursery tales about the dark warrior. But what did he have to do with Leopardstar? She leaned closer to Blossompaw. "He was *ShadowClan's* leader, wasn't he?"

Sandstorm glanced sharply over her shoulder. "Yes," she hissed. "But it was a bit more complicated than that. Now hush!"

Dovepaw bit her tongue as Mistystar went on.

"We are pleased to have Petalfur back and we grieve for Rippletail, who died bravely fighting the beavers."

Dovepaw's heart tightened. She hadn't thought of the RiverClan warrior in days. She didn't want to forget him, not ever.

"I am sure," Mistystar added, "that he and Leopardstar walk now among StarClan and watch over their old Clanmates."

Sighs of sympathy spread through the Clans as Mistystar sat down.

Blackstar took her place. "Leopardstar will be missed." The ShadowClan leader seemed to speak with genuine grief, his eyes glistening in the moonlight. "The loss of a leader is a loss to all the Clans," he went on. "But new blood brings new energy, and we wish Mistystar a long and happy leadership."

Dovepaw stared at the ShadowClan leader, surprised by his compassion. Why couldn't the Clans show this sense of friendship more often? Perhaps Mistystar's leadership would mark a new time, one based on trust rather than suspicion.

As hope flashed in Dovepaw's chest, the ShadowClan leader's eyes hardened. "And yet borders are still borders. They must remain unblurred."

Dovepaw saw Graystripe stiffen as Blackstar glared down at the ThunderClan cats.

"There's been too much activity on ThunderClan's border," Blackstar hissed. "Scent marks are becoming confused."

Thornclaw leaped to his paws, bristling. "How dare you! It

was ShadowClan who left scent on *our* territory!"

RiverClan and WindClan cats turned and watched, their eyes bright with interest as ShadowClan warriors began to get to their paws. Dovepaw noticed Graystripe unsheathe his claws.

"The truce!" Sandstorm hissed in the gray warrior's ear, but Graystripe only dug his claws hard into the ground, letting the fur lift on his shoulders.

"Don't stir up trouble you can't handle," he warned.

"Sit down!" Brambleclaw's growl made Graystripe pause. Snorting, he let his hackles fall, but kept his claws unsheathed.

Blackstar's eyes gleamed. "We aren't stirring up trouble," he argued. "It was ThunderClan who started the accusations."

Graystripe's tail was twitching as the ShadowClan leader went on. "One of my warriors inspected the so-called scent you found inside your border, and he couldn't tell which Clan it belonged to. As usual, ThunderClan is looking for any chance to tell the other Clans what to do."

Sandstorm pressed against Graystripe, as though reminding him to control his temper.

Dovepaw wriggled forward so that she could glimpse Tigerheart. The dark brown tabby warrior was keeping his head down. *He knows he's guilty. But do his Clanmates?*

As she stared at Tigerheart, the scent of blood touched her nose and she suddenly realized that the young tom was scratched. His fur was ruffled by wounds, not embarrassment, and one of his ears was torn. Perhaps his Clanmates *did* know he had left scent on ThunderClan's territory and had decided to punish him.

She frowned, her thoughts wandering. *Poor Tigerheart!* ShadowClan warriors must be every bit as vicious as the nursery tales said.

A sharp nudge made her jump. "Stop staring at Tigerheart," Sandstorm snapped. "You look like an owl!"

Was I staring? Dovepaw turned her gaze back to the Great Oak. Blackstar was still lecturing.

"If ThunderClan can't keep its borders marked and stay inside those markers, then ShadowClan *will* react." He sighed dramatically. "Why does ThunderClan always seem to think the other Clans are in their debt after a mission that involved all of us?" He let his gaze grow mournful and drift over RiverClan and WindClan, as though they shared a common burden.

Dovepaw winced. Had Blackstar somehow found out about her visit to Sedgewhisker?

Blossompaw gave her a shove. "Stop fidgeting!"

"Sorry!" Dovepaw hadn't realized she'd been shuffling her paws so much.

"Be quiet!" Sandstorm hissed at them. "Or I'll send you both home early!"

Dovepaw pulled in her paws and pressed her lips together, vowing not to say another word. What would StarClan think if she was sent home from a Gathering?

At last Blackstar stopped complaining and Firestar padded to the center of the branch, his chin and tail held high.

"Welcome, Mistystar," he began. "You have earned your leadership and ThunderClan wishes you well." He blinked warmly at the RiverClan leader. "We shall miss Leopardstar. I remember her from all the way back when I was an apprentice in ThunderClan." A purr rose in his throat. He was acting as though Blackstar's speech had never happened. "I always respected her, and, though her loyalty to RiverClan never wavered, she was a leader who understood the importance of keeping *every* Clan strong." Firestar flashed a glance at Blackstar before going on. "She had the heart, courage, and strength of the mighty cat she was named for."

As he dipped his head, a mew sounded from behind Dovepaw. The WindClan warriors were grumbling again.

"Firestar's always acting like everyone's ally!"

"Trying to make friends to avoid battle."

"Never did like the smell of blood."

"Just like a kittypet."

Dovepaw whirled around. "Just because he's friendly doesn't mean Firestar *or* ThunderClan is weak!"

Oops! Remembering Sandstorm's warning, she shut her mouth quickly and turned back to the Great Oak.

"Blackstar." Firestar used his smoothest mew to address the ShadowClan leader. "We understand borders, and their importance in keeping peace among the Clans. We also know they are worth fighting for." His voice was suddenly edged with threat. He held Blackstar's gaze for a moment; then, just as the ShadowClan leader opened his mouth to retaliate, he turned back to the gathered cats. "Good news in ThunderClan," he mewed brightly. "Cherrykit and Molekit are our newest members, born to Poppyfrost." He waited while warm murmurs of congratulations echoed through the Clans before concluding, "At this rate, we'll have to make the warriors' den even bigger." He dipped his head. "With the blessing of StarClan." Then he jumped down from the oak.

Dovepaw lifted her head, feeling very proud of her leader. Around her, the cats began to drift across the clearing. Apprentices mingled, sharing training gossip, and warriors gathered in knots while elders swapped their own news.

Blossompaw and Briarpaw were heading for a cluster of ShadowClan and RiverClan apprentices.

"Are you coming?" Briarpaw called.

Dovepaw blinked. She'd been looking for Tigerheart. "In a while," she promised.

Where had he gone? Snowbird and Redwillow were gossiping with two WindClan warriors. Tigerheart was nowhere to be seen. She breathed deeply, trying to make sense of the jumble of scents on her tongue.

There!

She tasted his scent at last. Her gaze darted toward a bramble bush at the far side of the clearing. He was crouching in the shadows beneath.

"Hiding?" she mewed, trotting up to him.

He sat up. "What from?"

"Me." Dovepaw stared boldly at him. "You promised you'd explain what you were doing in our territory."

Tigerheart's eyes grew wide. "Keep your voice down!"

He glanced nervously around. "Follow me." Creeping away, ears and tail lowered, he led her through the bramble thicket and into a small dip behind a cracked willow tree. Dovepaw blinked, her eyes adjusting to the shadows. The willow blocked out the moon and half of Silverpelt.

"Look," Tigerheart whispered. "I can't tell you exactly what I was doing, but we're not planning an invasion, I promise."

Dovepaw cocked her head. The young warrior was definitely up to something. "You were on *my* territory," she reminded him. "I have a right to know why. And if you don't tell me, I'm going to report you to Firestar!"

Tigerheart dropped his gaze. "You do have a right to know." His mew was soft, apologetic. "But, please, I need you to trust me." He raised his eyes and gazed into hers. They were round, almost black, and glittering with worry.

Dovepaw felt a rush of sympathy. The young tom was clearly torn. Something was bothering him. She nodded, distracted for a moment by the soft fur edging his face. He seemed desperate for her to understand. She curled her tail to touch the tip of his. He stiffened at her touch, but didn't draw his tail away; instead, he leaned forward and rested his nose against her ear fur.

"Thank you."

The warmth of his breath on her ear made her shiver. It smelled sweet, for a ShadowClan cat's breath.

"Okay." She made an effort to focus on the reason she'd wanted to talk to him. "But if something is threatening the forest, I need to know."

"Nothing's threatening the forest," Tigerheart promised. "I would tell you if something were." His eyes grew rounder until Dovepaw felt his gaze reaching into hers. "On the journey upstream, we were almost . . . friends."

Dovepaw found herself nodding vigorously.

He sighed. "If we were in the same Clan it would be so easy. . . ."

No! Dovepaw drew back, suddenly aware that she was leaning far too close to this handsome young ShadowClan warrior. She had to change the subject! "H-how did you get those scratches?" She stared at the fur on his shoulder, still clotted with blood. "That one looks nasty."

Tigerheart sat back and shrugged. "Battle training."

Dovepaw shuddered. Did ShadowClan warriors train with teeth and claws bared? "Has Littlecloud treated it? It may get infected."

Tigerheart turned away so that his shoulder was hidden in shadow. "It's not that bad, honest. It only hurts when I—" He broke off.

The bramble bush rustled.

Tigerheart crouched and flattened his ears. Dovepaw drew back into the deeply shadowed cleft between the roots of the willow tree.

"Blasted prickers." It was an old mew, croaking with irritation. Dovepaw sniffed and smelled WindClan. It must be an elder looking for a quiet spot to make dirt.

Tigerheart scooted backward. "Got to go," he murmured, and disappeared over the roots.

Dovepaw stared after him. Why was he acting so odd? Puzzled, she hopped out of the dip and onto a thick root. "It's quiet over there!" she called to the grumbling WindClan elder, pointing with her tail to a clear spot a few tail-lengths farther into the woods.

The old cat dragged himself free of the brambles. "*Now* you tell me!" he rasped. "Once my ears have been shredded and half my pelt is hanging in this fox-toothed bush."

Whiskers twitching, Dovepaw scooted back to join her Clan. Sandstorm saw her and nudged Whitewing.

"Dovepaw?" The white warrior was calling for her anxiously. "There you are!"

"I wasn't far away." Dovepaw wove past Thornclaw and Graystripe, while Firestar circled his Clan, his shoulders rippling with tension. "What's going on?"

"Blossompaw! Briarpaw! I've found her!" Whitewing called back the two apprentices who had been scooting around the edge of the clearing, sniffing the bushes. "Where were you?"

"Over there." Dovepaw nodded vaguely toward the cracked willow. "Why isn't anyone sharing tongues anymore?"

The Clans had separated and were eyeing one another warily.

Sandstorm flicked her tail. "WindClan and ShadowClan started fussing over boundaries again," she huffed.

Ratscar paced around his Clanmates, his eyes burning in the moonlight as he glared at ThunderClan.

Breezepelt sat bolt upright, eyes slitted, his tail sweeping the ground behind him. "Borders are borders," he growled at

Lionblaze, who was staring back at the furious warrior.

"You share a mission with ThunderClan and they think they own the whole lake!" Crowfrost hissed.

Foxleap clawed at the ground. "But we saved the lake!"

"We *all* saved the lake!" Onestar hissed. "Cats from every Clan. So why are you crossing borders like you own us now?"

Darkness slid over the clearing. Dovepaw looked up. The clouds that had been bubbling on the horizon had begun to drift across the moon. Pale light still filtered through, but the wind was picking up and the thickening clouds were swallowing Silverpelt star by star.

Firestar lashed his tail. "Let's leave before StarClan calls a halt to this Gathering altogether." He shot an angry look at Onestar and Blackstar. "ThunderClan is not making trouble and you know it."

Dovepaw felt herself swept along by her Clanmates as they headed for the edge of the clearing. Blossompaw nudged her forward, while Millie, Brightheart, and Brackenfur jostled behind her.

Firestar held his ground a moment longer. "Think carefully," he warned the WindClan and ShadowClan leaders, "before you accuse us of something we didn't do!" He turned, curling his lip, and followed his Clan into the trees.

Chapter 10

Bright flowers nodded around the apprentice as she wove, slender as a pine marten, through the grass. She sneezed as pollen dusted her soft muzzle. Then, relishing the sun on her back, she lifted her forepaws and peered over the curving stems. Wide-eyed, she gazed at the broad green pasture and breathed the soft scent of the shimmering grass.

A huge gray mare ambled past, its wide hooves thumping the earth and tearing trails through the grass. The she-cat scooted backward and sheltered beneath the lush leaves of a dock. Butterflies whirled up as the horse sauntered away. The apprentice scampered and leaped after them, swiping the air as they jerked on the breeze and scattered like windblown petals into the blue sky.

The air was heavy with greenleaf scent and, as the cat tasted the breeze, she caught the musky tang of prey. Nostrils flaring, she followed the scent, tail down, ears flat. She tracked it through dark green clover and around a clump of bobbing white flowers before catching sight of a tiny flicker of movement.

Mouse!

Nibbling at the juicy roots of a cowslip, it didn't even flinch as she began to wiggle her hindquarters. Confident, she pounced, but as her front paws left the ground, her back brushed against a thick poppy stem. Red petals flashed and the mouse whisked into the clover, diving under cover so thick that the cat lost sight of its tiny brown body. She plunged in her paws, patting the ground crossly, claws plucking but finding nothing but earth and roots.

Mouse dung!

"Bad luck."

The apprentice spun around as a deep mew sounded behind her. She blinked at the broad-shouldered tom gazing at her. His muzzle was scarred, and when he lifted a paw to flick away a fly, his long, hooked claws glinted in the sun.

"I-is this your field?" she mewed nervously.

"I visit here, just as you do," the tom replied. He rested his paw on the ground and cocked his head.

"This is the first time I've been here," she admitted.

"Well, I'm glad you've come," purred the tom. "It gets lonely sometimes."

"Do you live nearby?"

The tom didn't answer, but nodded toward the patch of clover where the mouse had disappeared. "Too bad you lost it," he commented. "I could show you how to pounce without arching your back, if you like."

She nodded shyly. This tom didn't smell like a Clan cat, though he was as smooth pelted and tightly muscled as any warrior. His scent was strange and reminded her of walking in the forest at night.

"Watch this." Crouching, the tom leaped forward, skimming the ground, keeping his back smooth and straight as he landed so that only his flank grazed the overhanging stems without disturbing them.

The apprentice watched wide-eyed.

"You try it." The tom nodded to a knot of moss. "Aim for that."

The she-cat nodded and squatted down, ready to pounce. Wriggling her hindquarters, she bunched her muscles and sprang, but she skimmed the ground too closely and came to a skidding halt before her front paws reached the moss.

"Try again," the tom coaxed.

Again the apprentice pounced, this time keeping farther off the ground, but when she tried to flatten her spine she lost her balance and landed clumsily, stumbling to one side and sending shivers through the grass.

"Again," came the quiet encouragement.

Thinking hard this time, the apprentice backed up, stared at the moss, and let awareness of every muscle spread through her body. Then she jumped, raking the ground, curving her body to weave around the stems before landing perfectly, the ball of moss falling between her paws as naturally as if StarClan had placed it for her.

"Wow!" She sat up, pleased with herself. "I'll show my sister that move."

The tom looked around. "Is she here?"

The apprentice shook her head. "It's just me." She frowned,

aware how strange it felt to be here alone, without the company of her littermate. "Maybe I can bring her next time."

The tom looked quizzical. "Don't you like to do things by yourself?"

The apprentice shook her head. "It's much more fun with two."

"Well, there are two of us." His blue gaze reached intently into hers. "Is that okay?"

She nodded.

"I could show you a stalking technique, if you like," the tom offered.

"I know all the basic ones," the she-cat told him.

"I bet you haven't seen this one." He crouched down and began to draw himself forward, chin stretched out, whiskers drawn back so that he wove through the grass like a snake. Suddenly his muzzle darted forward, and he grasped a flower stem in his jaws so quickly that the apprentice gasped.

"That was so fast!"

"Good for catching fish."

"Fish?"

"Mice too," the tom added. "Any prey that's quick."

"Can I try?"

"Of course."

As she flattened herself to the ground, the tom sat up and wrapped his bushy tail over his paws.

"What's your sister like?" he asked.

The apprentice was focusing on a long blade of grass a tail-length ahead. "She's clever," she mewed, pulling herself slowly forward. "And funny." She crept closer to the grass. "And the bravest cat I know." With a lunge, she snapped at the grass stem, grabbing it in her jaws before spitting it out, coughing. "Yuck! Bitter!"

The tom purred. "I suppose you mean the grass, not your sister."

"Of course!"

A faint yowl drifted across the meadow. A cat was calling.

The she-cat turned her head. "I've got to go now." She started to pad toward the voice, the grass stroking her back.

The tom called after her, "Don't you want to know my name?"

The apprentice turned, blinking.

"I'm Hawkfrost."

"Good-bye, Hawkfrost." The name felt strange on her tongue.

"Aren't you going to tell me yours?"

"Oh, yes. It's Ivypaw."

Ivypaw shook herself awake, surprised to feel chilly air around her muzzle after the warmth of her dream. Cinderheart was peering through the den entrance. "Ivypaw!" she hissed.

Dovepaw was still asleep, tired after the Gathering, and Cinderheart was clearly trying not to wake her. But Blossompaw's, Briarpaw's, and Bumblepaw's nests were all empty.

Dazed from her dream, Ivypaw hauled herself to her paws. "Coming!" She picked her way on half-numb legs past Dovepaw's nest and padded out into the damp dawn air. Briarpaw and her littermates were pacing the clearing, Blossompaw mumbling under her breath as though running through answers while Bumblepaw kept stopping to crouch and pounce.

Ivypaw remembered through the haze of her dream that today was their final assessment. Mist hung in the camp, shrouding the dens so they looked eerie and far away. The dawn sky was obscured by thick, dark clouds.

Ivypaw shivered. "What did you want?" she asked Cinderheart.

Her mentor was already halfway across the clearing, heading to where Hazeltail, Mousewhisker, and Thornclaw sat like stones, eyeing their apprentices with anxious interest.

Ivypaw glanced up, past the rocky walls of the hollow and the trees crowding the rim. The clouds were darker than ever. There would be rain before long. Ivypaw shuddered. Why couldn't she have lingered longer in her dream meadow with Hawkfrost?

"The assessment will be carried out in pairs this time," Cinderheart told Ivypaw. "We need you to pair up with Blossompaw."

"No way!" Blossompaw's horrified mew took Ivypaw by surprise. "She's not properly trained! Can't I have Dovepaw? At least she can *hunt*."

Ivypaw glared at the tortoiseshell-and-white cat. "I know how to hunt!" Hawkfrost had just taught her two new moves!

"You've hardly caught more than a mouse!" Blossompaw

complained. "Dovepaw's brilliant! She can hear prey anywhere!"

Self-conscious and disappointed, Ivypaw felt her shoulders begin to sink.

You're just as good as your sister.

The words rang in her head. Another voice, not here, though she couldn't place it. She straightened up and lifted her chin. "I'll do my best," she promised. "Besides, you're the one being assessed, not me."

"Well said, Ivypaw." Hazeltail padded through the mist and stood beside her apprentice. "Ivypaw is doing you a favor," she scolded Blossompaw. "*You* should be doing the work, not her."

The warriors' den rustled as Dustpelt and Spiderleg padded out. "Are we ready to go?" Spiderleg asked, yawning.

Cinderheart nodded. "You'll be assessing Bumblepaw with Hazeltail," she informed him. "I'll help Mousewhisker with Briarpaw. Dustpelt, you and Thornclaw can assess Blossompaw."

Hazeltail looked surprised. "So we're not assessing our own apprentices?"

"Firestar wants us to try a different way," Cinderheart reminded the small gray-and-white she-cat.

"Firestar has a new training technique every moon these days," Thornclaw muttered, padding toward the entrance. "This is pointless," he growled. "By the time we've figured out this way of training, Firestar will have come up with something else." He disappeared through the tunnel, the mist closing after him.

"Come on," Cinderheart urged.

Ivypaw hurried after Blossompaw and her littermates as they pushed their way out of the camp.

"You two will hunt by the lake," Cinderheart announced. She signaled to Briarpaw and Bumblepaw with her tail and the apprentices darted away, heading for the shore. Cinderheart looked at Ivypaw. "Be careful," she warned. "Don't forget you're just helping. You've got nothing to prove."

Except that I'm as good a hunter as my sister. Wait till they see what I learned in my dream!

Ivypaw dug her claws into the soft, damp earth as she watched Cinderheart trot toward the lake with Mousewhisker, Hazeltail, and Spiderleg, quickening their pace as their apprentices hared off, clearly keen to make their first catch.

"Where are we hunting?" Blossompaw asked Dustpelt.

Dustpelt glanced questioningly at Thornclaw. "The abandoned Twolegplace?"

The golden brown warrior nodded. "Sounds good to me."

Blossompaw flicked Ivypaw's flank with her tail-tip. "Come on." She pelted into the trees and Ivypaw raced after her, wishing she had longer legs as the older apprentice gathered speed and leaped the ruts and gullies in easy strides.

She was panting by the time she spotted the cracked stones of the abandoned Twolegplace. Blossompaw was waiting on the wall surrounding the tumbledown nest. "You can't even keep up," she scoffed.

"We're supposed to be showing them we can work together," Ivypaw snapped.

"Like I'm going to give you the chance to hold me back." Blossompaw jumped down from the wall and headed past the plants Jayfeather had carefully nurtured. The scent of them made Ivypaw's mouth water, but she knew the warning given to every Clan cat: *Stay away from the catmint*. It was the only cure for greencough, and more precious than poppy seeds.

As she disappeared around the corner of the wall, Blossompaw called over her shoulder, "Just stay out of my way!"

Ivypaw's heart quickened with rage. How come everyone thought Dovepaw was so great and she was just a mouse-brain? *I'll show them!*

She padded past the wall and ducked into the echoing Twoleg den. A jagged stone slope rose up to a hole in the roof and she scooted up it and peeked through a gap in the wall at the top. Blossompaw was tracking something in the unkempt grass below. Ivypaw couldn't see what, but the tortoiseshell apprentice was moving intently through the tangled weeds.

Suddenly Ivypaw spotted movement at the bottom of the wall. Peering to see what it was, she pushed away a wave of dizziness, then turned and pelted down the jagged slope, the neatly cornered stones a blur beneath her paws. Treading lightly but fast, she nipped out of the nest and darted around the corner. There it was! A squirrel, rummaging in the plants at the bottom of the wall.

Remembering Hawkfrost's instructions, she crouched down, keeping her back low so that it didn't brush the branches arching from the rocks.

The squirrel was busy feasting on seeds it had shaken from

a clump of dried-up flowers. Ivypaw slowed, preparing, letting awareness spread through her muscles, then sprang, flattening her back as she swerved around the plants. Her paws reached the squirrel with a curling swipe before it could see her and she grasped it and nipped it with a single killing bite.

Thanks, Hawkfrost!

"Impressive!" Thornclaw's mew startled her and she swung around, the squirrel dangling from her jaws. The warrior was trotting toward her with Dustpelt on his tail.

"Where did you learn *that* move?" Dustpelt asked, his eyes wide. "You looked like you were hooking a fish out of water!"

Ivypaw gazed back innocently. There was no reason she had to give away her secret. "I guess it was just . . . instinct."

The tall weeds beside them swished and Blossompaw came stomping out. "What's all the noise about?" she spat. "I was stalking a rat and you scared it away!"

Dustpelt tipped his head to one side. "Weren't you helping to catch this squirrel?"

"I thought you were working in pairs," Thornclaw added.

Blossompaw bristled. "She was supposed to be helping *me*, not the other way around."

You told me to stay out of the way! Ivypaw glared at her denmate but kept her mouth shut.

"Then why was she *here* while you were trawling through the undergrowth?" Dustpelt queried. "You're supposed to be organizing a hunting pair. You should have told her where you wanted her."

"Okay," Blossompaw huffed. She flicked her tail at Ivypaw.

"Come with me." Turning, she pushed her way back into the jungle of weeds.

Ivypaw dropped the squirrel and flashed a rueful glance at the two warriors before following.

"What did you have to show me up for?" Blossompaw hissed as soon as they were out of earshot. "This is *my* assessment, remember?"

"Okay, then." Ivypaw was still feeling pleased from her catch. "What do you want me to do?"

Blossompaw nodded toward the pine trees on the far side of the abandoned Twoleg nest. "We'll hunt in there."

They padded between the trunks. The crowded trees blocked the daylight, which was dull anyway. Ivypaw could taste the coming rain. Wisps of mist still lingered, but little undergrowth thrived here and it was easy to spot prey.

"There!" Blossompaw hissed.

A blackbird was rooting along the needle-strewn floor. There was no cover to hide their approach, but if they worked as a team, they might be able to trap it between them.

"Perfect," Blossompaw murmured. "You head that way; I'll come at it from the other side." She nodded Ivypaw away, adding, "Keep low, and don't drag your paws."

"I'm not a kit!" Ivypaw hissed back.

Before Blossompaw could give her any more obvious instructions, she crept fast between the trees, keeping down but not letting her belly or tail brush the floor. She fixed her eyes on the blackbird, not allowing her gaze to stray even when trees passed between her and their quarry. It had hold of a worm and was struggling to drag it out of the ground.

Blossompaw's pelt flashed at the edge of Ivypaw's vision. She ignored it, padding closer and closer until she was only a few tail-lengths from the bird. Then she halted. *This is Blossompaw's assessment,* she reminded herself, fighting the urge to pounce. She knew she could get it, with Hawkfrost's lesson still fresh in her mind.

Where was Blossompaw? The blackbird was winning the struggle with the worm. It would fly away any moment. Ivypaw narrowed her eyes. Perhaps she should catch it, just to make sure. She began to waggle her haunches, ready to leap.

A flash of tortoiseshell fur made her freeze as Blossompaw flew at the bird, paws outstretched, hind legs hitting the ground a moment too early. She managed to clasp the blackbird in her forepaws but there was no grace in the catch. The blackbird struggled, frantic wings battering the earth and sending pine needles flying while Blossompaw regained her balance enough to make the killing bite.

Hawkfrost would have sneered at such a clumsy catch. For a moment the scent of night washed over Ivypaw's tongue, bringing a vivid image of the warrior tom to her mind and the dark forest musk that clung to his thick pelt.

Was he a StarClan cat? Had he come especially to teach her?

Dovepaw has never been visited by StarClan! Ivypaw felt a prick of satisfaction. *She would have told me.*

Rain began to patter on the canopy high overhead as Dustpelt and Thornclaw caught up. Dustpelt was carrying

Ivypaw's squirrel. He dropped it and nodded toward the blackbird. "Nicely caught."

Thornclaw shrugged. "Whatever Firestar says, I don't see the point of hunting in pairs. Blossompaw would have caught it if Ivypaw were somewhere else catching her own prey." He snorted. "Seems like a waste of warriors." He glanced up as the rain grew heavier and began to drip through the branches. It splashed on his nose, making him sneeze.

"Come on," he meowed, shaking his head. "I think we've seen enough. Let's get back to camp before the downpour starts."

Blossompaw lashed her tail. "But I've only caught one bird!"

The rain began to pound through the trees until the pine needles bounced on the forest floor.

"We've seen enough," Thornclaw repeated. He flicked his tail toward the squirrel. "You may as well carry your own catch," he told Ivypaw.

Pleased at the thought of walking into camp carrying such a fat piece of prey, Ivypaw grasped the squirrel in her jaws and began to head through the trees.

By the time they reached the thorn barrier, the forest was drenched. Ivypaw could hardly see her Clanmates through the fog of rain. Her paws squelched on the muddy forest floor, each sucking paw step filling with water behind her. After so many moons of drought, the elders couldn't complain now. There was enough water to fill the lake even if every stream dried up.

Blossompaw trotted past Ivypaw, quickening her pace to enter camp first, and tripped on the wing of the blackbird. "Fox dung!" She cursed through her mouthful of feathers. "One wretched bird while you have to catch a squirrel!" She glared at Ivypaw. "If I fail this assessment, it's all your fault."

She ducked into the tunnel, leaving Ivypaw startled. At the start of the morning Blossompaw had been complaining that she'd be no help. Now she was upset because Ivypaw had been too much help.

Ivypaw dragged the squirrel through the thorn tunnel. Whitewing and Millie hurried to greet them.

"You're the first back," Millie meowed.

Whitewing's eyes glowed with pride as she gazed at the squirrel hanging in her daughter's jaws. "Well done!"

Millie glanced at Blossompaw's blackbird. "You two obviously work well together."

Yeah, right!

Ivypaw lifted her chin to keep the squirrel out of the mud as she carried it to the fresh-kill pile.

Dovepaw ducked out from the apprentices' den, her shoulders hunched against the battering rain. "Great catch!" she called. "It's nearly as big as you!"

"Thanks." Pride rushed through Ivypaw as she dropped the squirrel beside Blossompaw's blackbird. She wanted to tell Dovepaw about Hawkfrost. She glanced around the clearing. Millie and Graystripe were crowding around Blossompaw to find out how the assessment had gone, while Thornclaw and Dustpelt sheltered beneath Highledge, conferring with Firestar.

"Come with me." Ivypaw beckoned with her tail before scooting toward the thorns.

"Why?" Dovepaw sounded puzzled as she hurried after her. "What's going on?"

Wait till she hears how a StarClan cat taught me how to hunt!

Ivypaw was bubbling with excitement. She slid through the tunnel and waited in the clearing outside, pummeling the muddy earth impatiently till Dovepaw caught up.

"What is it?" Dovepaw's eyes were wide.

Ivypaw glanced around, making sure no cat was listening. "A StarClan cat came to see me," she breathed.

"When?" Dovepaw blinked away raindrops.

"In my dream!" Ivypaw explained. "He was teaching me how to hunt!"

Dovepaw leaned closer. "Tell me more."

Suddenly Ivypaw felt self-conscious. Did Dovepaw believe her or was she humoring her? Perhaps it had just been an ordinary dream. "This cat . . ." She fumbled for words. "He taught me some new hunting moves. . . ."

Dovepaw was staring at her. "Who was it?"

"It was . . ."

The undergrowth shivered. "What are you doing out here?" Brightheart burst from a clump of ferns, panting. She was clearly racing for the shelter of the hollow. "You'll catch your death!" She circled them, pressing them toward the thorn tunnel. "Inside, both of you! What would Whitewing say? Or Jayfeather? We don't want to start leaf-bare with a medicine den full of sneezing apprentices!"

Sparking with frustration, Ivypaw allowed herself to be

herded into camp. Praying the apprentices' den would be empty, she headed straight for it, beckoning to Dovepaw. Her sister kept close as they slipped into the dry den and shook the rain from their fur.

Ivypaw turned and started to explain about Hawkfrost. "He was a warrior. . . ."

"Dovepaw!" Lionblaze was calling through the den wall.

Ivypaw unsheathed her claws. *Can't he wait?*

"Sorry." Dovepaw looked apologetic as she backed outside. Ivypaw ripped a pawful of bracken from her nest and flung it down. Dovepaw was always racing off to talk to warriors without her. Didn't she care about her? And since when did the least experienced cats run the Clan? Couldn't Lionblaze manage a few moments without his precious apprentice?

The yew bush shivered as Blossompaw, Briarpaw, and Bumblepaw came bouncing in, water spraying from their pelts. "We passed! We passed!"

"Great!" Ivypaw slunk into her nest. "Congratulations!" She closed her eyes, blocking her ears to the mews of excitement as her denmates congratulated one another. If she went to sleep, Hawkfrost might teach her some more hunting moves until she wasn't just as good as her sister—she was *better.* Then the Clan might start paying some attention to her as well.

Chapter 11

Rain dripped at the mouth of Firestar's den. As Jayfeather slid in, he brought a scattering of raindrops with him. Lionblaze shuffled closer to Dovepaw.

"Any news?" Firestar asked. He glanced uneasily at his den entrance, as though he was afraid they would be disturbed.

Lionblaze, Jayfeather, and Dovepaw shook their heads.

"No word from StarClan," Jayfeather mewed.

"No more ShadowClan scents on our side of the border," Lionblaze reported.

"Dovepaw?" The ThunderClan leader gazed at the pale gray apprentice. "Have you sensed anything?"

She stared at her paws. "Nothing," she mumbled.

Lionblaze guessed she was uncomfortable being used as a spy. It seemed that, while Jayfeather secretly relished being able to creep into other cats' minds, Dovepaw wasn't used to following her senses farther than any ordinary cat could go.

She'd better get used to it. She'd been given her power for a reason.

"ShadowClan is up to something," Firestar warned. "Border incursions are bad enough, but telling lies about them is low, even for ShadowClan."

"They've always been sneaky," Lionblaze reminded him.

"We must be even more vigilant," Firestar growled.

"Extra border patrols?" Jayfeather suggested.

Firestar shook his head. "They'll see it as provocation."

Outside, the haze of rain that had obscured the camp all morning was lifting; sunshine was arcing into the hollow. But the gale that had blown the clouds away was roaring through the forest and buffeting the dens. It whined at the den entrance.

Lionblaze noticed Dovepaw stiffen. "It's just the wind," he murmured.

She shook her head, her eyes widening. "There's something else."

Lionblaze leaned closer. He recognized the distant look in her eyes. "What?"

"A sucking noise." Fear lit her gaze. "Roots." Her breath quickened. "Roots coming out of the ground." She stared directly at Lionblaze. "A tree is falling. One of the trees at the top of the hollow." Her shrill mew echoed around the cave. "Clear the camp!"

Firestar was on his paws in a moment. "Is it true?" he asked Lionblaze.

"It's true." Lionblaze had no doubt that Dovepaw was describing something real. "We've got to get everyone out."

He pelted out of the cave, taking the rockfall in three bounds. "Everyone leave the camp!" he screeched. The wind howled around him, almost drowning his words.

Faces peeped out from the den entrances. Dustpelt and Brightheart, who had been picking through the fresh-kill pile, spun around.

"What's going on?" Alarm filled Dustpelt's call.

"A tree is falling!" Lionblaze stared up at the rim of the hollow, trying to spot the tree that was losing its grip on the rain-drenched earth. The whole forest was swaying in the gale. It was impossible to tell if one was about to crash down onto the camp. "Clear the dens!"

Brambleclaw skidded from the warriors' den as Firestar scrambled down the rocks from Highledge. "You heard him!" Firestar yowled. "Clear the camp!"

Brambleclaw headed straight for the nursery.

Firestar nodded to Dustpelt. "Apprentices' den." He turned to Brightheart. "Elders' den."

Jayfeather raced over the clearing. "The medicine den's empty."

"Double-check it!" Firestar ordered. He turned to Lionblaze. "You check the warriors' den; I'll check the rest of the camp." The ThunderClan leader pelted past the warriors' den as warriors began to stream out.

Lionblaze pushed his way in between Thornclaw, Foxleap, and Toadstep as they crowded through the entrance, ripping it wide in their rush to escape. Frantically he began searching the dark thornbush. "Hurry up!" he snapped at Cloudtail, who was stretching in his nest.

The white warrior blinked sleepily at him. "What's happening?"

"Just go!" Lionblaze ordered. "Get every cat out of camp!"

He wove through the nests, reassuring himself that each one was empty, then darted outside. The Clan was bunched together at the entrance to the tunnel through the barrier of thorns.

Brambleclaw stood at the nursery entrance, pulling Ferncloud by the scruff as she squeezed through the brambles after Daisy. He ducked inside, then hopped out. "Nursery clear!"

Poppyfrost was running for the tunnel with Molekit swinging in her jaws. Cherrykit sprawled on the ground behind her, wailing, her eyes glazed in terror. Daisy scooped her up and headed after Poppyfrost.

"Apprentices' den clear!" Dustpelt's yowl rang across the clearing.

"Warriors' den empty!" Lionblaze called.

"No one in the medicine den!" Jayfeather's fur was barbed with prickers from the brambly entrance.

Firestar emerged from behind the nursery. "Perimeter clear!" He charged over to Brambleclaw, who was guiding his Clanmates through the barrier. "Slow down!" he ordered as Rosepetal slipped and Brackenfur tripped over her.

Lionblaze glanced at the elders' den. Brightheart hadn't made her report yet.

Purdy was plucking anxiously at the ground outside the entrance. "Hurry up!" he hissed through the honeysuckle.

Why were they dawdling?

"Dovepaw!" Lionblaze caught sight of his apprentice. She was circling the clearing, staring up at the rim of the hollow.

"Which tree is it?" he demanded.

"I don't know!" Terror filled her mew. "I can hear its roots slipping through the earth. It's the rain. Too much rain! It's loosened the roots!"

Ivypaw paused beside the halfrock and stared at her sister, bewildered. "Get out of the camp!"

"I can't go till I'm sure!"

Ivypaw blinked. "Sure of what?"

"Which one is falling!"

"Why in the name of StarClan do you need to know?"

Lionblaze lashed his tail. "It doesn't matter which one!" he screeched. "Just get out of the hollow! Both of you!"

As the two apprentices scooted from the clearing, he turned back to the elders' den. Still no sign of Longtail, Brightheart, or Mousefur. He pelted for the den, skidding past Purdy, and ducked inside. "What's going on?"

Brightheart was staring in panic at Mousefur.

Mousefur glared back at her indignantly. "If I leave my bed, the moss will get wet!"

Longtail was thrusting his muzzle under his denmate's flank. "Just get up!" he urged. "We'll get dry moss when we come back."

"Where are we going to find dry moss?" Mousefur objected. "It's been raining all moon!"

Fury surged through Lionblaze. "Get out!" His order barked like cracking wood, and Mousefur jumped to her paws, gazing at him in shock.

"Get out!" he repeated, unsheathing his claws. He wasn't

going to let this stubborn old cat die for the sake of a dry bed!

Brightheart rolled her eyes thankfully as Mousefur headed for the entrance. She nudged Longtail, herding them both through the trailing honeysuckle and into the clearing.

Lionblaze darted after them. The camp was empty apart from the elders hobbling across the clearing. He stared around the top of the hollow, wondering again which tree was falling, praying that Dovepaw had overreacted, though his gut told him she was right.

As Brightheart and Purdy steered Longtail and Mousefur through the tunnel, Firestar and Brambleclaw barged back in. Dovepaw slid in after them, her fur on end.

"Is the camp clear?" Firestar demanded.

Lionblaze nodded.

Brambleclaw darted from one den to another, poking his head in.

Dovepaw's ears were pricked. "It's clear," she assured them.

"Come on, then," Firestar ordered. "Let's join the Clan. They're sheltering along the gully on the way to the lake." He glanced at Dovepaw. "You're sure they'll be safe there?"

Dovepaw was looking up to the top of the cliff that overhung Highledge. "It's falling!" she whispered.

She knows which tree it is. Lionblaze followed her gaze to a tall beech that still had nearly all its leaves. He could see the danger clearly now. The wind kept tearing at the tree's heavy branches as it began to slip from the earth and slide toward the rim of the hollow.

"Come on!" Firestar insisted. He prodded Dovepaw toward the entrance. Lionblaze ran across the clearing and followed her out, Brambleclaw and Firestar on his tail. As he ran, Lionblaze glimpsed the pelts of his Clanmates through the trees, huddling in the gully several tree-lengths from the entrance to the hollow. Then he spotted Mousefur stumbling toward him. She was trying to dodge back into the camp.

Longtail stood in her way. "Leave the mouse! We can catch another."

"I'm not wasting prey!" Mousefur growled. "It's an insult to StarClan!"

"Then I'll get it!"

Before Lionblaze could stop him, Longtail had darted back through the thorn barrier.

Briarpaw raced after him, a blur of dark brown fur. "Come back! It's not safe!"

Lionblaze slowed to a halt and spun around. He pelted after Longtail and Briarpaw. "The tree's going to fall!" he shrieked, tearing through the thorns in time to see Longtail and Briarpaw disappear into the elders' den. "Get *out*!"

His yowl was smothered by a great creaking roar from the top of the hollow. With a deafening crack, the beech toppled over the rim and hurtled down the cliff. Its branches scraped the rocky walls like claws, showering thorn-sharp stones over the camp. Lionblaze shrank back against the barrier, shards of rock raining around him, terror pulsing through him as the clearing disappeared under a storm of flailing branches. He flattened his ears against the snapping, splintering wood and watched, frozen in horror, as the honeysuckle den caved under a tangle of branches. With a wrenching crunch, the beech trunk hit the ground and split like a shattered bone.

He felt a pelt trembling next to his. Dovepaw was beside him, mouth open, eyes so wide he could see their white rims.

"Briarpaw," she breathed.

Lionblaze charged toward the den, slithering through the tangle of branches, clambering over the ripped wood. He could hardly see the honeysuckle underneath the fallen beech. The tree was half propped against the far side of the hollow, its muddy roots reaching like talons around the nursery. Half the warriors' den was gone, and branches obscured the entrance to the medicine den.

"Wait!"

Lionblaze halted when he heard Firestar's yowl. He turned, balancing on the jagged end of a shattered branch.

The ThunderClan leader was clambering after him, Dovepaw following on shaky paws.

"Can you hear anything?" Firestar asked.

"No." Lionblaze glanced at Dovepaw.

The gray apprentice shook her head. "Nothing."

"They still might be alive." Firestar leaped past Lionblaze and began to wriggle through the fluttering golden leaves toward the flattened den. Lionblaze struggled after him, wincing as the jagged wood scraped his pelt.

The tree creaked.

"It's not safe!" Dovepaw's wail sounded behind them.

Lionblaze felt the tree move around him.

"It's slipping down the side of the hollow," Dovepaw warned.

"I can see a shape," Firestar called from inside the debris.

Lionblaze squirmed deeper into the snarled branches, feeling a surge of hope as a honeysuckle tendril snaked out, whipping him across the muzzle. "Who is it?"

"I can't tell," Firestar called back. "But I think it's moving."

"The whole *tree's* moving!" Dovepaw shrieked. "Get out of there!"

With a groaning, scraping sigh, the beech began to slide down the wall of the hollow.

"Out!" Firestar ordered sharply.

Lionblaze hesitated. He couldn't leave his Clanmates! He yelped as teeth clamped around his tail.

"It's collapsing!" Dovepaw's mew was muffled by fur as she dragged him backward and the tree shivered beneath his paws. Firestar was scrambling out beside him.

"Jump!" Dovepaw yowled.

The three cats hurled themselves onto an empty patch of ground beside the apprentices' den. Behind them, the tree groaned and dropped down, its branches caving beneath it as crumpled into the base of the hollow.

Dovepaw let out a whimper.

Lionblaze strained to see the elders' den. Strands of honeysuckle snaked among the branches. There was still a chance that part of the den wasn't crushed.

"Firestar?" Brambleclaw was crossing the wreckage toward

them. As he jumped down beside them, Lionblaze saw the rest of the Clan streaming back into camp. They barged through the barrier of thorns until it was as tattered and wrecked as the rest of the camp.

"Stop!" Firestar yowled at his Clanmates.

They froze and stared at the ruins of their home. Leafpool closed her eyes, as though praying to StarClan.

"Where's the camp?" Cherrykit mewled.

Daisy bent to comfort the kit as Poppyfrost stared blankly at the fallen tree. "It's gone," she breathed.

"It's still there," Firestar growled. "We just need to stay calm."

"Where's Longtail?" Purdy asked shakily.

"Briarpaw?" Millie's mew cracked.

"I'm going to find them!" Lionblaze promised, bracing himself to force his way through the smashed branches. If he thought of the tree as an enemy in battle, would that protect him from getting hurt?

Firestar turned to his deputy. "Brambleclaw, I want a patrol to clear a way to the elders' den and I want the rest of the Clan outside the hollow and taken care of."

Brambleclaw studied the tree. "We'll need to clear the branches we can move and prop up the ones we can't." He called to Dustpelt, "How many warriors will you need to do that?"

Dustpelt narrowed his eyes. "Four," he meowed. "Any more would get in the way."

Lionblaze remembered how they had destroyed the dam.

"We could use logs to lever the heaviest branches out of the way."

Squirrelflight stepped forward. "I'll organize a team to find logs and props." She glanced at her Clanmates. "Millie, Brackenfur, Birchfall, and Thornclaw, you can help me."

"Sorreltail, Graystripe, Cloudtail, and Berrynose." Dustpelt nodded to his denmates. "Come with me."

Lionblaze stiffened as he heard a faint mewl from where the elders' den had been. "There's definitely a cat still alive in there."

Firestar nodded. "Then there's not a moment to lose." He flicked his tail at Whitewing. "Get everyone else back to the gully. Jayfeather, do what you can to treat any cat with shock. Daisy, I'm putting you in charge of the elders, queens, and kits. Keep them calm." He nodded at Brambleclaw. "Work with Dustpelt and Squirrelflight."

Mousefur paced back and forth, a wail sobbing in her throat. "This is my fault! I should be buried under there, not Longtail!"

Purdy wove around her, steering her away through the shredded thorns. "They'll find him," he promised.

Dovepaw was shaking from nose to tail-tip. "Why didn't I hear it earlier? I could have stopped this!"

Firestar glanced at the horror-stricken apprentice, then called softly to Whitewing. "Take Dovepaw with you. Make sure she's okay."

Gently, the white warrior led her kit out of the camp.

Blood pulsed in Lionblaze's ears. He wanted to launch

himself back among the tangle of branches and haul Longtail and Briarpaw out. But how? Even if he found them, how would he get the two cats past the shattered branches without hurting them?

Dustpelt was already nosing around the edge of the beech. Reaching up with his forepaws, he snapped the first branch out of the way.

Squirrelflight hurried to his side and grabbed the branch in her paws. "We can use this as a prop."

Dustpelt pushed deeper into the tree, forcing an arching bough up with his back long enough for Squirrelflight to wedge her branch underneath.

"Briarpaw!" Millie wailed into the gap. "Longtail?"

Sorreltail and Thornclaw shoved her away as they squeezed after Dustpelt, snapping branches where they could, propping others out of the way. Graystripe plunged in beside them, claws fraying as he ripped at the mangled beech wood.

"Briarpaw!" Brackenfur rolled a log toward a heavy bough, and while Birchfall and Cloudtail levered it up with a long splinter of wood, he pushed the log underneath. The beech creaked, but stayed still. They were making progress.

"Longtail? Can you hear me?" Lionblaze peered down the tunnel that was beginning to form.

No answer.

Tendrils of honeysuckle shivered tantalizingly beyond the tangle of branches still blocking their way. Lionblaze turned to see his brother behind him, blind blue eyes glittering with worry.

"I need to get to my den," Jayfeather meowed.

Branches blocked the entrance.

"Poppyfrost's in shock and Mousefur is beside herself with worry. And if you get Longtail and Briarpaw out alive, I'll need to treat them."

"Can't you gather fresh herbs?" Lionblaze suggested.

Jayfeather's eyes blazed. "It's *leaf-fall*! There are no fresh herbs!"

Firestar turned away from helping Dustpelt roll a log. "Fetch Rosepetal," he ordered. "She's skinny like her father." It was true. She had the same lithe body as Spiderleg. "She might be able to find a way through." He cast a glance at the branches blocking the cave. "It's a mess, but there may be enough gaps."

Jayfeather turned and hurried away.

"Lionblaze!" Squirrelflight was trying to wedge a forked branch into place.

Lionblaze scooted over and helped her to push. The tree seemed to sigh as they lodged the branch under the trunk.

"We're nearly at the elders' den," Dustpelt announced. His pelt was threaded with splinters, and blood oozed from his paws.

Lionblaze looked down the tunnel to the last pair of branches blocking their way. "I can push my way through."

"Do it," ordered Firestar. "We'll shift them while you're inside so that you can get Longtail and Briarpaw out."

Millie and Graystripe stood side by side, looking past the rescue operation at the crumpled honeysuckle. Their daughter was somewhere in the wreckage.

"Please, StarClan," whispered Millie. "Let her be okay."

"She'll be fine," Firestar vowed, his eyes dark.

Jayfeather raced back with Rosepetal. As he passed Millie and Graystripe, Lionblaze noticed him stiffen as though he'd stepped on a thorn. *He can feel their grief.*

Rosepetal was peering through the fractured branches into the medicine den. "I can get through," she announced. Paws first, she wriggled between the spars, grunting a little as her hind legs and tail disappeared into the golden leaves. "What do you want me to get?" she called out.

While Jayfeather began to describe the herbs he would need, Lionblaze padded down the tunnel toward the honeysuckle bush. His heart was pounding and he could feel Graystripe's and Millie's worried gazes on his pelt. What if he found only dead bodies? He pushed away the thought and shouldered his way past the two remaining branches. The bark tore his fur as he squeezed his way through, hope pricking as he felt soft honeysuckle tendrils beneath his paws. Delving into the crushed heap, he squirmed into what was left of the elders' den.

A tiny space opened up in front of him. Only Mousefur's nest remained; the others were hidden underneath shattered branches.

Then he saw the body.

Twisted. Limp. Lifeless.

As he stared, stiff with grief, Dustpelt squeezed in beside him.

"We've cleared the last two branches," the tabby warrior

began. His voice trailed away when he saw the body. "Longtail." The name caught in his throat.

With a strange choking feeling in his throat, Lionblaze lifted the pale tabby elder by the scruff and dragged him from what was left of the den. The old cat was light as a squirrel in his jaws as Lionblaze pulled him through the tunnel and laid him on the bare ground.

Firestar dipped his head while Graystripe pressed close to Millie.

"Did you see Briarpaw?" the gray warrior whispered.

As Lionblaze shook his head, Dustpelt called from inside the den, "She's alive! Quick!"

Lionblaze dashed back with Graystripe pressing on his tail. As they raced along the makeshift tunnel, an ominous snap cracked the air. A prop snapped beside them, spraying splinters. The tree shivered as another prop broke.

"It's not going to hold!" Millie's terrified mew wailed behind them.

Ignoring her, Lionblaze ducked into the remains of the elders' den. Graystripe squashed in beside him. Dustpelt was crouching on Mousefur's nest, his muzzle probing a branch where the beech had crushed the honeysuckle into a mangled mass of tendrils. As Lionblaze slid in beside the tabby tom he saw Briarpaw looking up at him, her face twisted with pain.

"I can't move," she croaked.

Her hind legs were pinned. She screeched as the beech trembled again.

Lionblaze tensed at the sound of another prop splintering

behind them. "We've got to get her out now!"

"How?" Dustpelt gasped. "The tree's collapsing and she's trapped."

"I'll get her!" Graystripe grabbed her scruff.

As Briarpaw squealed in terror and pain, Lionblaze knocked the gray tom away. "You'll kill her," he warned. Without thinking, he pressed his back against a wide branch that spanned the crushed den. Pressing his paws to the ground, he arched his spine, forcing his shoulders up until he felt the whole weight of the tree. The branch shuddered and creaked and began to shift upward.

"Y-you're moving it!" Dustpelt whispered.

"Grab her now!" Lionblaze panted as he felt the tree move another whisker.

Graystripe leaned forward and grabbed his daughter's scruff.

"Gently!" Lionblaze warned. The weight on his shoulders was agonizing. But he wouldn't leave his Clanmate to die. Outside the den, wood splintered and cracked.

"The props are going!" Millie shrieked.

Slowly, carefully, Graystripe drew Briarpaw from under the branch. "I've got her," he mewed through her fur.

Briarpaw whimpered as her father pulled her out.

Dustpelt stared down the tunnel as the pair disappeared.

Lionblaze felt his lungs screaming as he fought for breath, his legs trembling beneath him.

"They're clear!" Dustpelt reported.

"You go too!" Lionblaze yelped.

Dustpelt scooted away between the branches as the tree groaned and wood splintered.

With a last heaving gasp, Lionblaze ducked out from underneath the branch and dived after Dustpelt. The tree crumpled around him and he shot from the tunnel a moment before the last prop gave way and the tree fell to a shuddering halt, its roots slamming against the nursery. With a heaving crash, its branches flopped to the ground like corpses.

Darkness crowded Lionblaze's vision as he struggled to catch his breath. His legs shivered but he refused to let them buckle. He waited, letting strength gather within him and spread through his limbs. Then he stretched and blinked the darkness away.

A tail smoothed his back.

"Well done, Lionblaze." Firestar was at his side.

Graystripe and Millie were crouching beside Briarpaw. Jayfeather grabbed a mouthful of herbs from the pile Rosepetal had passed through the branches. He dropped them next to Briarpaw and began to sniff her limp body.

"Will she be okay?" Millie rasped.

The young cat's breath was coming in gasps and her eyes were glazed.

"I don't think she can see us," Graystripe wailed.

"Out of my way!" Jayfeather scooted around Briarpaw, sniffing her pelt, his eyes narrowed in a frown.

"Longtail?" called a trembling voice. It was Whitewing.

Lionblaze turned and saw the Clan creeping back into the hollow. They padded slowly, edging what was left of the clearing, and sniffing at the remains of their devastated camp. Blossompaw and Bumblepaw broke away and raced to Graystripe and Millie, pressing hard against them.

"Will Briarpaw be okay?" Bumblepaw whimpered.

Mousefur darted from Whitewing's side and began to circle Longtail's body. "No, no, no, no, no," she moaned.

Purdy shuffled close to the old she-cat as she dropped to her belly and pressed her nose into her denmate's chilly pelt.

Dovepaw and Ivypaw stared in horror at Briarpaw's unmoving body.

"Is she dead?" Ivypaw whispered.

"Don't just stand there like rabbits," Lionblaze snapped. "Go and fetch her some moss. Try to make her comfortable!"

The two cats sprang away and raced from the hollow. They passed Leafpool, who padded through the thorns and halted. Through slitted eyes, she watched Jayfeather work.

Jayfeather lifted his head to face her. "Well?" he snarled. "Are you going to help me or not?"

Leafpool blinked, pain flashing in her eyes. Then her gaze hardened. "What do you want me to do?" She slid in beside Jayfeather and sniffed at Briarpaw.

"Shock's setting in fast," Jayfeather reported.

"She needs thyme," Leafpool instructed. "I'll make pulp." She took a mouthful of leaves from the pile and began to chew them.

Jayfeather sat up. "I can't find where she's hurt. There's not a scratch on her." He sounded perplexed.

Briarpaw's eyelids flickered. "I—I c-can't feel my hind legs."

Jayfeather leaned forward and gently took one leg in his jaws to lift it up. He let go and it dropped to the ground like dead prey. "Is that thyme ready yet?" he called to Leafpool.

"Yes." She began wiping the pulp around Briarpaw's lips with her paw. Instinctively Briarpaw licked it off and Leafpool applied more.

Millie was pacing around them, her eyes clouded with grief. "What's wrong with her?" she begged.

Jayfeather didn't answer. Instead he glanced up at Lionblaze. "Comfrey, please."

Lionblaze hurried to the medicine den entrance and called through the branches to Rosepetal, "Jayfeather needs comfrey!"

"I've got loads," Rosepetal meowed back. She began stuffing pawfuls of leaves through the branches.

Lionblaze grabbed a mouthful and carried them to Jayfeather. "Will she be okay?" he whispered.

"Her heartbeat is getting steadier, but her legs . . ." Jayfeather's words trailed into a frustrated growl. He flicked Lionblaze away with his tail.

Ferncloud was trying to comfort Graystripe and Millie. "If anyone can save her, Jayfeather can." She glanced at Jayfeather as he began rubbing a dark green poultice into Briarpaw's hind legs. "And he's got Leafpool helping," she added in a hopeful whisper.

Firestar straightened up. "Dustpelt!" he called. "See if the nursery is secure. We can at least make sure the queens and kits have some shelter." He glanced around the camp, which was half-hidden by the beech. "The apprentices' den looks okay." He nodded to Cloudtail and Squirrelflight. "Check that it's secure. Then collect bedding. As much as you can find. The elders and queens and kits will sleep inside tonight. But the rest of us will still need nests."

Squirrelflight nodded and beckoned to Berrynose, Thornclaw, and Brackenfur with her tail before charging out of the camp.

"Should I go with them?" Lionblaze offered.

Firestar gazed at him. "You've done enough for the Clan for today," he murmured. "Thank you. And thank StarClan we have you. If it wasn't for you, Briarpaw would be dead by now."

Lionblaze looked at Briarpaw lying on the sodden ground. Leafpool was massaging her chest with a firm paw, her eyes more focused than they had been in moons.

Briarpaw opened her eyes and stared at her father and mother. "Where are my back legs? Are they still there?"

Millie let out a muffled squeak, and the fur rose along Graystripe's spine. Briarpaw's hind legs were stretched out behind her, looking just as they always had, strong and glossy. But she couldn't feel them—and if she couldn't feel them, she couldn't stand or walk or run. . . .

A torrent of grief swept through Lionblaze, and for one unbearable moment he wondered if the lively young apprentice would thank him for saving her life.

CHAPTER 12

Jayfeather lifted his head and sniffed the dawn breeze. The air was fresh with the tang of sap from the fallen tree and musty with wet leaves and mud. He felt the warmth of Millie's pelt against his. The gray queen was wrapped around her kit.

Briarpaw slept on, the poppy seed he'd given her last night still heavy on her breath. He could sense the weight in her limbs and the emptiness of feeling in her hind legs.

Aching with the strain of yesterday's disaster, he sniffed at his patient, his whiskers brushing over Millie's pelt as he leaned into Briarpaw's nest.

Millie raised her head. "How is she?"

"She's safe from the shock," he told her. Briarpaw's heart beat steadily beneath her clammy pelt.

"What about her legs?" Millie's mew trembled.

"I don't know." Jayfeather stifled a growl. He hated being so helpless.

Outside, warriors were moving in the half clearing. Jayfeather could hear Brambleclaw issuing orders.

"Patrols will carry on as normal. We must hunt. Dustpelt, how many cats do you need to help you clear the debris?"

Jayfeather pricked his ears. The wreckage of the beech muted sound. The mews of his Clanmates no longer rang against the rocky walls of the hollow but soaked into the soft mass of sodden branches and leaves.

"Four or five should be enough for the first shift," Dustpelt answered his deputy resolutely, but Jayfeather felt the sting in the warrior's paws, raw from yesterday's work. "Birchfall and Brackenfur? They could start with the bigger branches. Rosepetal and Hazeltail could help with the smaller ones."

A path had been cleared to the medicine den. The nursery was safe, enfolded in a tangle of beech roots. The apprentices' den had survived unscathed.

Briarpaw was stirring. As Jayfeather bent to sniff her muzzle he felt her eyelids flicker on his cheek.

"How are you?" he asked gently.

He could feel panic pricking from Millie and tapped her with his tail-tip. *Don't let her smell your fear.*

"Don't know," Briarpaw answered groggily.

"Any pain?"

"No. Just sleepy."

"That's because of the poppy seed."

"Is that why I can't feel my hind legs?"

Jayfeather felt Millie's gaze burning his pelt. She wanted him to say yes. She wanted it to be true.

Perhaps it was. Perhaps once the trauma of the accident had worn off Briarpaw would be up and about, her hind legs fine. After all, he hadn't felt any breaks in the bones. There was no reason why they shouldn't work.

"Well?" Briarpaw pressed.

"I think they're just recovering from the accident a little more slowly than the rest of you," he told her. "Let's wait and see. StarClan willing, they'll wake up before too long."

Briarpaw hooked her claws into the bracken of her nest. "I hope it's soon. I've just passed my assessment. I can be a warrior now!"

Millie swallowed hard. "Go back to sleep," she whispered. "The more you rest, the quicker you'll recover."

Briarpaw rested her chin on her paws and within moments her breath deepened into slumber.

Millie followed Jayfeather out of the den. "What's wrong with her?" she demanded as soon as they were beyond the trailing brambles.

Jayfeather winced as his paw stubbed a branch littering the pathway to his den. The camp had changed shape, distorted by the fallen beech, and he had to pick his way carefully through it, not knowing what might be jutting out, waiting to trip him. He snorted with frustration. The camp had been the one place he could move around without concentrating. Now it was as foreign to him as RiverClan territory.

"What's wrong with her legs?" Millie pressed as he licked his paw fiercely to ease the pain.

He paused, fixing his gaze on her. He knew that cats listened harder when he looked at them, though it made no difference to him. "I don't know."

"You must!" Fear and frustration edged her mew.

Jayfeather was relieved to hear Graystripe's paw steps

approaching. The gray warrior could comfort his mate.

Graystripe's fur brushed Millie's. "No change?" His voice was taut with worry.

"We're just going to have to wait," Jayfeather told them. "At least she's not in pain."

He began to pad away, his mind whirling. Why couldn't Briarpaw feel her legs? They were bruised, but not broken. Jayfeather frowned. He'd never come across that before.

"Can we see her?" Graystripe called after him.

"Sitting with her won't harm her, though she needs her rest," Jayfeather meowed over his shoulder. "She's your kit. You'll know best how to keep her spirits up."

Jayfeather's belly growled. The prey pile smelled freshly stocked. He figured that he'd better eat. There hadn't been time last night. He padded toward it, tasting the familiar scent of Lionblaze, mixed with heavy, wet earth.

Jayfeather plucked a mouse from the stack. "Have you been burying Longtail?" He knew his grief for lost Clanmates was less than that of other cats. *He* would see Longtail again, free from blindness and aches, basking in the warmth of StarClan's hunting grounds or sitting with old friends in the ranks of starry-pelted cats who visited the Moonpool.

Briarpaw's problem upset him more. If her legs didn't recover, she faced more suffering than he wanted to imagine.

Lionblaze flicked his tail against the ground. "I was helping Mousefur and Purdy. They were tired after sitting vigil all night." He pushed the blackbird distractedly with a paw. "I sent them to rest in the nursery, but I don't think Mousefur will sleep. She's still very agitated."

"I'll take her a poppy seed once I've eaten," Jayfeather promised. "Is Dovepaw any calmer?"

"A little." Concern edged his mew. "She should be proud that she saved so many lives by warning us."

"She feels the responsibility of looking after the Clan more heavily than ever," Jayfeather guessed.

"She's young." Lionblaze sighed. "And being one of the Three *is* a great responsibility."

Jayfeather nodded. He and Lionblaze were older, surer of their abilities, and they still found it hard.

"I'll take her hunting with Ivypaw this morning," Lionblaze decided. "I want her to remember what normal Clan life feels like."

"Good." As Jayfeather bent to pick up his mouse he heard pattering paw steps. Blossompaw and Bumblepaw brushed against him.

"Can we see Briarpaw?" Bumblepaw circled anxiously.

"She's sleeping at the moment," Jayfeather answered. "But I don't see why not. She's not in pain. Company will be as good a medicine as any."

The two young cats hurried away to the medicine den while Lionblaze headed for the tattered thorn barrier. Jayfeather bent again for his mouse.

"How's Briarpaw?"

Leafpool's mew took him by surprise. She was the only cat who could creep up on him. Perhaps her scent was too familiar. Too close to his own. He shook the thought away.

"Why don't you check on her yourself?" he suggested, trying to keep his fur lying flat.

"I'm a warrior now," she reminded him gruffly.

Disappointed, he snatched up his mouse and began to pad away.

"I'd go and see Littlecloud."

Leafpool's suggestion stopped him in his tracks.

"Really?" He turned back to her. "I thought you weren't a medicine cat anymore."

"I meant, if I were you."

"But you're not me!"

Leafpool took a steadying breath. "Littlecloud's dealt with an injury like Briarpaw's," she explained. "A cat whose legs were crushed. He might have ideas about how to help Briarpaw."

Jayfeather didn't reply.

"It's not that I don't trust your judgment," Leafpool went on. "It's just what I would do."

Jayfeather dropped his mouse, his appetite gone, and padded away. He climbed the rocks to Firestar's den, pushing all thoughts except Briarpaw from his mind.

Sandstorm was sitting with the ThunderClan leader, grooming his shoulders, her rough tongue scraping his sleek fur. She paused as Jayfeather padded in.

"News?" Firestar's voice was pricked with worry.

Jayfeather shook his head. "I want to travel to the ShadowClan camp to speak with Littlecloud," he meowed. "Leafpool says he's dealt with injuries similar to Briarpaw's."

"Very well." Firestar didn't hesitate. "But take Squirrelflight with you."

Jayfeather's heart sank. "I can manage by myself."

"I know," Firestar agreed. "But if one tree can fall after so much rain, so can another. We can't risk losing you. Take Squirrelflight."

Jayfeather could sense that there was no point arguing. But why Squirrelflight? He couldn't think of any cat he'd like to travel with less. Except Leafpool.

Was Firestar forcing them together on purpose?

Jayfeather left the leader's den and picked his way across the clearing. Grief pricked the air, the cats speaking only when necessary.

Foxleap and Icecloud were dragging a rustling branch past the apprentices' den. They stopped as Jayfeather passed.

"How's Briarpaw?" Icecloud called.

"No better, no worse."

Farther on, Thornclaw was gnawing at a branch, trying to loosen it from its thick bough. "How's Briarpaw?"

Jayfeather hardly broke pace. "No better, no worse."

"How's Briarpaw?" Brightheart padded across his path.

Jayfeather growled. "No better, no worse."

Sympathy flooded from the one-eyed warrior's pelt. "We ask only because we care."

Jayfeather's shoulders slumped. "I don't like being helpless," he confessed.

"Is there anything I can do to help?"

"Actually, there is." Jayfeather nodded. Brightheart was

used to helping in the medicine den. "I have to go out. Can you give Briarpaw poppy seeds if she starts to complain of pain? No more than one at a time. I don't want to dull her feeling any more than necessary."

"Okay."

"And take one to Mousefur as soon as you get a chance," he added. "She's still very upset."

"Right." Brightheart ducked away toward the medicine den.

Jayfeather wanted to check on the elder himself before he left. He slid into the apprentices' den, where Purdy and Mousefur were crouched in thickly padded nests.

"It was my fault," Mousefur was muttering. "All my fault."

Purdy forced a loud purr. "I bet he's walking with StarClan now," he mewed. "Hunting in lush forest, warm and happy."

"How will he manage without me to guide him?" Mousefur fretted.

"I wish I'd known him longer," Purdy pressed on. "I heard he made the Great Journey while he was blind."

"He never seemed to get tired." Memory distracted the old she-cat for a moment. "Always first up and ready to move on. Never afraid of what lay ahead."

"What was he like before he lost his sight?" Purdy prompted.

"Eyes like a hawk," Mousefur remembered. "Could spot prey under a rock a tree-length away."

Jayfeather felt Purdy's gaze flit over his pelt. For the first time, Jayfeather thanked StarClan for the garrulous old loner.

"Tell me about his best catch," Purdy urged Mousefur. "I hear he once caught an eagle."

"Well, it wasn't exactly an eagle, though he did fight off an owl when it tried to snatch a kit."

Relieved, Jayfeather backed out of the den.

As he neared the barrier, branches swished. Cloudtail and Brackenfur were heaving them up against the ragged thorn-bush.

"Wait!" Squirrelflight was hurrying after him. "Sandstorm told me to accompany you to ShadowClan's camp."

"I'm going to speak to Littlecloud." Jayfeather didn't turn to greet the orange warrior before he ducked through a gap in the barrier.

She hurried after him but kept a few paces behind as they headed into the forest. The wind was cold: the first promise of leaf-bare. Jayfeather shivered, then jumped as a tree creaked beside him. He had never considered the fragility of the trees before. They stood so strong and tall. How could rain have defeated one?

Squirrelflight quickened her pace and fell in beside him. "It's not right to fear the forest."

"It's not right for a tree to crush the camp," Jayfeather growled. "But it did."

Squirrelflight moved a little farther away and padded on in silence. Jayfeather relished the tension sparking between them if it meant she would keep her distance. He had not been alone with the cat who had raised him since the truth came out: that she had lied to him and his littermates all their lives, that she wasn't their mother at all, but their mother's sister.

"I remember when you, Lionblaze, and Hollyleaf were still kits," Squirrelflight meowed suddenly.

Jayfeather stiffened.

"A leaf landed on Hollyleaf's head. She thought the forest was falling and hid in the nursery and wouldn't come out for three days."

Shut up! Jayfeather flattened his ears.

"I couldn't have loved you more," Squirrelflight murmured.

Anger flashed through his pelt. "If you'd really loved us, you wouldn't have lied!"

Squirrelflight bristled. "Well, the *truth* is just great, isn't it!" She whipped her tail though the air. "Look at Leafpool. She's lost everything she ever cared about."

"Her choice," muttered Jayfeather.

Squirrelflight ignored him. "She lost you, Lionblaze, and Hollyleaf."

"She gave us away."

"Other cats have been hurt too!" Squirrelflight snapped. "This was never just about you, and I'm sick of you flapping your wings like an injured sparrow, feeling oh so sorry for yourself. You're not the only cat suffering. Your pain is not the hardest to bear. I suppose I expected more from you because you're the medicine cat; I suppose I forget how young you are!"

As she lectured him, Jayfeather's rage spiraled alongside hers. "Leafpool made this happen. *I* didn't go looking for mates in another Clan. *I* didn't have kits and give them away!

I didn't lie and let every cat think I was something I wasn't!"

Squirrelflight drew in a long breath and let it out slowly. "Try to remember," she meowed quietly, "that we did what we thought was best. Remember that you were always loved."

Yeah, right.

Border markers crossed their path.

Jayfeather padded past them.

"Wait," Squirrelflight ordered.

Jayfeather dug his claws into the ground. Was she going to argue with everything he did or said? They had to speak with Littlecloud as soon as possible! But he waited while she tasted the air, her paws shifting the needles on the forest floor as she scanned the woodland.

"Patrol," she warned.

Jayfeather sniffed, and scented the fresh tang of Shadow-Clan warriors. Oakfur and Ferretpaw were padding close by.

Squirrelflight hailed the ShadowClan warrior. "Oakfur?"

Jayfeather felt surprise spark from the ShadowClan cats' pelts. Paw steps came hurrying.

"So Blackstar was right!" Oakfur growled. "You *are* trying to invade."

"Keep your fur on!" Jayfeather realized he was on the wrong side of the border. "I just want to see Littlecloud."

Ferretpaw swarmed around him, whiskers twitching. Jay-feather stood still and let the young cat sniff.

"Do we look like a battle patrol?" Squirrelflight asked.

"There may be more of you." Oakfur sounded suspicious.

"Can you smell any others?"

Ferretpaw snorted. "The others may be disguised."

Squirrelflight sighed. "We really haven't come to invade. Can you take us to see Littlecloud, please?"

Oakfur hesitated. "Okay," he agreed. "But Blackstar will send a full patrol to check the rest of the area." His mew rang through the trees, clearly aimed at the invasion patrol he suspected was hiding behind the trees along the border.

Squirrelflight padded across the scent line and fell in behind Oakfur. Jayfeather followed, his irritation with Ferretpaw growing as the apprentice trotted around him as though he were guarding the Clans' most dangerous warrior.

"What's the matter?" Jayfeather muttered. "Worried I might give you some medicine?"

Ferretpaw bristled. "Shut up!"

Jayfeather recognized the ShadowClan camp as they approached. He'd been here before, with Sol. He padded across the clearing, confident the way was clear, aware of Kinkfur and Ivytail peering from the nursery, of Tawnypelt and Scorchfur crowding from the warriors' den, and hearing fur brush the earth as Starlingpaw and Pinepaw leaped to their paws on the edge of the clearing where they'd been sharing a shrew.

Oakfur gave a warning yowl, which brought Blackstar from his den.

"What's going on?" the ShadowClan leader demanded.

Squirrelflight's paws scuffed the clearing. "May we speak to you in private?"

Oakfur brushed past her. "They want to see Littlecloud."

Surprise bristled in the ShadowClan leader's pelt. "Then

go get him," he ordered. His fur snagged the brambles as he disappeared back into his den. "Come inside," he called.

Jayfeather followed Squirrelflight through the entrance. The stench of ShadowClan was strong and he wrinkled his nose.

Blackstar sat down. "What's wrong?"

"A beech tree fell into the hollow," Squirrelflight explained. "We have an injured cat and we were hoping Littlecloud would be able to advise us on her treatment."

"Just *one* injured cat?" Blackstar's mew croaked with surprise, then hardened. "StarClan must have been keeping a close eye on you."

"Yes," Squirrelflight replied. "We managed to clear the camp before it fell."

"Longtail died," Jayfeather told Blackstar bluntly.

The ShadowClan leader sighed, sympathy flashing briefly like sunlight between clouds. "StarClan will welcome such an old friend, though his Clanmates will miss him."

Littlecloud poked his head through the entrance. "Did I hear you say a tree fell?" He gasped.

"Yes." Squirrelflight was keeping her answers short. "It fell into the hollow. Briarpaw was injured. Longtail died."

"Thank StarClan it wasn't worse," Littlecloud breathed.

"It's bad enough." Jayfeather flicked his tail. "Briarpaw can't move her hind legs."

He let Littlecloud's thoughts flood his own. He saw images of a tom howling in agony, then lying in a nest, limp with fear, unable to move, anguish clouding his gaze.

"I had a case like that." Littlecloud's mind cleared as he

began to speak. "Back when I was Runningnose's apprentice. Wildfur's legs were crushed by a collapsing burrow."

"Leafpool told me." Jayfeather wanted to hear about the cure, not the cause. "But Briarpaw's legs aren't crushed. No broken bones."

"Same with Wildfur," Littlecloud told him. "His legs were only bruised. It was his backbone that was broken."

Jayfeather felt sick. He was suddenly aware of the arch of his own spine. The strength in it. The fragility of it. "Did he recover?"

"He died," Littlecloud mewed quietly.

"But Briarpaw's alive and feels no pain."

"Same as Wildfur, to begin with. I don't think it was the broken backbone that killed him."

Jayfeather leaned forward. "Then what killed him?"

"He couldn't walk."

"Didn't you feed him?" Squirrelflight gasped.

"Of course we did," Littlecloud snapped. "But he kept getting a cough, over and over. Each time we treated it, it came back. He found it harder and harder to breathe."

"Did the loss of feeling spread to his chest?" Jayfeather wondered.

"No. I think it was because he never moved from his nest." Littlecloud spoke slowly, thoughtfully. "It seemed as if he never had a chance to shake the sickness from his chest. As though it filled with disease, like a pool filling with water until there was no air left."

Jayfeather shivered, picturing Briarpaw curled in her nest.

Had she coughed this morning? Was she coughing now, while he was here, away from his patient? His paws suddenly itched for home.

Squirrelflight's tail-tip brushed the roof of the den. "Then we must keep Briarpaw moving."

Jayfeather blinked. "Do you think that would work?" he asked Littlecloud.

"If you can manage it, then it's worth a try," Littlecloud murmured. "And you could try making her a nest that lets her sleep sitting up. It might help keep her chest filled with air." There was doubt in the medicine cat's mew. "But it will be uncomfortable. And keeping her moving will be hard for her and for the rest of the Clan." He paused. "I wish you luck."

Jayfeather bristled. "Luck will have nothing to do with it."

Littlecloud brushed his tail over the ground. "Let me fetch you some herbs to help with her chest and belly. That's where you must focus your healing. Her legs are beyond your powers."

The ShadowClan medicine cat padded from the den, and Jayfeather and Squirrelflight waited in awkward silence with Blackstar until the tang of strong herbs touched Jayfeather's nose. He padded out to meet Littlecloud.

"The coltsfoot will ease her breathing." The ShadowClan medicine cat pushed a bundle of leaves toward him. "The juniper berries will keep her belly soothed."

"We have these herbs already," Jayfeather told him.

"You'll need all you can get." Littlecloud sat down. "Come back if you need more. Or if you want to share any more ideas.

We can all learn from this."

Jayfeather picked up the bundle. As Squirrelflight squeezed out of Blackstar's den, he headed for the camp entrance.

"May StarClan watch over you and Briarpaw," Littlecloud called.

They may watch, Jayfeather thought. *But I won't let them take her yet.*

As Jayfeather followed Squirrelflight back to the hollow, he kept trying to work out ways to keep Briarpaw healthy and moving.

Squirrelflight paused outside the hollow. "I'm proud of you," she meowed. "If any cat can help Briarpaw, it's you."

Jayfeather turned to her, searching for words. He wanted to believe it. That she *was* proud. That he *could* help Briarpaw. "Thanks," he mumbled through his mouthful of herbs, and ducked into camp.

Cloudtail and Brackenfur were still hauling branches against the tattered barrier, slower now as weariness dragged at their paws.

Firestar stood in the empty patch of clearing, talking with Brambleclaw and Dustpelt. "How much of the tree do you think you'll be able to clear?" the ThunderClan leader asked his senior warriors.

Jayfeather sensed the weight of worry in Dustpelt's chest. "We may need to wait for wind and weather to destroy the larger branches and trunks."

"We could make use of them to construct new dens,"

Brambleclaw suggested. "And looking at how much of the debris we've cleared already, I think we can rebuild most of our camp in less than a moon."

"But we can't neglect hunting and border patrols," Dustpelt warned.

Firestar's attention swung toward Jayfeather. "What did Littlecloud say?" he called across the clearing.

Jayfeather padded to the leader's side and dropped his bundle of herbs. "He had some good advice," he reported. "I want to share it with Graystripe and Millie first."

"I sent Graystripe on patrol," Brambleclaw confessed. "I wanted to keep him busy."

Jayfeather picked up his herbs and left the warriors. He could hear Brightheart and Millie in the medicine den. Anxiety was sparking from them, and he sensed Briarpaw's agitation growing as the two she-cats fussed over her.

"Just eat a little!" Millie begged. Jayfeather could smell the shrew dangling from her claws.

"I'm not hungry!" Briarpaw complained.

Jayfeather pushed through the trailing brambles and put down the herbs. "Leave her alone," he ordered.

Millie rounded on him. "She's my kit!"

"I'm her medicine cat!"

Briarpaw churned her nest with her forepaws. "I just want to help my Clanmates rebuild the camp!" she wailed.

Brightheart crossed the den and whispered in Jayfeather's ear, "We told her about Longtail. She's still distressed, but I didn't want to give her poppy seed, after what you said."

Jayfeather nodded. "Good. She's going to have to learn to deal with distress." He felt Brightheart stiffen at the darkness in his mew. "We have to face the truth," he explained. "Briarpaw has a difficult path ahead, but I will do everything I can to save her."

"Save her?" Millie nudged between them, her pelt prickling. "What did Littlecloud tell you?"

Jayfeather wasn't ready to share what he'd learned. "Wait." He needed to check Littlecloud's theory first. There was still a chance Briarpaw's legs were only bruised. That her backbone wasn't damaged. He padded to her nest.

"What are you going to do?" Anxiety tightened Millie's mew as Jayfeather leaned into Briarpaw's nest.

"I need to be sure." He ran his paws down Briarpaw's back. He felt her twist to see what he was doing.

"Sure of what?" Millie fretted.

When Jayfeather didn't answer, Brightheart padded closer and nudged Millie gently away. "He knows what he's doing," she whispered.

The backbone felt smooth: nothing out of place. Hope sparked in Jayfeather's chest. He sniffed her legs. Definitely swollen. Perhaps when the swelling went down . . . ? He lifted a leg in his teeth as he had done yesterday. It dropped, still lifeless. More comfrey might quicken the healing.

One last test.

Leaning farther into the nest, he nipped Briarpaw's backbone in his teeth, just below her shoulders.

"Ow!" Briarpaw stiffened in alarm.

"I'm testing something," Jayfeather reassured her. "It'll prick, but I won't damage you." He put his muzzle close to hers until their whiskers brushed. "Do you trust me?"

"Yes," she breathed.

"I need you to be brave while I do this."

"Okay."

Millie tried to move nearer the nest.

Brightheart blocked her. "Give him room to work."

Jayfeather nipped Briarpaw's backbone again, a little farther down.

"Ow."

He nipped again, working his way gradually toward her tail.

With each nip she stiffened, but stifled her mew.

He nipped her lower.

"Aren't you going to do it again?" she asked.

The question turned Jayfeather's blood cold. He reached into the nest with one paw and poked a claw into the same spot. "Did you feel that?"

"Feel what?" Briarpaw twisted around to see.

"No, don't look," said Jayfeather. He dug his claw in harder. "Now?"

Briarpaw started to shake. "I can't feel anything." Panic edged her mew.

"What are you doing?" Millie barged past as Jayfeather stuck his claws in hard. "You're making her bleed!"

"Is he?" Briarpaw struggled to see.

Jayfeather hardly heard them. "You couldn't feel my claws, could you?" he murmured numbly.

"No," Briarpaw whispered.

"Your backbone is broken," Jayfeather told her. "There's no pain because there's no feeling past the break." He pressed his paw gently against her flank. "I'm sorry."

"Why?" she squeaked. "If I can't feel pain, surely that's a good thing?"

"You won't ever be able to feel pain in your legs again," Jayfeather told her slowly. "You won't ever feel *anything* in your hind legs again."

Millie gasped. "What do you mean? Broken bones mend."

"Not backbones."

"How do you know that?"

"Littlecloud had a warrior with the same injury," he told her.

Briarpaw was craning her head toward him. "What happened to him?" she mewed.

Jayfeather didn't answer.

"He died, didn't he?" Briarpaw whimpered.

Jayfeather felt Millie barge into his shoulder, shoving him until she had bundled him right out of the den.

"How could you tell my kit she was going to die?" she hissed. "She can't feel her legs, that's all! You're not fit to be a medicine cat! *Do* something!"

"What's going on?" Squirrelflight dashed across the clearing and slid between Jayfeather and her snarling denmate.

"He says she's going to die!"

Squirrelflight stiffened. "Did you say that, Jayfeather?"

Jayfeather shook his head.

"I didn't think so." Squirrelflight's voice grew calm.

"Littlecloud's patient died. It doesn't mean Briarpaw will."

"We can feed her and help her move to keep her healthy," Jayfeather put in. "If we keep her active, she stands a good chance of beating this."

Millie's breath was coming in quick gasps. "She'll recover?"

"Her legs won't," Jayfeather meowed gently. "But she doesn't have to die."

Squirrelflight's tail swished the air. "We need to keep her as active as we can, so that her chest stays clear. If we can do that, she'll be okay."

"Okay?" Millie sobbed. "She'll never hunt. She'll never be a warrior! She'll never have kits!"

Graystripe bounded into camp. "What's happening?" He skidded to a halt at Millie's side.

"Our poor kit!" Millie buried her muzzle in his shoulder.

The trailing brambles at the entrance to the den swished. "Briarpaw can hear you!" Brightheart hissed. "I think you should come in, Jayfeather, and explain to her exactly what's happening."

Squirrelflight's nose brushed his cheek. "I'll look after Millie and Graystripe," she told him.

Heart heavy as a stone, Jayfeather padded into his den. He settled beside Briarpaw's nest. Panic was flooding in waves from the young cat.

"I'm never going to walk again, am I?"

Jayfeather rested his muzzle on her trembling head. "No," he whispered. "I'm so sorry."

Chapter 13

"StarClan honors your courage and spirit." Firestar touched his muzzle to Briarpaw's head. Watching, Dovepaw felt a surge of excitement.

"I name you Briarlight."

Bumblestripe and Blossomfall, already named, were the first to start the cheering for ThunderClan's newest warrior.

"Briarlight, Briarlight!"

The voices of the Clan shook the chilly air and rang up through the hollow into a clear blue sky. Millie and Graystripe pressed against each other, their proud gazes sharpened with grief.

Briarlight shifted her forepaws, propping herself higher, raising her chin. Dovepaw tried not to look at her hind legs, splayed uselessly behind her.

It had been a quarter moon since the tree fell. Dovepaw was weary, like the rest of her Clan. The work of clearing the camp of debris on top of the regular patrols had left every cat exhausted. And with each shortening day, prey was starting to grow leaner and scarcer.

Dovepaw longed for a good night's sleep. She had been

plagued by terrible dreams. If only she'd given more warning, then Longtail might have been saved and Briarlight would be scampering around her littermates right now. A dream had woken Dovepaw only last night: the tree splintering into the clearing yet again, a trapped cat wailing.

Ivypaw!

In every dream it was Ivypaw who was trapped underneath the beech tree, not Briarlight; and in every dream Dovepaw struggled in vain to reach her sister.

"Dovepaw?" Whitewing's mew brought her back. "Are you all right?"

Dovepaw shook herself. "I'm just glad Briarlight's got her warrior name."

"She's a warrior at heart," Whitewing murmured.

It was true. Briarlight had never stopped fighting for a moment. Jayfeather had devised exercises to keep her chest clear and strengthen her forelegs. And Briarlight never missed a chance to practice them: stretching and twisting, reaching out with her forepaws until she trembled with the effort and her pelt grew matted. The past few days she'd insisted on fetching her own food from the fresh-kill pile, though her Clanmates often tripped over one another trying to be the first to carry the tastiest morsel to her nest in the medicine den.

"I'll get my own," Briarlight had told Cherrykit, who had tried to give her own meal to the injured young cat.

Cherrykit had stared with round eyes at Briarlight as she hauled herself with her forepaws across to the fresh-kill pile.

"Look, Molekit!" Cherrykit had called. "She's doing it herself!"

Molekit had come running. "Go, Briarlight!" he cheered.

Dovepaw secretly thought the two kits and Jayfeather had been Briarlight's greatest allies; they alone accepted her entirely as she was now. Millie's gaze was still clouded with grief, and pity flashed in every warrior's eyes when they saw the young cat hauling herself across the camp. Mousefur could not even look at Briarlight. She still blamed herself for the tragedy that had killed her best friend and crippled the young warrior.

In spite of their horror, most of the Clan was getting used to Briarlight's injury. They no longer stared with startled eyes at the medicine den when she wailed and yowled under Jayfeather's instruction.

"It'll keep your chest clear," he'd encouraged. "Yowl your head off if you have to. Your Clanmates won't mind."

The treatment seemed to be working. Briarlight's hind legs were no better, but her fur was sleek, her eyes brighter each day, and her forelegs as strong as any warrior's.

They didn't even tremble now as Molekit clawed his way up the newest warrior's pelt and balanced on her shoulders. "Briarlight!" he cheered.

Millie nosed him off crossly. "Be careful!"

"It's okay," Briarlight insisted. "I bet I can carry both of them."

"Really?" Cherrykit's eyes sparkled.

"Don't you dare!" Millie warned the kits.

Graystripe softly pushed his mate away. "Let them have some fun."

"We'll be warriors, too, soon!" Molekit bundled his sister over in a surprise attack.

"You're not even apprentices!" Briarlight teased.

Dovepaw gazed at her old denmate. How could she act so cheerful?

Whitewing leaned forward and licked her daughter's ear. "Don't forget, we're gathering moss for the new elders' den."

How could she forget? For days, she'd been helping to weave the honeysuckle around what was left of the beech branches where the old den had stood. The new den was spacious and strong. Purdy and Mousefur would move in as soon as the new nests were built.

She gazed around the camp, accustomed now to its new shape. The warriors' den was lost for good, crushed by the trunk. But the thick boughs of the beech, which arched over half the clearing and pressed against one side of the hollow, gave plenty of new shelter. There were plans to shape a brand-new warriors' den around the thickest of them; rescued branches had already been stacked, ready for construction to begin. The nursery looked safer than a badgers' set, enclosed in a thick tangle of roots that had been woven where possible to form a protective shell around the old bramble bush.

"Come on." Whitewing flicked Dovepaw's flank with her tail-tip. She beckoned to Toadstep and Rosepetal. "Are you ready?"

The two warriors trotted to meet them.

"Where's Ivypaw?" Dovepaw glanced around the clearing, and spotted her sister slipping in from the dirtplace tunnel.

"I'm coming!" Ivypaw bounded across the clearing. "See you later, Briarlight!" she called cheerfully.

Briarlight had lain down in a spot of weak sunshine, while Molekit and Cherrykit clambered over her. She lifted her head and purred at Ivypaw. "Can't you take these two with you?"

"I'm afraid you're stuck with them for another moon yet," Ivypaw joked.

"Hey!" Molekit objected. "We'd come if we could!"

Ivypaw bounded to a halt beside Toadstep. "A dawdling cat gathers no moss," she teased the black-and-white tom.

Dovepaw wove around them. "I bet I collect the most," she challenged.

Ivypaw shrugged. "If you say so."

Dovepaw tensed. Ivypaw was acting really weird lately. She'd been like this since the tree fell. Had she guessed Dovepaw's powers? Was Ivypaw blaming her for not warning the Clan sooner? Dovepaw shook the thought away. *Impossible.*

She watched her sister race after Toadstep and Rosepetal toward the camp entrance, still not sure if she was imagining Ivypaw's coldness.

"Watch this!" Ivypaw called to Toadstep as they reached the slope leading down to the shore. She skidded onto her belly and slid three tail-lengths down the soft grass.

"You look like a duck!" Toadstep huffed with amusement.

Rosepetal was watching the pair through narrowed eyes. Had she seen the change in Ivypaw too?

"Right." Whitewing gazed along the shore. "Let's see if we can find swan feathers. After all they've been through, I expect Purdy and Mousefur will appreciate soft nests."

"And Briarlight," Dovepaw added.

Ivypaw rolled her eyes. "Well, *of course* Briarlight."

Whitewing flashed her daughter a stern look. "Seeing as you and Toadstep seem to be getting on so well . . ."

"Not that well!" Toadstep shifted his paws, his fur spiking up with embarrassment.

"*However* well," Whitewing went on, "you may as well gather bedding together."

Ivypaw nudged Toadstep, her eyes sparkling as she relished the young warrior's discomfort. "Come on," she mewed. "I'll race you to the water." She charged away down the bank, pebbles crunching as she landed gracefully on the shore.

Dovepaw flicked her tail. Ivypaw was even *moving* like a different cat.

"You and Rosepetal can work together," Whitewing told Dovepaw. "I'll be upshore if you need me." She flicked her tail toward WindClan territory and headed away.

"Where do you want to start?" Rosepetal asked.

"You're the warrior," Dovepaw replied. Ivypaw had left her feeling ruffled.

"Yes," agreed Rosepetal. "But I was hoping you'd have as good a nose for moss as you do for prey."

Dovepaw glanced at her paws. "I guess the trees around the stream will have the most moss, and there might be feathers caught there too."

"Right." Rosepetal headed downshore to where trees lined the stream that raced into the lake.

Dovepaw padded after her. By the time she'd caught up, Rosepetal was already stripping moss from the roots of a tree.

"You head farther upstream," the dark cream she-cat ordered.

Dovepaw nodded and walked into the chilly shadows of the trees. The stream chattered past her paws as she searched for the mossiest roots.

Suddenly a white flash caught her eye. A feather was bobbing on the breeze. It danced along the forest floor and Dovepaw gave chase. It was long and downy and would make great bedding. She wove after it through the trees, then pounced, flattening it between her forepaws. "Got you!"

"There you are!" Lionblaze slid from a clump of ferns. "Whitewing said you'd gone this way."

Dovepaw sat up, startled. "What is it?" A breeze rustled the ferns and lifted her feather, carrying it away through the trees. "Mouse dung!" Dovepaw started after it.

"Feathers can wait!" Lionblaze called her back.

"What about Mousefur's nest?"

The fur rose along Lionblaze's spine. "There are more ShadowClan scents inside the border," he growled. "Something's going on. The sooner we find out what, the better. They might be planning to invade. They know about the tree. They probably think it's weakened us."

Dovepaw sat down crossly. ShadowClan had known about the tree for a quarter moon. They hadn't invaded yet. She watched her feather flicker out of sight. *It's probably just Tigerheart again.* Only StarClan knew what he was up to, but he'd promised there was no danger to ThunderClan. Why would he betray her? They were friends.

"Well?" Lionblaze stared at her. "Have you heard anything from ShadowClan territory? Are they planning something?"

"How would I know?" she answered stubbornly.

Lionblaze rolled his eyes. "Your *powers*?"

Dovepaw lashed her tail over the forest floor. "If I'd heard something important, don't you think I'd have told you?"

"You might not know what's important!"

Dovepaw stood up and faced her mentor. "It's *my* power!" A growl rose in her throat. "I don't tell you how to fight, do I?"

A bramble rustled a few trees farther upstream and Ivypaw popped out. "Hello," she mewed, her eyes darting from Lionblaze to Dovepaw. "I-I've just found the best patch of moss."

Lionblaze flashed anger at Dovepaw and bounded away into the forest.

"What did he want?" Ivypaw asked. Her mew was softer than it'd been in days.

"He's my mentor; he was just checking up on me," Dovepaw snapped, still prickling from Lionblaze.

"But it sounded important." Ivypaw padded closer. "Why does he think you know what's going on in ShadowClan?"

Dovepaw tensed. How much had her sister heard? "I don't know," she mewed quickly.

"You're lying!" Ivypaw scowled.

Dovepaw flinched.

Ivypaw leaned closer still. "What is it with you? Why are you always going off to talk with Firestar? Why is Lionblaze always calling you away for secret conversations?"

"They're just interested in my training." Dovepaw hated this. With every lie she felt another barrier of thorns spring up between her and Ivypaw.

Ivypaw curled her lip. "Firestar never asks about *my* training! What makes you so special?"

"It's not like that, honestly!" Dovepaw's heart fluttered with panic. "I don't think I'm special. It's . . ." Her voice trailed away. "It's just complicated."

Ivypaw took a step backward. "Too complicated to tell your sister? I thought we were best friends!" She glanced away through the trees, her eyes darkening. "Well, you have your secrets; I'll have *mine*!"

Secrets? What was Ivypaw talking about?

Suddenly, Dovepaw remembered Ivypaw's story about the StarClan cat who'd visited her. She dug her claws into the ground, annoyed with herself. Why hadn't she shown more interest?

"Have you had another dream?" she guessed. "Another visit from StarClan?"

"Jealous now?" Ivypaw sneered. "You weren't that interested when I tried to tell you before. Too busy chitchatting with Lionblaze. Why should I tell you now? Are you worried I might be more *special* than you? Are you worried the senior warriors might start taking an interest in me instead?"

Rawness edged her mew, and Dovepaw felt a wave of dismay. She hadn't realized Ivypaw felt like this.

"I-I'm sorry," she began.

But Ivypaw was already bounding away into the trees. She glanced over her shoulder. "Clearly not sorry enough!"

I'll explain it all one day! Dovepaw vowed silently to her. *Then you'll understand!*

Back in the hollow, Rosepetal and Toadstep dumped the moss in the new elders' den before hurrying off to find out what duties Brambleclaw had planned for them next.

"You'll be okay straightening it out?" Rosepetal called to Ivypaw over her shoulder.

"No problem." The feather wrap muffled Ivypaw's answer as she slid under the branch arching over the entrance.

Dovepaw followed her sister inside. They worked silently, draping the moss over the bracken that Icecloud and Birchfall had already patted into place at one edge of the den. Late sunlight rippled through the honeysuckle roof, making the den seem underwater.

Wordlessly, Ivypaw unfolded the wrap and placed a pawful on the nest that Dovepaw was shaping.

"Aren't you going to speak to me at all?" Dovepaw begged.

Ivypaw ignored her. The honeysuckle rustled and Dovepaw turned to see Purdy leading Mousefur into the den.

"See," purred the old loner. "I told you they'd have the nests ready." He nodded to Dovepaw and Ivypaw. "They look lovely. Thank you."

Mousefur stared blankly around the new den. "It's very big," she murmured.

Dovepaw waited for her to start complaining about drafts, but the old she-cat didn't say anything else, just curled into one of the nests and rested her nose on her forepaws.

Dovepaw wished she'd planted a burr in the moss. Anything to get the elder complaining again. It wasn't right, seeing her so sad. "Not too damp?" she prompted.

"I preferred the old nests." Mousefur sighed. "They smelled of Longtail."

Purdy glanced at the apprentices and Dovepaw guessed that he wanted them to leave. As she turned to the entrance, she saw him circle down into his nest, pressing close to Mousefur. With a pang she wondered if she and Ivypaw would ever curl up together like that again. Watching Ivypaw stomp out ahead of her, she guessed not.

"Hey!" Rosepetal called as they reached the clearing. She was standing beside the fresh-kill pile. "Do you want a mouse?"

"Yes, please!" Ivypaw trotted away as if Dovepaw didn't exist.

Dovepaw was too sad to feel hungry. Maybe Briarlight wanted company. She padded toward the medicine den, her paws scuffing through the beech leaves that littered the ground outside. She paused outside the den to listen to Jayfeather and Briarlight working on exercises.

"That's it," Jayfeather urged. "Stretch just a little bit more."

"Oof!" Briarlight panted. "A few more of those and I'll be able to wrestle Thornclaw!"

"Good!" Jayfeather purred. "I would love to see the look

on his face!" The tang of fresh herbs was drifting through the brambles. "Three more stretches, and then you should have your medicine."

"Can't I just go outside and enjoy the last of the sunshine?" Briarlight pleaded. "The Clan will be sharing tongues soon and I don't want to be stuck in here."

"Eat your herbs first," Jayfeather insisted. "Then you can share a mouse with your littermates."

"Are they back from patrol?"

Dovepaw looked around the clearing. Blossomfall and Bumblestripe were padding into camp, carrying fresh prey. She should have known that as well as Jayfeather. She'd been so busy worrying about Ivypaw that she'd forgotten to keep her senses open to movements around the camp.

"Yuck!" Briarlight gagged on the herbs. Then Dovepaw heard her hind legs dragging across the den floor. She backed out of the way as the brambles swished and Briarlight's head poked out. "Can't you find a way of making them taste better?" she called back to Jayfeather.

"I'll do my best," he promised.

Briarlight hauled herself from the den and over the shifting leaves. Her eyes were bright but her teeth were clenched with effort. She spotted Dovepaw.

"Hi!" The greeting came as a hiss. "Sorry," she groaned. "This is hard work! It'll get easier."

She headed toward the fresh-kill pile, where Blossomfall and Bumblestripe were arriving with their catches. Their eyes lit up as they spotted her.

"Briarlight!" Blossomfall hurried to greet her sister, a

mouse dangling in her jaws. She dropped it at Briarlight's paws. "Want to share this?"

Dovepaw ducked into Jayfeather's den. "Hi," she murmured wearily. She needed advice. She wanted to be friends with Ivypaw again. She wanted to share a mouse with her littermate, like Blossomfall and Briarlight.

Jayfeather was sweeping herb fragments with his tail into a dusty pile. He looked up as Dovepaw padded in. "Would you rather eat herbs sweetened with nectar or mouse blood?"

"Mouse blood," Dovepaw answered absently.

Jayfeather let his tail lie still. "What's wrong?" His blue eyes glowed in the dim light of the den.

"Please can I tell Ivypaw about the prophecy?"

Jayfeather sighed and went back to his sweeping. "No."

"But it's making it really hard to stay friends with her."

"How?"

"She thinks I'm getting special treatment."

"She's jealous?"

"No!" Dovepaw suddenly felt defensive of her sister. Then she sighed. "Well, yes, sort of. I guess."

"Lionblaze and I never told any other cat," Jayfeather pointed out.

"But you had each other!"

"Not to start with." Jayfeather began to pick the cleanest fragments out of the pile. "I was the first one to find out, and I couldn't share it with Lionblaze and Hollyleaf until I was sure they were the ones."

"But Hollyleaf wasn't one of the Three."

"I thought she was." Jayfeather shook out another herb fragment. His eyes darkened. "She thought she was too." He put the leaf shred carefully down. "Not being one of us was the hardest thing for her to live with in the end."

"She didn't know how lucky she was," Dovepaw muttered under her breath. Curiosity pricked her pelt. "What *did* happen to her?"

"She went away." Jayfeather picked up another shred. "She couldn't stay here."

"Because she wasn't included in the prophecy?" Dovepaw frowned. She sometimes tried to imagine what it would be like to be an ordinary warrior. It had to be easier, surely?

"Partly," Jayfeather mewed.

"Partly?" *What was the other reason?*

Jayfeather scooped the pile of shreds in his jaws and carried them to the split in the rock where he stored his herbs. Clearly he wasn't going to give any more information away.

Secrets! Always secrets! Crossly, Dovepaw pushed her way out of the den.

Blossomfall, Bumblestripe, and Briarlight lay in a patch of dying sunshine sharing their mouse. Ivypaw was lying beside Rosepetal, sharing a blackbird.

Dovepaw gazed at her sister. *I would tell you if I could.*

Ivypaw swallowed her last mouthful and began grooming Rosepetal.

But I have to keep this secret. Even if it means losing my best friend.

CHAPTER 14

Ivypaw shivered. A chilly wind had stripped the flowers from the meadow and driven pale gray clouds across the sky. The ground trembled beneath her paws. The horses were running, crowding along the edge of the meadow, their eyes wild and their ears flat back.

Where was Hawkfrost?

Ivypaw felt nervous. She didn't want to be alone in the wide pasture today. The breeze was moaning across the dull, dry grass, ruffling her fur the wrong way.

There! A dark rump showed above the grass, thick, bushed tail flicking.

She scampered toward the RiverClan warrior.

"You're here!" she puffed, relieved when he turned and fixed his familiar dark blue gaze on her. "I thought you weren't coming! I've been looking for you for ages."

Hawkfrost sat up and gazed at her lazily through half-closed eyes. "Lucky you found me today, then."

"Teach me something new!" she begged. Cinderheart was already impressed by the progress she had made in training; she wanted to please her mentor again today when they practiced battle moves.

Hawkfrost yawned, hunching his shoulders as he stretched his spine.

"Just one battle move," Ivypaw pleaded.

"Haven't I given you enough to practice already?"

"I've practiced it all. Now I need something new." Ivypaw widened her eyes hopefully. "Please!"

Wearily, Hawkfrost stood up. "Do you pester your Clanmates this much?" he murmured.

"They don't teach me such interesting stuff," Ivypaw mewed.

"Watch carefully." Hawkfrost lunged for her, hooking her hind legs under her and rolling her over with his forepaw till she found herself splayed on her back.

"Wow!" she squeaked, springing to her paws. "Let me try it."

She leaped at Hawkfrost, curling a paw around his hind legs and tugging.

Nothing happened. The broad-shouldered warrior turned his head to look back at her. "Have you started?"

Frustrated, Ivypaw backed away and tried again.

Still, the RiverClan warrior didn't budge.

Ivypaw put her head to one side. "How did you do that, exactly?"

"Run your paw along my hind legs," Hawkfrost ordered. "Can you feel the tendon along the back of the joint?"

Ivypaw felt a tough cord behind the crook of his legs, like a stretched mousetail.

"Aim there," Hawkfrost told her. "A sharp jab. Try to hit both legs at once."

Excited, Ivypaw crouched down, fixing her gaze, then leaped. She brought her forepaws down hard, hitting the tendon, and Hawkfrost's legs buckled beneath him. Seizing the advantage, she used her shoulders to shove him sideways. Unbalanced, he toppled over and she threw herself on top of him, pinning him to the ground.

"Good," he grunted. He got to his paws, shaking her off. "But make more of your advantage. The surprise will last only a moment. You must use that moment. Try again."

Ivypaw tried the move again, but this time swept his forepaws from under him too. Her teeth were at his exposed throat before he could recover himself.

He shoved her off with a hiss. "Not bad."

Pride rippled through her pelt.

"We might make something of you after all," he conceded.

She lifted her chin. "Of course!"

A shadow rippled through the grass some distance away. Ivypaw jerked her head to look at it and saw eyes glinting at her. Some cat was watching. She stiffened. "Who's that?" As she spoke, the cat ducked lower in the grass and slunk away.

Hawkfrost shrugged. "I mentioned you to a couple of friends," he meowed. "It was probably one of them. No doubt he wanted to see the apprentice who keeps badgering me for extra training."

Ivypaw tossed her head. "He probably wanted to learn from me."

"Yeah, right." Hawkfrost cuffed her softly over the ear. "Come on, try that move again. See if you can do it twice."

"Okay!" Ivypaw crouched down. "I want to get it perfect before I show Dovepaw."

Hawkfrost blinked. "Who's Dovepaw?"

"My sister." Ivypaw wriggled her hindquarters, ready to pounce. "The one I told you about. Remember?"

She sprang up, hitting the tendon harder this time, feeling a surge of triumph as the broad-shouldered warrior crumpled and she rolled him to the ground.

Sitting back on her haunches, she wiped a paw over her whiskers while she got her breath back. "All the senior warriors think Dovepaw's the best apprentice ever." She shrugged. "They're always asking her stuff, like she knows something no other cat does."

Hawkfrost sat down and lapped at his chest. "And does she?" he asked between licks.

"There's *something* she's not telling me, but I can't figure out what it is." Ivypaw cocked her head. "I just wish she wouldn't act like she's so special. She's always got her ears pricked like she's on guard: like no one else in the Clan can keep us safe."

Hawkfrost finished grooming his chest and ran a claw across a clover leaf. The soft green tissue split and darkened beneath his touch. "Did you tell her about me?"

"I was going to," Ivypaw mewed, irritation prickling as she remembered their interrupted conversation. "But I didn't get a chance." She sniffed. "Now I don't want to tell her." The tip of her tail twitched. "Why should I? She has her secrets, so I'll have mine."

Hawkfrost plucked at another leaf. "Probably a good idea. It sounds like . . ." He paused. "Dovepaw—is that her name?"

Ivypaw nodded.

"It sounds like Dovepaw would get jealous and want to learn all your moves."

Ivypaw unsheathed her claws.

"She's your littermate," Hawkfrost pressed. "Not your echo, right?"

"Right!" Ivypaw declared. "Why should I give her the chance to copy me?"

Hawkfrost stretched his hind legs. "No more echoes. Let's try something new."

Ivypaw woke up. Her shoulders were stiff. She wriggled them into the soft moss of her nest, wondering if she'd slept awkwardly. Then she remembered: Hawkfrost had worked her hard, until her muscles ached. She sat up, surprised. Wow! What a vivid dream!

Dovepaw was snoring. Curled in her nest, her eyes closed, the gray apprentice looked small and fluffy. Far more like the innocent kit she had been than the knowing apprentice she pretended to be now. With a surge of affection, Ivypaw longed to tell Dovepaw about her dream, just like they used to when they shared a nest in the nursery with Whitewing.

No. Ivypaw pushed away her nostalgia. Dovepaw had a secret. *I'm going to have one too.* It was probably a far better secret than Dovepaw's anyway. *She* was being trained by a StarClan warrior! She was going to be the best warrior ever. She'd be even better than Lionblaze!

"Ivypaw!" Cinderheart's mew rang through the wall of the den.

Ivypaw crept out into the cold, gray dawn. Blossomfall and Bumblestripe were stretching in their makeshift nests beneath the arching bough of the beech. Cinderheart beckoned them over with her tail.

"You three will be training together today," she announced.

Blossomfall sat down, yawning. "You want us to train Ivypaw?"

Cinderheart shook her head. "You will be training *together.*"

"We're not apprentices!" Bumblestripe shook out his fur, fluffing it against the cold air.

Cinderheart's gaze flashed to the slope of rocks. Firestar was leaping down into the clearing.

Blossomfall rolled her eyes. "Let me guess," she grumbled. "A new idea about training."

Ivypaw could hear Thornclaw's irritated sigh echoing in her mew. Blossomfall was obviously quoting her denmate.

Firestar halted beside them. "There's nothing wrong with trying something new," he meowed.

Blossomfall looked at her paws. "I guess."

Firestar straightened his tail in the air. "We don't want the Clan getting stale. And there's no harm in warriors practicing their skills. Would you rather we started battles to keep our paws nimble?"

"I suppose not," Blossomfall conceded.

Ivypaw glanced at the apprentices' den. "What about Dovepaw? Will she be training with us?"

Cinderheart shook her head. "She'll be training with Lionblaze."

"Of course." Ivypaw's fur pricked along her spine. "Why should she train with ordinary warriors?"

"Pardon?" Cinderheart pricked her ears.

"Nothing," Ivypaw mewed quickly. She felt hot as she noticed Firestar staring at her. "I just don't get to train with her much these days."

Dustpelt, Birchfall, and Leafpool were stirring in their nests beneath the fallen tree.

"I hear Firestar put you in charge today, Cinderheart." Dustpelt yawned, padding under the snaking branch. "Are we ready to go?"

Birchfall and Leafpool followed him, neither looking excited at the prospect of a training session.

"Yes, we're ready," Cinderheart meowed. "Come on; follow me."

They stopped in a clearing where bracken edged a leafy patch of forest floor. Leafpool flicked her tail restlessly as Cinderheart wove between the warriors. Ivypaw circled Bumblestripe and sat down.

"It's weird training with senior warriors," she whispered in his ear.

"It's certainly different." The young warrior's eyes were bright. "I wonder if we'll be able to beat them?"

"Maybe." Ivypaw stretched her claws. The run through the forest had warmed her up and loosened the stiff muscles in her shoulders. She was ready to try out some of Hawkfrost's moves.

"Now," Cinderheart began, "we're going to set up a mock battle." She flicked her tail toward the hazel bush at one end of the clearing, then at the clump of ferns at the other. "I'm going to split us into two patrols." She nodded to Dustpelt. "You lead Leafpool, Blossomfall, and Ivypaw. I'll lead Bumblestripe, Hazeltail, and Birchfall. If that's okay with you, Birchfall?" The tawny tom dipped his head to the younger warrior. "We'll try to take the hazel. You"—she nodded again at Dustpelt—"try to take the ferns."

Ivypaw padded after Bumblestripe into the center of the clearing. She crouched beside him, preparing for the attack, while Leafpool and Dustpelt flanked them. Cinderheart's patrol lined up opposite, so close that their whiskers almost touched.

Bumblestripe narrowed his eyes, concentrating on the hazel bush a tree-length behind his opponents. Hazeltail and Birchfall pressed their bellies to the earth.

"Remember," Cinderheart ordered, "claws sheathed. We're not ShadowClan."

The warriors nodded and Ivypaw quickly curled her claws away beneath the soft fur of her white paws.

"Go!"

At Cinderheart's command, Ivypaw rolled over. She heard Cinderheart's paws thump the ground where she'd been.

"Nice!" Cinderheart's praise was cut short as Leafpool bowled the gray she-cat over and bundled her with flailing paws to the end of the clearing.

Ivypaw jerked around, ready for an attack. Bumblestripe was wrestling with Blossomfall.

Blossomfall wriggled from his grasp. "Don't forget I learned all your moves before you were out of the nursery."

"Bet you don't remember this one." Bumblestripe jumped in the air and landed, belly first, flat on her spine.

Blossomfall collapsed, her legs crumpling beneath her. "Hey! That's unfair. That's a kit move!"

"But it still works," Bumblestripe teased, refusing to budge as Blossomfall struggled underneath him.

Ivypaw stiffened. Birchfall was streaking toward the fern clump. If he reached it, his patrol would win. She raced after him, spraying dirt with her hind legs. He was nearly at the ferns. She pounced. Reaching out, she jabbed his hind legs, aiming for the tendons. He stumbled and fell and she leaped onto his shoulders, fighting to cling on with unsheathed claws while he writhed beneath her.

With a fierce shove he flung her away and she landed heavily, the wind huffing from her. Narrowing her eyes, she sprang to her paws. She wasn't going to let Hawkfrost down! Birchfall was on his paws but looking bewildered, his hind legs trembling. She dived underneath him, curving her body and hooking herself under his belly. With one paw on either side of her, she knocked a foreleg and hind leg out from under him. Then she darted out of the way before he collapsed.

Where was the rest of her patrol? She couldn't defend the ferns without help. She scanned the clearing.

Leafpool was staring at her, her eyes wide. *I bet she's impressed with my moves,* Ivypaw thought.

Leafpool blinked as Dustpelt blindsided her. Rolling over onto her side, the pale tabby warrior scrabbled to escape, but Dustpelt held her down and she could do nothing but lash her tail.

"I give up!" Leafpool yowled.

"You've lost anyway!" Cinderheart was standing beside the hazel bush. "I claim this bush for CinderClan!"

Birchfall was scrambling to his paws. He dipped his head to Ivypaw. "Good moves for an apprentice."

Leafpool struggled out from under Dustpelt and padded across the clearing. "Yes," she agreed. "Very nice moves. Where did you learn them?"

Ivypaw wasn't going to give her secret away. "I k-kind of worked them out for myself." Why shouldn't her Clanmates think she was as talented as Dovepaw?

"That last one looked like a RiverClan move," Dustpelt commented, padding over.

Ivypaw shrugged, making her eyes as round and innocent as she could. Dustpelt was wrong. It was a *StarClan* move!

"Whatever it looked like," Birchfall meowed warmly, "it was a good one. I'll remember to look out for it in the future."

Leafpool was still staring at her quizzically. "Do it again," she suggested. "We could all learn it."

Ivypaw opened her mouth. "I—I don't remember exactly what I did." She didn't want to share her secret moves with any cat. Nor did she want Dustpelt analyzing it any more. Leafpool already looked suspicious. They both might have known Hawkfrost when he was alive, and recognized his special technique.

Dustpelt flicked his tail. "Too bad." He turned and called to Cinderheart, who was still proudly guarding her captured ferns. "Are you going to give us a chance to make it even?"

"Okay," Cinderheart agreed. "But this time we start from the bracken. Your patrol on one side, ours on the other."

Relieved that the attention had slipped away from her, Ivypaw followed Blossomfall, Leafpool, and Dustpelt into the bracken on one side of the clearing. She crouched among the brittle branches and peeped out into the clearing.

The bracken opposite trembled as Cinderheart's patrol prepared for the attack.

"Blossomfall," Dustpelt hissed. "You're fast. I want you to race for the ferns while the rest of us stop them from reaching the hazel."

Blossomfall dropped into a crouch with her haunches bunched underneath her.

"Ready?" Dustpelt whispered.

Before any of them could answer, the bracken on the far side of the clearing crashed apart and Cinderheart's patrol pelted out.

"Go!" Dustpelt yowled.

Blossomfall dashed toward the ferns while Ivypaw hurtled out beside Dustpelt and Leafpool and raced to block the path to the hazel. Birchfall and Bumblestripe were already charging for it while Cinderheart and Hazeltail rushed to stop Blossomfall from reaching the ferns.

Blossomfall tried to zigzag out of their way, but Cinderheart and Hazeltail brought her down.

"Help her!" Dustpelt yowled to Leafpool. As Leafpool veered away, Ivypaw pelted beside Dustpelt, stretching her stride to match the warrior's bound for bound. Bumblestripe was almost at the hazel.

You're not winning again! Ivypaw sprang forward, stretching her forepaws to grasp Bumblestripe's tail. She tugged it and he stumbled. She hauled herself close enough to nip his hind legs.

"Ow!" He flicked his haunches up out of the way, then spun and swung a clumsy paw at Ivypaw's muzzle.

She ducked and swerved, hooking a forepaw around his and sending him crashing onto his side.

"Too easy!" she crowed, leaping on top of him.

He didn't even struggle, but gazed up at her, his eyes dark with sadness.

"What's up?" Surprised, she sat back on her haunches and let him clamber to his paws.

A yowl sounded behind them. Dustpelt was wrestling with Birchfall. But the battle could wait. Something was wrong with Bumblestripe.

"Are you okay?" Ivypaw prompted.

The warrior was staring sadly at the hazel bush. Was he just trying to trick her? Was he about to make a sudden dash for it? Ivypaw narrowed her eyes, tensing.

"Briarlight would have loved this," Bumblestripe mewed quietly. Anger flashed in his gaze. "It's just not fair!" he growled. "She was trying to help Longtail. Why did StarClan have to punish her?"

Ivypaw wished she had an answer. "Sometimes bad things happen." The words felt lame on her tongue.

"Then what's the point of StarClan?" Bumblestripe looked utterly defeated.

Ivypaw padded to his side and pressed her head against his shoulder. "Briarlight won't let this beat her," she murmured.

"No." Bumblestripe sighed. "But it didn't have to happen."

Feeling her Clanmate's grief in every shaking breath, Ivypaw imagined Dovepaw dragging herself around the hollow like half-dead fresh-kill. She understood Bumblestripe's fury. It was so unfair.

"We won!"

Leafpool had captured the ferns. She pressed a frond beneath her paws while Hazeltail circled her, snorting. Cinderheart dipped her head in gracious defeat, then glanced over to Bumblestripe. Her eyes narrowed in puzzlement. She was clearly trying to guess why the two young cats were sitting so close.

Then she blinked and nodded.

She understood.

"Hey! You two!" Cinderheart turned to Dustpelt and Birchfall. The toms were still fighting. Dustpelt thrust Birchfall away with his powerful hind legs, but Birchfall landed on his paws and spun around, ready to attack again.

Cinderheart cleared her throat. "I hate to break it up," she called. "But the battle's over."

Dustpelt and Birchfall halted and stared in surprise at the gray she-cat.

Birchfall sat down, the fur ruffling on his shoulders. "We were just practicing battle moves," he meowed self-consciously.

"Yes," Dustpelt agreed. "That's what training's all about, isn't it?"

Cinderheart's whiskers twitched. "And I suppose if we happen to enjoy it, StarClan won't mind too much," she teased.

The sun was lifting over the trees, brightening the sky. "Looks like it'll be a good day for hunting," Leafpool commented.

Cinderheart nodded. "Let's get back to camp and see if Brambleclaw wants us to join a patrol."

Dustpelt nodded. "The Clan needs fattening before leaf-bare."

Birchfall led the way through the bracken and disappeared among the trees. Cinderheart, Blossomfall, and Dustpelt followed.

Bumblestripe drew away from Ivypaw, his pelt smooth where she'd pressed it. "Thanks," he murmured. He hurried to catch up with his sister and fell in beside her.

Ivypaw followed, feeling left out as the two young warriors

walked side by side, speaking softly to each other.

"Ivypaw." Leafpool's gentle mew made Ivypaw jump. The pale warrior had caught up to her and was padding at her side. Leaves crunched underpaw, golden as Brackenfur's pelt.

"Those were pretty advanced moves," Leafpool commented.

Ivypaw glanced sideways but the she-cat's amber gaze was fixed on the path ahead.

"I guess I just did them accidentally."

"Lucky," Leafpool commented.

"I suppose." Guilt itched in Ivypaw's pelt.

"And you're sure you couldn't do them again?" Leafpool pressed.

Leave me alone! Ivypaw quickened her pace, irritated when Leafpool kept up. Every other cat in the Clan had secrets—including Leafpool. Why wasn't she allowed to have her own?

Chapter 15

"Why didn't you want me to bring Dovepaw?" Lionblaze sat down beside the wall. The abandoned Twoleg nest loomed above them, stark against the leafless forest.

"I didn't want to scare her." Jayfeather patted earth around his precious catmint, shoring up its delicate stems against the snow he knew would come too soon.

"She's got to know sometime," Lionblaze pointed out.

But not yet.

Jayfeather stiffened.

Paw steps.

He lifted his muzzle and tasted the air.

Lionblaze jerked around. "What is it?" His pelt was pricking. "Oh, it's just Sandstorm's patrol."

Bushes swished as Sandstorm and Cloudtail raced through the trees nearby. Squirrelflight and Spiderleg pelted after them.

"So what did you want to know?" Lionblaze swished his tail over the cold earth.

"Have you had any dreams about Tigerstar lately?"

"None."

Jayfeather sighed.

"What's on your mind?" Lionblaze kneaded the earth.

"He's not just going to give up, is he?" Jayfeather sniffed at a patch of borage that he'd discovered growing wild beside the Twoleg wall. "Help me with this." The biggest leaves had withered, but he could scent new shoots near the base that he wanted to collect. They were good for treating fever. He parted the dying stems so that Lionblaze could see the young growth. "Can you pick those?" he asked, holding back the foliage.

"Okay." Lionblaze began to pluck out the shoots, making the air sharp with the scent of sap.

"So?" Lionblaze prompted. "Who do *you* think Tigerstar's visiting?"

"Definitely Breezepelt. Why else would he attack me?"

Lionblaze plucked another pawful of shoots. He was quiet but Jayfeather could sense his mind turning. Finally he spoke.

"I thought I was special," he murmured. "I thought that's why he visited me. Because we were kin and he thought I'd make the best warrior."

"You *are* special," Jayfeather insisted.

"But Tigerstar never believed in the prophecy."

"No."

"And we were never really kin," Lionblaze pointed out. "He knew all along that Brambleclaw wasn't our father."

"Yes."

Lionblaze sat back on his haunches. "So why did he visit *me*?"

Jayfeather let go of the stems and they swished back together. "Even without kinship or the prophecy, you're one of our strongest warriors," he reasoned.

"Is that all he wants?" Lionblaze asked. "Strong warriors?"

"He clearly needs warriors to fight for him." Jayfeather began to bank earth up around the broken stems to protect them. "He's already using Breezepelt. And remember the ghost warrior who fought with Breezepelt? Tigerstar must have found allies in the Dark Forest."

"Allies?" Lionblaze growled.

"Not all cats go to StarClan," Jayfeather reminded him. "But why is he doing this now?"

"He hates Firestar. All the Clans know it. What could be better than raising a force against him when he's least expecting it?"

"I suppose."

Lionblaze lapped at his chest. "Breezepelt seems like a strange choice for a recruit. He doesn't have any kinship with Tigerstar."

"But he does resent us because we are Crowfeather's kits." Jayfeather pawed the shoots into a pile. "Tigerstar's clever. He knows most warriors are too loyal to break the code. So he has to exploit weakness."

"He couldn't exploit me!"

Jayfeather felt a surge of affection for his brother. "Of course not. But he tried. Who knows who else he may be trying to influence?"

Lionblaze's paws shifted. "So we have to work out which

cats have weaknesses he might use?"

"Or kinship." Jayfeather sensed Lionblaze stiffen. "What is it?"

"That must be how he got to Tigerheart!" Lionblaze's tail was flicking over the ground. "Do you remember me telling you the battle moves he used on the beavers were pure Tigerstar?"

"Of course!" Jayfeather's belly tightened. Things were beginning to make sense. "And I found him at the border that night WindClan brought Dovepaw home, remember?"

"So all those ShadowClan scents we've been finding could be Tigerheart, scouting out the border on Tigerstar's command?"

"Right," Jayfeather agreed. "Tigerheart's an obvious choice, right down to his name. Which means we can pretty much assume that Tigerstar is exploiting both kinship and the weakness of other cats to recruit them to his side."

A growl rumbled in Lionblaze's throat. "How do we stop him?"

"We can't, not yet. We'll just have to be on our guard," Jayfeather warned. "We can't prove any of this, and no cat will admit their loyalty lies outside their own Clan."

"We could try to find out if more cats are being trained by him."

Jayfeather gave the borage another sniff. "Watch them at Gatherings," he instructed. "See if any others cross our borders. I'll find out what I can at the medicine cat Gathering tonight."

"Okay," Lionblaze agreed. "So far we know of one WindClan

and one ShadowClan cat. What about RiverClan?"

Jayfeather narrowed his eyes thoughtfully. "Is there a RiverClan warrior who hates us as much as Breezepelt? One whose weakness Tigerstar could exploit?"

"I can't think of one," Lionblaze answered. "But . . ." His voice trailed away.

Jayfeather leaned forward. "What?"

"Tigerstar had a son, didn't he?"

"Hawkfrost?" Jayfeather gasped. He'd never seen him in StarClan. There was a good chance that he walked the Dark Forest with Tigerstar. "He lived in RiverClan. He'd know exactly which cats to approach."

"So Tigerstar might not be the only cat training warriors in their dreams," Lionblaze guessed.

Jayfeather shrugged.

"Oh, great," Lionblaze growled.

"Let's head back to camp," Jayfeather meowed. "I want to rest before the Gathering."

He padded into the trees. The ferns stroked his pelt as he pushed his way through.

Lionblaze rustled behind him. "Will the herbs be okay?"

"I hope so." Jayfeather sent a silent prayer to StarClan. "It's good to know that I have fresh supplies."

"You seem to enjoy looking after them."

"Plants do what they're told," Jayfeather commented. "Unlike apprentices."

Lionblaze purred. "Have you thought about taking on an apprentice?"

Jayfeather tensed. "Not while . . ." The words were hard to say. "Not while Leafpool is around."

"Are you hoping she'll be a medicine cat again?"

Jayfeather twitched one ear. "Maybe." He wasn't being sentimental. "It just seems like a waste of training for her to turn her back on it. She knows so much, and sometimes I feel that I know so little. The Clan still needs her, Lionblaze. Maybe more than ever."

"Jayfeather!" Sorreltail was calling from the clearing. "Littlecloud's here."

"Coming!" Jayfeather gave Briarlight a sniff. She was fast asleep in her nest. No smell of sickness. He hurried out of his den. He could sense the fragile half-moon hanging over the hollow. The air smelled fresh with a tang of frost. Hard weather was on its way. He trotted across the clearing, finally sure of a route that wouldn't trip or snag him.

"I thought you usually met the other medicine cats at the border when you go to the Moonpool," Sorreltail whispered as Jayfeather passed.

"I think he wants to see the tree damage for himself."

Littlecloud was standing just inside the thorn barrier. Jayfeather could sense the ShadowClan medicine cat's shock as he stared around the camp.

"I'm amazed you lost only one cat," Littlecloud commented as Jayfeather reached him. "How's Briarpaw doing?"

"She's Briarlight now."

"Really?" Littlecloud sounded surprised, but Jayfeather

didn't comment as he followed the ShadowClan medicine cat out through the thorns. Flametail, Littlecloud's apprentice, was waiting outside the tunnel.

Good. He was Tigerheart's littermate. If any cat's dreams held a clue to the warrior's intentions, it would be Flametail's.

Unless Tigerstar was training him too.

A medicine cat? No way!

Jayfeather tried to push the thought away, but it clung to the back of his mind like a tick, making him wary of saying too much.

Littlecloud let Jayfeather take the lead as they headed for the WindClan border. They would meet the other cats there.

"So Firestar made her a warrior anyway?" Littlecloud pursued the news about Briarlight.

"She's as brave as any warrior." Jayfeather felt for Flametail's reaction. How much interest was the young cat taking in their conversation?

"Has she had any sickness?" Flametail stuck his muzzle close to Jayfeather's.

"None. We've kept her moving," Jayfeather explained. "She does exercises every day and fetches her own food from the fresh-kill pile. It seems to be keeping her chest and belly working fine."

"How are you keeping her spirits up?" Flametail asked.

Was he looking for a sign of weakness? "No need," Jayfeather meowed. "She's very positive."

He was relieved as they padded from the trees and he

scented Kestrelflight, Mothwing, and Willowshine waiting on the WindClan border. He pushed ahead, hurrying over the grass to meet them.

He leaped the stream in a practiced bound. "It's cold," he remarked in greeting. An icy wind was whipping off the moorland and ruffling every cat's fur.

"Not once we get moving." Kestrelflight was stamping his paws against the chill. The WindClan medicine cat began to lead the way upstream.

"Mothwing." Jayfeather greeted the RiverClan medicine cat formally. He felt her cool gaze touch his pelt.

"Jayfeather." There was an edge to her mew. Did she think he'd give away her secret? She was wrong if she did. What would he gain by telling the others she had no connection with StarClan?

"Hopefully the hollow will be sheltered from this wind," Littlecloud grumbled.

"You sound like an elder," Kestrelflight teased.

Flametail joined in. "He almost is one."

"Cheek!" Littlecloud pretended to sound offended, but there was warmth among the medicine cats as they trekked up the stream.

Any other moon, Jayfeather would have relished the lack of boundaries and suspicion. But tonight he was worried. The old trust he felt with his fellow medicine cats felt threatened by the ghost of Tigerstar. He walked behind the small group of cats as they followed the stream to the waterfall. As he concentrated on picking his way over the rocks, he felt the distance between them stretching.

"Do you want us to slow down?" Littlecloud called back.

"I'll catch up," Jayfeather replied, scrabbling between two boulders. He wondered again if Tigerstar and his Dark Forest Clanmates would visit any of the medicine cats tonight.

Absurd! he told himself. But was it really? They were used to being visited by StarClan cats. Why not cats from the Dark Forest, the Place of No Stars?

Jayfeather skidded as he landed on a slippery rock.

"Careful." He felt Littlecloud's steadying paw. The ShadowClan tom had waited for him.

He paused as Jayfeather padded on a few steps, then fell in behind. "How's Leafpool?"

Jayfeather detected worry in Littlecloud's mew as he asked about his old friend.

"How is she managing as a *warrior,* I mean?" Littlecloud uttered the word as though he still didn't quite believe she'd made the decision.

"She's fine." Jayfeather picked up his pace. Why did he have to explain her behavior?

"Doesn't she miss it?"

Jayfeather turned on him. "No cat forced her to leave!" he snapped. *But how could she remain a medicine cat after she'd broken the code?*

Jayfeather pushed away the prick of sympathy plucking at his heart as they headed on; then Littlecloud spoke again.

"We all make mistakes," he murmured. "Some have echoes that last forever."

Flametail was already scrambling up the waterfall a few tail-lengths ahead. By the time Jayfeather had clawed his way to the top, the ShadowClan apprentice and Mothwing were already settled beside the Moonpool. Willowshine was still looking for a space.

Littlecloud padded down to join them.

"You were right, Littlecloud," Kestrelflight called. "It *is* more sheltered here."

Jayfeather followed the paw prints spiraling down to the pool, dimples made over countless moons. He waited for the whispers that always called him to share with his ancestors, but heard only the wind whining above the rocks.

A desolate pang opened in his belly. No ancient pelts brushing his? No murmuring welcome? No half-familiar scents?

Were they angry he'd broken Rock's stick?

I'm sorry! he wailed silently.

Mothwing's breathing had already deepened into sleep by the time he settled beside the Moonpool. It would be pointless probing her dreams. If StarClan never visited her, it was hardly likely any cat from the Dark Forest would make it through her barrier of disbelief.

Flametail was most likely to hold clues about Tigerheart. But Littlecloud or Willowshine might betray fresh information. They might have their worries too. They may have seen a Clanmate acting strangely or have treated unexplained wounds.

Perhaps it was best simply to walk alone among his ancestors?

Jayfeather touched his nose to the cold, clear water and closed his eyes.

A world opened before him, green and lush. Warm breezes enfolded him and the smell of fresh prey touched his nose. Sunlight slanted through the trees as he padded through the long grass.

A familiar, matted pelt moved through the undergrowth ahead. Jayfeather recognized it at once. He broke into a trot. He was about to call out when another cat jumped out from the long grass and greeted the shaggy StarClan warrior.

"Yellowfang!"

"Hi, Flametail!"

Jayfeather halted, pricking his ears.

"Runningnose wants to speak with you," Yellowfang told Flametail.

I wonder what the old ShadowClan medicine cat has to say?

Jayfeather ducked into the ferns and began to shadow Flametail's path through the trees.

"Don't you ever learn?"

Jayfeather reared in surprise as Yellowfang landed a whisker ahead of him.

He bristled. "He jumped into *my* dream!"

"And asked you to follow him?" Yellowfang's amber gaze was sharp with rebuke.

"You don't know everything!" Jayfeather growled. He could see Flametail disappearing into the undergrowth.

"I know you need to trust him," Yellowfang snapped back. "He's a medicine cat."

"*Leafpool* was a medicine cat." Jayfeather snorted.

Yellowfang narrowed her eyes and Jayfeather tensed, waiting for the lecture. But no lecture came. Instead she looked thoughtful. "You said I don't know *everything*," she murmured. "Tell me, what don't I know?"

"Where do I start?" Jayfeather huffed.

Yellowfang growled. "There's no time for smart replies." Her eyes darkened. "Several StarClan cats are troubled. Something bad is coming. This might be what the Three will be needed for."

Jayfeather tensed. "Something bad? Do you know what it is?"

Yellowfang shook her head. "We were hoping you'd know."

"All we know," Jayfeather told her, "is that Tigerstar is training warriors from different Clans in their dreams. Hawkfrost might be working with him."

Yellowfang's eyes stretched. "Training them? Why?"

"The Dark Forest is rising." Jayfeather heard the words fall from his lips. His heart quickened. "The Dark Forest is rising against us."

"What do you mean?" Yellowfang's fur was on end.

"Tigerstar is training cats to fight us. He's already trained Breezepelt. I fought him by the Moonpool. But not just him. Another cat fought with him. A cat from the Dark Forest."

"Who?" Yellowfang pressed her muzzle closer.

"I don't know," Jayfeather answered. "He was big and dark pelted. I didn't recognize him."

"You think he's working with Tigerstar?"

"And Hawkfrost." Jayfeather felt suddenly cold. "I don't know how many there are. But they're entering cats' dreams—cats who have a grudge against us or who are kin to them. They're training them to fight."

"You suspect Flametail's one of their recruits?" Yellowfang's eyes flashed with horror. "He's a medicine cat!"

"We don't know who we can trust," Jayfeather fretted. "Tigerheart's been crossing our border at night. And he might not be the only one. I promised Lionblaze I'd try to find out if there are others. Perhaps RiverClan cats. Kin of Hawkfrost."

Yellowfang sat down, forcing her fur flat. "Then they were right to be worried." She was muttering to herself.

"*Who* was right?" Fear pricked in Jayfeather's paws. "StarClan?" How could StarClan be worried? It was *StarClan*. Dread began to run like cold water along his spine. "What should we do?"

Yellowfang looked into the distance, her grave amber gaze stretching far past Jayfeather.

"We must go to the Dark Forest."

Chapter 16

Trees in full leaf whispered gently in the breeze. Yellowfang hopped over a narrow stream that meandered through the long grass. Jayfeather followed, relishing the warm lushness underpaw after walking the dried-leaf floor of the forest. She led him through flourishing bushes that brushed their pelts with dew and pollen as they passed.

A meadow stretched ahead, graced by trees, flecked with flowers, aglow in the slanting sunlight. Warriors, sleek and content, walked through the long grass, or stretched in sunny hollows, their pelts soft in the sun. A tabby crouched, rump waggling, before pouncing after a plump mouse. A white cat with rose-tipped paws stretched up the cracked trunk of an ash tree and plucked happily at the bark while she watched a squirrel bobbing along a high branch. With a sudden bound she scooted upward and was swallowed by the fluttering leaves.

Jayfeather tasted the air. Half-familiar scents floated in the breeze: WindClan, ShadowClan, ThunderClan, and RiverClan.

"Hi, Silverstream," Yellowfang purred to a gray tabby

padding from a swath of ferns.

"Yellowfang." The tabby nodded. "Have you seen Feathertail?"

"She was resting at Warm-rocks earlier."

"Thanks." Silverstream slid away through the grass, her tail-tip flicking.

Jayfeather narrowed his eyes. "No quarrels. No leaf-bare. No hunger," he observed. "No wonder everyone seems so content."

Yellowfang's eyes darkened. "We never cease watching and worrying over those left behind."

Jayfeather shrugged. "If this is where we're heading, what is there to worry about?"

"No cat enjoys another's suffering. And not every path leads here," Yellowfang answered.

With a shiver, Jayfeather remembered where they were going.

Another familiar pelt caught his eye. *Frighteningly* familiar. Blazing ginger fur, large pricked ears, emerald gaze—the slender tom wove through the bushes ahead. He seemed paler than the other cats, almost invisible. And yet he *was* there.

"Firestar?" Jayfeather breathed.

"Not quite," Yellowfang mewed gently. "Five of his lives are here, but he won't be able to hear or speak until his ninth life has joined us."

Jayfeather watched the ghostly cat disappear behind an oak. Could Firestar feel his lives ebbing away? *No.* He shook off the thought. How could he stay such a strong leader if he did?

Jayfeather began to realize that other pelts were paler too. Some were so ghostly they hardly seemed there at all. More like mist than flesh.

"Are those cats half-dead too?" he asked Yellowfang as a wraithlike tortoiseshell crossed their path, hardly acknowledging Yellowfang's greeting nod.

She shook her head. "They've been here a long, long time," she explained. "So long that they're forgotten."

"By everyone?" The thought chilled Jayfeather.

"Being forgotten is nothing to fear. Not even the stars last forever. All cats fade and disappear eventually. They've earned their peace."

Jayfeather imagined Yellowfang fading into nothing and was surprised to find grief pricking his heart.

"Don't worry," Yellowfang purred, as though she could read his mind. "Who could forget a cantankerous old badger like me?"

"Hey! Yellowfang!" A pretty tortoiseshell hailed them from the rocks above a waterfall churning above a sparkling brook. She leaped down, disappearing into the long grass for a moment before bounding up toward them.

Jayfeather recognized Spottedleaf at once. "Hi." He dipped his head as she reached them and shook the grass seeds from her dappled pelt.

Her eyes were bright as stars. "Where are you going?" They dimmed as they met Yellowfang's tough gaze.

"The Dark Forest."

"You mustn't!"

"We must."

Jayfeather watched the exchange, tipping his head to one side. It was hard to tell which cat was most frightened, though both fought to conceal it. "Tigerstar is plotting against us," he told her. "We have to find out what he's planning."

Spottedleaf bristled at the name. "Is it wise to go alone?"

"We have each other," Yellowfang told her.

"I'm coming with you," Spottedleaf decided.

Yellowfang flinched. "I don't want to attract too much attention."

Spottedleaf held the old cat's gaze. "Firestar would never forgive me if I let anything happen to Jayfeather."

Jayfeather lifted his nose. "I'm not helpless," he objected.

Spottedleaf turned her amber gaze on him. "You're going to find *Tigerstar*," she reminded him. "Against that fiend, every cat is helpless."

Jayfeather lashed his tail. "Then maybe it's time for things to change!"

They padded through the trees, the lushness fading with every paw step. The trunks grew thinner and smoother, the branches too high to reach. The sun faded from the sky, leaving white, eerie light that permeated the woods like water flooding through a reed bed. Jayfeather drew a breath of cold, damp air, tasted nothing but decay, and shivered. The grass had thinned and disappeared, and mist wreathed the bare forest floor. It rose and thickened, enfolding them in fog until Jayfeather realized with a tremor that he could no longer see Yellowfang's thick, matted pelt or hear

Spottedleaf's soft tread.

Gulping air so thick that it made him cough, Jayfeather quickened his pace, hoping to catch up. He was too scared to call out, in case other ears heard him.

The ground grew peaty underpaw as he hurried into a trot.

Where are they?

His heart began to pound, the blood rising and roaring in his ears. He broke into a run.

Yellowfang! Spottedleaf!

He couldn't see. The mist was choking him. This was worse than running blind through ThunderClan territory. He bolted through the trees, paws tripping on a gnarled root snaking across his path. Pain seared his leg but he raced on. A yowl echoed through the fog, and paws began to thunder on the ground behind.

Someone was chasing him.

He pushed on harder, weaving around trees, cutting so close that they ripped at his fur. The paw steps were gaining on him, rhythmic, powerful, pounding the forest floor in his wake.

Panic seized him. He was hardly breathing now, just running.

Crash!

Shock rang through him as he hit a tree. It sent him reeling, chest first, into a puddle. Twisting onto his back, he saw a figure looming over him, a broad face leering down through the mist.

"No!" His voice cracked into a whimper.

"It's Yellowfang, you mouse-brain!" The she-cat grabbed him by the scruff and hauled him to his paws.

Spottedleaf came skidding to a halt beside them. "You found him," she puffed.

Yellowfang was trembling with rage. "We have to stay together!" she hissed.

Jayfeather had seen her cranky, but never this furious. That was when he realized how frightened the tough old she-cat was.

He nodded, gulping for air.

"Come on." Yellowfang began to head away, then paused to make sure that Jayfeather and Spottedleaf were following. They padded through the sucking mud until the fog began to clear.

Jayfeather recognized the trees, the eerie light, the echoing silence. He'd met Tigerstar here once before. Spottedleaf had come and guided him home that time. She wasn't pleased to be back in the Place of No Stars now, her pelt pricking, her eyes stretched wide. But it was Yellowfang who was really afraid.

Jayfeather glanced nervously at the tattered old she-cat. He'd never imagined she could be scared of anything. But there was a stiffness in her movements that betrayed real terror. He probed her mind.

A flash of panic flooded him. A hulking, dark-furred cat stalked her thoughts. The glow of bright red berries like drops of blood. Searing grief and fury.

Curiosity enticed him on, further into her thoughts. *No!* He must concentrate on where he was. There was enough danger without losing himself in another cat's nightmare.

Jayfeather jerked his head as he heard rustling in the sparse undergrowth, the pattering of paws. He glanced questioningly at Spottedleaf.

She shook her head. "No prey here."

Jayfeather's fur rippled, chilled by the gaze of watchers in the shadows. He scanned the trees. Eyes glowed from the gloom.

Jayfeather drew closer to Spottedleaf. "Who are they?" he whispered.

"Cats, dead and long forgotten," Spottedleaf murmured. "Ignore them."

How? Jayfeather could feel menace in their stares, their minds haunted by evil beyond the reach of every memory but their own.

Yellowfang paused and tasted the air. "We have to find Tigerstar and figure out what he's up to."

Spottedleaf blinked. "You think we're going to stumble over him plotting?" She narrowed her eyes. "He knows this forest too well. He'll know we're here long before we find him."

Jayfeather headed along a trail weaving between the gray, whispering trees. "We've got to try. Otherwise, why did we come?" He smelled tom. The scent was darkly familiar, but he couldn't tell which Clan it belonged to. He glanced over his shoulder, checking that Yellowfang and Spottedleaf were close behind.

Spottedleaf's mouth was open, her nostrils twitching.

"Can you smell that?" he whispered.

"Wait!" Yellowfang was staring wildly into the trees. "Let's go back. We can't do any good here."

Jayfeather shifted his paws. What was spooking the old cat so much?

"Hello." A deep growl sounded on the path ahead. Jayfeather jerked his head around.

A huge black cat blocked the way. "What are you doing here?"

Jayfeather froze, the scent of the tom stirring his memory. Where had he met this warrior? He lifted his chin bravely, preparing to answer the tom's question.

Then he realized that the cat wasn't talking to him. The warrior's hard amber gaze was fixed on Yellowfang.

At once Jayfeather found himself plunged into a whirl of memories. Yellowfang yowling as she kitted, squirming in the shadows, hiding from her Clan. A small bundle of fur dropping into another cat's nest—a queen who did not care for her new charge, who bit it and nipped it and deprived it of milk as punishment for being born at all. Then the kit, fully grown. *Brokenstar.* The name blazed in Jayfeather's mind. A strong, well-muscled warrior, fattened by his own hunting skill, as hungry for power as a fox was for rabbit. The death of a leader and darkness descending over a Clan in chaos. Then suddenly he saw Yellowfang again, powerful now; the warrior weak, blind, battered, imprisoned, but still with the murderous glint in his eye. Through Yellowfang's eyes Jayfeather watched the cat struggle as she forced him to eat deathberries, saw him convulse and die, swearing hatred and vengeance. He felt searing guilt slice through his heart: the guilt of a queen who had brought such a monster into the world. The guilt of a mother who had driven him from it.

I murdered my own son!

Shuddering as he drew in a deep breath, Jayfeather struggled out of the nightmarish visions and back into reality.

This was Brokenstar. Yellowfang's *kit*!

The cat was staring at his mother with cold contempt, his bared yellow teeth glinting in the eerie light.

Jayfeather backed away, pressing against Yellowfang's pelt. "You were his mother?" he breathed. "But you were a medicine cat!"

Yellowfang dragged her gaze from her son and stared at Jayfeather. "Mistakes happen," she growled.

Jayfeather flinched away. *Mistakes happen? Is that how she sees me?*

Spottedleaf's sweet breath brushed his ear fur. "You weren't a mistake, Jayfeather. Your mother always loved you." She glanced at Brokenstar. "You were *always* loved, Jayfeather."

Brokenstar hissed, "What do you want?"

Jayfeather opened his mouth, reaching for something to say. But his mind still whirled with everything he had seen and learned about Yellowfang in those few moments of shared memory.

I trusted her!

She was no better than Leafpool!

Spottedleaf pushed past both of them and faced Brokenstar. "What are you doing?" Her mew was commanding.

Brokenstar looked at her as if he had only just noticed she was there. "Nothing."

"I'm talking about training the cats from the Clans by the lake," she pressed.

Brokenstar blinked, his eyes softening into enticing pools. "Training cats by the lake?" Brokenstar's mew rang with the innocence of a kit. "Why would we do that?"

Spottedleaf refused to be swayed. "That's what we want to know."

Brokenstar swept his tail behind him. "Look around," he purred invitingly. "Explore a little."

Jayfeather found himself following the warrior's gaze as it flitted over the dank, gray trees and wreaths of mist.

"See as much of my home as you like," he urged.

"Okay." Spottedleaf took a step forward but he blocked her.

"But of course," he murmured sweetly, "if I let StarClan see the Dark Forest, then StarClan must allow me to visit their hunting grounds." He showed his teeth. "Isn't that only fair? Surely the warrior code would expect it." His mouth twisted into a sneer.

Yellowfang leaped forward and crouched, bristling, in front of him. "That will never happen!"

Brokenstar shrugged. "Then you can't come any farther into my territory."

He turned away.

Jayfeather leaped after him, hackles up.

"No!" Spottedleaf blocked his attack, shouldering him away. "It's not a fight you would win," she insisted, holding his gaze.

Disappointed, Jayfeather nodded. She was right. If only Lionblaze could come here!

"Come on." Spottedleaf turned and gently nosed Yellowfang back along the path. The old cat's eyes stared blankly ahead of her. Jayfeather had no wish to probe her thoughts now. Her eyes showed nothing but pain.

They padded along the path until Brokenstar had faded into the mist behind them.

Jayfeather stumbled suddenly as Spottedleaf nudged his shoulder. Bundling him off the path, she pushed him into the low verge of wilting gray ferns. Yellowfang halted and stared around, confused.

"Over here!" Spottedleaf hissed at her.

Bewildered, Yellowfang slid in beside them. "What are you doing?"

"Go home," Spottedleaf ordered. "You're no help to us while Brokenstar is around. He clouds your judgment." She touched her muzzle to the old cat's shoulder. "Go back to StarClan," she murmured, "where you are loved."

Yellowfang blinked at her and sighed. "Very well."

"If we don't return," Spottedleaf added, "send a patrol for us."

Yellowfang nodded. "I'll wait for you by the waterfall." She nosed her way through the ferns. "Be careful!"

"We will," Spottedleaf promised. She led Jayfeather farther from the path, weaving through the dank undergrowth, only half-visible in the mist.

Jayfeather kept close, his paws wet and cold as he padded over the sticky earth.

Water murmured ahead of them as they crept from the ferns. A sluggish river heaved its way through the forest, its waters dark and lifeless.

Spottedleaf scanned the bank. No fallen tree spanned the water. No rocks dotted its course. Jayfeather shuddered. He hoped she wasn't going to suggest they swim across.

"Look!" she hissed.

There were figures moving among the trees, beyond the water. Half-shrouded in mist, warriors gathered.

"Always aim for the throat." A shadow-pelted tabby was lecturing the others. He grasped a wiry brown tom, hooking his claws into his ragged fur and hurling him to the ground. "See?"

The tom struggled helplessly as the tabby ran a claw along his throat. Blood rose in its trail.

Jayfeather felt Spottedleaf stiffen beside him. "Darkstripe," she breathed.

The tabby turned and stared in their direction.

Jayfeather ducked, his heart pounding as Darkstripe blinked.

"It's okay; he hasn't seen us," Spottedleaf whispered.

A low growl set Jayfeather's pelt on end. Hawkfrost padded from the shadows, knocking Darkstripe away from his victim. "Concentrate on what you're doing!" He grabbed the bleeding tom and shoved him back toward the line of watching cats.

The brown tom shook himself and lapped at his wound.

Hawkfrost snarled. "Worry about your pelt later!"

The tom stopped midlick and stared at Hawkfrost with rounded eyes.

"You wanted to learn some killing moves!" Hawkfrost hissed at him. "Stop acting like a frightened kit and listen." He turned to a skinny white tom who was watching with half-closed eyes. "Come here, Snowtuft!"

Warily the white tom crept forward.

"Are *you* ready to learn?" Hawkfrost sneered.

Eyes glinting, Snowtuft nodded. "That's why I'm here," he spat.

"Good." Hawkfrost lunged and grasped Snowtuft by the throat. Lifting him with powerful paws, he spun around to face the others. "Shredtail, come here!"

As Snowtuft's paws churned helplessly in the air, a dark brown tabby crept forward.

"Slice his belly open," Hawkfrost growled.

Shredtail's eyes gleamed with blood-hunger.

Jayfeather's breath quickened. Bile rose in his throat. "No!" he breathed. "The warrior code would never allow such vicious battle moves."

Spottedleaf dug her claws into the earth. "These cats have always lived outside the code." Her mew was thick with disgust. "They were rogues within their Clans. They are rogues now. That's why they're here. They never deserved to be called warriors."

Foul breath stirred the fur on Jayfeather's spine. "You're wrong."

The two cats spun around.

Tigerstar sat in the middle of the trail, staring at them, his eyes lazy with contempt. "There's no code to say what can and can't happen here." His gaze flicked to Hawkfrost. "It's your world that's restricted by petty rules and expectations."

Anger surged through Jayfeather. "A true warrior's heart needs no rules! It can do no evil!" he blurted.

Amusement lit Tigerstar's amber gaze. He turned to Spottedleaf. "Don't you just love his innocence?"

Spottedleaf straightened. "It's goodness, not innocence."

"Do good cats creep around and spy on others?"

A low growl rumbled in her throat. "They do when there is no other way to find out what's going on."

Tigerstar's eyes rounded. "You could have just come to me and asked whatever you wanted to know."

"Very well." Jayfeather sat up, forcing his trembling shoulders to relax. "Why are you training cats from the Clans?"

Tigerstar gazed around the forest. "I see no Clan cats here." Then he fixed Jayfeather with a look so cold, Jayfeather had to sink his claws into the ground to stop his legs from shaking. "The only Clan cats here are you two. And you're trespassing." His foul breath washed over Jayfeather's muzzle as he leaned closer. "Which makes you the only cats here breaking rules." He blinked. "Didn't Brokenstar order you to leave?"

How does he know that?

"Why bother training these cats in killing blows?"

Spottedleaf glared at Tigerstar.

The warrior flicked his tail. "Why not?"

"You're already dead!"

Tigerstar shrugged. "That's no reason to lose our fighting skills."

Jayfeather let out a low hiss. "What do you need fighting skills for here?" he challenged.

"Once a warrior, always a warrior," Tigerstar purred.

Spottedleaf took a step forward. "You gave up the honor of being a warrior in the heartbeat you decided to kill Bluestar!" she snapped. "You can't steal warriors from the Clans and turn them against their own Clanmates!"

"Really?" Tigerstar lifted a paw and unsheathed his claws. "Says who?"

Jayfeather thrust his muzzle into Tigerstar's face. "*We* do!"

Tigerstar batted him away.

Jayfeather huffed as he hit the floor, wincing at the pain burning his ear. He scrambled to his paws and faced Tigerstar again. There was no way Jayfeather was going to let this dead warrior think he was scared to fight him.

"Don't bother," growled the dark warrior. "It's a fight you can't win." He turned away. "Now get out of here before I pass you over to my friends for practice."

"Come on," Spottedleaf whispered. "There's nothing more we can do here."

Jayfeather hurried after Spottedleaf, gagging as Snowtuft's agonized yowl rang through the trees behind them.

Chapter 17

Lionblaze couldn't sleep. Had Jayfeather discovered something at the Moonpool? Was he walking in another cat's dreams right now? They had to find out who their enemies were before it was too late.

Lionblaze sat up and gazed past the bough that arched over his nest. The half-moon trembled through the rustling leaves, and Silverpelt glittered beyond. Bathed in crystal light, his Clanmates huddled in nests around him. Were any of *them* being trained by Tigerstar in their dreams?

Brackenfur? The golden warrior twitched his flank. *No way.* What weakness could Tigerstar exploit in him?

Squirrelflight? However much Lionblaze resented her for the lies she had told, for letting him, Brambleclaw, and every cat in every Clan believe that she was his mother, he couldn't believe she would ever be persuaded to betray her Clanmates.

Dustpelt? The dusky tom often argued with Firestar, but Lionblaze suspected the two warriors relished their disagreements, sparking off each other and never holding grudges.

Whitewing? Never. Just . . . never.

His gaze rested on Thornclaw. *Maybe.* He had been good

friends with Ashfur. Perhaps he should ask Jayfeather to visit Thornclaw's dreams.

Leafpool? No cat from the Dark Forest would be mouse-brained enough to think she'd turn against her Clanmates.

What about Cinderheart?

The gray she-cat lifted her head. "Lionblaze?"

Lionblaze blinked. What was he thinking? How could he doubt his Clanmates? "I can't sleep," he whispered.

Cinderheart yawned. "Let's go for a walk." She hopped from her nest, landing delicately between the pools of bracken, and wove her way into what was left of the clearing.

Lionblaze followed, glad of her company. If anyone could chase away his dark thoughts, it was Cinderheart.

Her gray pelt shone under the stars, her eyes almost black in the half-light. "Look out!" she hissed over her shoulder as Lionblaze's tail brushed over Graystripe's nose. "He might dream it's a mouse and bite off the tip."

Lionblaze stifled a snort of amusement. Graystripe probably *could* eat in his sleep.

"Come on." Cinderheart bounded to the thorn barrier. Newly shored up with fresh branches, it shielded the opening to the hollow as well as ever. She squeezed through the gap and Lionblaze headed after her.

Outside, a cold breeze stirred the empty trees.

"Forest or shore?" Cinderheart offered.

"Forest." Lionblaze didn't feel like wandering along the exposed lakeside. The pathways of the forest were easier to move along unnoticed. And if they reached the ShadowClan border, he could check for Tigerheart's scent. He padded along the gully, wading through dead leaves. Cinderheart scampered past, kicking them up so that they showered his pelt. She raced ahead before he could retaliate and waited, puffing, for him to catch up, her soft form silhouetted in the moonlight.

"Have you noticed that Ivypaw and Dovepaw are avoiding each other?"

Her question took him by surprise.

"No."

"You should watch them," Cinderheart suggested. "They hardly ever share a mouse anymore."

"Littermates argue." Lionblaze shrugged. He and Hollyleaf had always bickered, especially when she was at her bossiest. Grief pricked him and he pushed away the thought.

"Not Dovepaw and Ivypaw," Cinderheart persisted. "They've always been so close." Her blue eyes grew wistful. "But I guess I used to quarrel with Honeyfern and Molepaw when they were alive."

Cinderheart looked so sad that Lionblaze wanted to remind her she still had kin in the Clan. "You haven't fallen out with Poppyfrost in moons."

"She's too busy with Cherrykit and Molekit to argue." Cinderheart brightened. "They're a pawful, aren't they?"

"Only when they're awake," Lionblaze purred. They hadn't come out here to grieve for lost littermates. He wanted to forget his worries for a while. He padded up a slope and headed around a swath of brambles tumbling between the oaks.

Cinderheart padded at his side, her pelt occasionally

brushing his as she squeezed past snagging branches. "But I do wish Ivypaw weren't so competitive with Dovepaw." She sighed.

"That's natural with apprentices."

"It's only since Dovepaw was chosen to go on the quest," Cinderheart commented. "I think that's what started it." She turned her gaze on Lionblaze. "Why did Firestar choose her? She's only an apprentice. I heard some cats saying she had a dream from StarClan. Is that true?"

"That's what she said," Lionblaze answered evasively. "Whatever it was, we were lucky."

"Perhaps she's special, like Jayfeather," Cinderheart pressed. "Should she be training as a medicine cat? Would Jayfeather take her on?"

Lionblaze shook his head. "Don't even suggest it to her. She'd be horrified. She's warrior to the bone."

"It's great that you have such confidence in her, and I wouldn't want to undermine that, but . . ." Cinderheart cast him a sideways glance. "Maybe you could talk to her about being a bit more considerate of Ivypaw?"

"She seems to be making great progress," Lionblaze pointed out. "Perhaps the competition is doing her good."

Cinderheart flicked her tail irritably.

"Let's race." Lionblaze didn't want the night spoiled by bickering over their apprentices. "It'll warm us up."

Cinderheart shrugged. "Okay." Then, gasping, she stared into the branches overhead. "Oh, no!"

Alarmed, Lionblaze looked up.

"Ha, ha! Got you!" Cinderheart hared away into the trees.

"You sneak!" He pelted after her.

As he closed on her she darted through the hollow trunk of a tree. He veered to the side, overtaking her as she emerged with cobwebs trailing from her bushy tail.

Now Lionblaze was in front. He scrambled up an outcrop of rocks. Cinderheart leaped after him, and he felt her muzzle brushing his tail. As the stone scraped beneath his paws, he thought of Heathertail and the way they'd played in the cave.

He halted, panting at the top. "Wait!" he called as Cinderheart shot past him.

She skidded and turned to look challengingly at him. "Are you tired already?"

"No."

"We could climb trees instead." A mischievous sparkle glinted in her eye. "Oh, I forgot," she added innocently. "You don't like climbing trees."

"Why climb when you can run?" Lionblaze jumped past her and charged through the trees. This wasn't the cave and Cinderheart wasn't Heathertail. This she-cat was ThunderClan from her nose to her tail-tip. There was nothing wrong with being with her. Feeling freer and happier than he had in moons, he swerved and headed for the lake.

I'm not skulking in the shadows like prey!

Cinderheart pounded after him as he pelted around a clump of ferns and skidded out from the trees. His paws slithered down the grassy slope. Cinderheart hurtled past him and bounded onto the shore, rattling pebbles under her feet.

She charged into the lake and stood waiting, belly-deep in the rippling waves. "I dare you to get your paws wet!"

"No way!" Lionblaze skidded to a halt at the water's edge.

Cinderheart plunged her shoulders under and began to swim, gasping at the cold. Lionblaze had forgotten that Jayfeather had taught her to swim to strengthen her leg after her accident as an apprentice. "You look like a RiverClan cat!" he called from the shore. "Why don't you catch me a fish while you're in there?"

Cinderheart splashed out onto dry land and shook out her pelt. Lionblaze shied away as the water showered him.

"Don't you call me RiverClan!" she huffed, eyes sparkling. "I'm ThunderClan through and through!"

"I'm glad you are." Lionblaze pushed away all thoughts of Heathertail and admired his feisty denmate, her pelt spiked with water.

Cinderheart blinked. "Of course!" she declared. "It's the best Clan to be in."

Lionblaze glanced at his paws. He hadn't quite meant it like that. Hot with embarrassment, he padded along the shore, not sure if he was glad that she had missed the clumsy compliment. *She must think I'm a mouse-brain!*

"Brrr!" Cinderheart caught up to him. She was shivering.

"Let's get you back to camp before you catch a cold." He steered her up the bank and into the trees, pressing close to share the heat of his pelt. She smelled sweet—mossy and damp, like a warm nest.

"Thanks for coming out with me," he murmured as they neared the hollow.

"No problem," she answered. "It was fun." She yawned. "We'll be tired in the morning."

"It was worth it," Lionblaze purred, glad that for a few brief moments the prophecy and the Dark Forest had been pushed to the back of his mind.

He woke late. Brambleclaw was already organizing the early patrols when he opened his eyes. Shaking himself awake, Lionblaze scrambled from his nest and hurried out from under the beech.

Cinderheart was crowding around the ThunderClan deputy with her Clanmates. "Can Ivypaw and I join the border patrol?" she asked.

Brambleclaw glanced at Brackenfur, who twitched his ears in agreement. "Okay."

Lionblaze tried to catch Cinderheart's eye, hoping that some of the warmth of last night would linger in her gaze. But she only nodded briskly. "I'm taking Ivypaw on patrol."

He cut her off. "I heard." Was she being aloof on purpose, or hadn't she enjoyed their walk the same way he had?

Dovepaw interrupted his thoughts. "Brambleclaw wants us to hunt with Thornclaw," she told him.

The border patrol was already heading out of camp. Lionblaze watched Ivypaw's tail disappear through the gap in the thorns. "Don't you mind not going with your sister?" He remembered Cinderheart's worries about the sisters. Were they really not getting along?

Dovepaw looked at him. "Why should I?" She shrugged. "I'll know what she's doing wherever she is, anyway."

Lionblaze cocked his head. "Yes, of course." It felt strange to hear Dovepaw talking so calmly about her powers. She usually acted like they were a burr in her pelt.

"Are you coming?" Thornclaw called from the entrance. Icecloud and Sandstorm were pacing beside him.

"I'm going to make the first catch," Icecloud declared, glancing at Thornclaw and Sandstorm. The young warrior was clearly determined to impress them.

"Not if I can help it," Dovepaw mewed. She sped past him and ducked through the barrier first.

Lionblaze caught up to her in the gully. Thornclaw and Sandstorm were already ranging up the slopes, noses twitching. Icecloud hared past them, spraying leaves.

"You'll never catch anything making that sort of noise!" Dovepaw yowled after her.

"Hush!" Lionblaze warned her. "You'll scare everything away."

"*I'll* scare everything?" She stared after Icecloud, at the leaves resettling in her wake, then flicked Lionblaze with her tail. "What's gotten under your pelt?"

Lionblaze frowned. He wasn't going to admit that he'd been stung by Cinderheart's briskness.

But Dovepaw didn't seem interested in an answer. Her ears were pricked and her whiskers were quivering. "There's a mouse at the top of the rise," she announced. "Shall I catch it?"

"Give Icecloud a chance, at least," Lionblaze advised. According to Cinderheart, she'd already put Ivypaw's tail out of joint; he didn't want every cat in the Clan to be jealously competing with his apprentice.

"But she might take ages, and the mouse'll be an easy catch," she begged.

"Just wait, okay?" he snapped. "The Clan has managed so far without your powers."

He saw her flinch and instantly felt guilty. He hadn't meant to be so harsh.

Suddenly, farther up the gully, a bush exploded with a clatter of leaves as a pigeon erupted from it. Icecloud jumped, her paws flailing as the pigeon batted her away with panicked wings and disappeared into the branches of an oak. Landing clumsily, Icecloud straightened and shook herself, her fur ruffled with embarrassment.

"Let's split up!" Lionblaze called. He felt sorry for the young warrior. It might be easier if Icecloud didn't have to match Dovepaw's skills in front of Thornclaw and Sandstorm. "It'll be better with fewer paws stirring up the leaves."

Sandstorm called down from the top of the gully, "That's fine with me." She nodded to Icecloud. "Let's try the lakeshore." She raced away through the trees, Thornclaw and Icecloud on her tail.

"I'll get that mouse now, okay?" Dovepaw mewed pointedly.

"It's probably run for cover."

"I can still hear it." Dovepaw headed away up the slope and, with a deft pounce, captured the mouse and gave it a quick killing bite. She flung it down in front of Lionblaze. "You think it's unfair, don't you?" she challenged.

"What?"

"Using my powers to hunt!"

"Of course not." Lionblaze wished he hadn't been so sharp with her. She was just beginning to get used to hearing far beyond her Clanmates. "They're part of the prophecy; you may as well use them."

"But I thought the prophecy didn't just apply to ThunderClan," Dovepaw argued. "I thought it applied to every Clan. Wouldn't it be fairer if I used my senses to catch food for every Clan?"

"I don't think they'd thank you for the help," he pointed out. But he understood what she meant. He would leap into battle to defend his Clanmates from a rival Clan. But he always knew he'd win. Was that a fair fight? He shook his head, uncertain how to reassure her. "I think we just have to remember the good we've done with our powers already. After all, if you hadn't sensed the beavers, we'd have all died of thirst by now."

Dovepaw's eyes brightened a little.

Relieved, Lionblaze led her along the gully and up the rise. From the top, they could see Sandstorm's hunting party stalking the slope beside the lake. With a sudden lunge, Sandstorm flushed a pheasant from the grass, and Icecloud, crouching in wait, leaped and made a clean catch before it could escape.

"Well done, Icecloud!" Dovepaw cheered.

Lionblaze stiffened as her mew died away and she pricked her ears. "What is it?"

"Ivypaw's patrol."

He flicked his tail. "Have they found more ShadowClan scents?" Had Tigerheart crossed the border again?

Dovepaw shook her head. "No, but they're looking for them." She stood still with her ears stretched up. What was she searching for? Lionblaze stared through the trees, but saw nothing but branches and bushes blocking his view.

Dovepaw jerked, her eyes widening.

"What is it?" Lionblaze unsheathed his claws.

"Nothing," she answered quickly.

Lionblaze narrowed his eyes. She was definitely jumpy.

"Why don't we try closer to the WindClan border?" Dovepaw mewed suddenly. "I can hear a woodpecker. We can find its nest."

Lionblaze hesitated. Perhaps it was better to head that way. Brackenfur was already checking the ShadowClan border. He wouldn't thank his Clanmates for treading on his paws.

They tracked the tapping of the woodpecker to a tree at the edge of the forest. WindClan's moorland stretched beyond the border, gray beneath a gray sky.

"I'll climb up," Dovepaw offered.

"I'll come with you." Lionblaze didn't want to get a reputation as a reluctant tree climber. It was bad enough to have Cinderheart teasing him. He scrabbled up the shiny poplar trunk after Dovepaw and perched on a thick branch high above the forest floor.

The woodpecker's tapping had stopped, but Dovepaw clambered onto the next branch. "The noise was coming from here," she called down. "Look!" She shuffled out of the way to let Lionblaze climb after her, then flicked her tail toward a small nest lodged in the crook of the branch. There were no eggs or birds inside, but it was lined with soft feathers.

Lionblaze pushed his head into the nest, wrinkling his nose at the stench, and pulled out a mouthful.

Dovepaw purred. "You look like you just swallowed a starling!"

As Lionblaze twitched his whiskers, he heard voices.

Jayfeather.

The medicine cats were coming down from the Moonpool. He could hear them calling their farewells at the border.

"Let's wait for them." Feathers puffed from his mouth as he spoke and drifted down onto the forest floor. He could see Jayfeather padding from the border with Littlecloud and Flametail.

"Come on." Lionblaze scooted down the tree, landing a whisker in front of the ShadowClan cats.

Littlecloud jumped in surprise. "Are ThunderClan cats turning into squirrels?" He quickly smoothed his ruffled fur with a few sharp licks.

"Didn't mean to surprise you," Lionblaze apologized. "We were just collecting feathers."

"Are you planning to learn how to fly?" Flametail meowed.

As he spoke, Dovepaw clawed her way down the trunk,

sending a shower of feathers and bark ahead of her. Flametail ducked like a startled mouse.

"Sorry!" Dovepaw mewed. She glanced at Jayfeather. "How was the meeting at the Moonpool?"

Lionblaze searched his brother's face. Had he found anything out?

"It was fine," Jayfeather reported. He turned and dipped his head to the ShadowClan cats. "I'll head back to camp with my Clanmates," he told them.

"Okay." Littlecloud nodded. "We'll head for our border from here."

"See you next half-moon," Jayfeather called as the two cats walked into the trees.

"Say hi to Tigerheart from me!" Dovepaw mewed.

Lionblaze glanced at her. Why was she sending greetings to Tigerheart?

Her pelt ruffled as she caught his eye. "And, er, say hi to Dawnpelt too," she added quickly.

Jayfeather was already following the trail home. His shoulders were slumped and his eyes were glazed with tiredness.

Lionblaze fell in beside him. "So?"

"Wait, what about these?" Dovepaw was staring around at the feathers, scattered below the poplar.

"We can come back for them later," Lionblaze meowed over his shoulder. "What happened?" He pressed close to Jayfeather, guiding him with his shoulder. His brother seemed happy to lean against him.

"I visited the Dark Forest," Jayfeather began.

"What do you mean?" Dovepaw gasped.

"That's where our real enemies lie," Lionblaze told her.

Dovepaw blinked. "Dead warriors?"

Lionblaze felt a flicker of frustration. Why hadn't they told Dovepaw earlier? There wasn't time to explain it all now. "Just listen," he ordered. He turned his attention back to Jayfeather. "What did you see?"

"I met Brokenstar," Jayfeather meowed. "He's the one who fought against me with Breezepelt."

"The old ShadowClan leader?" Lionblaze's pelt bristled.

Jayfeather nodded. "And we saw Hawkfrost training warriors."

Lionblaze's heart lurched. "*Clan* warriors?"

"No. Dark Forest warriors."

"So we still don't have any proof they're recruiting Clan cats."

"No." Jayfeather sighed. "But they *are* up to something. Why else would dead warriors be training? Their fighting days are long gone. And they were using some pretty nasty moves."

Lionblaze felt Jayfeather shudder against him. But he wasn't afraid. He unsheathed his claws. Strength pulsed through the muscles beneath his pelt. He couldn't wait to take on Hawkfrost and Tigerstar in a battle! He knew he could beat them both.

Dovepaw padded after them, the fur bristling along her spine. "How could Dark Forest cats recruit Clan warriors?"

"Through their dreams," Jayfeather told her.

"But why in the name of StarClan would Clan cats listen to them?"

"You don't know Tigerstar," Jayfeather warned. "He preys on other cats' weaknesses. He can make them feel like they're strong and noble by doing what he wants them to. They probably don't even realize they're doing anything wrong."

Dovepaw's gaze was fixed on Jayfeather as she padded beside him. "How could any cat be so dumb?"

Lionblaze felt heat spreading under his pelt. Tigerstar had fooled him like that once. *Never again.*

Jayfeather shrugged. "All cats like praise," he meowed. "And Tigerstar is smart enough to exploit any grudges. He knows that there will always be warriors glad of a chance to settle old scores." He didn't mention Breezepelt's grudge against his ThunderClan kin.

Dovepaw stretched her eyes wide. "No ThunderClan cat would keep old wounds open once they'd healed."

Lionblaze was pleased to hear his apprentice speaking like a true warrior. As far as he was concerned, once a battle was fought, it was finished. But Dovepaw's innocence made her vulnerable right now. "We're just trying to warn you that not all warriors are perfect, and Tigerstar will be the first to take advantage of that."

"How can we fight Tigerstar if he's dead?" Dovepaw protested.

"We need you to keep your senses alert," Lionblaze mewed. "Listen for unusual signs in the other Clans. Tell us anything you hear or see that seems out of the ordinary. Anything that might suggest the Dark Forest cats are training Clan cats."

"You mean, spy on them?" Dovepaw sounded horrified.

"Yes," Jayfeather meowed simply. "And not just in other Clans. In ThunderClan too."

Dovepaw stood still. "Spy on my own Clanmates? No way!"

"It's not that we don't trust them," Lionblaze tried to explain. "We don't trust Tigerstar."

"You don't trust anyone!" Dovepaw accused. "Do you even trust me?" Her pelt was standing on end. "You're totally overreacting. You're just looking for a way to use your powers. Maybe the prophecy has nothing to do with Tigerstar. Maybe we're just meant to be the best warriors we can be. Why should I be responsible for every cat's destiny?" She darted forward, yowling over her shoulder, "I'm going back to camp! I just want to be normal! I'm not going to spy on any cat!"

She hared away through the trees.

"That went well," Lionblaze muttered. Then he sighed. "Maybe we're asking too much of her."

Jayfeather padded on. "She's part of the prophecy," he growled. "We didn't choose her. She has to be strong!" His voice softened. "I don't want Dovepaw to get hurt. But she's one of the Three, and she has to play her part."

One of the Three. Lionblaze's thoughts flashed back to Hollyleaf. Why couldn't it have been her? Grief stung as he remembered her wisdom and sharp thinking. She may not have been part of the prophecy, but she was his littermate, and sometimes that counted for more than anything.

Chapter 18

Dovepaw didn't want to go back to the hollow. Her fur was fluffed with anger. She wasn't a spy and she wasn't going to let any cat make her become one! That couldn't be what the prophecy meant!

She raced through the trees, swerving around bushes and charging through ferns. She didn't care if she was frightening off prey. With her powers, she could always find more. There was nowhere it could hide from her.

Fury surged through her muscles, driving her harder. Thanks to her power she could take care of everything.

Find prey, Dovepaw!

Save us from the beavers, Dovepaw!

Spy on every cat around the lake. Oh, and while you're at it, you may as well spy on your own Clanmates.

Yeah, right! Her mind fizzed. *Why don't* you *spy on your Clanmates?* She imagined Lionblaze's and Jayfeather's expressions as she told them what she really thought. *Oh, that's right. You want to have friends! I suppose I don't need friends. I suppose it's okay if my sister doesn't want to talk to me anymore.*

Resentment burned in her belly.

Her ears pricked up. Leaves were rustling. Bushes swished. The border patrol was nearby. Had she run that far already? She skidded to a halt and sniffed. She was almost on the ShadowClan border. She should have noticed the thickening brambles. She glanced around anxiously. How would she explain being so far from the rest of her patrol?

The ground sloped up beside her. She could hear Ivypaw's patrol just beyond the rise.

"See anything?" Brackenfur called.

"No tufts of fur," Ivypaw reported.

Dovepaw ducked into a bramble thicket.

"How fresh are the markers?" Whitewing prompted. Ivypaw scooted over the top of the rise and sniffed at a trunk. Dovepaw watched her sister wrinkle her nose.

"Scented a few days ago, and then again last night by the smell of it," Ivypaw answered.

Dovepaw felt a rush of pride. Her sister was going to make a brilliant warrior. Everyone would think she was great.

Unlike me.

Dovepaw sighed. Every cat in the Clan would turn against her if they knew that she was supposed to be using a secret power to test their loyalty. *A true warrior trusts her Clanmates!*

Brackenfur, Bumblestripe, and Whitewing had appeared over the rise now. They were checking every tree and bush. Dovepaw scooted farther into the bramble, gritting her teeth as the barbs scraped her pelt. Brackenfur was padding nearer.

Mouse dung!

She wriggled deeper into the brambles as Brackenfur began

sniffing at the edge. Then, in desperation, she scrambled up one of the thick stems. Biting her tongue against the pain of the thorns, she squirmed to the top of the bush and wormed her way along it. Prickers tore her pelt and scratched her muzzle. Wincing, she peered through the tangle of stems and saw Brackenfur following a scent the other way. He must be ignoring ThunderClan scents in his hunt for traces of ShadowClan. She felt a wave of relief and struggled on through the prickers and scrabbled down the far side, the bramble thicket a perfect barrier between her and her Clanmates.

Her paws slid on the smooth needles covering the ground.

Oh, StarClan!

She sniffed the air.

She'd dropped down into ShadowClan territory.

She glanced along the thicket. If she nipped around the far side she could be back in ThunderClan territory without leaving a trace. Keeping low, she slid along the edge of the bush.

"Hello!"

Tigerheart!

Heart thumping, she spun around to greet the ShadowClan warrior. "Sorry! I didn't mean . . . I mean, I wasn't planning . . ."

Tigerheart shrugged. "It's okay. I trust you. We're friends, right?"

Dovepaw felt her ears burn. "I guess."

Tigerheart's sleek tabby pelt shone in the light rippling through the pines. He padded toward her and touched her muzzle with his. "It's nice to see you," he meowed. He sat down and licked a paw before running it along his whiskers. "I've missed talking to you since the quest."

"Me too." Dovepaw felt her fur flatten. Once a friend, always a friend. Why should borders stop that? "I mean, there are the Gatherings," she went on, "but it's not the same."

"I know what you mean," he agreed. He began licking his flank, smoothing a stray tuft into place. "It was fun, wasn't it? Building nests beneath the stars and waking up each morning in a new place, but with the same familiar faces." He sounded restless, and Dovepaw wondered if he was frustrated at being confined to his territory.

"I tried to visit Sedgewhisker, you know."

"You did?" Tigerheart looked up from his washing. "How is she?"

"She was bitten by a dog, but nothing serious."

"I noticed the wound at the Gathering." Tigerheart narrowed his eyes. "I wondered what it was."

"But everyone got so angry with me!" Dovepaw's pads itched with frustration. "All they were bothered about was that I'd crossed the border. But I was *worried* about her. We're all Clan cats, aren't we? Is it wrong to care about one another?"

Tigerheart gazed into her eyes. "No, it isn't."

Suddenly feeling self-conscious, Dovepaw looked away.

"Do you remember when the dam burst?" Tigerheart's mew was brisk, as though he could sense her discomfort and wanted to distract her. "The river nearly washed us to StarClan." He stood up and began to knead the ground. "And we had to cling to nothing but branches to keep our heads above water." He leaped for a low twig jutting from a pine trunk and swung by his forepaws.

Dovepaw purred with amusement. "What about trying to drag the logs out of the dam? That was like trying to pull the forest up by its roots!"

"I thought you were so brave!" Tigerheart told her.

"You were braver," she argued.

"No way! I was terrified!"

"I couldn't tell." Dovepaw found herself staring into his soft amber eyes. Words dried on her tongue.

"Tigerheart!" The call of a ShadowClan cat made her freeze.

Tigerheart bristled, then quickly nudged her past the brambles and bundled her across the scent line. "See you soon!" he hissed before turning back to meet his Clanmate.

Dovepaw glanced around. No one had seen her. She scooted away from the border and headed home through the trees. Warm with thoughts of Tigerheart, she felt a purr rise in her throat. This was one friendship that Lionblaze and Jayfeather couldn't spoil, because they were never going to know about it.

She lifted her nose. And if they thought she was going to spy on ShadowClan for them, they were very much mistaken. Clanmates were Clanmates, but friends were just as precious.

Chapter 19

"Clanmates are everything. And we're your Clanmates now."

Hawkfrost gazed deep into Ivypaw's eyes, and she began to relax. The gray, mist-wrapped forest suddenly seemed less strange. The sound of warriors training beyond the half-shadowed trees felt familiar. She was with Clanmates.

At first, when Ivypaw had dreamed herself beyond the flower-flecked meadow and into the forest, she'd been nervous. She'd crept between the towering trunks with her fur prickling, stiffening every time a yowl drifted from the misty depths of the woods.

But then Hawkfrost had found her, padding out of the shadows, his blue gaze sparking with pleasure as he saw her.

"Don't be scared of them," he'd reassured her when she'd jumped at a sudden, muffled noise.

"But who are they?" Ivypaw flicked her tail toward two wraithlike forms wrestling in a clearing a few tree-lengths away.

"Your Clanmates," Hawkfrost answered.

"They're *ThunderClan*?" Ivypaw blinked. This couldn't be such a bad place if ThunderClan came here.

Hawkfrost didn't answer, just scraped a line in the moldering earth. "See if you can make it past this mark," he challenged.

More training!

Ivypaw crouched down, wincing at the ache in her shoulders. The pain followed her from dream to waking and back. As she'd hunted with Icecloud and Toadstep that day after sunhigh, she'd struggled to keep up. Nightly training with Hawkfrost had taken its toll, but Ivypaw knew she was growing stronger, and his praise was worth much more because it was so hard-won.

She swished her tail over the ground and stared at Hawkfrost. He sat calmly watching her behind the line he had drawn. She narrowed her eyes, keeping her rump still as he'd taught her.

Wait a moment. Then another. She ran through an old lesson in her head. *Until they're not sure what you're going to do.*

Ivypaw lunged, forepaws stretching, claws unsheathed. She looked for Hawkfrost's first sign of movement, knew he'd double-bluff, pretending to move one way, then another, then back. She kept her hind paws on the ground until she was sure of his direction, then used them to steer her pounce and caught him off balance, swiping his muzzle with one front paw.

He batted her back with a hefty blow to her shoulder, and she fell sprawling to the ground. She sat up, shaking the dizziness from her head.

Hawkfrost was staring at the line. The earth was scuffed, but only on her side.

"You didn't cross it," he growled. "Try again."

Ivypaw tucked her hind legs under her, concentrating. She barely saw the shadow move at the edge of her vision.

A voice rumbled from the mist. "Hello, Hawkfrost."

Stiffening, Ivypaw spun around. A massive dark tom padded out. *Brambleclaw?* No. This cat had the same broad shoulders and tabby pelt, but his eyes glittered like a fox's.

"Who—" Ivypaw didn't get a chance to finish her question. Hawkfrost slammed into her, flinging her down and pinning her shoulders to the ground. He leaned in close, baring his teeth. "I've warned you before about getting distracted," he growled.

She struggled to her paws, eager to examine the newcomer, but wary of taking her eyes from Hawkfrost.

The blue-eyed tom nodded. "Meet Tigerstar."

With his permission, Ivypaw turned to stare at the dark warrior. He was bigger than Brambleclaw and his pelt was crisscrossed with scars. "T-Tigerstar?" She'd heard many stories about this warrior, stories that made her paws tremble.

She was surprised when his gaze softened. "Don't believe everything you hear, little one," he rumbled.

Could he read her mind? "I—I wasn't," she stammered. "I mean, I didn't . . ."

Tigerstar wove around her, his pelt brushing hers. "You're among friends now, Ivypaw," he murmured. "I know what the Clan cats say about me. But they can't see into my heart." He sat down. "Success is lonely. I was punished for wanting to lead my Clan. They misunderstood my desire to guide them through hardship. And so they forced me to leave."

"You mean ThunderClan?" Ivypaw struggled to remember the details of the nursery tales she'd heard.

"They were my birth Clan." Tigerstar sighed. "If I'd led them, they would not have lost so many. Instead they drove me out. But they could not destroy my loyalty to the Clan that raised me."

Ivypaw narrowed her eyes. "But you led ShadowClan."

"What else could I do?" Tigerstar shrugged. "Turn rogue? What true warrior would do that?" He leaned toward her, his eyes round and sincere. "We are Clanmates in every way." He turned to Hawkfrost. "How's she doing?"

Hawkfrost flicked Ivypaw's flank with his tail. "Show him."

"Show him what?" Ivypaw suddenly felt nervous.

Hawkfrost cocked his head. "How fast you can turn. How accurately you can pounce."

Ivypaw dropped to her belly, then sprang up, pushing with her hind legs as hard as she could. She landed and turned instantly on one hind paw, then leaped again, landing on a twig that she'd fixed in her gaze. She plucked it up with her forepaw and snapped it in midair. Then she came to rest, paws straight, tail down, muscles tensed to leap again if she had to.

"Very neat," Tigerstar murmured. He padded toward her and without warning stretched out a massive forepaw and tossed one of the broken pieces of twig into the air. It arced over her head.

"Catch it!" he ordered.

Without thinking, Ivypaw jumped, twisted in midair, and stretched to pluck the twig from the air, catching it without effort and landing on three legs. Pleased with herself, she dropped the twig at Tigerstar's paws.

Tigerstar's amber gaze glowed. "She's ready," he purred to Hawkfrost.

Excitement thrilled through Ivypaw. "Ready for what?"

Tigerstar swung his gaze toward her. His eyes narrowed very slightly. "I hadn't planned on telling you yet. . . ." He glanced at Hawkfrost as though debating. "But I suppose the sooner we act, the safer your Clanmates will be."

Ivypaw leaned forward. Was ThunderClan in danger?

"ShadowClan is planning to invade your territory."

"Invade?" Ivypaw's heart quickened. She knew there'd been activity near the border, but not enough to suggest an immediate threat. "Why?"

With a sigh, Tigerstar began to explain. "Many moons ago, Firestar gave a large strip of your territory to Shadow-Clan. He told his Clanmates they had no use for it. That it would be a hassle to defend."

Ivypaw blinked. "He gave it *away*?" She knew it was only the piece of land Twolegs used to build greenleaf nests, but anything that pushed the ShadowClan border farther from the prey-rich forest must be important. And she had always assumed ShadowClan had won it by force. "Why?"

Tigerstar shook his head sadly. "Firestar's been afraid of ShadowClan since he left his kittypet life. The stories of their ferociousness always seemed to get under his fur."

"But Firestar's not frightened of anything!" Ivypaw objected.

"Really?" Tigerstar looked surprised. "I suppose he must appear that way to an apprentice. But I knew him before he was a warrior, when he was young enough to believe nursery stories."

"He wouldn't still believe such nonsense!" Ivypaw exclaimed.

"Of course not." Tigerstar tucked his tail over his paws. "What warrior would? But still he decided that it was easier to give up territory than risk lives defending it. And unfortunately ShadowClan saw it as weakness, not wisdom."

Suspicion pricked in Ivypaw's pelt. "Why are you telling me this?" she asked. "You were once ShadowClan's leader. Why do you want to give away their plans?"

Tigerstar's gaze sharpened. "ThunderClan is my birth Clan. My loyalty lies with them even though they drove me out and forced me to beg for a home with another Clan." He glanced at his paws. "I'd rather be a humble warrior than live outside the Clans, without the warrior code to guide my paws." He looked up. "ThunderClan must be warned of the danger."

"You really think they'll invade?"

Hawkfrost padded closer. "They've already had a taste of ThunderClan territory."

"How much more do they want?" Ivypaw's heart was pounding. She had to defend her Clan!

Tigerstar tipped his head to one side. "Only the land up to

the abandoned Twoleg nest," he told her.

"But that's where Jayfeather grows his herbs!"

"Do you think they don't know that?" Tigerstar murmured.

Ivypaw felt foolish. Of course! "What can I do?"

Tigerstar closed his eyes for a moment. "Are you sure you're ready?"

"Of course I am!"

"Then," Tigerstar mewed, "you must persuade Firestar to take back the territory he gave away to ShadowClan."

"Will that stop them?"

"It'll send them an important message," Tigerstar growled. "It'll prove that ThunderClan doesn't fear them."

Ivypaw clawed at the earth. "We don't!"

Hawkfrost pushed his muzzle close to Ivypaw's. "But does ShadowClan know that?"

"They will if we attack first!" Ivypaw exclaimed.

Tigerstar looked pleased. "Exactly."

Ivypaw frowned. "How can I get ThunderClan to launch an attack?"

"Speak to Firestar."

"He won't listen to me!" Ivypaw flattened her ears. "And if I tell him the message came from you, he'll never believe it!"

"Then don't tell him." Tigerstar stood up. "He'll believe anything you want him to, if you put it the right way."

Ivypaw's mind was whirling. How would she find the words to persuade Firestar? "I don't know . . ." she breathed.

Tigerstar caught her gaze and held it. "You'll find a way, Clanmate."

Chapter 20

"I'll find a way," Ivypaw murmured as Tigerstar led Hawkfrost away into the mist.

"A way to where?" Blossomfall's mew sounded in her ear.

Ivypaw blinked open her eyes. Early morning light filtered through the branches overhanging the den.

Blossomfall huffed at her and turned back to Bumblestripe. "It's bad enough that we have to sleep in the apprentices' den again," she complained, "without them chattering like sparrows in their sleep."

Alarmed, Ivypaw sat up. What else had she said?

Cold air nipped her nose. She smelled the sharp tang of frost. The first of the season.

Dovepaw was stirring in the nest beside her. "What's going on?" she mewed sleepily. She raised her gray head and gazed around the den, blinking.

"Nothing," Ivypaw told her. She hopped out of her nest.

"Where are you going?" Dovepaw called.

"To talk to Firestar."

Dovepaw sat up. "Why?"

Blossomfall's whiskers twitched. "I suppose Firestar's used

to consulting with apprentices these days," she commented with an edge to her voice.

Ivypaw ignored them both. She slid under the branch spanning the entrance and padded into the clearing.

Cinderheart was sharing tongues with Sorreltail and Poppyfrost outside the nursery. Molekit and Cherrykit tumbled over the frost-whitened ground, fighting to reach a rolling ball of moss. Millie was disappearing through the trailing brambles of the medicine den, while Cloudtail and Brightheart shared a mouse beneath Highledge.

"Ivypaw!" Cinderheart called.

"I'm busy," Ivypaw told her. She was already halfway to the rockfall.

Cinderheart stood up. "Where are you going?"

"I need to see Firestar." Ivypaw didn't stop. "It's urgent."

She began to scramble up the rocks. Cloudtail and Brightheart looked up from their meal and stared at her, round-eyed.

Self-conscious now that her Clanmates were watching, Ivypaw kept going. The future of ThunderClan depended on her. She paused at the entrance to Firestar's den, acutely aware of Cinderheart's gaze burning her fur from the bottom of the hollow. "Firestar?" She tried to keep the tremble from her mew. He might think she'd gone mad.

"Ivypaw?" Firestar's mew echoed from inside the cave.

"Yes," she replied. "I need to talk to you."

"Come in." The ThunderClan leader sounded surprised.

Ivypaw's heart quickened as she stepped into the shadowy

den. Graystripe and Brambleclaw were sitting with Firestar.

"That doesn't mean we shouldn't keep up the extra patrols," Graystripe was urging. The three senior warriors were clearly in the middle of a heated discussion.

Firestar nodded, then turned his attention to Ivypaw. "Well?"

She glanced around at the smooth rock walls and at the soft nest of bracken and moss in the far corner. She'd never been in here before. "Ummm." She suddenly wished she'd planned exactly what she was going to say.

Firestar turned back to his warriors. "While Ivypaw finds her voice, let's carry on."

"Are the extra patrols worth the effort?" Brambleclaw flicked his tail. "With leaf-bare coming, we should be hunting, and it looks like ShadowClan has stopped crossing the border—"

Heat surged under Ivypaw's pelt. "That's not true!"

The three warriors turned and stared at her.

"Have you seen them?" Firestar demanded.

"No." How in the name of StarClan was she going to explain that she knew something these cats didn't?

"I—I had a dream."

Brambleclaw flattened his ears. Graystripe put his head to one side.

"Go on," Firestar prompted gently.

Ivypaw blurted out the first words that came to her. "I dreamed that I was standing at the edge of ThunderClan territory . . . on that strip of grass beside the place where Twolegs come in greenleaf." She tried to read the warriors' expressions. Were they taking her seriously? "The place that used to belong to ThunderClan. The place you gave to ShadowClan."

Firestar narrowed his eyes. "How did you know that? It was before you were born."

"Probably heard it from Mousefur," Brambleclaw muttered.

Ivypaw shook her head. "It was all in the dream. How you gave it to ShadowClan because it was useless hunting, not worth defending."

"Go on." Firestar was leaning forward now, his ears pricked.

"I saw the stream and it was running with blood." Ivypaw felt her words coming quickly. Now that she'd started, this was easier than she'd thought. "*ThunderClan* blood. And ShadowClan cats were patrolling the edge, purring, and they were saying that soon the whole forest would run with ThunderClan blood and they'd own it all, because ThunderClan was no more dangerous than a swarm of beetles, and beetles could be crushed."

As Ivypaw took a steadying breath, she realized that the three warriors were staring at her, captivated. Encouraged, she went on. "So I ran back to the hollow, but ShadowClan cats were everywhere: all through the forest, hiding behind bushes, hunting for squirrels, training for battle, all the way up to the Twoleg nest. They were gathering Jayfeather's herbs and saying ShadowClan would never be sick again." She ran out of words. Had they believed her?

Graystripe's eyes were half closed. "There may be some

truth in it." He glanced at Firestar. "You used to have dreams that came true when you were an apprentice."

Brambleclaw flexed his claws. "Young cats also have vivid imaginations."

"But her sister warned us about the beavers," Graystripe reminded him. "That wasn't imagination."

"Is it worth risking trouble with ShadowClan?" Brambleclaw questioned. "We have no real evidence. I've already told you that ShadowClan cats have stopped crossing the border."

Graystripe shifted his paws. "That may be part of their strategy," he suggested. "To lull us into a false sense of security."

Ivypaw didn't take her gaze from Firestar. The ThunderClan leader wrapped his tail over his paws. "Who else knows about this dream?"

"No one," Ivypaw assured him. "I came straight to you."

"Were there any other cats in it besides you and ShadowClan warriors?" His leaf green stare was unwavering. "Any cats from StarClan?"

"She's too young to know any," Graystripe pointed out.

"Longtail?" Firestar wondered.

Ivypaw shook her head. "Just ShadowClan warriors."

"Did you recognize any of them?" Firestar pressed.

"Crowfrost . . . er . . . Scorchfur." Ivypaw's heart pounded as she tried to remember cats she'd seen at the Gatherings. It couldn't be wrong to lie, not when she was doing it to save her Clan. Anything to make them believe her.

"Okay." Firestar turned to Graystripe and Brambleclaw. "What do you think?"

Excitement itched beneath Ivypaw's pelt.

"It would explain why they were crossing the border," Graystripe growled. "They might have been looking for the best places to fight."

"And it's interesting that she saw the Twolegplace." Brambleclaw glanced at Ivypaw. "Surrendering it did make us seem vulnerable."

"It was a good decision," Graystripe defended his leader hotly. "It saved bloodshed. And we were never going to hunt in such an open space. Especially not if it's crawling with Twolegs when prey is richest."

"But giving it up may have sent the wrong message," Firestar conceded. "Maybe I shouldn't have handed it over so easily. That act of kindness seems to have left echoes of weakness."

They believe me! Ivypaw couldn't stay quiet. "If we take back the Twolegplace, then they'll know we can't be beaten!"

Firestar stood up. "Thank you, Ivypaw," he meowed. "We'll need to discuss this with the other warriors, and until we do I want you to keep it to yourself." He brushed past her. "Don't even tell Dovepaw."

Ivypaw nodded earnestly while the warriors filed past her out of the cave.

Firestar glanced over his shoulder. "Tell me if you have any more dreams," he ordered.

"I will." Ivypaw's heart was pounding. She'd done it! They were thinking about attacking ShadowClan! She couldn't wait to tell Tigerstar the good news.

Chapter 21

Briarlight was coughing.

The roughness in her mew that had begun last night had developed into a heaviness in her chest that Jayfeather could hear growing thicker every time he lowered his head to listen.

"Here," he mewed, pushing another pawful of herbs toward her. "Swallow these."

"No more," she complained. "I couldn't swallow a thing."

"I've flavored them with mouse," Jayfeather coaxed.

Briarlight let out a low moan, as if the thought of food made her feel worse. Jayfeather pushed away Littlecloud's dark memory of Wildfur's slow decline after his accident. He wasn't going to let the same thing happen to Briarlight.

Millie pushed her way through the brambles. "I've come to help Briarlight with her exercises. . . ." Her mew trailed away as she recognized sickness in her kit. "What's wrong with her?" Her voice was tense.

"Just a slight fever." Jayfeather deliberately kept his tone light. "A bit of exercise might help her fight it off."

"Shouldn't she rest?" Millie questioned.

Briarlight clawed at her nest. "I've been resting all night!"

she mewed. A cough gripped her but she swallowed against it.

Jayfeather heard Millie's paws hesitate for a moment before padding briskly across the den. "Come on, then."

Briarlight's breath rasped as she began to go through her strengthening exercises with her mother. Suddenly she stopped, and Jayfeather heard her flop down in her nest. "This is too much work!"

Jayfeather tensed. Briarlight had never given up before. "Come on," he urged. "It'll make you feel better."

"It's *all* too much work," Briarlight wailed. "Exercises morning and night. Dragging myself to the fresh-kill pile as if it were a mountain away. I can't even breathe or lie comfortably, let alone hunt or play with my littermates!"

Fear was flashing from Millie's pelt. "But think how much you have to be grateful for," she meowed as brightly as she could. "You can still share tongues with your littermates and enjoy a tasty mouse. And the whole Clan admires you." Jayfeather could sense the she-cat desperately searching for more reasons for Briarlight to be happy and grateful.

He padded forward and touched Millie's shoulder with his muzzle. "Why don't you see if you can catch her something really tasty?" he suggested. "I'll mix up some fresh herbs." He turned to Briarlight. "You've been working hard. A day's rest will do you good."

As Millie left the den, Jayfeather began to rub Briarlight's chest, hoping to stimulate her breathing.

"Your mother would gladly suffer your injuries for you," he murmured.

"That's dumb," Briarlight rasped. "Why would any cat *want* to be like this?"

"It's just how mothers think." His thoughts flashed to Leafpool. Would she have taken his blindness to spare him?

"Careful!" Briarlight's mew brought him back. "I smoothed that fur down earlier and now you're rubbing it the wrong way."

"Sorry." Jayfeather felt a glimmer of relief at hearing her old spark.

"Washing myself is about all I can do these days," she went on. "You don't have to mess it up."

Jayfeather purred and smoothed her fur back down with his tongue.

The brambles rustled.

"Jayfeather?"

Dustpelt was standing in the entrance. "Firestar's called a meeting of the senior warriors," he meowed. "He wants you there too."

Jayfeather hesitated. Who was going to watch Briarlight?

"I'll be okay." The young warrior guessed what he was thinking. "In fact, I'll enjoy the peace."

"Are you sure?"

"Positive."

"Okay."

He pushed his way out of the den and sniffed carefully. Firestar was sitting in the crook of a beech bough, out of hearing of the rest of the Clan. Graystripe, Brambleclaw, Squirrelflight, Dustpelt, Thornclaw, Sandstorm, Brightheart, and Cloudtail sat below him, flavoring the air with their anticipation. Jayfeather took his place beside them.

"Thank you for joining us." Firestar's tail brushed the beech bark. The leader was agitated. "Ivypaw has had a dream."

"What's that got to do with us?" Dustpelt called.

Firestar's claws scraped the bark. "I think it's a sign from StarClan."

"Ivypaw?" Thornclaw's mew was scornful.

"Why not?" Brightheart prickled in defense of her kin.

"Our daughter's kit wouldn't lie," Cloudtail growled.

Thornclaw's pelt bristled. "I'm not saying she'd lie," he retorted. "I just want to know the reason Firestar's taken it so seriously."

Graystripe's paws shifted. "She seemed to know more than she should."

Thornclaw huffed. "Apprentices always know more than they should!"

"This was different." Brambleclaw's tail swept the earth.

Jayfeather listened in silence. Ivypaw? Dreaming? What was StarClan doing sending her messages? He pricked his ears.

"Okay, okay." Dustpelt snorted impatiently. "Let's say this dream was a message from StarClan. What was it?"

"She dreamed that ShadowClan had invaded," Firestar told them. "That the stream along the clearing where Twolegs come in greenleaf was running with ThunderClan blood."

Jayfeather felt anxiety sweep through the warriors.

"Do we know what it means?" Thornclaw demanded.

"It's pretty easy to guess," Dustpelt scoffed. "ShadowClan wants to push the advantage they got from being given the clearing in the first place. They want more of our territory."

Anger flashed from Firestar, but he kept his voice level as he answered the dusky warrior. "The decisions I make may not always be right, but they are based on reason and experience."

"No cat doubts your reason," Dustpelt conceded. "But any cat with any experience must know that ShadowClan will always take advantage wherever they can."

A growl rumbled in Graystripe's throat. "There's always the hope that if we treat them like true warriors they'll start acting with honor instead of preying on weakness wherever they find it."

"Enough!" Firestar lost patience. "We're here to discuss the safety of ThunderClan, not ShadowClan's honor. If Ivypaw's dream is right, we must act."

"Good!" Dustpelt's claws scraped the ground.

"Jayfeather?"

He looked up.

"Have you had any warning from StarClan about ShadowClan?"

"No." *Not about ShadowClan.*

"We don't need warnings from StarClan!" rumbled Dustpelt. "We've had enough warnings from ShadowClan!"

"They have been crossing the border lately," Squirrelflight agreed.

"It might be best to nip any trouble in the bud," Sandstorm ventured.

"But how?" wondered Brightheart.

Dustpelt stood up. "Well, we gave the clearing to them. We should take it back!"

"It was ours to begin with," Cloudtail agreed.

"And with leaf-bare coming," Graystripe chipped in, "the extra hunting would be useful."

Jayfeather could feel unease pulsing from Firestar's pelt. "I don't like to go back on my word," he growled.

"This is ShadowClan we're dealing with!" Thornclaw reminded him. "A warrior's word means nothing to them."

"And if Ivypaw's right," Firestar murmured, "then we risk our lives by delaying."

Jayfeather sighed. He knew what this meant. In his head, he began to tally the herbs in his store. Was there enough marigold? It was the best medicine for gashes and bites.

"We must attack before they do," Firestar decided.

"Now?" Dustpelt was pacing.

"Not yet," Firestar cautioned. "I must warn them first."

"Warn them?" Brambleclaw sounded shocked. "You'll have lost the battle before you've begun it!"

"We can win any battle," Firestar told him. "I'm going to give Blackstar a chance to surrender the clearing peacefully."

Cloudtail spluttered with disbelief. "As if!"

"I must give him the chance," Firestar insisted. "No blood will be spilled needlessly." He leaped down from the bough.

Where's Lionblaze? Jayfeather suddenly realized that his brother wasn't in the hollow. He needed to know what was happening here. Jayfeather hurried after Firestar. "Can I go and find Lionblaze?"

"No time," Firestar replied. "I want you to come with me." He called to his deputy. "Brambleclaw! Let Graystripe finish organizing the patrols. I want you with us."

Jayfeather flattened his ears. It was a huge show of trust for Firestar to visit the ShadowClan camp with his deputy and medicine cat. Especially with a proposal like this one. Foreboding swelled in his belly.

What if this was exactly what Tigerstar wanted? After all, he'd won Tigerheart over to his side. How many other ShadowClan cats had he recruited?

Brambleclaw seemed less concerned about where they were going than what they were leaving behind. "Is it wise to leave the camp so vulnerable?"

"Vulnerable?" Graystripe echoed. "Are you calling us mouse-hearts?"

There was warmth in the gray warrior's mew. But he had a point. Even with Firestar and Brambleclaw gone, the camp would be well guarded.

But, Jayfeather wondered with a chill, what if they never came back?

Frost-hardened leaves crunched underpaw as they padded through the forest. When they approached the ShadowClan border, Firestar and Brambleclaw tasted the air. Hope prickled from their pelts. Jayfeather guessed they were looking for traces of ShadowClan this side of the scent line. Was Ivypaw's dream enough of a reason to attack? Had it really come from StarClan?

Firestar paused at the border, then crossed it. The air was fragrant with pine, the ground soft underpaw, thick with fallen needles. Jayfeather felt his leader push away his last tremor of doubt. Brambleclaw padded at his side, determined and calm, while Jayfeather trailed behind.

"Keep up," Brambleclaw ordered. "We're on enemy territory."

As he spoke Jayfeather felt alarm flare from among the trees ahead. "Patrol!" he warned.

Firestar halted. "We've come to speak with Blackstar!" His voice echoed through the pines.

Jayfeather recognized the scent of Toadfoot and Ratscar. Their paws scuffed the needles, wariness fizzing in their pelts.

"What do you want with him?" Ratscar growled.

"To talk," Firestar answered.

Jayfeather pictured Toadfoot and Ratscar exchanging questioning glances before Ratscar replied.

"Very well."

Jayfeather was familiar with the twisting route to the ShadowClan camp, but he had never felt this uneasy before, this unconvinced of his reason for being there. He followed the warriors through the prickly entrance. Surprised murmurs rippled through the ShadowClan cats.

"Firestar?" Tawnypelt's questioning mew rang across the clearing.

Ratscar was heading for his leader's den. "He wants to speak to Blackstar," he growled.

But Blackstar was already padding out. "Why has ThunderClan's leader come to ShadowClan?" His mew was sharp with suspicion.

"I need to talk to you," Firestar answered. "In private."

Blackstar's tail lashed the air. "In *private*?" He padded slowly around Brambleclaw and Jayfeather, his whiskers twitching audibly with distrust. "Why so secret?"

"Feel free to match my Clanmates with your own," Firestar offered.

"How generous of you," Blackstar sneered. "Russetfur! Littlecloud!" he called. "We have company."

Jayfeather sensed stiffness in Russetfur's limbs as she ambled across the clearing. Frailty oozed from her, and he could smell the scent of strengthening herbs on her breath. The ShadowClan deputy had grown old, and with a flash of surprise Jayfeather realized that she would probably not survive leaf-bare. Littlecloud hurried from the medicine den, paws still fragrant with the herbs he'd been mixing. Some cat had whitecough, by the smell of the coltsfoot and catmint on his fur.

Jayfeather let his mind roam the camp, searching the nursery first. No sickness there. Then he heard coughing from the apprentices' den. Pinepaw was sick, but not fevered. The strong young apprentice would easily shake off her illness.

Jayfeather followed Blackstar, Firestar, and Brambleclaw into the ShadowClan leader's den, nose wrinkling in readiness for the stench. He would never understand ShadowClan's taste for rat.

"What do you want?" Blackstar was brisk, and Firestar matched his briskness with his own.

"I want you to give the Twoleg clearing back to ThunderClan."

Shock pulsed from the ShadowClan leader. Russetfur's claws scraped the floor.

"What?" Blackstar rasped.

"We gave it as a gift," Firestar went on. "But you've pushed at our forest borders once too often."

"That's not true!" Russetfur hissed. "You just want extra hunting lands. Have your greedy warriors hunted the forest clean?"

"We have enough prey for ourselves," Firestar meowed evenly. "But our forest can't spare prey for ShadowClan hunting parties."

Rage filled the den, so thick in the air that Jayfeather's heart began to quicken and he felt as if there weren't enough air to breathe.

"You're accusing *us* of crossing borders?" Blackstar spat. "We were beginning to think ThunderClan had forgotten what scent lines mean."

Jayfeather felt tension seize Brambleclaw, as though he was holding back from lashing out at the ShadowClan leader. "We want our land back," he growled.

"It's *our* land now," Russetfur spat.

"Then we'll take it from you by force," Firestar warned.

Blackstar's tail scraped the side of the den, his fur snagging on the thorns. "If you want a battle, you'll have one."

"Very well," Firestar answered. "My warriors will be setting the new boundary tomorrow at dawn. It's your choice whether to stop them."

"Don't play that game!" Blackstar hissed. "*You're* the one leading your Clan into battle."

"Toadfoot! Crowfrost! Ratscar!" Blackstar yowled as they crossed the clearing. "Escort them from our territory." The rage in his voice set pelts prickling around the edge of the camp.

Paws itching with unease, Jayfeather followed Firestar, trying to keep his pace slow even though he wanted to run. The air in the camp had soured into enmity.

Toadfoot fell in beside him, knocking roughly against his shoulder. "Why can't you mind your own business?" the ShadowClan warrior growled.

Jayfeather shifted away from his escort. Closing his eyes, he prayed that Ivypaw's dream had been right.

CHAPTER 22

Ivypaw drew in a breath. The cold seared her tongue but the tang of fresh ThunderClan markers tasted warm. She puffed out her chest. Her Clanmates were lined along the border like hawks, poised to defend their new territory. Their breath billowed in the milky light of dawn, while mist drifted from among the dark trunks of ShadowClan's forest and rolled over the grass toward them.

"Are you okay?"

Dovepaw was trembling beside her.

"Fine." Dovepaw shifted her paws.

"Do you think ShadowClan will come?"

Dovepaw didn't answer. She was staring into the trees, her ears pricked, claws unsheathed.

For a moment, Ivypaw wished Dovepaw weren't there. She hadn't had extra training from Hawkfrost. How in the name of StarClan could she fight ShadowClan warriors? Ivypaw suddenly pictured Dovepaw horribly wounded, with claw marks scarring her flanks. She shuddered. Whatever arguments they'd had recently, they were still littermates.

She curved her claws into the damp earth, dragging her

thoughts back to the present. This was *her* battle. The new border was here because of her, and she was ready to defend it with her blood.

"Hold the line!" Lionblaze snarled at Blossomfall as the young tortoiseshell warrior took a step forward, whiskers twitching.

"I thought I heard something," Blossomfall protested.

"Get back in line!" Firestar growled. He swung his head to stare along the ranks of warriors. "Stay inside the border."

Blossomfall shuffled back into place.

Dovepaw flinched.

Someone was coming.

Ivypaw caught her breath as Blackstar padded out of the forest, flanked by Russetfur and Rowanclaw. His pelt glowed white in the half-light. He looked far more powerful than he did at Gatherings, his hackles raised, eyes glittering with anger. Ivypaw fought the urge to back away. *Hawkfrost has trained me!* She grasped the thought and hung on to it.

Courage began to seep back into her paws as Blackstar halted and wrinkled his nose. The clearing was drenched in ThunderClan scent.

"You have made your choice," he snarled to Firestar. "You gave us this territory. It's not yours to take back."

Firestar lifted his chin. "We have given you a chance to avoid fighting. Even now, no blood needs to be shed."

Blackstar curled his lip. "Blood will fall, and every drop of it will be on your conscience." He flicked his tail.

From the shadows and mist of the forest ShadowClan

warriors leaped out with their claws unsheathed, their teeth bared. The muted dawn was ripped apart by screeches.

Ivypaw froze. The warriors were huge! Then she felt the warm bulk of Hawkfrost pressing against her flank. She knew that if she turned her head, she would be unable to see him, but he was there, all the same.

"Defend what is yours," he growled. "You know how."

The first wave of warriors hit.

A dark tabby tom lunged toward her. Ivypaw was ready. She turned and flicked out her hind legs, catching him on the cheek and sending him reeling backward, a yowl of surprise choking in his throat.

Hawkfrost's breath stirred her pelt. "Don't spill all their blood at once, little one."

"Okay." Ivypaw swerved away from the fallen warrior and reared to meet a ShadowClan tom twice her size.

Ratscar!

Undaunted, she raked claws across his nose, drawing blood.

His eyes lit with surprise. "Don't think I'll go easy on you"—he batted her back with a hefty blow—"just because you're an apprentice."

Dizzy from the clout, she rolled sideways. His forepaws split the grass a whisker from her ear. She leaped to her paws and reared again.

Blossomfall appeared. "Want some help?"

"Yes, please," Ivypaw grunted. She began swiping with her forepaws and, as Blossomfall joined in, ducked and scooted behind Ratscar and crouched beneath his legs. Blossomfall drove him backward and, as he tripped, Ivypaw pushed herself up in a surging jump that sent him spinning away, shocked and unbalanced. Before he could find his paws she was clinging to his back, churning her hind paws mercilessly.

"Get underneath him!" she snapped at Blossomfall.

The young warrior obeyed and slid beneath the raging ShadowClan tom, unbalancing him again. Ivypaw let go before Ratscar tumbled onto his back, then plunged her forepaws down hard onto his belly. The breath huffed from his mouth and he lay stunned for a moment before scrabbling up clumsily, shaking his head as if trying to clear it.

"Wow!" Blossomfall breathed. "Cinderheart must be an awesome mentor!"

Ivypaw glanced at the young warrior, her mind fizzing. *I have a better mentor than you could ever imagine!*

Ratscar was snaking away into the writhing mass of pelts. Ivypaw searched the battlefield. ShadowClan had spilled over the new border and was pressing ThunderClan back into the long grass.

Dovepaw? She searched for her sister.

In the swirl of pelts and mist, Ivypaw couldn't pick her out. She plunged into the fray, shouldering her way between the wrestling bodies. The fighting was vicious. Dovepaw hadn't been trained by Hawkfrost. She must need help.

Chapter 23

Dovepaw dug her paws deeper into the grass as Blackstar strode from the trees, flanked by Russetfur and Rowanclaw. She would not give way, no matter what. Ivypaw was pressing against her flank. Dovepaw was aware of her sister's stillness beside her own trembling body. Wasn't Ivypaw scared?

She could hear ShadowClan coming, stalking through their territory, their paws scuffing the needle-strewn forest floor, their pelts brushing against pine trunks, their breath coming short and fast. She could picture them slicing through the sparse undergrowth, scoring marks on the ground with unsheathed claws. Their stench rolled over her, choking her until she felt as if she could no longer breathe.

Blackstar was challenging Firestar.

Blood roared in her ears. She could see her leader's mouth moving but heard nothing but her own blood pulsing through her.

Then ShadowClan warriors erupted like a flock of ravens from the misty pine forest.

"Make every blow count!" Dovepaw hardly heard Lionblaze's order before he leaped away.

Crouching low, she fought to remember her battle moves as her mind emptied of everything except panic. Cats lunged on either side of her and she shrank back, staring wildly around her.

Then the noise began. Every breath, every rip of fur, every scrape of tooth on bone. Growls and shrieks tore at her senses. As she struggled to shut out the chaos of sound, the scent of fear and of blood swamped her tongue. Was that Dustpelt's breath knocked from him as a warrior hurled him to the ground? Was that pain in Sorreltail's shriek, or was it triumph?

A cream pelt flashed toward her. Paws slammed her shoulders and knocked her flying; then claws gripped her flank. The ShadowClan she-cat smelled like Tigerheart.

Dawnpelt?

Instinctively Dovepaw battered the warrior's belly with her hind paws until the she-cat let go. It *was* Dawnpelt! Dovepaw jumped to her paws and ducked under Dawnpelt's belly, breaking from the line, racing forward, slipping through the ShadowClan ranks as she desperately tried to escape the shrieking mass of warriors.

Her ears twitched with too much noise. Was that the sound of *more* ShadowClan warriors pounding through the undergrowth toward her?

Her paws skidded underneath her. The ShadowClan cats had driven ThunderClan back toward the middle of the clearing. Dovepaw couldn't get a grip on the slippery grass. Her claws couldn't reach through to solid ground.

Dawnpelt was on her tail.

She turned and reared and met the ShadowClan warrior in a clumsy flurry of swiping blows. Dawnpelt fought back. Knocked her muzzle. Unbalanced her.

Help me, StarClan!

She tried to spring up but Dawnpelt held her down, raking her spine with hind claws. Pain seared her pelt and a yowl escaped her. Writhing to escape, she glimpsed golden fur.

Lionblaze was staring down at her. "You seem to have strayed from your Clanmates," he growled.

There was a blur of movement above Dovepaw, and suddenly Dawnpelt let go. Raising her head with a wince, Dovepaw saw Lionblaze fling the ShadowClan warrior away.

"Can you manage now?" he asked.

She nodded, hoping she could, and Lionblaze dashed back toward the battle line.

Ivypaw slowed to a halt beside her. "Are you okay?"

"Fine," Dovepaw panted. She fought to block out the yowling of her Clanmates.

"Look out!" Ivypaw warned.

Dovepaw spun around as Foxleap backed into her. His forepaws were raised as he swiped at an advancing ShadowClan warrior.

Crowfrost.

Two ShadowClan apprentices—Starlingpaw and Pinepaw—flanked the black-and-white tom, their eyes fixed on Foxleap as they drove the ThunderClan warrior toward the pine forest, separating him from his Clanmates.

Ivypaw darted forward and nipped Starlingpaw's foreleg. Dovepaw knew what she had to do. Yowling, she hurled herself at Pinepaw, knocking her backward with such ferocity that Crowfrost glanced up to see if his Clanmate was okay. In an instant, Foxleap regained his balance, dropped onto four paws, and launched himself forward. He sent Crowfrost hurtling backward and the pair rolled away while Dovepaw dug her claws into Pinepaw's flanks and tore until the she-cat shrieked and struggled from her grip.

Starlingpaw was dragging at the grass as Ivypaw pulled him backward and sank her teeth into his neck. Dovepaw froze. Her sister looked as though she were killing prey. She felt a flash of relief as Ivypaw let go and Starlingpaw raced back toward his Clanmates.

Ivypaw turned to face Dovepaw, curling her lip to reveal teeth stained with blood. "Who next?"

Suddenly Brackenfur and Thornclaw appeared, pulling up in front of Dovepaw and Ivypaw, their breath clouding the air.

"Brambleclaw wants us to try something different," Brackenfur panted.

His gaze fell upon Foxleap; the tawny tabby was beating Crowfrost backward, helped now by Toadstep. Overwhelmed, the ShadowClan warrior turned and slipped back among his own ranks. Brackenfur nodded approvingly and beckoned with his tail.

Foxleap raced over, Toadstep a pace behind. "What is it?"

"ShadowClan keeps regrouping," Thornclaw told them.

"They're pushing us back across the field."

Toadstep nodded. "It's impossible to get a good grip on this grass."

"Brambleclaw wants us to outflank them," Brackenfur told him.

Ivypaw leaned forward. "How?"

"I'm going to lead a separate patrol," Thornclaw meowed, "and try to draw ShadowClan away from the clearing, back into their own territory."

Brackenfur rubbed his muzzle with one paw. "We stand a better chance in the woods," he growled. "There are brambles and trees. The ground will feel more familiar. And we can try out our new tree tactics."

Dovepaw's eyes widened. "But won't ShadowClan just fight harder if we invade their territory?"

"That's a risk we'll have to take," Brackenfur muttered. "We'll never beat them out here in the open."

Lionblaze bounded toward them, Rosepetal and Sorreltail behind him. "Are you ready?" he asked Thornclaw.

Thornclaw nodded and headed toward ShadowClan's woods.

Dovepaw glanced at her sister. What if they were caught between two rows of ShadowClan warriors?

But Ivypaw seemed undaunted. She scrambled after Thornclaw. Dovepaw hurtled after, her heart pounding.

"Hey! Where are they going?"

She heard the shocked yowl of a ShadowClan warrior behind them.

"They've broken rank!"

Dovepaw tried to concentrate on her Clanmates, slipping after them through the pines, feeling the needles underpaw, adjusting to the gloom of ShadowClan's woods as she wove past a swath of brambles. Ivypaw was already scooting up a tree, gripping the bark like a squirrel.

Dovepaw glanced back through the bramble hedge at the battle still raging in the clearing. It looked like chaos. Where were the battle skills they'd all been taught? From here it looked like a tangled mass of writhing pelts, and she was agonizingly aware of each shriek of pain and fear, the tearing of fur, the crunch of teeth as each cat struggled in its own private battle. How could they bear to do this to one another?

"Dovepaw!" Lionblaze's mew dragged her attention back.

ShadowClan warriors were pounding toward the pines, thundering over the grass, spitting with rage.

"Quick, climb that tree!"

Dovepaw looked in dismay at the smooth, slender pine trunk. Her Clanmates had already scrambled up their own trees and were clinging to narrow branches, staring down, poised to drop on the fast-approaching ShadowClan warriors.

"Move!" Lionblaze nosed her upward and she clawed her way to the lowest branch.

Below, Lionblaze turned to face the ShadowClan attack as warriors streamed through the trees, Blackstar leading. The ShadowClan leader's face was twisted in rage. "Can't you even respect the border you just made?" He blinked in surprise at

Lionblaze and Thornclaw. "Where are the rest of you?" he demanded.

His warriors skidded to a halt beside him.

Lionblaze glanced up and Blackstar followed his gaze, his eyes widening as he spotted the ThunderClan warriors clinging to the branches above.

Brackenfur was trembling in an effort to hang on. He dropped a moment before Thornclaw gave the signal.

"Now!"

The other ThunderClan cats began to dive on the ShadowClan patrol. Dovepaw clung, trembling, to her branch. Pelts swam beneath her like fish. She fixed her gaze on the light brown pelt of Owlclaw, then leaped.

Oh, StarClan!

The branch sagged beneath her. Her paws slithered wildly. With a yowl of shock, she landed unevenly on Owlclaw's back. It was ungraceful but it was enough to floor him. He collapsed beneath her weight.

"What in the name of StarClan are you doing?" Owlclaw heaved her off and turned, his paws raised. Dovepaw ducked the first swipe and nipped at his leg.

"Need help?" Rosepetal appeared at her side and began to bat the tabby away, backing him against a bramble bush till he shrieked with pain.

Dovepaw scanned the fighting cats closest to her. Lionblaze had Ratscar pinned to a tree. Ivypaw was wrestling with Starlingpaw again. Hadn't the ShadowClan apprentice learned her lesson? Toadstep was squirming beneath a dark tabby tom, his tail lashing wildly.

Tigerheart!

"Fighting like squirrels!" Tigerheart hissed. "Doesn't ThunderClan have any pride?" He tore at Toadstep's spine with vicious hind claws, sending fur flying as Toadstep screeched in agony.

Anger surged in Dovepaw's chest. She had to help her Clanmate. Then she paused. It was *Tigerheart*! Could she really hurt her friend?

Oh, StarClan! Do we really have to fight each other?

As she hesitated, Foxleap knocked Tigerheart from Toadstep's back. Relief washed over Dovepaw.

"Help me!" Sorreltail's furious mew sounded behind her.

Dovepaw spun to see her Clanmate swiping at Smokefoot. The dark ShadowClan warrior was snarling with his teeth bared, sharp claws glinting. Sorreltail reared and fell against him, their chests clashing as Smokefoot rose to meet her challenge. Her hind paws scrabbled, sending needles showering against Dovepaw's pelt. Dovepaw sprang forward to help, knocking Smokefoot's paws from under him so that he landed with a grunt on his belly.

"Thanks," Sorreltail growled, and dived on the tom. Dovepaw leaned away from the flurry of paws and caught sight of Ivypaw. She was steadily beating Starlingpaw backward, her forepaws slashing with vicious accuracy.

Wow! Dovepaw was impressed. Ivypaw was a brilliant fighter. Then Dovepaw stiffened as a dark brown pelt flashed at the edge of her vision. She reared up to get a better look, staring over the tangle of pelts.

Tigerheart was streaking toward Ivypaw.

He mustn't hurt her!

Panic surging in her throat, Dovepaw barged through the battling cats. She dived beneath Crowfrost and burst out just in time to see Tigerheart leap for Ivypaw.

"Ivypaw!" Dovepaw's warning was lost in the shrieks of battle.

She watched her sister turn and spot Tigerheart lunging toward her. *Thank StarClan!* Dovepaw flexed her claws and prepared to go to Ivypaw's rescue. Then she paused.

Tigerheart had stopped midleap and landed clumsily on all four paws. His gaze caught Ivypaw's and the two cats stared at each other.

Dovepaw felt her chest tighten.

Tigerheart had nodded at Ivypaw. A tiny nod. So tiny that Dovepaw wondered if she had imagined it. Then the ShadowClan warrior turned and vanished into the battle, his pelt blurring alongside Owlfur's as he fought Thornclaw and Foxleap.

Dovepaw waited for relief to come. Her sister was safe. Tigerheart had not hurt her. But there was no relief inside her. Some other emotion jabbed her belly. A feeling that said she didn't want Tigerheart to look at Ivypaw that way. The same way he had looked at Dovepaw when he told her he wanted to stay friends.

Am I jealous?

Dovepaw tried to shake the nagging pang away.

Why had Tigerheart looked at Ivypaw like that? Had he

recognized the silver-and-white she-cat as Dovepaw's sister?

No. That wasn't the look. Something else had lit his gaze, something far more knowing. It almost looked as if they'd met before. *But I would know!* Dovepaw bristled. Had Ivypaw been sneaking out of camp to meet the ShadowClan warrior? Was that why there was so much distance between the sisters now? Was that why Tigerheart had sought Dovepaw's friendship?

There is no time for this! A voice inside her told her that she was putting herself and her Clan in danger. Her Clanmates needed her. She would have to wait to sort out what was going on with Ivypaw later. Right now, she needed to fight.

She turned and swiped at the hind legs of Owlclaw, then sank her teeth into Crowfrost's tail. His yowl of agony sent energy surging through her, and as he turned she reared up, ready to take him on.

A yowl of rage rent the air. Dovepaw ducked out of Toadfoot's way and spun around. At the edge of the trees, Russetfur was attacking Firestar. She held his throat in her jaws, a stream of drool swinging from her straining cheek. Firestar thrashed desperately but she didn't let go.

A golden pelt streaked through the trees.

Lionblaze!

Dovepaw blinked as her mentor hurled himself at Russetfur. At first the she-cat didn't move. Then, claws stretched, eyes wild, Lionblaze caught hold of the ShadowClan deputy and dragged her backward, off her hind paws. As he did, Firestar stumbled and collapsed to the ground, blood pumping from his neck.

CHAPTER 24

Lionblaze nosed Dovepaw up the tree trunk and turned to face the ShadowClan attack. Brambleclaw's idea had to work. The battle in the clearing was going badly, because none of them had figured they wouldn't be able to hold their footing on the smooth, short grass. They needed to take the fighting to somewhere ThunderClan held the advantage. Maybe Firestar was right to start training the apprentices up in the trees. Hopefully they'd fight better among the pines.

Blackstar burst out of the brambles. "Can't you even respect the border you just made?"

Lionblaze unsheathed his claws.

"Where are the rest of you?"

He felt a glimmer of satisfaction at Blackstar's confusion. Power pulsed through his paws and he braced himself for the attack. ShadowClan warriors streamed through the trees. They were furious, their faces twisted with outrage, their yowls edged with fury as they spun in surprise.

"Now!"

On Thornclaw's signal, ThunderClan warriors swooped like hawks from the branches. Lionblaze relished ShadowClan's yowls of bewilderment. The battle exploded around him, shrieks echoing through the pines.

Scorchfur.

Lionblaze glimpsed the streak of gray pelt a moment before the ShadowClan warrior rammed him. He fell skidding across the needles, slowing himself by digging his claws deep into the earth. *Scorchfur has no idea who he's dealing with.* Drawing himself to his paws, Lionblaze faced his attacker.

Scorchfur's face was a mask of anger. The gray tom's eyes were lit with a self-righteous rage, as though he'd been wronged by this battle.

Maybe he had.

Lionblaze felt his paws freeze.

All this because of the dream of one apprentice. An apprentice who'd never before shown any sign of a connection with StarClan.

He shook the doubt away.

Ivypaw was Dovepaw's sister. That was proof enough that they could trust her.

Scorchfur reared and clawed at his ear. Lionblaze felt only a distant prick of pain. Power was stirring beneath his pelt. Strength rose from his belly, flooding every muscle.

Around him the battle seemed to slow down.

The cats fought as if in water, each blow an arcing sweep of paw, each lunge a dragging leap that Lionblaze could watch unfold moment upon moment. Around him, the shrieking seemed to fade, and yet he saw curses billow from snarling jaws.

He saw Snowbird face Rosepetal, her green eyes betraying

every thought as they flitted like butterflies, assessing Rose-petal's position, moving to fix on her strike point, half closing as she bunched her muscles and prepared to jump.

This is too easy. Lionblaze strode forward, flipping Owlclaw from his path, knocking Redwillow backward as the warrior attempted to lunge. Lionblaze saw Rowanclaw's gaze fix on him, heard the breath gasp from his mouth as he crouched for the attack, felt the rush of air as slowly the warrior flew at him, teeth bared. Lionblaze had only to rear up and raise a paw to bat him backward into his Clanmates.

A yowl, deep and slow, sounded at the edge of the clearing.

Spinning around, he saw Firestar with Russetfur at his throat. The ShadowClan deputy had sunk her teeth deep into the ThunderClan leader's neck. Firestar was trying to shake her off, but she allowed her body to be thrashed back and forth, her jaws clamped shut while Firestar staggered, paws slithering in his own blood.

Lionblaze lunged for the ShadowClan deputy. He swiped at her, raking her flank with claws half-sheathed. He only wanted her to release her grip. But she writhed and lashed out, still holding Firestar's throat.

Firestar sank slowly to his belly, rings of white showing around the rims of his wide-stretched eyes.

Desperate now, Lionblaze flung his paws around Rus-setfur's neck and hauled her off. As she let go, he lurched backward, his paws still wrapped tightly around her scrawny body. He landed heavily, sprawling on his back, and Russetfur collapsed on him like a deadweight.

The noise of battle suddenly flooded his ears; the screeching mayhem crashed into his consciousness like a wave breaking.

"You killed Russetfur!" Owlclaw's wail split the air.

Lionblaze scrambled to his paws. The she-cat flopped, unmoving, onto the ground, her eyes wide-open but clouded with death.

His breath came in panicked gasps. "I d-didn't do anything!" He hadn't even scratched her. Only pulled her loose. How could she be dead?

Blackstar barged past him and crouched over her limp body. "Russetfur!" He shook his deputy with his heavy black paws, but she didn't stir. "Russetfur!"

"Enough!" Brambleclaw shook Ratscar from his back and sat up. "The battle is won," he growled. "The clearing is ours. Do you concede or shall we fight for it again?"

Blackstar flashed a look of burning hatred over his shoulder. "Take it," he hissed. "It was never worth the blood that has been spilled here today."

Around them the battle stuttered and stumbled. Confusion filled the air as Lionblaze stood, frozen, wrapped in horror until Sorreltail shrieked.

"Firestar!"

Turning in a daze, Lionblaze saw blood pool around Firestar's neck. The ThunderClan leader twitched, his flanks falling still. His tail snaked behind him, dead as prey.

He's losing a life!

The ground lurched beneath Lionblaze. This wasn't supposed to happen!

ShadowClan warriors began to gather around Russetfur's body. They pressed forward to lick her fast-cooling fur.

Lionblaze backed away.

Sorreltail leaned over Firestar, her eyes clouding as Sandstorm appeared at the edge of the trees.

"What's wrong?" The orange she-cat raced to crouch at her mate's side.

"He's losing a life," Sorreltail reported grimly.

Two deaths?

What kind of battle was this? StarClan would never have sent a dream to lead them into a battle this deadly. A thought flickered in Lionblaze's mind. His fur, sticky with the blood of other warriors, grew cold. A black, sucking hollow opened like a pit in his belly.

What if this dream hadn't come from StarClan? What if it had been sent from beyond StarClan's hunting grounds? Had *Dark Forest* warriors sent them on this fatal battle against their rivals? Two senior cats dead—one who would never recover—and many more warriors and apprentices badly wounded? Both Clans would be weak for a long time, right at the beginning of leaf-bare. StarClan would never have wanted this, not over a strip of grass that was useless to either Clan.

Lionblaze stared at Russetfur's and Firestar's unmoving bodies.

Warriors filed silently past him, gathering, dazed, beside the dead.

This battle should never have happened!

ERIN HUNTER

is inspired by a love of cats and a fascination with the ferocity of the natural world. As well as having great respect for nature in all its forms, Erin enjoys creating rich mythical explanations for animal behavior. She is also the author of the bestselling Seekers and Survivors series.

Download the free Warriors app and chat on Warriors message boards at www.warriorcats.com.

Visit www.warriorcats.com
to download game rules, character sheets,
a practice mission, and more!

Written by Stan! • Art by James L. Barry

THE PLAINTIVE HOWLS

Whichever previous adventure you played, consider that three moons have passed since then. Determine what age that makes all of the cat characters (including the one belonging to the person who will take the first turn as Narrator) and use the information found in the "Improving Your Cat" section of Chapter Four in the game rules to make the necessary changes.

Unless you are the first Narrator in this adventure, stop reading here. The information beginning in the next paragraph is for the Narrator only.

The Adventure Begins

Hello, Narrator! It's time to begin playing "The Plaintive Howls." Make sure all the players have their character sheets, the correct number of chips, a piece of paper, and a pencil. Remember that the point of the game is to have fun. Don't be afraid to go slow, and refer to the rules if you aren't sure exactly what should happen next.

When you're ready, begin with **1** below.

1. Yowls in the Night

Special Note: If the players' cats are not from the same Clan, play out this scene as though a similar string of events is happening in each of the cats' Clans. The Narrator should let each of the players ask questions and explain that all the Clans have the same worries. In the end, the various leaders decide that it is best to send a group of cats from different Clans to investigate. By the final part of this scene, all the players' cats should be together to make the important Skill Check.

Read Aloud: "You wake up in the morning to find the Clan in disarray. The queens are tending to frightened kits, and even the senior warriors seem a little bit unnerved. There were strange sounds in the night—sounds no cat can explain."

Narrator Tips: This adventure opens with a Clan meeting, which the Clan leader has called to talk about the alarming sounds in the distance.

In the middle of the night, the warrior on duty heard a far-off yowling. The commotion awoke other members of the Clan. If any of the players' cats have a level of 5 or higher in the Listen Skill, they were awakened by the sound, too.

Some Clan cats thought the sound was indistinct, like an animal howling in pain. Others thought that it sounded distinctly like a cat crying out for help. As the wind picked up, the yowling grew louder and clearer. It soon became apparent that it was more than just a single yowl—several different voices could be heard, some crying in pain or fear, others calling out for help.

As the Narrator, your job in this scene is to get the players to understand that this is a situation that none of the cats can explain. The answer to many of the players' questions will be: "No one knows yet. . . . It's your job to find out." Be sure not to rush through the scene. Let the players ask all the questions they want, even if the answers are not reassuring.

When the players have run out of questions to ask or are anxious to know what happens next, inform them that the Clan leader has chosen them to investigate this mysterious yowling. They are to follow the sounds for as long and far as it takes to find the truth and do whatever they can to help ease the suffering of whoever is crying out.

Again, allow the players' cats to ask as many questions as they like (though the answers still won't seem very helpful). If they ask for any reasonable supplies (for example, traveling herbs), the Clan leader will grant the request.

As the players' cats set out on the trip, the sound of the yowling rises and falls. Mostly it is a background noise that is hard to distinguish from the wind. But sometimes it grows loud enough that the cats can all agree that it is the sound of some unknown number of cats calling for help, though none of them are voices they recognize.

What Happens Next: After they have been on the trail for a while, ask each of the players what his or her cat's Focus score is (the number they get by adding their levels of Focus to their Spirit score). At this point they cannot use any Knacks or spend any chips to improve their results—this is simply testing their natural ability to concentrate and ignore the distractions around them. Add up the results of all the Focus Checks to get a group total.

If the group total is equal to 16 or higher, continue with **3**.

If the group total is lower than 16, continue with **2**.

2. Chasing the Wind

Read Aloud: "The sound is certainly coming from the north. No . . . wait . . . perhaps that's the east."

Narrator Tips: The wind is playing tricks on the cats as they try to follow the yowling. Describe their progress as they follow the sounds for a while until the noise disappears. Then a few minutes later the crying sound seems to be coming from a different direction entirely.

If any of the cats have the Pathfinder Knack, they realize that the sounds are leading the group in circles. If none of the cats has that Knack, tell the cats to each make a Ponder Check. The cat (or cats) with the highest total comes up with the same realization, but not as quickly or as certainly as a cat with the Pathfinder Knack.

As they follow the yowling sounds, one by one the voices fade out until there is just a single cat's voice crying on the wind—sad, mournful, and weak. This makes it easier to track. Now one cat must take the lead and use his or her Listen Skill to try to follow the sound. Have the players decide which cat that will be. Once the decision is made, tell them that their cats can help, too. Any cat that wants to help can attempt a single Listen Check. In this case, they can use Knacks and spend chips if they wish. Make a note of how many cats get a Listen Check total of 7 or higher.

Then have the lead cat make a Listen Check, using Knacks or spending chips if the player wants to. Increase this Listen Check result by +1 for every assisting cat who got a total of 7 or higher. Increase it by an additional +1 for every cat in the group who has the Pathfinder Knack.

What Happens Next: If the final Listen Check total, including all bonuses, is 12 or higher, continue with **3.**

If the final Listen Check, including all bonuses, is between 6 and 11, continue with **4.**

If the final Listen Check total, including all bonuses, is less than 6, continue with **5.**

3. The Culprit

Read Aloud: "The sound of the yowling is getting clearer, but it's also getting weaker. It seems you've found the source just as it is fading away."

Narrator Tips: The cats have found the source of the yowling—Burr, a cat trapped in a Twoleg cage. The difficult thing for you, as the Narrator, is that the cats don't really have words for things like "cage" so describing the scene may be tough. They will probably think of the cage as a "den" that is hard and cold to the touch. For your sake, here are the details in plain English.

Burr is a rogue who was traveling in the area to the north of the Lake. He smelled food and followed it to an area where humans from a regional animal shelter had set up some "capture and carry" traps. Burr wandered into one of the cages and became trapped. He's been here for almost a full day now and has been crying for help practically the whole time. As he did, he could hear other cats begin to do the same thing. He guesses they must be trapped in similar cages, but he can't see any of them.

At this point, Burr is weak from exhaustion. It is only pure luck and a strong wind that let his and the other cats' cries be carried as far away as the Lake. Or perhaps it was the desperation in their voices and intervention from StarClan. Let the players' cats talk to Burr for a while and consult among themselves about what to do. The cage is built out of steel and it is attached to the ground. In other words, nothing the cats do will damage or move it.

Burr will be as helpful as he can be, but he doesn't really understand what's going on. Also, he's stuck in a cage and cannot see what the cats are doing once they walk too far away. He'll still shout out whatever seems helpful, and you can use that as a way to give hints to the players' cats in any other scenes as long as they are relatively near Burr's cage.

There are two other bits of information that will become clear to the cats as they investigate the situation. First, there's a smell of food in the air—not good fresh-kill but definitely food. Second, there's a new sound on the wind—the sound of Twolegs as they chatter away somewhere nearby.

What Happens Next: If the cats decide to investigate the smell of food, this is the end of the chapter. Pass the adventure to the next Narrator and tell him or her to continue with **6**.

If the cats decide to investigate the sounds of Twoleg activity, this is the end of the chapter. Pass the adventure to the next Narrator and tell him or her to continue with **7**.

4. The Fading Voice

Read Aloud: "As darkness draws near, the sound of the yowling fades away completely. You'll have to find somewhere warm to spend the night and continue searching in the morning."

Narrator Tips: The cats were unable to find the source of the sounds, though they've come close. Still, with the light fading, they will have to camp for the night. Take this as an opportunity to let them do some more talking among themselves or perhaps a bit of hunting for fresh-kill to eat; then have them get what sleep they can.

If they want to set up a watch during the night, have each cat attempt a Listen Check during his or her turn. They do not hear any more of the yowling. However, if you as the Narrator want to improvise some excitement during the night, perhaps one of the cats can hear an owl or encounter a skunk or a raccoon. While such an encounter can be fun, make sure the players and their cats remember that the focus of the adventure is finding the source of the yowling.

In the morning, the cats smell a bitter, meaty scent on the wind. It's not fresh-kill, but it's definitely food. What's more, they hear a new sound—the sound of Twolegs chattering away in their strange voices.

What Happens Next: If the cats decide to investigate the smell of food, continue with **6**.

If the cats decide to investigate the sounds of Twoleg activity, this is the end of the chapter. Pass the adventure to the next Narrator and tell him or her to continue with **7**.

If the cats decide to avoid both of these opportunities and keep looking elsewhere in the woods for the source of the yowling, continue with **5**.

5. Lost in the Woods

Read Aloud: "The woods grow thick, and although you hear many sounds, none of them are the yowls for help that you were sent to investigate."

Narrator Tips: Let the cats investigate a bit further. Perhaps they find a grove of trees where some squirrels are scampering about, or a pond filled with leaping fish. But the one thing they do not find is any new sign of whoever was responsible for the yowls in the night.

After a little while make it clear to them that they have wandered so far off track that they've lost the trail entirely. There is no way they will ever solve the mystery.

What Happens Next: The cats will have to return to their camp and tell the Clan that they failed to find the source of the yowling. The Clan leader will tell them that the yowling has stopped, so maybe there was nothing to worry about in the first place. Still, the night guard will be doubled for the next moon, just in case the yowling returns.

Although they tried hard, the cats do not get any Experience rewards for this adventure. The group can, however, play the adventure again, hopefully changing some of their tactics so that they get a better result the next time.

6. A Strange Den

Read Aloud: "The food smell is coming from a peculiar pile of leaves. At first you thought it was a small bush, but no bush actually grows like that. It looks like the leaves and branches were torn off the plants from which they came and placed here intentionally like some kind of nest. But why? And why is the food smell coming from within this nest?"

Narrator Tips: Although the cats can't figure it out for certain yet, the leaves and branches were put here by humans in an attempt to camouflage a cage. The food smell is from a small mouse that has been placed inside the cage as bait. To Clan cats it is obvious the mouse has been dead too long to make a good meal, and it smells strange—unnaturally clean and with a lingering scent of Twolegs.

Let the cats poke around and investigate as they like. Depending on what they do, you may want to allow them to

try Ponder, See, or Smell Checks to see if they notice particular details (in general, a total of 6 should be enough to allow them to observe interesting details, all of which should point to the involvement of Twolegs). Remember not to use words like "cage" or "metal." Try to describe the scene in terms that the cats would use—words like "den" or "thicket" or "nest."

The cats can pull the leaves off the "den," peek inside, sniff the food from a distance, or explore in any other way the players can think of. There is only one way to enter the cage and a particularly brave, curious, or foolhardy cat may try it. Other cats may avoid the cage and begin looking farther away. Those cats will discover more nests of leaves that have the same bitter food scent.

In addition, the cats now hear the sound of Twoleg voices chattering in the distance.

What Happens Next: If any cat decides to go into the cage, continue with **8.**

If the cats decide to investigate the other food smells nearby, continue with **9.**

If the cats decide to ignore the food smell and investigate the sounds of Twoleg activity, this is the end of the chapter. Pass the adventure to the next Narrator and tell him or her to continue with **7.**

7. The Twoleg Camp

Read Aloud: "Following the sounds of the Twolegs is easy. They apparently know nothing about stealth or subtlety. The question isn't whether or not you can find their camp; the question is what you'll do once you're there."

Narrator Tips: Finding the camp is so easy that the cats do not even have to make any Skill Checks. They can simply follow the chattering sound of the Twolegs calling out to one another. After a short journey, the cats find themselves atop a ridge that looks down on the Twoleg camp. It is a strange sight, not like a usual Twolegplace.

Two of the Twolegs' monsters (larger than average) sit there, and both appear to be asleep. There is also a strange den of some sort. It's made of some kind of soft skin that blows and flaps in the wind. And Twolegs are *everywhere*. There is also a faint cat scent coming from the Twoleg camp—enough cats to make up a small Clan—but no matter how hard the players' cats search, they can't see any cats down there.

The description above covers how the cats will see the scene, but as the Narrator you should have a clearer understanding. This is a temporary camp set up by people who work for a regional animal shelter. They have come to the woods to capture some of the wild cats, give them shots and other medical treatment, and take some of the healthier cats back to town where they can be adopted. In other words, these are good people who have only the best interests of the cats in mind, but the cats will think they are terrible threats.

The Twolegs have come in two vans (one contains supplies; the other has cages to capture, hold, and eventually transport cats). The Twolegs have also erected a tent where they've set up a makeshift animal hospital.

Allow the players' cats to look down at this scene for as long as they like. The players may speculate about what is going on, but don't give them any clear indications. Any cat that has the Twoleg Lore Knack can try to make a Ponder Check to get an idea of what's going on, but even that is quite difficult. The Check must have a total of 15 just for the cat to have a rough idea what all these sights and smells mean. Even then, the best he or she is likely to do is get a vague connection between these Twolegs and the "cutter" (a veterinarian's office), something that probably won't put the group's minds at ease.

The cats will have to decide on what their next move will be. The answers to the mysterious yowling lie somewhere in the Twoleg camp, but going there will pose a new set of dangers.

What Happens Next: If the cats decide to sneak into the Twoleg camp and take a closer look, continue with **11**.

If the cats are truly undecided as to what to do, or if they start and stop different courses of action, or if you as the Narrator think it would make the adventure more interesting, a few of the Twolegs can just happen to notice them up on the ridge. The Twolegs will try to approach the cats. Continue with **12**.

8. It's a Trap!

Special Note: It's possible for the cats to get to this scene while exploring a second or third cage. If they do, you'll want to improvise a more suitable description than the Read Aloud section below. If the cats have encountered one of these traps before, their focus will likely be on something other than the food inside.

Read Aloud: "The food inside the strange den smells awful, like kittypet food. Just as you're getting close enough to get a good sniff, the entrance to the den collapses with a loud crashing noise!"

Narrator Tips: Once the trap has been triggered, the cage door springs closed in an attempt to capture the cat inside. These are humane traps, meant to keep the cat from being hurt, but that doesn't mean they aren't frightening, so be sure to describe the scene in a scary way.

The cat may not be trapped in the cage. If the player wishes, his or her cat may attempt a Jump Check (using any Knacks or spending as many chips as he or she likes) to try to escape the "den" before its roof collapses. If the Jump Check total is equal to 13 or higher, the cat manages to get out before the door

swings shut. If the total is 12 or lower, the cat is caught inside.
What Happens Next: If the cat managed to escape the cage without being trapped, continue with **9**.

If the cat is caught in the cage and decides to eat the food, continue with **10**.

If the cat is caught in the cage and decides to search for ways to escape, continue with **13**.

9. More Dens

Read Aloud: "Scattered around the nearby woods you find several more leafy nests surrounding similar strange dens, each of which has the same bitter food smell coming from inside."
Narrator Tips: The Twolegs have been very busy in these woods. They have set a series of traps, hoping to capture as many "stray" cats as possible. The players' cats can't really understand that, but it should be clear that something strange is going on here and that the Twolegs are probably involved. The sound of their voices is now a constant background noise carried by the wind.

Let the cats explore as much as they want. Every new "den" they find is another opportunity for a cat to be tempted by the food scent or perhaps try exploring the cage out of pure curiosity. As before, you may want to allow the players to make Ponder, Smell, See, or other Checks for their cats. There isn't anything new to find here, but they can certainly discover any of the facts or clues that were present in earlier scenes. Again, the Twoleg Lore Knack will probably be the most useful information gathering tool at the cats' disposal.
What Happens Next: If the cats decide to investigate the sounds of Twoleg activity, this is the end of the chapter. Pass the adventure to the next Narrator and tell him or her to continue with **7**.

If any of the cats tries to enter one of the new cages, continue with **8**.

10. A Snack for Strength

Read Aloud: "This looks like a mouse—but it's not at all fresh and there are other bitter tastes in there, too."

Narrator Tips: To a Clan cat, anything but freshly killed meat is a very poor meal, and this one is especially bad. The humans have spiked the meat with mild sedatives to calm the captured cats and, hopefully, put them to sleep until they can be collected.

Any cat who eats this food immediately loses 5 chips because of the drugs. He or she must then make a Spirit Check. If the total of this Check is 9 or lower, the sedatives cause the cat to fall asleep. If the total is 10 or higher, the cat remains awake but is drowsy and will be unable to do much other than talk for at least the next few hours.

What Happens Next: Unlike in previous adventures, it is possible for some of the cats to be knocked out of the adventure while the rest of the group goes on. The cat who is stuck in this cage is now out of the game. However, tell that player there is a chance that the other cats will be able to rescue his or her character if they go through the rest of the adventure successfully. He or she should stay in the game and help the others, if only by giving advice.

The adventure may continue in several different ways, depending on what the remaining cats want to do.

If they want to explore some of the remaining cages, continue with **9**.

If Burr is still around and they want to talk to him more, continue with **3**.

If they want to investigate the sounds of Twoleg activity, this is the end of the chapter. Pass the adventure to the next Narrator and tell him or her to continue with **7**.

11. Sneaking into the Camp

Read Aloud: "The mixture of strange sights and smells is overwhelming. It's difficult at first to tell one sensation from another, especially while trying to stay out of the constant bustle of the Twolegs rushing back and forth."

Narrator Tips: Before getting any further into the scene, tell the players that it is now time to refresh their chips. Any chips that were spent on Skill or Ability Checks are now brought back into the cats' chip pool, but any chips lost to injury remain lost. (See Chapter Five of the game rules for a full explanation.) Note that this only happens the first time the cats play through this scene. The adventure may lead them back here several times, but they only get to refresh their chips once.

The point of this scene is to let the cats sneak into the camp and begin exploring. Because this action is so unpredictable, you as Narrator will mostly have to react to what the players want their cats to attempt. Your main job is to give them information about what they see. There are three main areas in the Twoleg camp for the cats to explore (though the cats will not know them by these names).

The Medical Tent: This is the "strange den" the cats saw in scene 7. As they get closer it will seem even stranger. The tent is set up to provide a fairly clean area for the vets to do medical examinations. Any cat who makes a Smell Check with a total of 5 or higher can tell that there are at least six separate cat scents in this area. But anyone whose total is 8 or higher knows that most of those are stale and that only two cats are in there right now.

The Supply Van: This is one of the "sleeping monsters" that the cats saw in scene 7. It is a minivan that the people from the animal shelter have used to carry their supplies to this remote location. The Twolegs are constantly going to the van, opening it, taking out some needed items, and closing it back up. Whenever the van is opened, the cats can catch a number of distinct scents. Any cat that attempts a Smell Check is at first overwhelmed by the mixture, but if the check total is 5 or higher he or she can identify a single specific item. For every two points the total is above that, the cat can identify another specific item (so if the total is 7 the cat can identify two items, if the total is 9 then three items, and so on). The items in the van include: The kind of food that's used in the traps, medicine, rubbing alcohol and other medical cleaning solutions, and any other items the Narrator thinks the animal shelter people would have brought with them.

The Transport Van: This is the other "sleeping monster" the cats saw in scene 7. It is a minivan that is set up to carry cats. The back of the van has been outfitted with a series of electronically locked cages, each large enough to hold a single cat. The Twolegs' plan is to bring back as many healthy, adoptable cats as they can, thinking that they are saving these cats from a life of hardship. The Twolegs don't open this van as frequently as they do the other one, but when they do, the unmistakable scent of live, healthy cats comes out. If the players' cats want to try to tell how many cats are inside the van, they have to make a Smell Check. If the total is 5 or higher, they know that there are at least eight cats in the van. If the total is 8 or higher, they know that there are exactly ten cats in the van. For every 2 points higher than that, they can pick out the scent of individual cats (so if the total is 10 they can smell one specific cat, if the total is 12 they can smell two, and so on). This may be important because any of the players' cats that got captured—either in the cages or by clever Twolegs—will be among those inside this van.

What Happens Next: The next step in the adventure depends entirely on where the cats choose to explore.

If the cats decide to explore the Medical Tent, continue with **15**.

If the cats decide to explore the Supply Van, continue with **16**.

If the cats decide to explore the Transport Van, continue with **17**.

If the Narrator thinks the cats are too bold and make it easy for the Twolegs to notice them, continue with **12**.

12. Spotted!

Read Aloud: "With a start, you realize that one of the Twolegs has seen you! It's heading this way!"

Narrator Tips: There are several ways the players' cats may end up in this scene and it may come up several times over the course of the adventure. Your job as Narrator is to improvise ways to make each one fit the current context.

Remember that while the cats see the Twolegs as threats, the Twolegs really just care about the health and well-being of all cats. They will try to be as friendly and calming as they can. They'll offer food and try to scratch the cats behind the ears and speak in a soothing tone. But the players' cats will misinterpret these friendly gestures as being aggressive moves.

There isn't really any more complication to this scene than figuring out if any of the cats get captured by the Twolegs. Any cat that lets the Twolegs get close enough to touch him or her is in danger of being captured. After petting the cat for a few moments, the Twoleg will try to grab him or her. At that point, the cat may make a Jump Check. If the total is 12 or higher, the cat escapes the attempted grab and can act freely. If the total is lower, though, the cat has been captured.

Any cat who eats the offered food immediately loses 5 chips because it has been drugged with sedatives. He or she must make a Spirit Check. If the total of this Check is 9 or lower, the sedatives cause the cat to fall asleep. If the total is 10 or higher, the cat remains awake but is going to be drowsy

and will be unable to do much other than talk for at least the next ten minutes.

Like in previous scenes, any captured cat has the possibility of returning later on in the adventure if the remaining cats can figure out how to free him or her. Beyond that, the only question is where the remaining cats go next.

If the cats stay away from the Twolegs and dash off into the woods or to another part of the camp, the Twolegs will not give chase. They have too much to do and too many cats to treat.

What Happens Next: Not all of these options will be available in each case. The details will depend on where the cats are spotted and what escape routes are possible.

If the cats decide they want to try to fight the Twoleg that is trying to grab them, continue with **18**.

If any of the cats are captured, continue with **14**.

If the cats escape into the outer camp area, continue with **11**, but do not refresh the chips again (that only happens the first time the cats go through scene 11).

If the cats escape to the Medical Tent, continue with **15**.

If the cats escape to the area near the Supply Van, continue with **16**.

If the cats escape to the area near the Transport Van, continue with **17**.

13. Difficult Choices

Read Aloud: "The strange den entrance has collapsed! You're trapped!"

Narrator Tips: One of the cats is trapped in a Twoleg cage. While the rest of the cats are nearby and can talk to the cat inside, this scene is about what that trapped cat does next.

To be honest, there are very few choices, and none of them are particularly appealing. But sometimes that's what happens when a cat pokes his or her nose into a dangerous place.

One choice is for the cat to eat the strange-smelling food

that has been placed in the cage.

Another choice is to try to push, claw, and squeeze his or her way out through the small gaps in the cage's construction. This is unlikely to succeed, and very likely to cause the cat some injury. Try to explain this clearly to the player before he or she decides on this course of action. If the player cannot be dissuaded, have the cat attempt a Strength Check to try to muscle his or her way out of the cage.

If the Strength Check total is 7 or lower, nothing happens. If the total is between 8 and 14, the cat is wounded by the sharp metal of the cage. The cat loses 4 chips due to the injury and is still trapped in the cage. If the total is between 15 and 20, the cat manages to squeeze out of the cage and is free, but still loses 6 chips in the process due to cuts, scrapes, and bruises. If the Strength Check total is 21 or higher, the cat manages to get out of the cage while suffering only minor wounds—he or she loses only 3 chips due to injury.

A final choice that a trapped cat may make is to simply sit down and wait. In this case, the cat will probably encourage his or her friends to search out some kind of way to open the cage (perhaps to be found wherever the Twolegs are).

If the player seems to be considering this course of action, assure him or her that there is a chance that the other cats will be able to rescue his or her character if they go through the rest of the adventure successfully. He or she should stay in the game and help the others, if only by giving advice.

What Happens Next: If the trapped cat decides to eat the food, continue with **10**.

The adventure may continue in several different ways, depending entirely on what the cats as a group decide to do. If the cat in the cage managed to escape, consult the choices below. Likewise, use those choices for the free cats if they want to search for a way to rescue their trapped companion. However, once the cats move along, the trapped cat will be collected by a Twoleg who comes by and carries the cage back to the Twoleg camp. As Narrator, you can tell the player this privately but be sure to also say that the adventure will provide the chance for the other cats to rescue his or her character later on.

If they want to explore some of the remaining cages, continue with **9**.

If Burr is still around and they want to talk to him more, continue with **3**.

If they want to investigate the sounds of Twoleg activity, this is the end of the chapter. Pass the adventure to the next Narrator and tell him or her to continue with **7**.

14. Captured!

Read Aloud: "With a quick snap of a massive paw, the Twoleg grabs you and lifts you into the air!"

Narrator Tips: There are several ways the players' cats may end up in this scene and it may come up several times over the course of the adventure. Your job as Narrator is to improvise ways to make each one fit the current context.

Once a cat has been captured, the Twoleg will carry him or her away, either to the Medical Tent (where the cat will get a sedative to calm him or her down) or to the Transport Van (where he or she will be placed in a cage to await medical treatment or the trip back to town).

Again, the humans are not doing this to be mean. They believe they are doing what's best for the cats.

As in previous scenes, any captured cat has the possibility of returning later on in the adventure if the remaining cats can figure out how to free him or her. Beyond that, the only question is where the remaining cats go next.

What Happens Next: Not all of these options will be available in each case. The details will depend on where the remaining cats are and what escape routes are possible.

If the cats escape to the outer camp area, continue with **11** but do not refresh the chips again. (That only happens the first time the cats go through scene 11.)

If the cats escape to the Medical Tent, continue with **15**.

If the cats decide to explore the Supply Van, continue with **16**.

If the cats decide to explore the Transport Van, continue with **17**.

If all of the cats have been captured, continue with **23**.

15. The Clean Den

Read Aloud: "By staying close to the edge of the soft-skinned den, you can sneak in close enough to stick your nose inside and see what's going on."

Narrator Tips: In this scene, the cats get to poke around in the Medical Tent. This is the busiest part of the Twoleg camp, so it is also the place where it is easiest for the cats to be seen and perhaps captured. Encourage the players to come up with clever ways for their cats to avoid detection and, if they seem reasonable, allow them to work.

Of course, you should still have the cats make a few Skill or Attribute Checks that seem appropriate for the situation—Sneak, Ponder, Focus, Listen, and Smell all could be useful depending on what the cats are trying to do.

This scene is called "The Clean Den" because that will be

the most striking thing about the tent from the cats' perspective. The tent has been set up like a little mini veterinarian's office in the woods. There is a small examination table, bright lights, and a cart filled with medical equipment, bandages, and useful drugs. It will smell strongly of antiseptics and the humans will do everything possible to keep dirt and other contaminants from the forest out of the tent.

While the cats are looking around, the doctors will be examining a cat. If possible, that cat should be a character the players have met before—either one of the captured player cats or Burr—just to give the scene a little more drama. If the cat is awake, it will be yowling angrily whenever the Twolegs poke and prod him or her.

Any cat that has the Herb Lore Knack may attempt a Ponder Check (using that Knack if the player so desires). If the Check total is 5 or higher, the cat notices some vaguely familiar scents mixed in with the antiseptics. If the total is 8 or higher, the cat realizes that some of the things in this den are similar to healing herbs that a medicine cat uses. If the total is 12 or higher, the cat is able to pick out a specific medicine smell and equate it to a specific healing herb.

Allow the cats to poke around for as long as the players remain interested. However, if they try anything particularly outlandish, there is a chance that the Twolegs will notice them.

What Happens Next: If the Narrator thinks the cats make it easy for the Twolegs to notice them, continue with **12**.

If the cats decide to attack the Twolegs in hopes of freeing their friend, continue with **18**.

If the cats return to the outer camp area, continue with **11** but do not refresh the chips again. (That only happens the first time the cats go through scene 11.)

If the cats decide to explore the Supply Van, continue with **16**.

If the cats decide to explore the Transport Van, continue with **17**.

16. A Sleeping Monster

Read Aloud: "The monster continues to sleep, despite the fact that the Twolegs keep coming over and trying to wake it up."

Narrator Tips: In this scene the cats can examine the Supply Van and watch as the humans come and go, taking things from the van and occasionally depositing bags of garbage generated by the work happening in the Medical Tent.

The Twolegs aren't doing anything special in this part of the camp, which makes it a good place for the players' cats to hide and catch their breath after being chased. This also may be the first time the cats have ever had the opportunity to examine a Twoleg monster. The fact that it is so soundly asleep should allow them to be bolder than they usually would be around such a beast. If the players decide their cats want to take this opportunity, be creative in your descriptions. Try to describe the various shapes and parts of the van as they would

appear to a cat and encourage an air of mystery and wonder.

This examination is interrupted periodically as the Twolegs come back and try to wake up the monster. (As the Narrator, you know they're really just getting supplies from the van.) Have the cats make Ponder Checks as they watch this. If the Check total is 6 or higher, the cats realize that the Twolegs are performing specific actions in order to get the monster to react in certain ways.

What Happens Next: If the cats want to keep examining the monster, this is the end of the chapter. Pass the adventure to the next Narrator and tell him or her to continue with **19**.

If the cats return to the outer camp area, continue with **11** but do not refresh the chips again. (That only happens the first time the cats go through scene 11.)

If the cats decide to explore the Medical Tent, continue with **15**.

If the cats decide to explore the Transport Van, continue with **17**.

17. A Wall of Dens

Read Aloud: "Like the other monster, this one appears to be sleeping, but the Twolegs do not seem to be trying nearly as hard to wake it up."

Narrator Tips: In this scene the cats can examine the Transport Van and watch as the humans occasionally carry over a sedated cat from the Medical Tent and put it into a cage inside the van. When the cats can see the inside of the van, they see a huge wall of metal dens (like those they saw in the early scenes in this adventure), many of which have cats inside them.

This may be the first time the cats have ever been this close to a Twoleg monster, but the fact that it is so soundly asleep should allow them to be bolder than they usually would be around such a beast. As the cats examine the situation, be creative in your descriptions. Try to describe the various shapes

and parts of the van as they would appear to a cat and encourage an air of mystery and wonder.

As they poke around the van, the players' cats can smell the fear from the cats inside the monster. Not only that, if they make a Smell Check with a total of 8 or higher, they can pick out all the individual scents of the cats inside (which include Burr and any of the players' cats that have been captured).

This examination is interrupted occasionally as the Twolegs come back and place more cats inside the monster. Have the players' cats make Ponder Checks as they watch this. If the Check total is 6 or higher, the cats realize that the Twolegs are performing some kind of specific action in order to get the monster to react in certain ways.

What Happens Next: If the cats want to stay and keep examining the monster, this is the end of the chapter. Pass the adventure to the next Narrator and tell him or her to continue with **19**.

If the cats return to the outer camp area, continue with **11** but do not refresh the chips again. (That only happens the first time the cats go through scene 11.)

If the cats decide to explore the Medical Tent, continue with **15**.

If the cats decide to explore the Supply Van, continue with **16**.

18. A Desperate Fight

Read Aloud: "The Twolegs are big and they're strong, but sometimes being a warrior means standing your ground and fighting, even when winning seems impossible."

Narrator Tips: Clan cats fighting against humans is a lost cause, but that doesn't mean that some of the players won't want their cats to try it.

One thing that a cat can do effectively is intimidate a Twoleg opponent. Despite their smaller size, cats that show enough ferociousness can cause a Twoleg to hesitate and be more careful, shifting the odds considerably. A cat who performs a Hiss or Arch Check with a total of 15 or higher will get an automatic +3 bonus to all Bite, Swat, and Wrestle Checks for the rest of the fight. If the cat can get totals of 15 or higher in both Checks, he or she can double that bonus, getting a +6 in those Checks for the rest of the fight.

While it's not possible for a cat to severely hurt a Twoleg opponent, he or she can get in some painful scratches. Twolegs do not Jump out of the way in combat; they pull their hands back out of reach. That movement functions the same way a Jump does for a cat. Treat attacking Twolegs as though their hands have Jump scores of 10.

Treat this the same as if two or more cats were Wrestling, though the Twolegs' Checks always have a total of 13. In order to pick up a cat, the Twolegs must win a Wrestling Check. As long as the cat wins, he or she is writhing around too much for the Twolegs to pick up him or her.

Once a cat has been lifted into the air, the fight is over.

Any time before that happens, the cat may decide to end the fight by running away.

What Happens Next: If the cat is lifted into the air, the Twolegs will put him or her into a cage. The adventure is over for that cat, though he or she can still be rescued if the other cats manage to figure out how to release the trapped cats from the Transport Van.

If all the cats are captured, continue with **23**.

If the cat decides to run away, or if the other cats run away after their friend is captured, the next step in the adventure depends on where they decide to go.

If the cats escape to the outer camp area, continue with **11** but do not refresh the chips again. (That only happens the first time the cats go through scene 11.)

If the cats escape to the Medical Tent, continue with **15**.

If the cats escape to the Supply Van, continue with **16**.

If the cats escape to the Transport Van, continue with **17**.

19. The Monster's Secret

Read Aloud: "As you watch the Twolegs walk up to the monster, briefly wake it up, then leave as it falls back to sleep, you notice that there's some kind of pattern involved. Is this some kind of ritual that only partially wakens the monsters?"

Narrator Tips: The secret is that these are the kind of vans where you can set the side door to automatically open, and the people from the animal shelter have done just that to make their coming and going easier. This would be very easy for another person to figure out, but it wouldn't be nearly so obvious to a cat.

This is another scene where your job, as Narrator, is to describe an ordinary action in a way that seems strange and exotic as seen through the eyes of the cats. There are several parts of what the Twolegs are doing that the cats are likely to focus on.

- Some cats may think it has something to do with particular sounds the Twolegs are making—a song or phrase that makes the monster partially wake up.
- Some cats may think that it is a ritual involving the Twolegs walking around the camp. They leave the monster, walk a specific pattern, then come back and the monster

will wake up only for a few brief moments.

- Some cats may think that it has to do with some special shiny stones a few of the Twolegs carry with them (the keys to the van). While that is partially true, the keys are not necessary to open the door at this time.
- Finally, some cats may think correctly that it is the act of giving the monster's side (the van's sliding door) a solid hit.

Let the players talk about it for a while; then have the cats all make Ponder Checks. Add the totals of all the Checks together to get a group total. As long as that group total is 12 or higher, the cats have the right idea—that the key is hitting the side of the monster in a special way.

If the group total is less than 12, tell the cats that they are certain that the correct answer is one of the choices above *other* than the real one. This will result in some strange behavior by the cats—behavior that will *not* open the van door. Once they have tried and failed once or twice, let them make another round of Ponder Checks and use them to increase the group total. Repeat this as necessary until the group total is 12 or higher.

Once the cats have the right idea, if their group total is equal to 18 or higher, the cats have figured out *exactly* what they have to do. If the group total is 17 or lower, they do not have all of their facts straight. This will have repercussions in the next scene.

What Happens Next: If the cats try to perform the ritual on the Supply Van, continue with **20**.

If the cats try to perform the ritual on the Transport Van, continue with **21**.

20. Inside the Monster

Read Aloud: "The Twolegs keep waking up this monster and it seems to be filled with all sorts of incredible things. It's possible there may even be some more trapped cats in there. Are you curious enough to check for yourselves?"

Narrator Tips: In order to get the monster to wake up, the cats know they must hit it on its side. Unlike the Twolegs, they cannot just walk up and Swat the monster—they're too small. However, they are sure that if they run up and Pounce on the monster, they can cause the same effect. The cats are correct in this assumption, but depending on the result of their Ponder Checks, they may or may not know exactly *where* on the side of the van to Pounce.

In order to succeed, the cats will have to Pounce on the monster more than once. Each time a cat Pounces, note that cat's Strength—that is, how many points of Force the Pounce inflicted. If the group total from scene 20 was 18 or higher, the cats must inflict a total of 12 points of Force in order to get the door to open. If the group total was 17 or lower, the cats' aim is a little off and they must inflict 16 points of Force to get the door open. If the cats have previously succeeded in opening either of the van doors, they only have to inflict 8 points of Force to do the same thing again.

Once the door is open, the cats will see a wall of human supplies. Some are in boxes, others are in plastic containers, others are just in big piles. There are drugs, food, bandages, blankets, medical supplies, and any other kind of thing you as Narrator think the humans would have brought with them. However, the cats are incapable of understanding what most of these items are. Describe them in terms the cats would get, referring back to the events earlier in the adventure whenever possible.

If the players want, their cats can explore the inside of the van—perhaps knocking over some supplies or unearthing a useful (or just entertaining) item or two. But if they make too much noise, they will attract the attention of nearby Twolegs. Indeed, if they spend too much time poking around in the van, someone is sure to come by and notice them.

Eventually it should dawn on the cats that if they can partially awaken this monster, then they can certainly do the same thing to the other one—the one that is surrounded by the scents of cats the Twolegs have put inside the monster.

What Happens Next: If the cats take too long or make a ruckus and the humans notice them, continue with **12**.

If the cats want to go try the ritual on the other monster, continue with **21**.

21. The Hungry Monster

Read Aloud: "Of all the places in the Twoleg camp, the area around this monster is the most intimidating. But many cats are trapped inside. Now that you know how to open the monster, you just have to summon your courage and do it!"

Narrator Tips: In order to get the monster to wake up, the cats know they must hit it on its side. Unlike the Twolegs, they cannot just walk up and Swat the monster—they're too small. However, they are sure that if they run up and Pounce on the monster, they can cause the same effect. The cats are correct in this assumption, but depending on the result of their Ponder Checks, they may or may not know exactly where on the side of the van to Pounce.

In order to succeed, the cats will have to Pounce on the monster more than once. Each time a cat Pounces, note that cat's Strength—that is how many points of Force the Pounce inflicted. If the group total from scene 20 was 18 or higher, the cats must inflict a total of 12 points of Force in order to get the door to open. If the group total was 17 or lower, the cats' aim is a little off and they must inflict 16 points of Force to get the door open. If the cats have previously succeeded in opening either of the van doors, they only have to inflict 8 points of Force to do the same thing again.

Once the door is open the cats smell the scents of all the

cats held within. What's more, those cats start calling out for help. If any of the players' cats were captured during the earlier part of the adventure, they are now here, as is Burr. If the players' cats wish to speak with the others, they can gather the following pieces of information:

- Not all of the cats were captured here in these woods. At least five of them were captured a day ago in another stretch of wilderness, put into the cages, and driven here. They are afraid that the same thing will happen today.
- All the cats that were brought into the Clean Den were given something that made them sleepy; then they were poked and pinched and made to eat foul-tasting food. But they all agree that the Twolegs didn't do them any harm.
- Each cat may be in a separate, small, cold den, but the Twolegs seem to be able to open or close them all simultaneously by touching some small stones and tugging on a stick near each monster's opening.

Opening the cages is another complicated matter that the cats will have to figure out using a combination of the descriptions of the cats in the cages and a series of Ponder Checks. The simple truth (which the players' cats won't understand) is that the cages are controlled electronically. If a person pushes a certain button then pulls a lever, all of the cages will open. But the cats cannot understand the apparatus in that way. Luckily, though, pushing the buttons and pulling the lever are things the cats can do quite easily once they've figured out the details.

Have all the players' cats involved in this process, even the ones trapped in cages, make Ponder Checks. Add all the totals together to get a group total. If the players' cats asked the advice of the other cats trapped in the cages, add an additional +6 to the group total.

If the group total is equal to 30 or higher, the cats have

successfully hit the right combination of buttons and levers and unlocked the cages.

If the group total is less than 30 then there is a chance that the Twolegs will notice what the cats are doing. This chance is 50/50, so flip a coin or use some other fair method to decide whether or not the Twolegs come to interrupt.

As long as the Twolegs do not come over to try to capture the cats, they may make another set of Ponder Checks and add their results to the previous group total.

What Happens Next: If the cats have succeeded in unlocking the cages, continue with **22**.

If the Twolegs notice what the cats are doing, continue with **12**. However, if this is the third time that cats have come back to retry this scene, the Twolegs realize what they're doing and lock the van. There is no longer any way for the cats to open the van door, so instead continue with **23**.

22. Released from the Monster

Read Aloud: "With a loud clanking noise, the mouths of all the caves open and all the trapped cats leap out! Although the Twolegs immediately notice and begin making very unhappy-sounding noises, there is nothing they can do as all the cats run into the woods, free once again."

Narrator Tips: The players have successfully completed the adventure, but there still is room for a little bit of storytelling.

At the very least, the players' cats can talk with the newly freed cats. They are all rogues from areas outside the Clan territories and they are anxious to get home. First, though, they will express their deep thanks for the work the players' cats have done. They may ask for permission to travel across Clan territory, but only so they can get back to the areas they were captured from.

Burr plans to stay in the general area. He will, however, agree to stay out of the Clan territories.

What Happens Next: The players' cats head back to their camp and regale the Clan leader and the other members of their Clan with the exciting tale of their adventure. Certainly, many of the other cats will have a hard time believing some of the details, particularly that the cats were able to survive being so close to *two* Twoleg monsters. In the end, the success of the mission will be self-evident, and no one will be able to argue that the players' cats did an excellent job.

23. In the Belly of the Beast

Read Aloud: "The den you're in gives you room to move around—a little. There's water here, but it isn't fresh. Food, too, though it's the same bitter stuff you smelled when you first discovered this awful place. There are other cats nearby. You can smell them—and their fear."

Narrator Tips: If you've ended up here, then the adventure has gone badly. Some or all of the players' cats have been captured and are about to be driven off in the animal shelter's van.

You can let them engage in a bit of storytelling by having the various captive cats talk to one another from their cages. This at least would give you a chance to help explain some of what happened and give the players a sense that their cats will not be harmed. These humans will not hurt the cats, just try to find them homes to be adopted into. Perhaps, eventually, the cats might be able to escape and rejoin their Clan.

What Happens Next: The adventure ends as the Transport Van starts up and drives off into a very different world than these cats have ever known before.

AFTER THE ADVENTURE

After the last scene of the adventure has been played, the game itself is not necessarily over. There still are a few things you can do if the players want to keep at it.

Lost Cats

One of the saddest parts of any tale is when a character we care about leaves. As fans of the Warriors series, we're all keenly aware of the mixed emotions that come along when that loss is part of a great story, but it's different when the character is your own.

If "The Plaintive Howls" ended badly, some or all of the character cats were left to an unexpected and uncertain fate. They are still alive, but no cat is quite sure where they are, where they're going, or if they'll ever return. This can be quite frustrating to the cat's player, who put in a good deal of time, effort, and emotion to create and develop that character.

So what can you do?

Make a New Cat

For some players, having a character meet an unexpected fate is just a good excuse to go back to the rules and make a new character from scratch.

You no doubt learned a lot while playing your cat character; maybe you even saw some things in the rules that you'd like to try out but that didn't mesh with the character concept of your previous cat. Now you can dive right in and explore those possibilities by making a new cat.

You can build a beginning warrior, just like you did the first time around. Or, if you and the other players agree, you can build a character and improve him or her quickly until your new character is just as many moons old as the others—that way you'll still be at about the same experience level as the others.

Either way, the next time you and your friends sit down to play the *Warriors Adventure Game*, there will be a new character for everyone to meet.

Write the Next Chapter

Perhaps you want to continue exploring the character of your old cat. That's certainly still possible, too, and the clues for how to do it are right there at the end of the adventure.

In the final scene, as the van pulls away carrying your captured cat, the text suggests that in time your character may yet escape from wherever the Twolegs are taking him or her. Then it would just be a matter of finding the way back to the Lake and your Clan territory.

Try making up a story about what happens to your cat—maybe about where the van takes him or her, or what other cats he or she meets along the way. There is a lot of adventure in the world, and a lost cat is sure to find plenty of it. And the best part is that when the story is over, your cat will be back home where he or she belongs and ready to take part in the next adventure.

Play It Again

Maybe you just want to try the whole thing a second time, starting back at the beginning or perhaps picking up somewhere in the middle where it feels like things went wrong. In either case, your cat would be right back where he or she was and have another chance to try to find a more favorable outcome.

One of the great things about storytelling games is that you can always tell the story again. And, since so many of the events depend on timing and Skill Checks, it won't always go exactly the same way.

Plus, there may be parts of the adventure that the cats

never got around to exploring (especially if the Twolegs kept noticing them as they moved around). Playing again will let everyone see all the parts of the story and give other players the chance to try their hands at being the Narrator.

Experience

If the cats completed the adventure successfully, then they all get Experience rewards. It is important to note, though, that each cat can only get experience from this adventure once! If you play through and successfully finish the adventure several times, your cat only gains the rewards listed below after the first time he or she completes the adventure.

If you use different cats each time, though, each one can get the Experience rewards. The rule is not that a player can only get experience once; it's that a cat can.

Age: Although the action in this adventure clearly all happens over the course of a handful of days, the presumption is that this is the most interesting and exciting thing that happens to your cat during the whole of that moon. Increase your cat's age by 1 moon and make any appropriate improvements described in Chapter Four of the game rules.

Skill: On top of the improvements your cat gets from aging, he or she also can gain 1 level in one of the following Skills: Focus, Ponder, See, Smell, Swim.

Knack: For surviving such close and prolonged interaction with Twolegs, your cat also gains one level of the Twoleg Lore Knack.

More adventures can be found at the back of each novel in the Omen of the Stars series, and you can find extra information at www.warriorcats.com.

DON'T MISS

OMEN OF THE STARS

WARRIORS

BOOK THREE: NIGHT WHISPERS

CHAPTER 1

A yowl sliced through the shriek of battle, sharp with grief more than rage.

Dovepaw ducked out of Toadfoot's way and spun around.

Firestar!

The ThunderClan leader was being dragged away across the battle-crowded clearing. The grass glistened crimson behind him. Birchfall sank his teeth farther into Firestar's scruff and heaved him over Spiderleg's shoulders, then helped to carry him away into the trees.

Horror pulsed through Dovepaw. Around her, the fighting was shuddering to a stop as cats sheathed their claws and stared in bewilderment. Firestar's deputy, Brambleclaw, his broad shoulders wet with blood, padded toward Blackstar. The ShadowClan leader didn't look up. His head was bent over a dark ginger pelt.

Brambleclaw dipped his head. "The battle is won," he growled. "The clearing is ours. Do you concede or shall we fight for it again?"

Blackstar flashed a look of burning hatred over his shoulder. "Take it," he hissed. "It was never worth the blood that has been spilled here today."

As Brambleclaw backed away, Dovepaw recognized the ginger pelt.

Russetfur! Is she dead?

The ShadowClan deputy lay unmoving, apart from the blood that trickled from her lips. Her Clanmates began to step carefully past the ThunderClan warriors and head for the pines. Scorchfur, Tigerheart, and Rowanclaw stopped beside their leader. While Scorchfur nudged Blackstar to his paws and guided him gently into the trees, Tigerheart grabbed Russetfur's pelt and slowly, gently, heaved her onto Rowanclaw's shoulders. Then in silence they followed their battered Clanmates into the mist-wrapped trees.

Dovepaw stared after them, the energy draining from her as she saw Tigerheart's tail snake into the shadows. She looked around for Ivypaw. Her sister was helping Blossomfall limp toward the forest.

"Come on, Blossomfall," Ivypaw was murmuring to her Clanmate. "Jayfeather'll fix you up." There was no hint of their past quarrels in her mew.

Squirrelflight was checking Leafpool's wounds, while Leafpool scanned the battlefield, her eyes round with worry. "Lionblaze is okay," Squirrelflight reassured her sister.

Brightheart lay panting on the grass, her one good eye so wide that a circle of white showed around the blue.

Cloudtail nudged her with his muzzle. "Come on, you'll feel better once you start moving," he urged.

Brightheart let out a low moan as she hauled herself to her paws.

Bumblestripe, one ear torn, surveyed the flattened grass. "I think we showed them," he declared.

Hazeltail glanced at him with scorn in her eyes and pressed closer to Mousewhisker, lapping at her sister's bleeding, ruffled fur. "Showed them what?" she muttered between licks. "How much blood can be spilled in a pointless battle?"

Only Lionblaze looked uninjured. A smear of blood stained his flank, but Dovepaw knew it wasn't his. She frowned, doubts flocking into her mind like starlings. Lionblaze was part of the prophecy, like she was. His power was the ability to fight any cat, any creature at all, without being hurt.

Why couldn't Lionblaze have saved Firestar? What's the point of having all that power if he couldn't help his leader?

In front of her, Brambleclaw crossed the stained grass where Russetfur had lain, and touched the tip of his tail to Lionblaze's shoulder. "Russetfur was too old for this battle," he murmured. "It wasn't your fault she died."

Lionblaze hung his head.

Oh, StarClan! Dovepaw's belly tightened. *Lionblaze killed Russetfur?* Her mentor looked shattered, his eyes dull. She hurried to his side and pressed against his flank. She felt utterly helpless. Her power was the ability to hear and see things that were happening far away, much farther than other cats could sense; she should have known what ShadowClan had been up to. Instead it had been her sister, Ivypaw, who had told Firestar that Blackstar was planning to invade ThunderClan's territory and steal more land for hunting. Had StarClan sent a dream to Ivypaw because Dovepaw had refused to use her powers to spy on the other Clans? Maybe if Dovepaw had been listening and watching, as Lionblaze had asked, she'd have known what ShadowClan was going to do. She could have warned Firestar about it before there was no choice left but to fight.

Could I have prevented this?

She felt Lionblaze's warm breath as he touched his muzzle to the top of her head. "Come on," he whispered wearily. "Let's go home."

Dovepaw pressed close to Lionblaze as they trudged on heavy paws through the whispering trees.

Chapter 2

Jayfeather reached a paw into the far corner of his medicine store. He could smell stale marigold tucked beneath the rock; it was the last of his supply and so old that he wasn't sure it'd be strong enough to keep infection from Sorreltail's wound. But he clawed it out anyway and pawed it together with the last of his dried oak.

"This might sting," he warned Sorreltail.

The tortoiseshell-and-white she-cat had been sitting patiently beside Briarlight's nest. "That's okay." From the echo of her voice, Jayfeather could tell she was watching the dozing young warrior. "Her breathing sounds rough."

Briarlight had fallen asleep before sunset despite the steady flow of injured warriors and apprentices through the den. Sorreltail was the last, having insisted on waiting until the others had been treated, though the gash in her shoulder was deep and still oozing blood.

Jayfeather pressed on the poultice and reached for cobwebs to cover it. "She has a chest infection," he explained, draping sticky white strands across the wound. "I'm not sure whether to make her exercise harder to clear her chest or to let her rest and fight it from inside."

Sorreltail brushed his shoulder with her muzzle. "Have you asked Leafpool?"

Jayfeather flicked his tail crossly toward the wads of blood-stained moss and herb fragments that littered the den floor. "Does it look like I've had time?"

"I just wondered," Sorreltail replied mildly.

"Besides," Jayfeather muttered, "Leafpool's busy checking injuries."

"I suppose." Sorreltail got to her paws. "Thanks for the herbs."

Regretting his sharpness, Jayfeather touched her flank with his tail. "Do you want poppy seeds to help you sleep?"

"No, thanks." Sorreltail padded away. "Brackenfur's snoring lulls me better than any medicine."

Jayfeather had treated the golden warrior earlier, snapping his wrenched shoulder back into place before sending him to his nest with strict instructions not to move until sunrise. The rest of the Clan had been spared serious injury. Only Firestar's wound had required careful attention. The tear in his neck had been closed with cobwebs and firmly bound. It would heal, but the life that had seeped away could never be replaced. Jayfeather pictured the faint warrior in StarClan, a little less transparent now, his flame-colored pelt one shade more vivid against the greenness of StarClan's hunting grounds.

As Sorreltail limped from the den, Briarlight stirred. "What a mess," she rasped over the edge of her nest.

"How are you?" Jayfeather sniffed her, relieved to find

that her ears were cooler.

"Sleepy. How's Firestar?" Briarlight blinked.

"Asleep in his den," Jayfeather told her. "Sandstorm's watching over him. He'll be fine in a few days."

"If only Russetfur hadn't attacked him." Briarlight had heard all the gossip from the other warriors. "Then Firestar would be fine, and Lionblaze wouldn't have killed Russetfur."

Jayfeather tensed. "Russetfur was *too old* to be fighting!"

The brambles swished, and Jayfeather breathed the familiar scent of Lionblaze. The warrior padded heavily into the den. "I should have realized that before I attacked her."

"What else could you do? She was killing Firestar." Jayfeather shook out his fur and crossed the den to greet his brother. "Is Dovepaw okay?"

"She's fine," Lionblaze reassured him. "Still quiet. But fine."

Dovepaw had returned from the battle shivering and speechless with shock. Jayfeather had offered her thyme, but she'd refused, saying she was just tired. Unlike her Clanmates, who were keen to share every battle move, Dovepaw had sat silently while Jayfeather checked her over, only mentioning when prompted that Lionblaze had saved her from Dawnpelt.

Is it fair to make apprentices fight alongside warriors? Worry for Dovepaw tightened Jayfeather's belly. Sometimes she seemed so young. At least Ivypaw was okay. She seemed rather pleased with herself, actually. And with only a bruised tail to show for her run-in with ShadowClan's fiercest warriors.

But she hadn't mentioned her dream again. The dream she'd blurted out to Firestar where ShadowClan had invaded

ThunderClan territory and set the forest streams running with blood. In fact, when Jayfeather had slipped into Ivypaw's thoughts, it had vanished from her mind. How could she forget a nightmare so vivid that it had sparked the battle between ThunderClan and ShadowClan?

Jayfeather turned his blind blue gaze on Lionblaze. "Was it worth it?"

"The battle?" Lionblaze stiffened. "Of course!"

"But to lose two lives over a worthless piece of grass!"

"We've sent ShadowClan a message they won't forget."

"At what cost?" Jayfeather sighed.

"We must not turn soft now." Lionblaze's voice dropped to a whisper as Briarlight's attention pricked across the den. "Who knows where the next blow might fall?"

Jayfeather's shoulders sagged as Briarlight began coughing again.

Lionblaze nosed him toward his patient. "We can't afford to ignore any signs now," he hissed. "Go on, see to Briarlight. We'll talk later."

As his brother swished out of the cave, Jayfeather began massaging Briarlight's flank with his paws. Her coughing subsided, and she laid her chin on the side of her nest, her breath quickly easing into sleep.

"Is she okay?" Leafpool's hushed mew sounded at the den entrance. She padded over to Briarlight's nest.

"A little cooler." Jayfeather could hear Leafpool scraping cobwebs from her paws. He could tell by the scent that she'd been repatching Cloudtail's gashes. "How's Brackenfur's shoulder?" He was worried that wrenching it back into place might have damaged more than it fixed. "Did you get a chance to look at it?"

"Y-yes." She hesitated. "What do *you* think?"

Jayfeather's belly knotted. In the past, her question would have been a test. Now Leafpool sounded like she *really* wasn't sure. Why mumble like a nervous apprentice? It was as though she was frightened of putting a paw wrong. His mind drifted back to when she used to boss him around in this very den. He'd answer back, and she'd snap in return. The air would fizz and crackle as he rebelled against her overcautious fussing.

The memory hurt. He'd *known* Leafpool in those days; he'd been able to predict her every objection. Since he had found out that she was his mother, he felt as if he didn't know her at all.

Ignoring her question, he dismissed her. "Will you check on Firestar, please?" He lifted a paw to wash.

Leafpool's whiskers brushed his toes as she dipped her head. "Of course."

Stop acting like a mouse! Jayfeather thought indignantly, while he tugged a sprig of thyme from between his claws. The brambles swished, and Leafpool's pads scuffed away across the clearing.

Jayfeather paused from washing and listened to his Clanmates settling down for the night. Poppyfrost was washing Molekit and Cherrykit inside the nursery. Purdy's rumbling mew droned in the elders' nest. Brackenfur was snoring just as Sorreltail had predicted. Blossomfall was fixing her nest in the warriors' den underneath the fallen beech; perhaps she was trying to make it the way it was before the tree had crashed into the hollow.

Jayfeather shuddered as he remembered the day it had fallen. Its roots had been loosened by rainfall, and the great tree had slid from the top of the cliff and smashed down into the camp, crushing the elders' den and demolishing the thornbush where the warriors used to sleep. Longtail had died. Briarlight had been crippled, her back broken so that she could no longer feel her hind legs. It was only Dovepaw's powerful hearing that had prevented more cats from being killed or maimed.

For half a moon the Clan had worked to rebuild their home, clearing twigs, leaves, and branches as much as they could. They had rebuilt the elders' den by weaving the old honeysuckle tendrils around a frame of splintered wood. The beech still spanned the camp, its trunk like a spine, its boughs a rib cage jabbing into the clearing, its roots gripping the bramble nursery like claws. Every night was filled with the sound of leaves and twigs being tugged and adjusted as the warriors worked on their nests in their new den beneath the strongest bough of the fallen tree.

Jayfeather was still finding it hard to navigate the camp, tripping on unexpected branches or piles of twigs that had been brushed to one side but not yet cleared. Longtail, the blind elder, would have struggled even more to adjust. Perhaps he was lucky to be with StarClan, luckier than Briarlight. She had a chest infection now because she couldn't run and hunt like her Clanmates. She could only drag herself to and from the clearing, her hindquarters dead as fresh-kill.

Jayfeather shook himself. Fretting wouldn't help. He rinsed his paws in the pool, shuddering at the chilliness of the water, then padded to the bracken pile beside Briarlight's nest.

As Jayfeather curled into the smooth stems and closed his eyes, Ivypaw's dream pricked his thoughts. Why had StarClan set this battle in motion? He couldn't shake the nagging suspicion that StarClan would never share dreams with Ivypaw. Why choose *her* and not one of the Three?

I'll talk to Lionblaze about it in the morning. Tired to the tip of his tail, he let his mind drift into sleep.

The stench of decay made him shudder. Blinking open his eyes, he found himself in the Dark Forest. Shadows pressed like dark pelts around him. He glanced nervously over his shoulder. What was he doing here? Was Tigerstar planning to recruit him?

No. Tigerstar was no fool.

He tasted the air. A familiar scent bathed his tongue. Stiffening, Jayfeather peered through the gloom.

"Hello!" A cheerful mew sounded in a clearing ahead.

Ivypaw?

A gruff mew answered her. "Sorry if I scared you today."

Who is she talking to?

"You didn't scare me at all." Ivypaw didn't sound frightened or even surprised to be in the Dark Forest. "I knew you wouldn't hurt me. You're one of the Clanmates, aren't you?"

The Clanmates?

Crouching low, Jayfeather ducked into the mist and crept

forward. Ivypaw stood a fox-length away, ears pricked, tail high. Beside her, Jayfeather recognized the broad shoulders of a dark brown tabby.

Tigerheart!

The ShadowClan warrior leaned close to the ThunderClan apprentice. "I saw you with Hawkfrost the other night while I was training with Brokenstar. I never guessed you'd be one of us."

One of us? Jayfeather crept closer.

Tigerheart circled Ivypaw. "You're good." Ivypaw fluffed out her chest as Tigerheart went on. "It was a shame our Clans had to fight, though. How did that happen?"

Tell him about your dream!

Paw steps scuffed in the shadows, and cold fear traced Jayfeather's spine as a rumbling mew interrupted the two young Clan cats.

"Come on, Ivypaw! You're wasting time!"

Jayfeather's breath caught in his throat as he recognized the speaker. *Hawkfrost.* Tigerstar's son, endlessly furious that he had been killed by his half brother, Brambleclaw, when he was trying to take Firestar's remaining lives and leave ThunderClan leaderless and vulnerable for his and Tigerstar's own cruel ambition.

"You fought well today," the former RiverClan warrior growled. "But you got the move wrong when you attacked Scorchfur. Never turn on two legs when you can manage on one!" He beckoned Ivypaw away with his tail. She followed without question, disappearing after him into the mist.

Hawkfrost's growl shot back from the shadows. "Wait there, Tigerheart. Brokenstar's coming for you soon."

Jayfeather stared in horror, his paws frozen to the chilly earth.

As the mist swirled around him, mews and growls began to rise from the shadows; young voices chirped with questions and called for approval while older mews snarled in reply, urging them on, pushing them ever harder. It was the noise of training sessions from any Clan by the lake—except this wasn't the lake, it was the Place of No Stars. Jayfeather glimpsed sleek, oily pelts wrestling in the shadows and smelled RiverClan. Beyond a line of gray ferns, lither shapes reared and swiped at each other.

WindClan, too?

"Unsheathe your claws!"

"Fight like a warrior, not a kit!"

The scents of decay swamped Jayfeather's tongue.

Then Breezepelt's mew rose from the shadows. "I wish I'd fought in the battle today." The WindClan warrior sounded tense with frustration. "I'd have fought on your side if I'd been given the chance."

Who is he talking to?

Jayfeather tasted the air, reaching through the foul tastes of the Dark Forest and shuddering as he recognized a ShadowClan scent. Breezepelt was swearing allegiance to a ShadowClan cat!

Another shape moved between the trees. Jayfeather spotted the long dark spine moving through the mist like a snake.

Yellowfang had given this cat a name on his last visit to the Dark Forest—a name she had spat from her tongue like poison.

Brokenstar.

"Don't worry, Breezepelt," the black-furred warrior growled. "There'll be many more chances to fight. We'll destroy the warrior code. Once it's gone, there'll be no limit to what we can achieve."

Breezepelt growled excitedly as Brokenstar went on. "With no mouse-hearted rules telling us what to do, we can rebuild the Clans stronger than ever."

Jayfeather shivered against the dread hollowing his belly. Clan cats, cats who lived beside the lake during their waking moments, surrounded him. He could feel their warm hearts beating, quickened by the lies of the dead. There was no hiding now from what was happening: Cats from *every* Clan were being trained by Dark Forest warriors to rise against their Clanmates, trained to break every part of the code the Clans had long fought to protect.

THE TIME HAS COME
FOR DOGS TO RULE THE WILD

SURVIVORS

BOOK ONE:
THE EMPTY CITY

Lucky is a golden-haired mutt with a nose for survival. Other dogs have Packs, but Lucky stands on his own . . . until the Big Growl strikes. Suddenly the ground splits wide open. The longpaws disappear. And enemies threaten Lucky at every turn. For the first time in his life, Lucky needs to rely on other dogs to survive. But can he ever be a true Pack dog?

WARRIORS: THE NEW PROPHECY

In the second series, follow the next generation of heroic cats as they set off on a quest to save the Clans from destruction.

HARPER
An Imprint of HarperCollinsPublishers

www.warriorcats.com

WARRIORS: OMEN OF THE STARS

In the fourth series, find out which ThunderClan apprentice will complete the prophecy.

HARPER
An Imprint of HarperCollins*Publishers*

www.warriorcats.com

WARRIORS: DAWN OF THE CLANS

6

In this prequel series,
discover how the warrior Clans came to be.

New Look Coming Soon!

HARPER
An Imprint of HarperCollinsPublishers

www.warriorcats.com

WARRIORS: BONUS STORIES

Discover the untold stories of the warrior cats and Clans when you download the separate ebook novellas—or read them in two paperback bind-ups!

HARPER
An Imprint of HarperCollinsPublishers

www.warriorcats.com

WARRIORS: FIELD GUIDES

Delve deeper into the Clans with these Warriors field guides.

ALSO BY ERIN HUNTER:
SURVIVORS

SURVIVORS: THE ORIGINAL SERIES

The time has come for dogs to rule the wild.

HARPER
An Imprint of HarperCollinsPublishers

www.survivorsdogs.com